Best Wishes!
Joanna

SILENT INLET

Silent Inlet

Joanna Streetly

OOLICHAN BOOKS

LANTZVILLE, BRITISH COLUMBIA, CANADA

2005

Library and Archives Canada Cataloguing in Publication

Streetly, Joanna
Silent Inlet / Joanna Streetly

ISBN 0-88982-207-7

I. Vancouver Island (B.C.)—Fiction. 2. Indians of North America—British Columbia—Vancouver Island—Fiction. I. Title.

PS8637.T74S54 2005   C813'.6   C2005-900680-3

We gratefully acknowledge the financial support of the Canada Council for the Arts, the BC Ministry of Tourism, Small Business and Culture, and the Government of Canada through the Book Publishing Industry Development Program, for our publishing activities.

Published by
Oolichan Books
PO Box 10, Lantzville, British Columbia
V0R 2H0
Canada

Cover photograph by Adrian Dorst

Printed in Canada

Author's Note

When I began this book, I didn't write, I drew. I drew people, houses, floor plans, maps, maps and more maps. I named every street in town and every river in the Sound. Hanson Sound came alive for me, even though it is completely fictional.

And while the characters in this book are imaginary, to be authentic, they must be recognizable as west-coasters. I hope all non-fictional west-coasters find fragments of themselves in these pages. Then I will have accurately portrayed us.

Acknowledgements

The excitement and pleasure of writing would be so much less without a community of other writers. I am fortunate to have such a community, with whom to share ideas, words, pages, and manuscripts. For their talent, friendship and dedication, I would like to thank Frank Harper and Janice Lore.

Similarly, I would like to thank the Clayoquot Writers' Group—Nicole Gervais, Chris Lowther, Shirley Langer, Janice Lore, Jan Jansen, Adrienne Mason, Jackie Windh and others past and present—for prodding me into writing things other than this manuscript and for being a thought-provoking sounding board. Thanks also to Kathleen Shaw and Mike Laanela for their suggestions.

Grants from the Canada Council and the BC Arts Council allowed me precious time to write this book; while the enthusiasm, skill and hard work of Hiro Boga and Ron Smith have brought the story to its full potential, and to publication.

James Roth gave me legal information and Dr John Armstrong helped me with the medical details. By their resilience, weirdness and wit, residents of coastal communities—Native and non-Native—from Port Renfrew to Winter Harbour, have unwittingly inspired me to represent this geographical area, which I love so much. Thank you.

And thanks to Marcel Thériault, who has never allowed my faith to lag, constantly encouraging me towards the next step. Marcel, Toby and Relic are the best peanut gallery a girl could ever have.

BIG MACK

A small, strong hand reaches into the man's chest. Where his windpipe meets his lungs, the fingers take hold. The squeezing sensation is familiar, otherwise Big Mack Stanley might shout out loud in the dark. As it is, he just opens his eyes. There is no hand in his chest. Instead, from his belly pulses a sense of anxiety and dread so heavy that he can barely move. And as his mind flounders towards consciousness, he exhales and turns on his side, grasping a pillow. He curls his knees upwards, pressing the pillow tighter.

Depression is no stranger to Big Mack. It often grips him like this—by the throat, by the belly—darkening his days with gloom. He sighs, the despair pouring out of his massive body into the room. From the floor comes a stirring of limbs and an answering sigh, this one full of sleep and dreams. Big Mack's son, Sam, and his nephew, Lonny, are sharing a mattress. They're ten years old and inseparable.

Big Mack lets his eyes drift in the darkness. Gradually he is able to make out the shapes on the floor—a pile of skinny legs and arms, both boys sprawled and tangled in the blankets. As he stares at them, Mack feels the sensation of dread overflow, spill into all of his limbs, until even his toes begin to twitch. Today, or tomorrow, or this week, he is going to disappoint these boys. He is sure of it. Suddenly, the pillow is not enough anymore. Nothing is enough any more. If he sighs now, it will be a great animal groan that will wake the house, have people running to the source of the sound.

Christmas is party time in North Hanson. Accidents happen. Houses burn; people drown, fall down stairs or kill themselves. There have always been funerals at Christmas; always people broken with grief, clustered together in overbright rooms, passing sandwiches and sipping coffee from styrofoam cups. If Mack yells right now, friends and neighbours will wake up instantly, fearing the worst, ready for anything. He pushes the covers aside and gropes in the dark for his jeans. Dressing quietly, he makes his way out into the kitchen.

The electric light makes him blink, so Mack rummages around until he finds a candle. He lights it, pours coffee and water into the percolator and switches the overhead bulb off. When the coffee is ready, he leaves the candle in the kitchen and heads over to his father's chair by the window. He hates having to be quiet. Right now he wants to thump something, anything—the couch, the wall, the window. He checks his watch, squinting wearily at the luminous marks: 5:30 a.m. Fuck! Two hours to sit here! Normally, the old man would be the first to wake up and the two of them would chat quietly until breakfast. But his father and his brother took the boat up the coast to a potlatch yesterday. Just before dark they radioed in, saying that the party looked like it was going to be an all-nighter. They would return the next day. Without his father here Big Mack has little desire to be in the house, but realistically, he has nowhere else to go. This is his temporary home. And if he doesn't have a home, he can't have his boys.

Huh. *His boys*. The words flutter through his mind as he swallows his first mouthful of coffee, the bitter liquid easing the knot in his gut. He realised a long time ago that Lonny was as much his own son as Sam. Lonny's mother died several years ago and his father, Big Mack's brother, is in jail. Lonny has done the rounds of the family, being looked after by various relatives. The only constant thing in his life is his connection to Sam and he hangs onto this like a lifeline. Whenever Lonny moved homes, he would always ask if he could stay with Big Mack. But often Mack didn't have a home, or money. He would explain this to Lonny, gently, trying not to let him down. You're like a son to me, Lon, he would say, but for now you'll have to stay with your auntie. She can help you more than I can.

Then he would see that look come over Lonny's face and he would feel the rejection, just as he himself had felt it when he was a boy: I am nobody's kid. Nobody really wants me.

Big Mack puts down his coffee and fishes in a pocket for his rolling papers. The scissors and his stash of pot are under the cushion where he left them. Picking up an old newspaper from the floor, he lays it on his lap and begins to cut up a sticky green bud. He wouldn't be rolling a joint in the house if his father were here. Old Mack calls the stuff "devil weed" and loathes it with a vengeance. Big Mack, himself, finds it soothing—too soothing sometimes. But while he reckons, privately, that his habit is acceptable, he always feels guilty about it when he thinks of the boys.

He comforts himself with the fact that things are a lot better for the boys than they were for him when he was a kid. Life was brutal, back then. At least his boys are wanted. And loved. Big Mack draws hard on the joint to get it going. He barely stifles a cough before breathing in another thick lungful of smoke. Love. They sure missed out on that as kids, Mack and his sister, Lila, and the twins, Silas and Nelson.

The twins . . . .

Big Mack sighs and re-lights his joint.

LONNY

Lonny wakes up when his uncle gets out of bed, but he stays where he is, almost dozing—happy. His cousin, Sam, likes to sleep late, but Lonny loves this time of day, when it isn't quite light yet. The house is warming up and usually at this time he hears the deep-voiced murmurs of his uncle and his grandpa as they drink their first coffee and talk about the weather, or fishing. They never say much, but their quiet, rumbly voices are comforting. Just knowing they're there.

This morning is different, though. After dozing for a while Lonny realises that there are no voices, just silence. Then he remembers: his grandpa, Old Mack, is at a potlatch. His older cousin, Raylene, is in the house, but she never gets up this early, even when her baby cries.

Right now, Uncle Mack must be all by himself. And he might like it if Lonny went out there to sit with him.

Lonny creeps out of bed and into the corridor, the soles of his feet suddenly cold. He peeks around the corner.

In the dim light, his grandpa's chair seems to have disappeared under his uncle's huge body. His uncle, Big Mack isn't fat, exactly, but he's twice as tall and big as anyone else Lonny knows. Hmmm. Since Uncle isn't on the couch, Lonny won't be able to slide in next to him. There's no room.

While he's thinking this, Lonny sees his uncle lean forward, strike a match and breathe in some smoke. Thick, shoulder-length hair hides his face, but Lonny can hear him wheeze and gasp. His chest shakes and he clamps his hand over his mouth. Lonny keeps watching. Uncle is smoking pot! Lonny and Sam already know that Uncle smokes pot. They've seen older boys do it, too. But they didn't know Uncle smoked it now—so early in the morning. They never dreamed he would smoke it in Grandpa's house.

Breathing hard, Lonny eases back down the corridor and into the bedroom. He's about to crawl back in with Sam when he sees

12

that his uncle's bed is empty, so he climbs into it instead, burying his head under the covers and breathing in the smell. He feels excited and happy, like a bear cub in a den. He decides he'll stay where he is until it's time to wake Sam up and tell him what he's seen.

It's pretty dark though. And warm.

He'll just close his eyes for a while.

BIG MACK

The marijuana is just beginning to take effect. Big Mack pulls the lever on the reclining chair, finishes off his coffee and lies back, letting the tension wane and the edges blur.

Soft.

Grey.

At least Lonny and Sam will never be taken away from each other.

And things are better now.

Now.

Better now.

Are they better now? In some ways, nothing has changed. Sometimes he comes close to being happy. Then, just when he is finding his way up and out of depression, another tragedy washes over him: an accidental death or a suicide—the sudden vanishing of a cousin, an uncle, a friend. And back to the depths he goes, new hurts pouring on top of the old ones, burying him in sticky silt.

Time wanders.

Big Mack lies in the chair without moving. Despite the pot, he can feel the effects of the coffee. The next cup will bring a better buzz. He pulls the window open to let the wet, dark air wash away the smoke. Then he levers the chair back down and shuffles towards the percolator, his socks finding torn patches on the linoleum. He stops to re-fill the woodstove. It has been a mild winter, with enough rain to let the salmon run. The chunks of hemlock that he pushes into the stove are soaking wet, but it doesn't matter. The old stove will burn anything. It hardly ever goes out, even when people forget to check it.

Big Mack settles back into the shiny leather chair. The first hint of light brushes the sky and he watches as his village quietly grows, house by rectangular house, out from the darkness. He can feel his own darkness slipping away from him, too, but he knows it won't leave him completely.

He knows it will hang on, there in his stomach, waiting to taint the events of the day.

LONNY

Lonny dreams that he is fishing with Sam. They're leaning over the edge of a dock, looking for perch and shiners. Suddenly, he hooks a big salmon and when he finally lands it on the dock, it becomes his uncle. Big Mack ruffles Lonny's hair, then sighs and walks slowly up the ramp. Lonny stares at his hook and then turns around. Sam's still fishing. He hasn't even noticed what happened.

As Lonny wakes up, he turns over to nudge Sam, but Sam isn't next to him. Surprised, Lonny realises that he's in his uncle's bed. Then he remembers what he saw. Excited, he tumbles onto the mattress on the floor and pummels Sam repeatedly, trying to wake him up. Sam grumbles and complains as usual and it takes a while before he's really awake.

"He did what?" Sam croaks.

"He was doing pot," whispers Lonny. "In Grandpa's chair. This morning. I saw him and he coughed."

"No way!" Sam says. "Grandpa would get mad."

"Grandpa's not here. He went to a party, remember?"

Sam's quiet.

"He really did, he did," Lonny goes on, "I saw him. But he didn't see me. And I had to wait so long to tell you."

"Is he still out there?" asks Sam.

"How do I know? I only just woke up again—stupid!"

"Well, go and see."

"I'm getting up anyway," says Lonny. "I'm hungry."

Lonny gets dressed in record time and races out into the kitchen, stumbling over the edge of a rug. The electric light is on now and Big Mack is standing at the table, slicing bread.

"Are you hungry?" he asks.

Lonny nods, suddenly shy. Then he remembers his dream and blurts it out. ". . . and Sam never even saw!" he finishes, as his uncle listens seriously. That's one thing about him. He always listens.

"Huh. So you were fishing for me, were you?" Big Mack questions him, half joking, half serious.

"No," says Lonny, a little confused. "I was just fishing."

"Well I've been here all morning, so I guess it really was a dream, Lon." Uncle Mack transfers the slices of bread to the toaster, not looking at him.

"I know it was just a dream," says Lonny, defensively. "But after breakfast, can me and Sam go fishing?"

Big Mack laughs. "Sure," he smiles. "Just don't ask me to cook myself, if that's who you catch."

Lonny blinks, unsure of what to say. Then he takes the bonus jar of peanut butter in both hands and heads to the table, to wait for breakfast.

BIG MACK

After the boys have gone off fishing, Big Mack has to convince himself to go to work. He's a handyman and Mr Stimpson, over in Hanson Bay, needs his front steps repaired. The problem is, Mack doesn't have the energy to fix stairs today. He's not sure he has the energy to do anything.

But it's also Christmas and he doesn't have money to buy presents for the boys.

Fucking Christmas. Just because you live on the west coast of Vancouver Island doesn't mean you can escape Christmas. That whole month of feeling confused. A dark, gloomy month, to boot.

Mack is just heading back over to the chair when Raylene's baby starts to squall in the back room. Raylene is his niece, a quiet, depressed seventeen-year old. She has a boyfriend of sorts—Kenny—who shows up once every six weeks or so and talks her into going out with him. Then she and the baby will be gone for a few days. When she comes back the baby will have a cold, streaming nose, gummy eyes. Raylene herself will be covered in hickeys. Kenny always leaves his mark.

In between bouts with Kenny, Raylene stays at Old Mack's, speaking when necessary, cleaning the house sometimes and cooking often. She doesn't mind keeping an eye on the boys, but sometimes Mack wonders how much she notices them, or anyone else. Still, her presence makes his life easier, that's for sure.

Today, however, Big Mack doesn't feel like being around Raylene. His own hopelessness is bad enough, he doesn't need hers, too. He grabs his bag of tools and a jacket and heads out the door.

Raylene pokes her head out of the side window: "Where you going, Uncle?"

"Hanson Bay. For a job. The boys are down the dock."

Raylene raises her eyebrows in acknowledgement and closes

the window. Mack can still hear the baby wailing when he's a hundred yards away. The rain has tapered off, but the breeze is still damp, heavy.

Jack Stimpson is a small, white man with a beaky nose and sun-marked skin, deeply creased. He's lived on the coast some sixty-odd years, but he doesn't act as if a lifetime of living here gives him special status. His voice is a gentle west coast drawl and he never forgets a name, always greeting you with what seems like genuine pleasure.

Today is no different and Mack's glad he's come, after all.

"Come on in and have a coffee, there, Mack," Jack calls. "Can't start a job without one, you know."

Mack picks his way gingerly onto the porch of the little shingle house. Should have done the stairs weeks ago, he thinks, picturing them crumbling into mossy chunks under Jack's feet. He has to duck his head to get through the front door.

"Can't get over your size, Mack," chuckles Jack. "Can never believe that a bruiser like you came out of a little bird like your mother!"

Mack stops.

Nobody ever speaks of his mother. She disappeared when Mack was eight years old. His father wouldn't talk about it and no one ever went to look for her. To this day Mack has no idea where she is. Photographs are scarce and Mack himself has very few memories of her. Several years ago his curiosity got the better of him. He got up the courage to ask around for clues, or memories, but nobody seemed to know very much. Or else they didn't want to say. He gave up, then. There was no point. She knew where her kids lived. If she missed them enough, she could find them.

"Here you go. Sugar? Cream?" Mack shakes his head. Coffee should be black and thick.

"As outrageous as they come, your mother, " Jack continues. "Even the herring fishermen would blush when she started

19

running her mouth off. Smart, though. She always knew when Ada was low."

Ada was Jack's wife. She died a few years back—a kind woman, unable to bear children. Once in a while this would get her down. Most people could tell when she was feeling sad and they would try to cheer her up.

"Sometimes, your mother was the only person who could pull her out of it," Jack muses. "Shocked her out of it, probably. She was good at shocking people."

Big Mack stares at Jack, mute. Shocked. That's a good word. He swallows his coffee in one gulp. "I'll get started now," he says and heads for the porch. He feels bad, cutting Jack off, but he doesn't want to hear any more. He's done with his mother. He doesn't want her to exist.

That afternoon, though, in the rhythm of his work and his thoughts, Big Mack finds that his mother does exist. Through the swing of the hammer and the pull of the saw he sees her disappearing, like a wisp of fog, through the trees. He sees that image whether he wants to, or not.

LONNY

The railings of North Hanson's government dock gleam brightly, the scarlet paint almost neon against the fading afternoon light. A fine drizzle mists the water and veils the cedar trees lining the shore, their branches dangling to the high tide line where the salt water has trimmed them. From the reserve northwards, a long inlet reaches towards the Selkish river, its serpentine edges lined with virgin rainforest. This is wild land, which older boys sometimes explore. Younger kids have to stay closer to the village, at the dock, or on the beach. Lonny and Sam never venture beyond the dock because their favourite pastime is fishing.

Lonny is pulling a bunch of tubeworms off the dock piling when Sam first notices the compass lying underneath a pile of netting. It's about the size of a big grapefruit, swinging on gimbals. It's obviously been pulled out of someone's boat and abandoned. The boys examine it minutely, watching the needle swing as they move it around.

"It's so you don't get lost," Sam pronounces.

"I know," says Lonny. "It's like Grandpa's, only different."

The boys have fished all day. In the morning they hung out with their older cousin, Boy. Boy doesn't say much, but he likes fishing. He didn't catch anything, though, so he gave up and went home. At one point Lonny and Sam went back to the house for lunch, but they didn't stay inside long. There was too much to do. Sam caught three shiners, two kelp crabs and a starfish. Lonny got four shiners. He doesn't bother with other creatures. He's after fish.

By the time they discover the compass, the boys are ready for distraction. For a while they walk erratically around the dock following every quiver of the needle, holding the compass out in front of them as if it's a crown they're about to place on someone's head. Then they start inventing stories about the compass: it's an alien's brain, a talking robot.

Eventually, they can't resist climbing into Big Mack's canoe. It's a wide aluminum canoe, with a square end and a tiny outboard motor. It leaks, but there's a bailer. They make a special spot at the bow for the compass, but with the boat tied up to the dock, they can't change directions.

"Hey, Lon."

"Uh-huh."

"Let's untie the boat."

"We can't."

"Why not?"

"Uncle will be mad. We're not allowed."

"We'll be right here, though. It's not like we're going anywhere."

"Uncle will still be mad."

"He won't."

"My dad would be mad."

"Your dad's in jail."

"So? He would still be mad."

"How do you know? You never even see him."

"I just know."

"No you don't. You're just making it up because you're chicken."

"Am not!"

"So. Untie the rope then."

In the end, Sam unties the canoe and they venture off, wherever the compass needle points, taking turns with a broken paddle. Over time, the canoe travels beyond the confines of the dock. Soon they've paddled around the point, then they cross over to the Otter Islands. Sometimes the canoe gets too full of water. That makes it tippy and once they nearly do tip, so Lonny has to keep bailing.

At first they're whalers. Then they're fishermen.

"I want to be Uncle Silas," says Lonny. "That's who my dad looks like."

"They're twins," says Sam. "They look the same."

"Do you think that maybe Uncle Silas is really my dad?" Lonny asks. He sometimes hopes this, just so that he might have a father who is real, not imaginary. A father who other people talk about.

"Nah," Sam replies. "Your dad's Uncle Nelson and he's in jail forever."

Lonny's chest hurts. "Let's go back. I'm tired."

A strong gust of southeasterly catches the bow of the canoe, turning it sideways. The movement startles a perching blue heron and it flaps away on heavy wings, croaking its strange, prehistoric cry.

A rush of cold air swishes over Lonny's shoulders and he shivers.

BIG MACK

Big Mack wanders home barely aware of the road under his feet. He managed to finish today's job quickly, but then he went straight to the bar. This time, though, the bar didn't make his mother go away. Half way through his third beer, a hint of the morning's dread had brushed his chest, like a feather. Plonking the unfinished beer glass on the counter he hefted his bag of tools out the door, deaf to the voices that called him back.

Now, Big Mack walks past Coast Convenience and the 2nd Wave Thrift Store. As he heads for the highway, he passes weathered wooden houses with steep, shake roofs. The fresh air helps, but should he be mad at himself for drinking, or pleased with himself for getting the hell out of the bar?

Cars pass on the highway, a blur of noise and motion. He doesn't stick out his thumb. The drink makes his feelings so clear, then so fuzzy; he finds a thought, loses it, finds it, loses it. His feet move steadily over the hard gravel, scratching a rhythm in his head. His sadness ebbs and flows, from a murky interior source. He wishes he could stop this pain, but first he would have to know where it comes from. He doesn't. He plods on. By the time he gets home, he's exhausted.

Raylene is baking bread. Normally he loves the smell of it, but today it just blends into the haze surrounding him.

"Dad back?" he asks, hopefully.

Raylene shrugs. She doesn't know.

"The boys?"

She nods in the general direction of the dock. "Still fishing," she manages, pulling a cigarette out of its package.

Mack turns around and heads back out the door. It'll be dark soon.

The boys aren't at the dock, but Mack isn't surprised. They're probably at someone else's house, most likely his sister Lila's. Mack surveys the dock from the top of the ramp, before turning around. He starts walking, then stops. He looks once more. Huh. His canoe is missing. And right next to where it should be lies a pile of tubeworms, half pulled apart. Bait.

Mack scans the shoreline. Nothing.

He checks the tide. Gray water ebbing. Swirling out to sea.

He checks the wind. Southeast—mild, but building for another blow. He hurries down the ramp, squeezes into the cabin of his cousin's boat and turns on the VHF radio. He calls Lila. She hasn't seen the boys. He calls his father's boat, to see if it's close by. It is. They're coming in. They'll be home in ten minutes, his brother Silas reckons. They haven't seen anything, but they'll watch for the canoe and the boys.

Climbing back onto the dock, Mack grabs an old dinghy, turns it right side up and pushes it over the edge, into the water. Further along he finds some oars—different lengths, but functional. He clambers into the little dinghy and pushes off, rowing strongly into the oncoming tide.

The water gurgles, wrapping around each oar before eddying away downstream. Parallel sets of oarprints twirl behind the dinghy. Mack looks over his shoulder as he rows.

LONNY

Lonny is in the front of the canoe, so he is the first to see the dinghy. One glance tells him it is his uncle, come to look for them—no one else makes a dinghy look so small.

Lonny puts down his paddle and turns to Sam, fear written all over his face.

"Uh-oh," Sam breathes.

"I told you we shouldn't have," says Lonny. He hates when his uncle is mad. It's the worst feeling in the world. He looks at the water swilling around his feet, feeling its coldness for the first time. He braces himself for what's to come. He will say nothing, he decides. Nothing at all.

Pressure gathers at the back of his eyes. Uncle Mack might not want him now. He might have to live with Auntie Lila. Being in trouble is okay for Sam. He has a mom *and* a dad. Sam's mom is a nice lady that Sam can live with anytime—if he wants to. A tear spills out and Lonny hunches over, holding other tears in. He fiddles with the bailer, not paddling. Why bother? They're going with the tide, anyway. Drifting right towards Big Mack.

BIG MACK

As Big Mack pulls on the oars, a new jumble of thoughts runs through his head: "Should've been a better father; should've spent more time with them this morning; should've been a better father, like my dad was when I was small."

He remembers all the hours he has spent rowing boats with his father. By the time his mother disappeared, he knew where to find the biggest clams and how to sneak up on ducks. He'd known a lot for an eight-year old boy. But there was something else that he knew, back then—something important, that had carried him through hard times.

When Old Mack was teaching Mack about the water, they rowed, side by side, to a place of no words. An unspoken current of understanding flowed between them. Has Mack developed such a current with his own boys?

The top-heavy dinghy lurches along the shoreline, five pulls then a shoulder check. Rocks and tree branches; no leaky canoe.

From today, I will be a better father. Just let my boys be safe."

Big Mack's mom vanished from his world. Had she run away from her kids as well as her husband? Have his boys run away from him? He turns to look.

His eyes won't focus. He sees nothing. "If they're okay, I'll spend so much time with them, I promise."

Five pulls. Turn and look.

A shape. A floating log?

Five pulls. Turn and look.

Not a log. A canoe?

Five pulls. Turn and look.

A canoe. Definitely a canoe.

Heading home. His boys were heading home, not running away.

"Thank Christ. Thank Christ! The rotten little snotbags!"

The boys are wooden dolls. Not paddling. Not even looking at Big Mack.

Five pulls.

Lonny's face, growing closer. Mack sees that look: I am nobody's kid. Nobody really wants me . . . .

Big Mack sighs. Puts his oars up. The dinghy spins sideways. The canoe drifts closer. Deep breath.

"Well, what are you waiting for? You got yourselves here, now get yourselves home! And bail that canoe before it sinks!"

The boys don't move—heads down, fingers fiddling. The canoe drifts closer. "NOW!" roars Big Mack.

The canoe jerks forward. Lonny bails. Sam wields the lone oar. Big Mack watches the canoe zigzag away from him. His boys are ten years old and they don't even know how to paddle in a straight line. He hasn't taught them.

Mack takes a joint out of his pocket and leans back, tilting the dinghy's gunwales within an inch of the water. As he lights the joint, he imagines the boys being swamped by storm waves, washed overboard into the frigid water. Mack knows what drowned bodies look like. He tosses the joint overboard and takes off after the boys.

HANNAH

Hannah had flown from Whitehorse to Vancouver, where she's staying overnight before catching the bus to Hanson Bay. She could have driven. She has the time and—who knows?—it might have been good for her. What she doesn't have is the concentration needed for driving. Staring out of windows is about the most she can do right now. The noise between her ears is loud, a jumble of thoughts clamouring for attention. Even the hubbub of the city is diminished by the struggle in her head. In Vancouver she wanders the streets in warm, drizzly rain, barely noticing the crush of people, feeling only the occasional poke of an umbrella.

At the hotel, she follows directions to her room, where she sits on her bed, tall and gaunt, bags at her feet, staring at the magnolia-coloured wall. Minutes pass.

A cacophany of horns blaring in the street outside startles her, bringing her out of her reverie. She blinks, looks around, then gets up and goes to the window. From there, she can see the north shore, the land rising steeply before disappearing into a swathe of damp, heavy clouds.

Hannah slides open the glass door and stands on the balcony breathing in the wetness. She hadn't noticed the rain when she was wandering the streets, but now she feels it, like wet hands on her face; now, she lifts her palms upwards, tilts back her head and opens her mouth, letting the water build up on her lips and her tongue. Her hair and cheeks glisten with water. It splashes into the deep hollows of her eyes and runs out of the sides like tears. A sudden gust of wind brings heavier rain and she delights in it, moving her head back and forth. Not until she's shivering with cold, does she think about going inside.

Hannah, dripping with December rain, is charged with energy. She goes straight to the shower to warm up, wondering what possessed her to stand outside like that. Is she losing it?

After her shower, she opens her bags, hoping her clothes aren't too crushed, because she had to leave her iron in Whitehorse. Her favourite jeans are still well pressed, though. Small mercies, she thinks as she slides into them. She's back on the coast again. Jeans are practical. So are raincoats.

She laces up her soft white runners and heads for Stanley park, where she walks briskly along the sea-wall towards Lions' Gate bridge. There she sits and watches the boat traffic, longing to be in her own boat—an open wooden Clinker, with an old diesel motor that she'd sold five years ago, before moving to the Yukon. Instead of using a wheel, she'd steered from the back, wielding a long tiller. As a teenager she'd been embarrassed by it—longed for a speedboat, something classy, that she wouldn't mind being seen in.

But that was then. Now she misses it. Seeing the ocean from the plane pulled a sliver of feeling from her, something that's been wedged in, niggling for too long.

She ponders the validity of the past five years, weighing them like a purchase, querying the purpose they've served. Perhaps her life would have taken a similar path, no matter where she'd gone. Perhaps she's destined to make bad choices. But nursing isn't a bad choice. It's a career that can take her anywhere. The important thing is that she left home. Flew the nest.

Hanson Bay is a small town on the west coast of Vancouver Island, miles from anywhere. It's natural that Hannah had felt smothered by the closeness of it—anxious to flee its incestuousness and curiosity. But the real issue that drove her departure was her mother, Harriet—Harry to everyone who knows her. Harry lives in a tiny cabin in the bush, twelve miles from Hanson Bay, on Fortune Island, four acres of windswept rock in the middle of Hanson Sound. What a place to live!

Growing up with Mother was difficult, to say the least. And like a tree growing away from the wind, Hannah fled towards normality wherever she could find it. But now she's jobless, and her boyfriend—well, she won't think about her boyfriend. Five years of normality later, she's running back to Hanson Bay, tail between her legs.

When the darkness increases, so she can no longer distinguish the yellow piles of sulphur glowing in the shipyards across the water, Hannah abandons the bench she's been sitting on. She strides back into the city for sushi and a movie. She loves the big screen, wants something gripping and dramatic. She's seen the ads for *The Perfect Storm* and it sounds exciting. It might help prepare her for going home, too. No longer feeling like a zombie, she sees that she might benefit from the distraction.

When she gets to the theatre, she joins a jostling line of people queueing for tickets. The people seem larger than life and she's distracted by the noise and laughter. When it's her turn she asks for two tickets. Not until she has them in her hand, does she realise her mistake. Instead of asking for her money back, she rips off one of the tickets and hands it to the pimply boy behind her.

"Amazing!" he exclaims, showing his friends. He walks past the booth into the theatre. Hannah stares after him, as she waits in line to order a coffee. When she gets her coffee, she blows on it to cool it and takes a long sip, trying not to taste irony: she's surrounded by people and she's never felt so lonely.

Getting to the ferry terminal in rush hour means leaving the hotel before seven. It isn't until Hannah is on the ferry to Nanaimo that she realises she has slept the whole night. It's amazing the difference seven hours of uninterrupted sleep can make. The last year at the hospital, there'd been a shortage of staff and she had often worked bizarre, exhausting hours. That, coupled with the state of her personal life, meant that over the last six weeks she's barely slept at all.

Hannah wedges herself into a seat, puts her feet up on her bags and stares out through the windows. Excitement wells up inside her, but she tries to keep it from showing, so that no one in the crowd will mistake her for a tourist. Keeping a low profile also means that she's less likely to run into anyone she knows. The problem with her homecoming lies in the volley of well-meaning (and some not-so-well-meaning) questions that she'll have to answer, once she arrives at Hanson Bay. She decides to invent some good one-liners. That way everyone will come away with the same story. Fewer rumours.

So? What is her story going to be? She's a dutiful daughter, home for the holidays. She's only visiting, though, and her two small bags will indicate a short stay. (In no way will the bags hint that the rest of Hannah's belongings are crated up in a storage depot in Whitehorse, waiting for her to send for them.) She'll say that nursing is a wonderful challenge. Whitehorse is a wonderful place; the snow is so much fun and the summer daylight hours amazing! Of course, she's missed the coast. Impossible not to. She'll be here for Christmas and New Year. After that she'll see how it goes. It all depends on Harry, how well she is. You know?

Hannah smiles at the image. She can almost see the heads nodding. She feels arrogant, deceiving people in advance like this, especially when there are people there who really do care about her. But one good thing about growing up in Hanson Bay is that she's learned how to skip around the nosy folks. Survival tactics.

She'll tell Jack, though. She'll tell him everything. Jack Stimpson has been like a father to her. She boarded with him and Ada while she went to high school and although she loved Ada, too, she needed a father figure and Jack was it. At a time in her life when she was desperate to fit in, she was magnetically drawn to Jack and Ada. That they had welcomed her so lovingly into their home still seems miraculous. Somehow, she'd risen out of the mess that was life with Mother and climbed to safety.

Hannah peers out at the descending clouds as they obscure the sharp rise of the mountains. This view always reminds her of the traditional Chinese watercolour painting she bought in Vancouver, from a store on Robson Street, and hung in her bathroom in Whitehorse. Last year in a fit of homesickness she'd taken it down, only to discover that it was easier to get rid of the picture than the sadness. Like the first rock of a landslide, so casually dislodged, the fall of that painting had started something. Feelings that she usually kept buried became harder for her to ignore. The life she had chosen started to disintegrate. Once the crumble began, she was reduced to scrabbling and flailing her arms.

Why did I let it happen? Hannah wonders. I'm intelligent, strong-willed. She tries to block out that last, crazy scene with her boyfriend, Rob, but her fingers slip under the pale blue angora sweater and touch her ribs, playing over one of the bruises. At least nobody can see this, she tells herself. Or the other ones. What would they think?

The ferry tilts suddenly as it comes into the open water of the Strait of Georgia. She thrills at the stormy pulse of the southeasterly. Even the ferry is affected by the weather, lurching and wallowing onto its lee side. Passengers spill their drinks, stumble into seats. Children play, as if at a fun fair, making the most of the strange motion, unafraid. Surprisingly, Hannah feels a wave of nausea pass over her. She's never been seasick in her life, not even on fishing trollers, with their rolling, ambling pace and stink of diesel. It must be nerves, she decides. I'm frightened of going home. Unfortunately, there's still a wide body of water to cover and Hannah's nausea only builds. Eventually, she curls in her seat with her eyes closed, trying to sleep. Her earlier excitement fades. Rain, fog and seasickness eclipse all.

HARRY

The bow of the *Polynesia* points into the south-easterly, disappearing from view with the onslaught of another wave. Salt water—a giant slosh of white-green noise—buries the windows of the little troller's cabin. Harry stands inside the cabin, at the wheel, holding tight. Under the green rubber raingear, her body braces, anticipating the heaving motion. Straight, grey-brown hair is pulled to the back of her neck in a clip. Her face lines with concentration as she bunches up her eyes for a clearer view. Under Harry's feet, Rustum sighs deeply before crawling under the table to hide.

"I'm sorry, Rustum," says Harry, with an apologetic glance. "It's a shitty day to be in the boat. But we're nearly out of the worst. Half a mile to Kingfisher Rock, then we'll be going with the tide. I promise."

Rustum is unresponsive. A hairy brown tail is all that can be seen of him. The rest of his body is squeezed as far under the table as possible. Were he visible, it would be hard to imagine that he could fit under the little table: he's huge—an aging mutt of doubtful origins. Harry claims he's half Bernese mountain dog, a quarter Malamute and a quarter Lab. When Hannah was around she used to complain that he was half bear—had to be, with a head that size. Whatever his parentage, he is brown and white and hairy, with great mournful eyes. And he is devoted to Harry. Rustum will follow Harry anywhere, never leaving her side except to swim, which he loves doing. Sometimes, when it's warm in the summer, they go for swims together. Harry tries to swim all year round, but in the wintertime she is usually reduced to a quick plunge once a fortnight. Still, she does it anyway; it's good for her constitution.

It's not so cold today. The southeasterly may bring rain, but it also brings warmth. Too bad the damp makes her fingers hurt.

Lately it's been hard to knead the bread dough. And without bread, there's no business.

Harry has made bread since she was twelve. She learned, initially, from her mother, Ruth, although Ruth's loaves were always small, grey, flat, lumpy. As a girl, Harry hoped that she could succeed where her mother failed. And she did. She had the knack for it, a fact that Ruth had difficulty acknowledging.

"This batch turned out okay," Ruth would begin brightly. "But it's too bad it's so salty."

"Great bread!" Harry's father would exclaim. "I think I'll have another slice."

It was a long time before the young Harry realised that her mother was jealous and that her bread was, in fact, good bread. That marked the point in her life when Harry began to understand that her mother was not infallible. Until then, the idea of her mother being jealous would have seemed impossible.

Harry tries to picture her mother's face—not her last mask, distorted by age and illness, but the vibrant, loving face of her younger days, the days when Papa was still alive and Ruth's life was sweet and full. Life was sweet and full for Harry then, too. That was before the stepfather, the drunken loutish bully, who beat Harry in secret, looking over his shoulder and threatening more if she told. Harry never told her mother about the beatings. They were all making the best of a bad situation—no need for her to make it worse. But she vowed that as soon as she could leave home, she would. Which she did. She came here.

Ploosh! Another wave over the bow. When the windows clear, Harry sees Kingfisher Rock poking up like a rotten tooth out of the lumpy water. She cheers loudly, but Rustum's tail doesn't even thump. He's been through this before and he won't come out until the sea's been calm for a while.

Harry ponders the necessity of going to town today. Normally she avoids Hanson Bay. She doesn't understand the intuition that drove her out to fight the twelve mile stretch on a day like this.

"Most people would just stay home," she says out loud to Rustum. "But sometimes there's a reason and maybe we'll even find out what that is."

Harry has lived without a telephone for most of her life. She keeps a VHF radio in her boat and in her cabin, so that she can call out if she has to. She turns it on for incoming calls at suppertime. Most people reach her that way, so if something urgent crops up, she'll go to town and deal with it. Often, the calls are from fishermen wanting bread the following morning. Oh yeah, and some fuel if you have any, they'll say, as an afterthought. Well, she always has fuel! She runs a gas station, for crying out loud! But Harry knows that people only buy gas from her out of a sense of obligation. She can't afford to sell fuel cheaply because she doesn't have huge tanks. She needs to sell something more than bread, but she doesn't want to feel like a charity case, either. *"C'est la vie,"* she sighs.

As she had thought they would, the waves soon diminish. The white boat slides easily through the rain, little puffs of diesel smoke blending with the cloud that is everywhere. Harry is quite pleased with herself. She likes to think she is a good judge of the weather and the water. Right now she is humming. Only three more miles to go, then she will tie up at the government dock and roll herself a smoke—*quishaa,* the natives call it. *Quishnuk* they call her: smoke-lover.

Harry forbids herself to smoke while the boat is going. Her reactions are slower now that she is older and besides, she shouldn't smoke in such a small cabin. When the summer comes and she can steer from outside, she might succumb to temptation. For now, she is surviving her decision.

Harry and tobacco, Harry and bread, Harry and Rustum, Harry and Fortune Island. These are the associations people make when they think of her. Once upon a time there used to be Harry and Hannah. But children do need to leave. Certainly she never stood in Hannah's way. She just wishes she could have influenced Hannah more. All her daughter ever seemed to want was to go to that horrible local high school, instead of doing her own thing with correspondence. Then she wanted a career, so she could have RRSPs, a house on a street, a car, a TV. Before long she will have mortgaged her soul, married and had two-point-two children.

Children. Harry worries about them. How awful to think that grandchildren of hers might be raised without all this . . . . She squints through the misty windows at the dripping, rainforested coastline. Thick pads of moss sit squarely on some tree branches, dangle dreamily from others. It's so lush here. Fortune Island, though only a few miles away from here, is much drier; an entirely different micro-climate. On Fortune Island there are shorepines, twisted and gnarled. Courageous Douglas fir trees corkscrew out from the rocks, bearing no resemblance to their textbook form. The granite substrate is covered with lichen and moss, dry-looking, nothing like this emerald green stuff. At home, she has made her garden from scratch, painstakingly hauling buckets of sand, seaweed, compost and the occasional sack of topsoil. She has gradually built up a variety of raised beds and learned which species survive the wind that blows constantly across the island. Harry pictures the heads of wildflowers nodding in that wind. In spring the island is covered in flowers: wild strawberries, chocolate lilies, Indian Paintbrush and yellow monkey flowers. Yes, Harry thinks, I would hate my grandchildren to miss those—or any of this. She sighs. It's all hypothetical at this point. Hannah doesn't even have a husband yet, or if she does, Harry doesn't know about him.

Harry never had a husband, herself. Hannah's father, Alain, left before Harry even knew she was pregnant. She's been single ever since.

It was her own mother's remarriage that made Harry stubborn

37

in her determination to remain single. Winters in the Interior were cold and snowy. Their cabin was remote and Ruth had been dependent on her husband for many things, not least of which was money. Through his labour and the earnings of their small farm, they made just enough to survive. Then he died. Without him, in a year when the harvest was ruined by storms, their situation was perilous. The community urged her to re-marry. She agreed, in order to provide Harry with food, clothes, a warm house—and a step-father.

Harry didn't want her own daughter to experience a step-father. Life has always been physically hard for Harry because she hasn't wanted to rely on others, the way her mother was expected to. Her initial flight to Fortune Island was to escape the stigma of single motherhood. But as Hannah grew, people seemed to forget her illegitimacy. Soon, the topic of marriage began to arise every time Harry came to town. She countered it by staying away for longer periods, working longer hours on other people's boats, or her own.

Eventually, the bachelors started "just dropping by" Fortune Island. She talked nicely to them, gave them tea and sent them home. She never considered them as potential mates. She didn't want another mate. She would never be able to look at these men without comparing them to Alain. That was no basis for a relationship, as far as she could see.

Hanson Bay looms out of the cloud and, as if on cue, Rustum squeezes out from under the table, shakes, then rubs up against the backs of Harry's knees. She bends down to stroke his ears, then eases back on the throttle in preparation for landing. There are several people milling around on the dock when she draws alongside it. Two Native boys grab her tie-up lines and pull the boat in snugly. She recognizes them, but has forgotten their names. The kids grow up so quickly these days, but these ones are Stanleys, she thinks. She can tell by their open faces, the lack of guile. She watches them tie the lines, expecting granny knots, but pleased to see clove hitches.

"Who showed you how to tie knots?" she asks.

"My dad," says the bolder one. "We know how to paddle and row, too."

Hannah feels the shyer boy staring at her. She can tell he wants to ask her something.

"What's your name young man?" she asks.

"Can I pet your dog?" he blurts out. Then the other boy elbows him and laughs. "Oh. Um. I mean, my name is Lonny. That's Sam."

"Oh right," she says, "you stay with Big Mack." Lonny's face lights up. Harry always asks who people stay with, rather than who their parents are. There's a lot of family juggling that goes on around here.

"Off the boat, Rustum," she says and watches with pleasure as the two boys become lost in the mass of brown and white fur. Harry approves of dog lovers, especially kids like this, who show no fear of Rustum. She ducks back into the cabin, grabs her pouch of tobacco and rolls a cigarette. Then she comes back out, shelters under the overhang of the cabin roof, lights up and inhales deeply.

Bliss.

She still doesn't know why she's here. Perhaps she should wander up to the post office. And if she finds there's no reason for her to be here, it doesn't matter.

BIG MACK

From his seat by the bar window, Big Mack sees a little white double-ender appear through the haze of wind and rain. Huh. It's the *Polynesia*, named after a parrot that the owner, Harry Farre, claims is the kind of creature you'd want to have with you in a crisis. He's pleased to see that his boys go straight over to help her tie up. He likes Harry—likes the way she talks to him, always really interested. Never faking it.

People laugh about Harry sometimes, call her weird, or a hippie. Mack doesn't think she's either. To him she's just a neat old lady who likes her own company. His sister complains about the dog—how it smells, how it sniffs her privates, how big it is. Dogs in the village have short, happy lives, running free, mating, fighting, chasing things. To Mack's sister, dogs are often a rowdy pack, uncontrollable unless you bend down to pick up a rock.

Dogs remind Mack of Sinbad, the black Lab he once loved at one of his foster homes. Funny how you can imagine that a dog loves you back.

Mack sighs, then chugs back the rest of his beer. He inspects his glass, but there's only froth dripping down the sides—no beer. He orders another one, looking down the dock again and feeling guilty. His campaign to be a better father has been backsliding right from the get-go. It's as if, as soon as he made that promise to himself, he had to break it, on purpose. What do they call that? Reverse something. Reverse psychology. Huh! Maybe he should set out to be a *bad* father. Then, if he failed, it would be a good thing.

Whatever! A good father wouldn't be in the bar, pounding back beers. At least he's got the boys rowing now—and paddling. He made them paddle him here, in the southeaster, even though he could have walked. He's fixed one hole in the canoe, so at least they don't have to bail every two minutes. Maybe tomorrow he'll fix up a couple of rowing stations. Yeah. That's what he'll do. They'll move faster that way, especially with his weight in the boat.

Hmmm. What are the boys doing now? he wonders. He sees them disappear into Harry's boat. The dog's still there, so Harry must be too. A rush of cars sluice dirty water onto the bar windows. The rain hasn't let up any. He supposes the boys must be wet by now. Maybe that's what they're doing on Harry's boat. Staying dry. He hopes they won't tell Harry where he is.

Mack stares, keeps staring out the window. He's drunk now. He can feel how stupid he must seem: big, fat, dumb. But the waitress comes by and he agrees to another mug.

Come on, they're all right, he thinks, hating himself. They're young. They'll survive. He turns in his seat and leans towards the next table.

"Anyone got a smoke?"

Ricky Nash gives him one, living up to his nickname, Ricky-nice-guy. Ricky's a faller, pulling trees down every day. In his time off he lives at the bar, where he's known for buying the beer. He doesn't have a wife or kids, or a truck, or a house. He's happy in the bar, playing pool or darts, getting drunk.

Big Mack turns back in his seat, taps the ash off the Export A tailor-made, then pulls on the beer. The windows have fogged up a bit so he doesn't see Harry, in her gum boots and rain gear, stumping up the hill towards the bar.

When he's sober, Mack never touches tobacco. Right now it feels wonderful.

Quishaa.

Nice.

In no time at all, the cigarette has crumbled into a pile of ash droppings. Big Mack is crushing it out, wishing for another one, when the waitress, Lisette, plonks a cup of coffee on the table. Then she puts down cream and sugar and another cup of coffee.

Mack knows he's staring at her, but the words haven't come yet. Finally he blurts out: "I didn't order any coffee."

"Nope," shrugs Lisette, "but she did."

Harry is walking through the bar from the ladies room. Mack's eyes won't focus. He closes them, but he knows she'll still be there when he looks up.

"Mack," nods Harry, sliding into the bench across from him. Mack returns the nod, but doesn't speak. He feels like a kid in school who's just been sent to the principal's office.

He drops his eyes and waits while Harry adds cream to her coffee. She stirs it and leaves it while she rolls herself a cigarette. Orange fingers, he notices. Bright orange, from the smokes. He begins to relax. She hasn't said much to him yet. Maybe she just wants a coffee. After all, it can't have been a fun boat ride if she's come from Fortune, on a day like this.

"What're you doing, Mack?"

He drags his eyes from her quick-moving fingers. In no time at all she's rolled two smokes. She hands him one and looks right at him, curious, like a harbour seal—big brown shiny eyes. He looks down again and fumbles with the roll-up, still lost for words. Between his massive fingers, it looks silly, like a matchstick.

"Oh. Nothing much." Mack's answer is delayed, like an echo, from far-off. "You?" He throws it back at her.

"I don't know," Harry admits. "I came into town because something kept telling me I had to. I couldn't stay home till I found out what it was."

"How was the water?" Mack asks. The water is common ground, like the weather, but more involved.

"Snarly until Kingfisher, then I had the tide with me after that. *Polynesia* can handle it, but sometimes I wonder why I bother. Rustum hates me for it. He hides under the table."

Mack raises his eyebrows as he tries to imagine that dog fitting under the little table space. Huh. The dog has the same problems as he does. Too big for everything.

42

"Your boys tie good knots," says Harry, unexpectedly. "You must be raising them like your father raised you."

Mack sits up nervously. He isn't expecting this from Harry and his brain is too foggy to see where she's going with it. He remembers now that Harry came to town when he was a kid, the year before he got shipped out. He takes a long swallow of coffee.

"Yup," he says. "I'm teaching them as much as I can."

"They're on my boat, Mack, waiting for you someplace dry."

Mack is mute, thinking of how it was when he was a boy, waiting in the rain. He can't believe he's blanked out the way he'd felt—cold, hungry, miserable.

"They're good kids, Mack. They're brushing Rustum. Ha!" she chuckles at the thought. "I'm going to the post office and then the grocery store and I'm going to make them supper on board. Grade A spaghetti. You're invited."

Mack hardly knows what Harry is saying anymore. She's inviting him for supper? Shouldn't he tell her to get lost, he'll deal with his boys himself?

"An hour," Harry says, sliding out of the seat. "See you later."

HANNAH

Hannah sits under the glaring lights of the bus depot, her body limp, her head lowered, a can of ginger ale at her feet. The seasickness is making her mind a blank. She'd boarded the bus on the ferry, but even the short journey to the depot turned out to be too much for her. Now, she can go no further.

Earlier, when the ferry neared the relative calm of Departure Bay in Nanaimo, she descended to the car deck with trembling legs, gripping the railings in the stairwell, praying she would not throw up. Other passengers had swarmed past her to their cars, appointments, journeys, lives. As she'd moved out of the stairwell toward the bus, a roar of noise had greeted her. Through the open bow gates she could see grey-green water rushing at the ferry as it steamed ahead. She'd vomited right there on the dark, steel floor, near the bus.

The bus driver was lanky and white-haired. He'd offered up the roll of paper towel he kept for wiping his dashboard. Hannah had cleaned herself with quivering hands, then bent to the puddle on the floor. She could feel the disgust of passers-by as they realised what she was doing. She felt humiliated, but as she was a nurse, she was accustomed to human messes. Cleaning them up was part of her job.

On the bus, she'd sat alone. She'd seen the faces of the passengers as she boarded. They were hoping that she would sit away from them. Despite the paper towel, the scent of sickness hung about her.

The short ride through the pouring rain to the depot told her the day's journey would have to be suspended.

Right now, the thought of moving makes Hannah nauseous. And since she's abandoning her plans, she doesn't need to move. She can sit here in the depot all day. She's washed her face and rinsed her mouth in the washroom. The water mingled with stubborn teardrops, surprisingly plump and viscous. Her face feels fresher, but her body feels old. She closes her eyes and lets her limbs droop in the yellow plastic chair. Around her, people move in patterns: coming through the doors, pausing, shaking off the rain, then getting into line for a ticket. Children squirm with impatience at journeys that have not even started yet. Mothers herd them into corners, hushing them with threats or bribes. Hannah sees only feet: theirs and hers. When the feet step out of the narrow slice of her range, her eyes do not follow, but return to the dark blue of her overnight bag or the wet footprints that splash across the grimy floor.

In her misery, she imagines that one pair of these feet belong to Rob. She pictures his shiny brown-leather-shod feet stepping purposefully towards her, escorting her back across the water and the mountains, to Whitehorse.

In the early days, Hannah was overwhelmed by Rob's attentiveness to her. "I'm old-fashioned," he'd said as he wooed her with roses. He never let her pay for a meal. He gave her his coat when she was cold. When they made love, he was solicitous. "You're the most beautiful woman in the world," he would proclaim, touching her hair, or her face. He was such a step up from the men she'd known in Hanson Bay.

Rob was an accountant. A popular man, with many clients, his own office and a secretary. His apartment was clean and spacious, with tall windows that looked out onto the city. The furnishings were rich, expensive. In memory, Hannah trails her hand over the fabrics, feeling the cool leather and rough velvet. In these surroundings she had recreated her life, become a woman of quality, not some backwoods girl.

Now, Hannah leans forward in her chair, examining her fingernails for dirt. The movement doesn't set her stomach heaving this time. Perhaps the nausea is finally settling. She thinks about her journey.

She was a different person in Whitehorse. In Hanson Bay, she'll be Fortune-Island Hannah again. It's a step backwards, but perhaps it'll be a relief, for a while.

Once, after they had been dating for six months, Rob had come to visit her at the hospital. It was an unexpected visit, one which changed things forever. She remembers every detail.

She's in the pale-green hospital corridor talking to Dr McNeill. McNeill is new, with curly brown hair and boundless energy. She's recounting the story of a recent admission, a woman with pneumonia, who keeps trying to lean out of the window and smoke. Hannah's caught her at it, twice.

Unknown to her, Rob is watching this conversation, taking in every detail.

That night, he waits for her outside the hospital.

"I saw you fawn over that doctor," he hisses. "I saw him lap it up. You think I'm dumb? Blind?"

"What?!" She gapes at him, winded by his venom.

"You're screwing him!"

"What do you mean, Rob? I don't know what you mean."

"Don't try to deny it!"

"Deny what?"

"Your affair with that doctor. I saw you talking to him today. You're having an affair. Don't try to deny it!"

"I'm not!" she gasps.

"You're telling me I'm stupid?"

"Not stupid. Wrong!"

His hands grasp her long hair, twisting and twisting, pulling her head back, pulling her eyelids wide. He bares his teeth at her and gives a vicious tug, then strides away, climbs into his canary yellow Mustang, squeals a U-turn.

That night he comes to her door, drunk, and accuses her repeatedly. They argue outside in the brown-carpeted foyer, which smells of stale air and the stink of yesterday's fried food. She tries to persuade Rob of her innocence, but nothing convinces him. He pokes his long, clean forefinger at her with violent jabs, as if she's his calculator, giving him the wrong sum. Every statement seems to feed his anger, give his argument more credence. He vibrates with a new frequency— unpredictable, irrational. He wants her to move departments, away from Dr McNeill. To do that, she'd have to move hospitals; quit her job. She slips away from him the instant he takes his eyes off her. He pounds on the door with his fists, while she pushes home the bolt, looks for a chair to wedge under the handle.

That week she stays home nights, avoiding the shimmering waves of anger and accusation. Then, one evening, she looks out of her window and sees Rob in his car, across the street, staring right at her. Cold fear runs through her. He stays there all night. It's another week before she's able to sleep again.

Hannah shivers, remembering her fear. After that week Rob seemed to pull himself back together. He came by one night and apologized. He poured wine, cooked omelettes, went home afterwards. He called her the next day. And the next. Soon things were back to normal. The incident was dropped, but it whined, like a mosquito, in the back of Hannah's mind. She found it impossible to equate the person she knew with the glimpse of the person she had seen. She was unable to shake off her fear of him. She stopped mentioning him to her co-workers. Her previously free-flowing conversation became staccato, constantly bumping into invisible barriers. She continued like this for another year. In all that time Rob stayed calm. His humour seemed restored, he treated her well and told her that he loved her more than anything in the world.

After a while, Hannah could find nothing visible to indicate that Rob was a jealous man. Only a strange numbness in part of her mind reminded her of what had happened between them. They made a handsome couple. His friends approved. They didn't see the glaze of change that had come over her.

That was before the drugs.

Hannah shudders as Rob's imaginary footsteps move past her and out through the twin glass doors of the depot. She wills the feet away from her, out of her mind and into another world. A hand touches her arm and Hannah gasps, but it's a small, sticky hand, belonging to a chubby, dark-haired, dark-eyed boy. The toddler is making his way around the room, holding onto the chairs. He needs to get past her to continue his route. She breathes out in one long, shaky breath and looks around for his mother. There's a petite Native woman behind them, with short, dark hair. She's waiting in line to buy a ticket. She looks like a girl Hannah went to school with, but Hannah doesn't remember her name.

Hannah holds her hand out, giving the boy his cue. He follows the length of her arm, then transfers his hands to her other, outstretched arm. This way he moves around Hannah's overnight bag and her legs. When he reaches the next chair, he looks up at her and grins. His small teeth gleam. Hannah smiles back. The toddler's grin grows wider and Hannah winks, making him laugh. Her thoughts left behind, she stands up gingerly, then bends to pick up her bag and the can of pop. She wiggles her fingers at the boy as he stands there, gripping the chair, beaming at her. Then she heads for the taxi rank, with plans to find a motel, bathe and sleep. As she passes through the doors of the depot a gust of wind comes sideways at her, showering her with rain. She ducks her head and aims for the nearest cab.

BIG MACK

Big Mack and Old Mack sit at the long kitchen table. Raylene has made breakfast, frying up bread and bacon. The boys have eaten already and have gone out. As usual, Old Mack takes a few bites and then gives up. He doesn't have much appetite these days and Mack is getting worried about him. He looks ghostly, with his white, white hair and clothes that seem empty, as if there's no body inside them. His head and hands stick out from his shirt as if to say: We know we're supposed to be here, so we'll hang around. It'll keep everyone happy.

Old Mack still has stamina, though. In his youth, this stamina had seen him through weeks of drinking. In middle age, some nuns helped him find the Lord and quit the alcohol. He became known for working long hours, logging or fishing. His pace is much slower now, but he can still work. And even though he's taken on a Catholic God, he never lets go of his roots. The potlatch he'd been to recently had gone on from noon one day until eight the next morning. He sat through the whole thing, never sleeping, his spine straight. He doesn't sing at potlatches any more, but at one time he had been a member of the singing group.

"Have some more, Dad," Mack urges. "I can make you some toast if you like."

"Just pour me some coffee."

Mack reaches for the pot and pours a cup for each of them.

"How long can I take the boat for?" he asks. There's a long silence. He isn't bothered by this. Old Mack likes to consider all angles of a situation. Sometimes he'll start talking about something completely different, but he doesn't usually forget what you've asked him. It just takes him a while to decide what he's going to say. Nowadays Old Mack uses the *North Wind* to carry freight up and down the coast. There isn't much fishing any more and he can make more money hauling freight.

Big Mack pushes some loose sugar crystals around the grey

arborite tabletop with his spoon. Even when it's clean, the table always seems to have sugar spilled on it. He starts to doodle on the back of an envelope.

"If it's nice I might need to take a load out the day after Christmas." Old Mack picks up his cup and slurps a mouthful of coffee. "I don't trust this weather, though. The waves have been coming at the beach funny. I could hear them first thing this morning. I never know what it means when they make that noise."

"Huh," says big Mack. "It's cleared up though. Maybe a change is coming. There's been too much rain anyway. I'm getting sick of it."

"It's winter," says Old Mack, his eyebrows raised. "It rains."

Mack's doodle turns into a picture of his canoe. He's trying to figure out how to make the canoe safer. Water leaks through the rivets and the ribs look like crusts of toast, crumbling to nothing. Whenever he sits on the seat in the back, he thinks about adding some floatation. The first thing to do is ditch the outboard—stop pretending that it works. Like the canoe, the outboard is a piece of junk.

Mack's doodle slowly becomes a shopping list. The reason he's asked to borrow his father's boat is to take a water tank out to Fortune Island. Harry roped him into doing this for her when he went for supper on the *Polynesia*. By suppertime that night he was even drunker than he'd been when she'd first found him at the bar. He didn't even know what he was agreeing to. She'd come to his house the next day to remind him. If he looked blank, it was because he didn't remember anything about it. Also because his head was pounding and red lights were pulsing behind his eyes. He had a vague memory of spaghetti and the boys pushing him home along the road. They left the canoe in Hanson Bay that night.

"I'll get someone to take the tank down to the dock," Harry had said, "but you'll need a hand loading it. It's huge. Too big for me to take. And anyway, I won't be able to get it off the boat once I'm home."

Mack wonders just how big this tank is. He doesn't really mind taking it out there. He needs to get away from home. Christmas is getting nearer, just a few days away now. He can feel the stress building, not just in himself, but in everyone else. It'll be good to get away. And the boys are excited about the trip.

Coffee.

Bread.

Bullets.

Peanut Butter.

Fish.

Mack gets up and looks in the cupboard. There are still about two dozen jars of fish left over from the summer. He pulls out three of them and goes to look for Raylene.

She's in her room, nursing the baby and smoking a cigarette. Raylene's always smoking. Old Mack doesn't notice because he smokes, too, but Big Mack doesn't think the smoke is good for the baby. He never says that, because Raylene might get mad at him. She doesn't say much at the best of times, but when she's in a temper she can go for days without speaking.

"Er, Raylene," he says quietly, not wanting to disturb her. "Were you thinking about making bread today?"

"There's no flour."

"Oh."

Silence.

"I'm going to town," Mack ventures. "If I got you some flour, would you think about making some bread?"

Raylene butts out her cigarette and exhales in a long, dramatic whoosh of smoke. "Haa-ah," she drawls, raising her eyebrows. "Get that Five Roses white flour. Get a bunch of it."

"Okay. Thanks, Ray," says Mack, slowly closing the door, then changing his mind and leaving it ajar so that some of the smoke can get out.

He goes to the front room and pulls on his boots and jacket. Stuffing the list in his pocket, he decides he'll just think of things when he's in the store. Old Mack has gone next door, so he takes a minute and rolls himself a joint. He decides to smoke half of it on the doorstep, before going down to the boat. The thought cheers him.

Cold, fresh air greets him as he steps outside. The sky is still grey, but harsh and bright. He feels a surge of energy. It'll be good to do something. Good to get away.

LONNY

Lonny races down to the dock. "I'm gonna beat you this time, Sam!"

"No way!" yells Sam. "You're too slow!"

Lonny pumps his legs and arms as fast as he can, running till his chest is bursting. It's no good. Sam is one of the fastest boys in the village. By the time Lonny gets to the float, Sam is sitting on a tie-up rail. He's not even out of breath.

"Told you I'd win!" gloats Sam.

The rain has let up and Lonny has a lot to do. Tomorrow, Lonny and Sam and Big Mack are taking Old Mack's boat to Hanson Bay to pick up a big water tank. Then they're going to take it to Fortune Island. Uncle has promised that they can take the canoe, too. On the way back they might try hunting or fishing. They might even spend a night on the boat. For sure, they're going to row around and look for firewood on the beaches. Uncle will cut the wood up with his chainsaw. Lonny and Sam will row it out to the boat.

Lonny can hardly wait. He likes the old lady from Fortune Island. She makes spaghetti and she tells stories. She says she's going to make them some cookies, too, when they come visit. And her dog will be there.

Lonny has never been to Fortune Island before. Sometimes he gets to ride on his grandpa's boat, but not often. It's a red seiner, called the *North Wind*. It's the biggest boat at the North Hanson dock. Nobody takes it out for fun. Only for work.

Uncle Mack has promised to fix up the canoe. They'll need it on this trip, so he's going to do it today. Ever since the day Lonny and Sam got in trouble for paddling, Uncle has been making them row everywhere. It's hard work, because he likes to come too. He sits in the back and the canoe tilts down real low. Once, the water even came in and he had to move forward more. It's pretty hard work rowing Big Mack around. He just sits there with his arms folded and hums the same Indian song over and over again. He only stops humming to tell them which way to go. He never takes a turn paddling, even when the boys are tired. Sometimes he bails, though. There's two bailers, but no lifejackets. Lifejackets are for sissies. Lonny and Sam are good swimmers. They don't need lifejackets.

Sam starts emptying out the canoe. They have to clean it before Uncle will fix it. Somehow, a bunch of sand got in the bottom. There's a dead starfish, too. It used to be purple and shiny. Now, it's grey. It smells. The fishing line is tangled up like a crow's nest in the back. Lonny can see a hook sticking through, ready to poke someone. He grabs the line and starts trying to unravel it. It used to be wound around a juice bottle, but he can't see the bottle anywhere. He's busy concentrating when something smacks into his feet. It's the dead starfish.

"Gotcha!" Sam laughs from the canoe.

Lonny is on the dock, so Sam is at his mercy. He throws the starfish and hits Sam in the chest, then he dashes back up the ramp, out of the line of fire. Looking over his shoulder he sees Sam getting out of the canoe. Then he sees Sam starting to grin.

He is so busy looking over his shoulder at Sam that he doesn't see his uncle coming. Bam! Lonny collides with Big Mack. It's like running into a punching bag, except that Big Mack doesn't move.

"Whoa there, Lon!" smiles Uncle, holding him at arm's length. "What're you trying to do? Push me off the dock?"

"Sam's gonna get me!" gasps Lonny.

"No way," calls out Sam from down below. "Lonny got me with a starfish. It was gross. I threw it over."

"Are you done with the canoe?" asks Big Mack.

"Pretty much," says Sam, looking down at the puddles of sand, as if he's wondering how they got there.

Big Mack walks down the ramp, propelling Lonny in front of him. He looks down at the rickety tin canoe.

"It'll do, I guess," he sighs. He climbs up onto the *North Wind* and comes back with a drill, some blocks of wood and some bolts. He puts down the tools and gets into the canoe. It tilts right down, but he doesn't seem to notice. He takes off the useless outboard motor and heaves it onto the dock. "No point rowing this around, eh?" he comments. Lonny doesn't answer. He and Sam together can't lift that motor. They tried one time, when they were by the beach. Big Mack used two hands but he could've done it with one. Lonny can tell. Nobody else is as strong as his uncle. It's a true fact.

Mack climbs back out of the canoe, and sits on the old grey planks of the dock. "What are we going to do with this?" he asks, looking at the motor. "It's not even heavy enough to be a good anchor." Lonny doesn't answer.

Mack gets up and grabs the bow of the canoe. Single-handedly, he pulls it up onto the dock, while Lonny and Sam look on.

"Get in," he tells them. "Let's measure where to put these oarlocks."

HARRY

Harry washes her face, then fastens her hair into a clip at the back of her neck. It's not raining any more, but she reaches her green raincoat down from the hook. Then she leans over and pulls on her rubber boots. Rustum's tail thumps loudly.

"Let's go, then," she says.

She opens the door of the boat and lets Rustum squeeze out ahead of her. Then she closes up and steps down onto the dock. It's a grey morning, but she can see the mountains. They aren't hidden by clouds. Instead, they loom large—a deep, dark blue that Harry seldom sees. She loves the vivid intensity of this colour. It's full of contradiction: dark and bright; gaudy and subtle. It's rare, so it makes her feel as if she's just encountered a wolf or a cougar. She fills her eyes as she stands on the dock, puffs of wind coming at her from different directions.

As she walks up the dock, she feels a stab of arthritis in her left hip. It's not enough to slow her down, but she hates the fact of it. Harry has lived life in pursuit of independence. Her boat, her cabin, living on the island—even raising Hannah. She's done all these things by herself. She doesn't want to think about being old and decrepit. It's too depressing. Perhaps the smokes will give her a heart attack—pow! dead, just like that! That would be ideal. But everyone hopes for a clean death, she thinks, and few people are so lucky.

Harry stops at the top of the ramp and looks up at the mountains again. She will lose sight of them as she walks into town, so this is her last chance.

She walks along Thornton Avenue, past the post office and the liquor store. A bit further down is the Seagull Café. That's where she's hoping to find Jack. She might be too late, though. Jack and his cronies make up the seven-o'clock club. They're all in their sixties or seventies with not too much to do, but after a lifetime of hard work, they can't shake the habit of rising early. Rather than being stuck at home in the dark, they get together at the Seagull as soon as it opens. There, they hash out age-old arguments and complain about new developments in Hanson Bay. The waitress, Darlene, knows what they like and only asks if they're eating, not what they're eating.

Harry can see the blue and white illuminated sign hanging above the sidewalk, its trademark seagull disappearing beneath a layer of green algae. The sign's light is still on, although it's not dark any more. It must be 8:30, by now. Jack might have gone home. His house isn't much further from the Seagull, but his coffee is instant and weak. Right now Harry wants real coffee—strong coffee. As she gets to the steamed-up window, she peers through it to the far right hand corner. Jack and his friends are in there, in their uniform buttoned shirts and suspenders, their heads bobbing. They *are* a bit like seagulls, she muses as she pushes open the door, smiling to herself as she overhears the tail end of a squabble.

The café is warm and overly bright. Moisture clings to the windows and a thick smell of smoke and bacon smears the air. Jack has his back to her, so he hasn't seen her yet, but the others have. Cutter McKay is staring sideways at Harry, his eyes narrowed, his mouth pursed. His cousin, Keith, looks at Harry and then at Jack, his expression warning of imminent disaster. Harry approaches them anyway.

"Good morning you old geezers!" she says as she pulls a chair over from another table. She hopes the false brightness will irritate Cutter. She calls over to the counter: "Darlene, can I get some of that black death, please? I'm truly desperate."

The men bob their heads at her and make small clucking noises. Jack smiles with genuine pleasure and asks her how she's doing.

"Well, it's December and I can see the mountains, so I suppose I can't grumble," Harry replies. "Eh, Cuthbert?" she adds, purposely using Cutter's full name, knowing it will embarrass him.

Cutter and Keith McKay look at each other and then pointedly at Harry. They push back their chairs and Cutter reaches for his hat. Keith says: "Well, we've sat around long enough; it's time to get to work."

"Really?" queries Harry, causing a cautious blurt of laughter. The two men glare at her, as if they really do have work to do. She's glad they're going. The unpleasantness will be over now. She moves into Cutter's still-warm seat and gratefully accepts the coffee that Darlene brings over. She pulls out her tobacco and rolls herself a smoke. The BC no-smoking laws haven't reached the Seagull yet, but the noisy extractor fans do a good job of pulling the smoke up and away from the food. Harry pulls the ashtray towards her. It already has half a dozen butts in it.

When the door swings shut behind Cutter and Keith, Harry apologizes.

"I'm sorry," she says to the remaining men. She'll apologize to them, but not to Cutter. The rift between her and Cutter is too deep, goes too far back.

Before Harry met Alain, she worked for Cutter, deckhanding on his father's fishboat. They would leave early in the morning and work hard all day. In all that time, Cutter never said much to her. She didn't mind. She liked being at sea and she was always busy. They ate their lunch at different times and she thanked him when he paid her. That was it. But when Cutter left the boat and moved on up to the bar, he let it be known that Harry was his woman. That she put out for him. Lionel Nieder asked Harry about it one day, when she was at the grocery store. He knew he'd made a mistake when he saw her face turn white. "Thank you Lionel," she'd said. "If you hadn't told me about this, I would never have known." She put her basket down, right at his feet, turned and left the building.

She went to the bar, of course, and there he was with a group of lads his age, all of them drunk, trying to get drunker. She confronted him right there, so his friends could hear.

"Cutter's looking for a new deckhand," she said, watching the collective rise of the group's eyebrows. Cutter said nothing and she took some pleasure from the look on his face. "Apparently he spends his time at sea dreaming up stories to tell you about me. That must be why he's so quiet all day. It's hard work dreaming up so many fantasies, hey Cutter?"

There were a few jeers then, eyes veering back and forth between Cutter and Harry, not sure who to believe. Harry remembers the awkwardness, the guys puffing on their smokes, Cutter staring, speechless. She felt bad hammering into him, when he was so obviously incapable of defending himself. But he started it.

"I don't work for liars," she told him. "So I guess I don't work for you. Better get one of these guys to help you tomorrow." She stared at the others, one by one. "If you can. They might not want you making up stories about *them* . . . ."

She heard the uproar begin the instant the bar door closed behind her, but she didn't stay to listen. She got back to the store before it closed, picked up her basket and continued her shopping. The next day she went down to the cannery and got a job cleaning fish, with a crew of women. Two days later she met Alain. Two weeks after that she was living with him.

Rumours about Harry and Cutter ranged from her version to his. Cutter grew up in Hanson Bay so he had more backers. It was unfortunate that Harry met Alain so soon after the little scene at the bar; people naturally assumed that she'd invented an excuse to throw Cutter over, thus leaving herself free for the new guy.

The seven o'clock club has heard most sides of this story. It's old news now and Harry doesn't feel compelled to defend herself to them. Instead, she smokes and swallows coffee while the conversation resumes. Danny Woollan and Arnold Brown are talking about fishing. They rarely talk about anything else. This time it's about whether there'll be any herring this year. Arnold asks Harry about her trip to town.

"Oh, I didn't come in today," she says, "I chose yesterday's horrible weather instead. It's funny, you know. I always thought that I'd get smarter as I got older."

"Yup," says Danny, "a year older and and a year dumber, that's what Annie always tells me. She has no mercy, that woman."

"Of course not, she's your wife," Harry spars, with shiny eyes. "She swore eternal honesty, right there at the altar."

"Ooooohhhh!" Danny cries with a smile, while the seagulls look on, squawking and flapping. The mood of the group improves and the repartee quickens. Harry enjoys the chance to use her wit and doesn't mind when the jokes are on her.

Eventually she gets onto her second coffee and has a chance to tell Jack what she's arranged. Her huge, black plastic water tank has been delivered to his yard, where it is taking up space, waiting for Harry to deal with it.

"If you can leave the tank where it is," she tells Jack, "the Peterson boys will come by this afternoon and take it down to the dock. Big Mack Stanley's going to come and get it with the *North Wind* tomorrow morning. Hopefully the two of us will be able to haul it into place, once he arrives."

"Hmm. I don't know about that, Harry," Jack says, pinching the bridge of his nose. "Mack's a big man, but that's a big tank you've got there. I suspect you'll need a come-along and some rollers."

"I was planning to push it off the boat and float it to shore at high tide, then use my firewood winch to get it as far as the woodshed. The rest of the plan, I haven't got to yet. But if I have to unbolt the winch, I can do that. Then tie it onto a tree somewhere and pull from there."

"Take my five-ton puller," interrupts Arnold. "That'll do the job, no problem."

"I can't do that." Harry replies, "I won't be back in town for a month."

"Oh shush," says Arnold. "You think I don't know that? I've used that thing twice in five years. Where's your boat tied up? I'll drop the puller off before you leave. It'll be perfect. You'll see."

Harry sips her coffee, grateful for the offer. This water tank has put her on the spot. She isn't really prepared for its arrival and would prefer to leave it in Jack's yard for a month. It would give her time to plan where it will go and how she will get it there. The tank is enormous, though. Much bigger than she'd pictured. It's taking up the entire spot where Jack parks his truck. She has to get it out of there. The puller will be a help. She must remember to bring Arnold some bread the next time she comes to town.

A few hours after the club has dispersed, Jack and Harry wander slowly through town together, heading for Harry's boat. Rustum is half a block ahead of them, on the other side of the road. Harry is smoking a pre-voyage cigarette, taking deep drags. She sticks the toe of her gumboot into every puddle in her path, kicking out splashes of water.

"I'm guessing Hannah's okay," says Jack, rubbing his chin. "It's been three months, though, eh? She used to write every two weeks. Even if it was only a postcard."

Harry is quiet, trying hard not to feel jealous. According to Jack, Hannah always sends her love to Harry. She usually only writes to Jack, though. She seldom writes home and the letters, when they arrive, are outdated and colourless. Harry's daughter might just as well be a foreigner these days. But then, she's been a foreigner to Harry since she turned fourteen.

"I did phone the Whitehorse hospital last Thursday," says Jack. "She wasn't working that day. I didn't try again."

Harry turns to face Jack.

"I just wish I could see her face. You know? Then I could tell if she was really happy. Sometimes I draw pictures of her, just so I have a face to pour my thoughts into. I miss her so much, Jack. But I can't force her to love me, or even to accept who I am." Her eyes brim with tears and she turns away, biting her lip.

Jack is quiet. Harry is seldom emotional, but the topic of Hannah is always a delicate one. He's an honest man and he wants to get it right.

"It's hard to say, there, Harry. Just don't go blaming yourself, that's all. You did your best with what you had. No one can say different. And one day Hannah may come to respect that. She's confused, is all. For now, she has to learn who she is. And we know she can't do that here."

"Until Hannah left, I never dreamed that the wilderness could be a bad place to raise a child," says Harry. "I still don't. In my dreams, children grow up loved and wild, with the land in their hearts."

They walk in silence for a while and turn down to the boat. Harry won't be back in town for several weeks. Even though she's a sociable person, it's usually the supplies that lure her to Hanson Bay, not the people. But it's going to be Christmas, so she's bought extra groceries. If the weather's nice, she might get visitors. She knows that Big Mack is coming tomorrow and hopes he brings his boys. One of the bags has chocolate chips in it, for cookies. Somehow it's different when people come to visit her. She loves to have company when she's at home. As long as there's an end date.

"That's the last telephone pole you're going to see for a while, Rustum," Harry calls out, breaking the mood. "Better make the most of it." Rustum looks up, bemused. He comes shambling across the street, completely missing the telephone pole.

Harry smiles at Jack and shrugs. "Did I claim that he was smart?"

The *Polynesia* starts easily, thrumming with all the bass tones of a well-loved diesel motor. Harry unties, and waits for the current to catch the bow and pull the boat away from the dock.

Inside the cabin she squints to find the green buoy. Near it is Bailey's Rock—not something she wants to run into. She steers outwards and keeps the rock on her right. Her route follows the curve of the land as it swings around to the northwest. She moves out into the channel, with the Hanson Bay mainland on her right and the protective barrier of Perez Island on her left. Behind Hanson Bay, the mountains rise up, still glowing with colour, now more violet than blue. The colour washes over Harry's melancholy, soft and sweet. She feels the fear and guilt ebbing away with the tide. The sadness is still there.

The sadness will always be there.

HANNAH

The bus speeds around a cliff corner, swaying out to the side, its three passengers clinging to their seats.

"You drive too fast!" yells the old lady in the front. She leans forward to see if the bus driver will respond. "My dentures are coming loose!"

Despite himself, the driver breaks into a smile. He's been poker-faced and gruff for most of the trip, which doesn't bother Hannah. His driving, on the other hand, does bother her. She's glad for the Gravol she took. This road is known for its potholes and switchbacks. Every year it claims its share of victims.

"I can slow down," the bus driver agrees.

"Yes, but can you drive better?" The old lady fixes him with an inquisitive look and the man behind Hannah laughs. Originally he'd been sitting at the back, but the swaying had been too much for him and he'd moved forward.

The bus driver reclaims his gruff face and mumbles a comment about back seat drivers that Hannah can't hear.

"But I'm in the front seat," the old lady says. "Right here where I can tell you what to do." She trills a little giggle, her fingers touching her lips. Everybody bursts out laughing, even the bus driver—even Hannah.

"Right on!" says the man behind Hannah.

The old lady turns and beams, her wrinkles creasing in arcs towards her ears. Her grey hair is immaculately pinned in a French roll. Hannah imagines touching it with the palm of her hand. She can tell from here that it will be rigid with hair spray.

Hannah's forefinger winds through her own hair, a constant motion. The closer she gets to Hanson Bay, the more trepidation she feels. She and Mother have never come to terms with each other. They might never come to terms. Hannah will have to visit her mother, but she isn't sure if she can manage more than one day at Fortune Island. Hashing out her childhood is not something she has the energy for.

"Hannah, why can't you just be yourself?"
"I am myself, Mother, I'm just not the person you think I am."
"You're trying to be someone you're not."
"You don't understand me! Leave me alone!!"

Hannah realises that something about the old lady in the front reminds her of her mother. Harry can be a bit of a show-off when she's in company. Hannah was embarrassed by this on countless occasions when she was younger. Still, she admires this old lady's feisty spirit. She's seen so many older people who wander the corridors of the palliative wing, looking at their toes. Their eyes are huge and empty, as if their spirits have fled. Hannah notices them because their expressions seem so familiar. She knows that when she was with Rob, she felt like this too—frightened and empty. She wonders where her spirit fled to. She wonders: if you lose your spirit, do you ever find it again?

The bus begins its slow descent, down the switchbacks to North Hanson and Hanson Bay. It's a grey day, but clear. Hannah can see the Sound stretching away northwest, into the distance. Soft blue-green islands seem to float on the water, like turtles surfacing. The curve of one inlet disappears behind a mauve-coloured ridge, while the steep straight sides of another knife their way due north. This is one of the most dramatic views of Hanson Sound and Hannah catches glimpses of the route she would take if she were driving to Fortune Island. At the next switchback, the bus turns and she's able to see to the south—one large, mountainous island dominating the view.

It's as if, with every inlet and island, Hannah's chest fills with compressed emotion. Her upper arms, ribs and breastbone tingle and her eyes mist with tears, but she feels unable to cry. Instead, the emotion pools inside her, flooding in from the trees and the creeks as they flash by her window. Seconds of pure elation are instantly replaced by seconds of confusion. Until now, she'd locked out this strange love she feels for the land, the mysterious way it creeps into her bones. Now that her defenses are low, she can't keep it out. Hannah's ribcage stretches and grows, tighter and tighter, until she presses her hands to her chest to stop it from exploding. Eventually she closes her eyes.

She can tell when the descent is over: the bus levels out and there are fewer corners. She opens her eyes again. Soon they're close to the water—calm grey inlet water, lapping at pebbly beaches—glimpsed through dripping cedar and hemlock trees. In Whitehorse, trees are a uniform height, their branches held tight to their trunks, poking out like hands, instead of outstretched arms. Now she's in the rainforest and the trees sprawl or swirl dramatically, embracing each other with greenery—bending and stretching, curling and spiking—a generous tangle of age-old cousins.

Hannah wasn't raised in the rainforest. Fortune Island is rocky and windy. The trees are mostly shore pines that struggle to grow, just as Hannah had.

What was I struggling against? she wonders, suddenly. When she thinks about it, she isn't sure she knows.

The bus slows and thrums into a deeper gear. They're arriving in North Hanson. The backs of brightly painted houses dot the road to Hannah's left. The highway passes inland of the village, whose houses and harbour face southeast. A small connecting road links the highway to the village. The bus jerks to a stop and the man behind Hannah gets up.

"*Choo*," he says, nodding to Hannah and the old lady. He turns to the driver and nods to him too.

"Well, at least you made it!" The old lady glances at the bus driver to see if she's annoyed him yet. He's grinning, apparently resigned to the ribbing.

Nobody is waiting for the bus, so he takes off again, continuing along the coast. It's only another mile before the first houses

66

come into view and the little wooden sign welcoming people to Hanson Bay. The suddenness of it takes Hannah by surprise and tears spill onto her cheeks. She tries to stop them, but they come anyway, until she balls her fists and blinks hard to stem the flow. The bus drives on, past the hardware store and the gas station, the Woollans' house and the Fyffes'. The road curves around the little south-facing bay the town has been named for, its harbour protected from storms by the narrow length of Perez Island.

Gradually, Hannah recovers her self-control. Dabbing her eyes with a tissue, she opens her purse and pulls out a bag of cosmetics. Looking in a mirror, she grimaces at the tell-tale puffiness of her eyes and decides to leave them alone; instead, she runs a comb through her straight brown hair and pulls it into a clip at the back of her neck. For courage, she dabs on a touch of shell-pink lipstick. Then she puts her things away, straightens her pale blue, high-necked sweater and brings her navy blazer down from the rack. When the bus pulls in to the flat, rectangular Co-op parking lot, she's ready. She stands up, smoothes the creases out of her jeans and slides her blazer on.

Moving up between the seats, she helps the old lady find her jacket and her bag.

"Thank you, dear," smiles the old lady.

Hannah smiles back and hefts her own bags. She doesn't pause, but heads up the street. Jack will be overjoyed to see her, she knows. She turns left on Fifth Avenue, and walks another two blocks to Alder Street. As she rounds the last corner, she sees a small man walking slowly up a flight of wooden steps and vanishing into the tangle of honeysuckle that consumes the porch. The little shingled house is exactly as she remembers it. The stoop of Jack's shoulders is more pronounced, but instantly recognizable.

"Jack!" she calls out, surprising herself with the volume of her shout. "Jack!"

There's a glimmer of movement from the porch. She sees his

pale, questioning face emerge from the shadows as she crosses the street. Her smile spreads wide as she strides towards him.

"Jack! I'm here!"

He's shrunk a lot in five years. He seems more vulnerable and his face is beakier than ever. But the smile that shines out of him is the same. Hannah drops her bags at the gate and runs up the steps. She sinks into his shoulder and hugs him and cries. They stand there for a long time, under the winter canopy of leafless, woody vines.

"You'll be fine," says Jack, into Hannah's shoulder. "You'll be fine."

BIG MACK

Big Mack is making fish sandwiches for the next day's journey when the phone rings. He puts down the jar of salmon and goes into the front room to look for the phone. Somehow, it always ends up under a chair or a couch somewhere. This time it's on the arm of Old Mack's recliner.

"Hullo?" he says, cautiously. He doesn't like telephones. Unless he holds the receiver with a thumb and two fingers, his hand tends to smother the mouthpiece and people can never hear him properly.

"Uh huh."

"Hmm."

"Okay."

"*Choo*."

Mack replaces the receiver with care and leaves the phone on the arm of the chair. He goes back into the kitchen and picks up the bread knife. Careful not to press too hard, he saws off a piece of the bread Raylene had made that evening. He loves the squishiness of fresh bread. And the smell. They had butter clams for dinner, but the combination of salmon and fresh bread is too good to resist. Mack takes the first sandwich, leans his back against the kitchen counter and eats.

From the corridor comes a shuffling noise and the creak of tired wood. Old Mack emerges from his evening bath looking younger and rested.

"Who called?" he asks.

"Eagle Jack," Mack says, after a moment of swallowing. A lot of people call Jack this, because of his nose. As he ages, he looks even more like an eagle—a small eagle, but an eagle.

"What does he want?"

Big Mack resists taking another bite of his sandwich. He puts it down on the counter. "He was just phoning to ask if I could take

69

Harry Farre's girl out to Fortune with me when I go tomorrow. She's here for Christmas, I guess."

"Huh." Old Mack muses. "I thought she *chii-et-shilth.*"

"I don't think she ran away," replies Mack. "I think she went to school or something." He picks up his sandwich again and eats half the remainder in one bite.

"It's right for her to come home," Old Mack states. He walks over to his recliner and picks up the TV remote. He'll probably stay in his recliner until midnight. Then he'll be up again at five or six.

Mack finishes his sandwich and resists eating another one. He makes four more: one for each of the boys and two for him. He wonders if he should make one for Harry's daughter, but that would mean opening another jar. And anyway, it's getting late.

He wakes when he hears his father moving around: ten to six. He isn't feeling too bad today. Maybe it's because of the journey. He wonders what Harry's daughter is like. He has a vague memory of a serious, high-school girl, brown-haired and gangly. She's probably about ten years younger than him.

Mack likes women. They're easier to talk to than men. More understanding. They're beautiful, too, with their dainty faces and bodies. He draws the line at admiring them, though. Big Mack had been with Sam's mother, Sara, from the time he was twenty-two until he was twenty-five. Then she ran off with someone. It was like losing his mother all over again, except that Sara didn't vanish. In the ten years that Sam has been alive, Sara has been through six boyfriends, including Mack. She's a nice lady—Mack still thinks that—but somehow she never seems happy. After Sara, he decided to go it alone, like his dad.

When he's in the bar, Mack sometimes gets offers from women. But it isn't as if he can bring them home to his dad's house. When he was with Sara he had enjoyed making love, and it became even more special after Sam was born—fathering a child was so magical! These days he can't seem to get interested in the offers. He's related to a lot of the women around here, anyway. He hates the thought of sleeping with someone and finding out later she's one of his cousins.

Mack pushes back the covers and feels for his clothes. He gets partially dressed, then goes down the corridor to the washroom. The showerhead screeches as he pulls the knob, but the water is hot. He climbs into the tub and pulls the plastic curtain shut. His head sticks out above the curtain rail. Showering is always frustrating for Mack. If he wants to wash his hair or his face, he almost has to sit down to do it. For now, he's content just standing in the steamy spray. It's a good way to wake up.

Three sleeping bags bounce, one by one, onto the cots in the dank front berth of the *North Wind*. Mack decides not to bother unrolling them. The boys are playing on deck, anxious to be off. High tide isn't until two o'clock, so they have lots of time, but he's promised Jack that he'll get to Hanson Bay by ten. The engine's been warming up for a while. It sounds fine, but needs another five minutes or so. Mack goes back out on deck to check that there's enough rope to tie down the tank. He shouldn't have worried, though. Since Old Mack is in the freight business, he has lots of ropes and straps, all neatly coiled, sitting on the smooth wooden lines of the deck. The deck is open and spacious because the drum and all the gear for the seine has been removed. The boat itself is fifty-five feet long and the deck takes up about two-thirds of that. Where the drum used to be, Mack has stored the canoe, with its new rowing stations and improved seats. He's even added some styrofoam floatation to the stern.

He looks down the length of the North Hanson dock. The other boats are mostly wooden day-trollers—twenty-five to forty feet—or small runarounds, aluminum or fibreglass. Fishing has declined so drastically in recent years, most of the day trollers only go out for home-use, now. It's crazy the way the government bought back all those troller licenses. It's like going to everyone in the village and saying: You know the job that you and your family have done for generations? Well, you can't do that anymore. The big fishing corporations from Vancouver have the licenses now. Maybe you can get a job with them.

Mack gets so mad whenever he thinks about it. His people have been fishing on this coast for thousands of years! He's heard the elders talk about how much fish there used to be. These stupid white people have ruined the fishery in under a hundred years and now, nobody can fish in this little town, this perfectly-located fishing village. Mack clenches his fingers. It's time to go.

"You sure you got everything?" he asks the boys.

"Yup!" they nod, in unison.

"Let's go, then!"

"Yeaaay!" cries Lonny and rushes forward to untie the lines. Mack can't help smiling at his enthusiasm. He can never understand how Lonny can be so happy, when his life's been so sad. He wonders how deep Lonny hides his hurts. He wonders how long it will take for them to surface.

Coming into Hanson Bay Mack can see the tank standing atop the main part of the dock. The tank is big, about eight feet tall, he guesses. He'll have to use the hand-winch to lower it onto the deck.

As he gets closer, he can see Jack with Harry's daughter. Mack manoeuvres the boat alongside the dock, then squeezes out of the cabin, goes forward and grabs a line. He throws it up to Jack, who loops it around a big old metal cleat, worn smooth by countless ropes. Then Mack grabs a stern line and throws it to the girl. She catches it and ties it on, no hesitation. Well, she must have tied up boats her whole life until recently. The boys are already climbing up the metal ladder to the dock. Mack waits until they're done, before following them.

"Hey, there, Mack, Lonny, Sam. Looks like a good day for a ride," says Jack. "You remember Hannah, don'tcha Mack?" Mack glances at the tall, thin woman. Her hair is dark, just a shade lighter than his own, and her face is as pale as fog. Her grey eyes are bloodshot and the hollows behind them are deep and dark. She's wearing pale blue jeans, clean white running shoes and a knitted cream sweater. She doesn't bear much resemblance to his image of a school-girl. She looks much older than he thought she would.

"I think so," he says. "You've changed."

The woman looks at him and her mouth smiles for a second. Then her eyes slide out to the ruffled grey water of the bay.

Huh, Mack thinks.

HANNAH

"Maybe Mother will be able to have a bath or a shower now, instead of swimming, or having a strip wash because she has to save the water for the garden," says Hannah, looking at the water tank.

Jack nods.

"At least in the wintertime, anyways," he adds. "That garden of hers drinks like a fisherman. If it's a dry summer, she'll still be scrimping on water, even with this."

"And when did you last have a dry summer?" Hannah asks, arching her eyebrows.

"Oh, you remember," Jack grins, "that heat wave fifteen years ago, or so."

Hannah laughs, glad for the distraction. She'd been expecting to spend a few days with Jack before going out to Fortune; instead, he'd talked her into leaving right away.

"You need to see her, Hannah," was all he said. She'd seen him blinking as he turned away. His words were spoken with such simple force that it stopped her from replying. Nor did he elaborate, which made her curious.

"You'll find Harry's made a lot of improvements," Jack told her later. "It's getting to be quite the comfy spot. Or so she tells me. I've not gone there myself, of course."

Of course. Fortune Island was in the middle of nowhere. It was a whole day trip to go there and back. There was nobody else to talk to when you were there, except for a large, foul-smelling dog. And maybe some fishermen, coming for gas. Hannah feels all her teenage resentments flooding back: no electricity, no running water, no friends. Nothing normal. Oh, and a cold, revolting outhouse to shit in. Let's not forget that, shall we? So nice to walk that path in the rain, at night. So nice to sit there and watch the giant slugs slide slowly towards you, or see the toilet paper in its jar and know that the mice would eat it if it weren't protected.

Yes. Fortune Island.

"There's the *North Wind*," Jack points as a scarlet seiner slips into view around the corner. The boat and the green marker buoy are the only spots of colour on the ruffled grey water. "I can't believe Mack's so prompt," he laughs. "He's usually a month or two late!"

"And you hire him to fix things?"

"He's a good carpenter, there, Hannah. I could ask a construction company to do stuff and they'd come over the next day. You've got to think about who you support, though. Eh? Life's hard for Mack. He's got the two boys, too."

Life's hard for all of us, Hannah thinks. She remembers Big Mack from her childhood. She'd see him sometimes, from a distance, like a giant from out of a fairy tale. Every year, he seemed to grow bigger.

The *North Wind* slows as it comes around the rocky point and nears the dock. It's a sleek boat and unlike many wooden boats, which need constant upkeep, it's well maintained. There are two kids on board, boys in sweat pants and t-shirts, apparently not cold, despite the winter breeze. The boat turns easily in the confined area between the main dock, the shore and the floats, spinning gently into place beneath them with a muted, last-minute roar of reverse.

Big Mack emerges, wearing jeans and a grey Stanfield work sweater. It stretches across his broad chest and shoulders, stressing the wool and opening the weave. Straight black hair fringes his face and falls unevenly to his shoulders. He's clean-shaven, with a scar that stands out whitely against the cedar-coloured skin of his forehead. He moves quickly, despite his size and throws the rope upwards with ease, so that Jack and Hannah only have to open their hands to catch it. Hannah winds the rope around the smooth metal cleat, enjoying the remembered action.

Within seconds the two boys have scrambled up the ladder and are on the dock. Jack shakes hands with them in a serious, man-to-man way, while Big Mack climbs the ladder. Up close, Hannah can see rips and stains on the boys' clothes. A big toe pokes out of a running shoe that had once been white.

This is it. The last stage—for now. So many journeys—each one a step closer to Harry. Hannah has almost forgotten about Rob in her anxiety about returning to Fortune Island. She has also taken a Gravol tablet today. A hint of nausea touched her at breakfast and she didn't want to risk getting seasick again. Fishboats are notorious for causing seasickness. Even without high seas, the smell of diesel is usually enough to send most landlubbers to the edge. Hannah realises that she's a landlubber now. That explains her new susceptibility to motion sickness.

Jack introduces Hannah to Big Mack, who says he thinks he remembers her, but that she's changed. Hannah wonders how many more people will say those same words to her in the next few weeks. Small talk. She's thankful that Big Mack doesn't say much more to her; instead, he sets about securing the tank with ropes and attaching it to the hand crane. He doesn't ask for help, nor does he seem to need it. He pushes the tank off the edge of the dock with ease and it dangles for a moment in mid-air while he cranks the wheel to lower it.

"I can't promise to stay long," Hannah says as she kisses Jack's cheek.

"Start from the beginning," he replies. "Put the past away, eh? Start again."

Hannah doesn't respond.

"Don't forget, you can always count to ten. Or leave the room. Just remember: whatever happens, she loves you."

Hannah's glad that Big Mack can't hear what Jack is saying. He's already clambered down the ladder with her bag. She lays her hand on Jack's shoulder for a moment, then turns to confront the ladder. Between the dock pilings, the dark water seems to sway with the movement of the ladder. Water drips from pale dangling anemones, limp and lost, waiting for the tide to return. The drips ring out into the cavern-like space, as Hannah's feet and hands negotiate the slimy rungs and she descends to the worn wooden deck of the boat.

The tie-up ropes slither down from above as Jack casts them off. The boys compete to catch them and put them away, the taller boy winning both times. With ease, the *North Wind* spirals away, out into the sound.

Water tumbles upwards from the *North Wind's* propeller, bubbling chaotically before weaving itself into an orderly white spread. Hannah gazes at the wake from the stern of the boat, feeling the reassuring vibration of the motor through her feet. Beyond the ever-widening white lines, Hanson Bay fades into the rainforest. To the south, Quiistuu Island forms a perfect mirror to the wake, its wide green shores ascending symmetrically to a softly curving peak. The island is almost completely round and conical, a distinctive landmark for the flocks of geese and shorebirds that pass by on their journeys north or south. Today, strange layers of cloud flow up and over the highest point of the island, clinging to it. The same effect is apparent over the other mountains, too. There's something eerie about it, as if the clouds have been painted with precise contour lines and colour changes to denote their elevation. Hannah has never seen clouds like this before. Behind them the iron sky is smooth and fluid, undulating with moist, subtle curves. The same colour changes are apparent, but on a grander scale.

On Hannah's right lies Perez Island and memories of summer swimming with high school friends. The lagoons on the island's rocky outer shore warm up a lot, compared to the seawater elsewhere. It's an easy hike to get to them, as the island isn't even a kilometre wide in places. The log-strewn coves gather quantities of shells and pebbles, each tiny beach distinct in its bounty.

Hannah remembers one beach that consists entirely of smooth black stones.

Hannah can only see the retreating view but she can tell when they cross Myrtle Channel. Swells from the open ocean sing by, from right to left, lulling her. Each slow-rolling wave is a hand smoothing her hair or her brow. For a moment she imagines that the water can take away her bruises, too. They haven't faded yet, still causing her to wince when she knocks them accidentally. The ones on her ribs are the most painful, but there are a couple on her upper arms that pinch whenever she moves. She felt them when she was descending the ladder from the dock.

What stopped me from telling Jack? Hannah wonders. The two of them had talked late into the night, but Hannah had told him nothing about the previous week. She told him instead about life as a nurse: the good things, the bad things; the patients who wanted to live and the ones that complained about living.

"Any young men in your life?" Jack asked at one point.

"Not right now," Hannah replied, half-truthfully.

"I thought maybe you had gone to ground because you were in love."

Ironic.

"I stopped writing because I was planning this trip. I wanted it to be a surprise." She evaded the truth. Why? She's never concealed things from Jack before. He's too straightforward and honest. Perhaps she was just tired. She flopped into bed soon after.

"My dad wants to know if you want sugar," announces the taller of the two boys—*Sam?* Hannah gropes in her mind for his name. His wide child's face seems too big for his skinny, pre-pubescent body. Soon he'll fill out, though, she thinks. He'll be good looking, too. Strong, straight features, like his father. He's holding a large mug in his hands and Hannah can see where the coffee has slopped out, staining—and probably scalding—his fingers.

"Are your hands okay?"

78

"It doesn't hurt," he says.

The coffee looks black and smells stewed.

"Do you know if there's any milk?"

"There might be some. There's a fridge, even."

"I'll come and get it," she says, sparing him two more trips with the mug, after which there might not be much coffee left. She gets up from her seat on the upturned hull of a dilapidated aluminum canoe. Squeezing around the water tank she arrives at the door and steps over the sill, down into the warm cabin. The smell of diesel is strong, but bearable.

"The boys could've brought you the sugar," Mack tells her, over his shoulder as he steers.

"Actually, I was wondering if there was any milk?"

"There's a can over there, but you'll have to punch some holes in it."

Oh yes. Evaporated milk. A staple on the coast. She's forgotten about that. She picks up the can and a can opener.

"Figured you might like some coffee if you were coming from Jack's place," Mack chuckles under his breath.

Hannah wonders what he's referring to. "Oh, you mean his instant coffee?" she asks.

"It's real horrible."

"Ada made the coffee when I lived there," Hannah muses, "But I wasn't really into coffee at the time. I didn't get very far with this morning's batch, I have to admit."

"I drink it when I'm there. It won't kill me and he's a good person. I like that he offers it to me." It's a moment before Mack continues: "Your mom refuses to drink it. She says it turns her stomach."

It's odd to hear a stranger talk about Harry. Mack speaks with a familiarity that Hannah doesn't think she'll ever feel. Hannah wonders how they know each other. Probably because of the gas station. People never come to Mother's gas station for a quick fill.

They always stay for coffee, clustering around the woodstove in the winter, spilling out their life stories.

As a little girl, Hannah was shy and hid in her loft bedroom, making up her own stories to go with the muffled voices. Later, she found that the conversations took a different turn when she appeared, as if people saw her and instantly sealed their mouths, leaving their expressions behind, like unfinished letters. Hannah knew that people brought their secrets to Mother, who soothed them with words that Hannah could never hear. Hannah felt left out, but she had only barged in on a heart-to-heart once. Mother's icy look had frozen her at the door. Afterwards, Harry had been furious, trembling with an anger that Hannah rarely saw.

"It must be a while since you've been out here," says Mack, still sipping his coffee, his fingers obscuring the mug.

"Five years," says Hannah. "I went to nursing school. Then I got a job in Whitehorse."

"Different up there, huh?"

"Well, yes, but I like it." Hannah moves up to the seat across from Mack. From here she can see out. They've passed between Haich Island and Hobb Rock. She can see Kingfisher Rock in the distance. "The scenery's not as beautiful as this, although I've been in the city most of the time, so I haven't seen a lot of the land."

"Sometimes I think I'd like to travel," ponders Mack. "But I've always lived here, and my family's here."

"Are they twins, your boys?" Hannah asks.

"They might as well be, but they're not. Sam's my son and Lonny's my nephew. Lonny stays with me because his parents aren't around. He's my boy as much as Sam is, by now."

Hannah wonders what Mack means about Lonny's parents not being "around." It sounds evasive. She decides not to pry. "I guess that's like Jack," she says. "He's been like a father to me."

"Then you were pretty lucky with your parents," Mack says.

Lucky.

Hannah doesn't reply. She breathes in the steam from the coffee and clasps the mug tight.

As Kingfisher Rock approaches, the *North Wind* slows, rocking in the steep sharp waves and general turbulence.

"I promised the boys they could jig for a while," says Big Mack.

"I'm just going to get them set up. Can you watch the wheel for a moment?"

Hannah fumes in silence. She hadn't really wanted to go to Fortune Island this soon. But they were underway so she'd resigned herself to it. Now they're stopping. Putting her on hold. How long are they going to fish for? Why didn't Mack mention this earlier? Her agitation increases at the idea of steering this huge boat. There are so many submerged rocks around here. The boat she used to own hardly drew any water, but this one must draw a lot. What if she hits a rock? She pulls herself into the driver's seat and eases back on the throttle. The boat rocks more noticeably. She sees that the momentum had helped to combat the water conditions. She pushes the throttle forward again. *Christ.* Too much! The boat jerks and Kingfisher Rock leaps out at her.

Hannah's hands are trembling. She takes a deep breath and slows the boat a touch. Mack ducks back in the door.

"Here," she says, abandoning her post. "You do this."

Mack squeezes up into the seat and steers straight for the rock. What the hell does he think he's doing? Then he turns sharply to the north, pulls into the lee of the rock and stops the boat a few metres from the rock. To her amazement he leaves the boat in neutral and goes straight back out onto the deck again. She follows him.

On deck, the boys have thrown out hand lines and are jigging. Mack tests each boy's line to make sure it's close to the bottom, but not so close that it will get hooked up. The boat spins again and Hannah can't take her eyes off the rock. It's brownish-black, volcanic, sharp-edged and inhospitable. Water crashes around it, in sudden surges. Birds like this rock and it's decorated with white spills of guano. The smell gusts down into her nostrils from time to time.

"Are you crazy?" she blurts, staring at Big Mack. "Are you trying to kill us all? This is dangerous. One big wave and we'll be on the rock!"

Mack looks surprised at her outburst, as if none of this had occurred to him.

"It's okay. I come here all the time."

"How can you say that?" she demands. "It's unsafe!"

"It's okay," Mack repeats. Then, as an afterthought, "We'll just catch one fish."

Hannah storms off into the cabin, where she paces up and down, checking through the window from time to time. Strangely enough, the boat stays in place; the rock never grows closer. She pours another cup of coffee from the pot on the stove, knowing that it might jangle her nerves further, but needing something to do.

From outside, there's a burst of cheering. She hopes the boys have caught a fish. Footsteps thump through the boards of the deck, running toward the door, which slams open. The smaller boy, Lonny, puts his head in.

"Come and see!" he cries. "Quick! Come and see!"

She puts down her coffee and follows him outside. A fish as long as her arm lies on the deck, mottled green and brown, with a wide, ugly mouth and head, tapering to a narrow tail. There's a pool of dark blood under its head and the hook is still inside the mouth, the translucent line trailing out between thick lips.

"A *tush-co*!" squeaks Lonny. "I got one!"

"My, that's big," says Hannah, observing protocol. "Is it a ling cod?"

"It's a *tush-co!*"

"Yeah, it's a ling cod," says Mack, bending over the fish with a knife.

"I dreamed I caught one just like this," continues Lonny, drenched in excitement. "This is bigger, though!"

"Come here and learn how to clean it," commands his uncle. Hannah checks the water, but the boat is still holding its own, away from the rock. She sighs and sits down on a crate, resigned to the interruption. She can see straight up Dagger Inlet, its fjord walls scarred brown with clear cuts and logging roads on the east side only. The other side is lush and green, its smooth cloth-like folds sinking into the frigid inlet water.

Fortune Island lies on the other side of the water tank. She can imagine its shape—like the swirl of a cochlea—and its colour, grey-mauve in today's light, and the two little islands, like a semi-colon out in front, suggesting more to come. If she gets up, Hannah will be able to see her former home. She stays put, though.

Near her, the guts of the fish flop loudly onto the deck—a dark mess of visceral convolutions.

HARRY

What a relief to be home! Harry sleeps deeply the night she returns, waking to the plaintive call of an eagle. The house is cool, but the stove still holds a treasure of coals, allowing her to add a few chunks of cedar without rebuilding the fire. Heat soon floods back into the wooden house, while Harry brews her coffee and tries to talk Rustum into leaving his warm bed.

"It's not raining," she promises.

He doesn't move; his eyes are squeezed shut, his nose is hidden under a swatch of fur.

"It's warmer than yesterday, too."

When his eyes still don't open, Harry gives up. Rustum can match her own stubbornness sometimes. She takes her cup of coffee over to a deep, plum-coloured armchair by the woodstove and sets it down on the threadbare arm. The sweet smell of cedar mingles with the bitter steam from the coffee. The only thing missing is a cigarette, but Harry is trying to refrain. She lets herself smoke by the open woodstove in the evenings, but forces herself to go outside during the day. If the weather is foul, which it often is, she compromises by smoking in the mudroom with the outer door open and the inner door closed. Eventually, she wants to quit smoking. But she wants it in the vague way that people want to go to the North Pole, or some other exotic place. It's a distant goal and so far she's taken few steps towards quitting.

She curls her aching fingers around the warm cup and stares out of the window behind the woodstove. An outcrop of granite slopes gently down towards the house, fingers of tree roots knotting and sliding across its smooth face. Pockets of moss and lichen find homes in any crevice or irregularity.

Harry stares at this rock for a long time every morning, sometimes finding strange shapes and patterns, sometimes finding only the blind workings of her own mind. Problems creep out of her head like the roots running down the rock. After two cups of coffee, her equilibrium, if previously unbalanced, is restored. Of course, some problems never go away entirely. They linger, like the moss and the lichen; little pockets of refugia in her mind.

Hannah is one such problem. Harry examines a large, amber-coloured cushion of moss on the middle left side of the rock. Her conversation with Jack has left her with a host of possibilities to consider, one of which is that her daughter has severed the last links to her childhood. She doesn't buy the argument that Hannah might be in love. She doubts Hannah is ready to be in love. In a relationship—yes; in love—no. To be in love Hannah would have to be willing to let go, lose old pieces of herself, find new ones. Hannah is flexible in some ways, but her self control is implacable. The sweet abandon of her child's nature vanished at puberty. Harry was shut out. Frustrated, she watched and wondered. Looking into Hannah's mind was like peering into the waters of Deep Bay; the only thing visible was Harry's own reflection and, on some days, the clouds behind it.

Grey brightness glows in through the window from the overcast sky, causing Harry to squint as she refills her coffee cup. Since she lives without electricity, she has designed her home to capitalize on natural light, adding windows and skylights as money has permitted. The kitchen and study windows catch the first hint of light in the east and spread it as far as the sitting area. The bay window at the front takes over when the sun swings southwards, lighting all but the deepest corners of the house. Finally, a shimmer of sunset filters through the window above Harry's small bed along the western wall. Sunsets and sunrises are dramatic from here at any time of year, but Harry prefers the lingering winter salutes—special treats in an otherwise wet, dark world.

Today the clouds look liquid and steely-grey—ominous, she thinks—and she can see a dark wind teasing the water. She turns on the VHF radio and tunes it to the marine weather forecast, then returns to her chair with her cup, to plan her day.

Bread is first. No questions there. She has to keep a supply of bread on hand for the squatters and homesteaders who, like her, "live out." There are five homes within a short radius of Fortune Island: two families, two bachelors and one childless couple. All of them buy gas and baked goods from Harry, even though most of them do some baking themselves. For the children, going to Harry's is a treat—an excursion that wouldn't be complete without a pocketful of cookies or a sticky bun.

Harry's closest neighbours live in Swan Bay, behind Fortune Island. San is Japanese, small and darting, while Clarissa is Native, imperturbable, with a deep placid voice and smiling face. San's story is a famous secret in Hanson Sound. He was a newborn during the second world war when the Canadian government rounded up all the Japanese-Canadians and sent them to internment camps. San's mother feared that her first child would die on the boat. He was not suckling well and was losing weight. Nobody knew where they were being sent—the Rockies? the prairies?—or how long they would be gone. In desperation, San's mother begged the Matthews family, Natives from North Hanson, to foster her son.

Alice Matthews had three children already and was expecting another—a boy, Sylvester, who was born soon afterwards. She hadn't understood much of what San's mother had said—the words were like bird song to Alice—but she knew the strange plight of the Japanese and felt bad for them. She raised the two boys as brothers, waiting several months before registering them as twins. Of the woman's fluttering Japanese syllables, only "san" stood out. On his birth certificate the name was recorded: San Matthews.

San's dark hair and eyes helped him blend into his new family although there was a pallor to his skin and a pull to his eyes that told a different story to some observers. His origins were known by the adults in North Hanson, but the kids were not told. The secret didn't spread to the white community until much later, by which time it was a rumour that no one could prove.

86

When San was nine, a Japanese woman arrived in North Hanson on the bus. She walked straight to the Matthews' porch and knocked on the door. She stayed behind their door for a day and a night, while the community watched and waited, fabricating rumours to keep themselves busy. But Alice never told anyone what had taken place and the woman left, as she had arrived, on the bus.

San grew to be energetic, intelligent and skilled. He won a scholarship to a college in Victoria, a city which became his home for many years. In his mid-forties he returned to the coast, married one of Alice's great-nieces and made a new home in his old stomping grounds.

Clarissa has borne four healthy, active kids: Naomi, Midori, Sonny and Bear. San teaches them to read and write, shows them how to build toys and furniture and keeps them active whenever they aren't asleep. One of their chores is going to Fortune Island for bread or gas. They haven't been over for a while, Harry realises, but they'd better not come today. The forecast is poor: gale-force south-easterlies, building to storm-force this evening. The low pressure system is deep—under 900 millibars—which is always a bad sign. Harry taps the barometer on the wall. The needle jerks, then drops.

Harry wonders if Big Mack is on his way, or not. He has promised he will come and she hopes he will. It will be good for him—keep him from brooding. She has urged him to bring the boys, too; they are well-behaved and respectful. Cookies, she thinks, as their faces spring into her mind. Bread first. Then cookies.

Tobacco first.

Then bread; then cookies.

She pulls herself out from the recesses of the armchair and puts two resinous sticks of fir into the stove. Fir burns hotter than cedar and she needs the added heat for the bread dough to rise. Straightening her back with an audible crick, Harry digs in her pocket for the dog-eared package of Drum tobacco. She pinches a rolling paper from its pale blue envelope and piles it with fragrant, dark tobacco. In seconds she has rolled a well-packed cigarette with only one hand, delicately wetting the glued edge of the paper with the tip of her tongue.

"That's it, Rustum!" she commands. "We're going outside, you lazy bum."

The dog uncurls himself with pleasurable deliberation, then rolls onto his back, forepaws raised, pleading for a belly rub. Harry resists his plea, picks up her lighter and thrusts her feet into her clogs. As soon as she opens the door Rustum abandons his pose and scrambles to his feet, rushing to barge out ahead of her.

Mmmm, Harry sighs, as the first pull of smoke reaches her lungs and the delicious ache rushes through her. Sometimes smoking is just routine, but today it is a delight. She sits down on a block of wood and gives the moment her full attention, while Rustum wanders off, sniffing.

A warm gust of wind spins around the corner of the house, likely the first of many. She should do the rounds: see what was damaged in the last blow; make things snug and ready for the next one. The weather can be cruel to her garden. She blankets the plants with masses of seaweed and still they get torn and battered by vicious gusts. Sometimes, in her bed at night, she imagines the wind moving the house, inch by inch, down the slope towards the bay. The wind batters the heavy wooden walls until they vibrate with storm-spun riffs and chords, the sheer volume of the gale keeping her awake. Some storms are bearable, passing off after twenty four hours. Other systems stall overhead for days at a time, rain-filled clouds blotting out light and hope.

Harry walks along a pathway that is lined with broken clam shells. Their fractured white shapes delineate what she considers hers. The island, she believes, belongs to the wild creatures. The outbuildings and garden beds belong to her. She is fiercely possessive of what is hers, shooing off crows and trapping mice.

When she first built this house, Harry had a calico cat, Diana, for mouse control. She loved Diana, but gave her away after a dead hummingbird arrived on the doorstep for the second time. Since then she has battled the mice on her own; with regular attention, the problem is manageable.

Fortune Island is almost a horseshoe, two arms of land embracing a basin of water. The north shore of Deep Bay is lined by steep forbidding cliffs and straggly trees. Even the healthy young trees have dead silver tops; weather and scanty soil conspire to dilute their aspirations of grandeur. From Harry's position on the trail, the exposed bones of the trees make the forest seem on guard, as if thousands of spears are being held high in defense of the land.

From the northern arm travelling counter-clockwise, the other end of Fortune Island's curve can be reached in an hour's hike. Here, a narrow, treeless wrist connects to a webbed hand of rock, thumb pointing into Deep Bay, little finger poking southeast. Harry's trail circumnavigates this knob of rock, connecting her home and her garden.

When she first moved to Fortune Island, Harry lived in the old A-frame hunting cabin that had been built many years before. It was mouldy and dark and small. The mice were everywhere, no matter how many traps Harry set. At night they would keep her awake with their scrabbling and squeaking. Sometimes they even got into her hair. She wanted to get a cat back then, but waited until Hannah was a little older, because Cilla Tate told her that cats liked to lie on babies and smother them. "They think a baby's a hot water bottle," she warned, "especially put out for them." At times the mice made Harry scream out loud in the dark and then baby Hannah would wake up screaming, too.

Back in those days, Harry had a rowboat with a two-horsepower engine, which went about as fast as she could row. Getting to town took several hours and could only be done on calm days. In town, her popularity ebbed as her pregnancy grew. People who had been her friends now treated her with contempt. So there she was, confined to her island, with no one to help her, or to talk to. That summer was dry, and fresh water was hard to come by. She would bind Hannah to her chest and row around the island to the creek. She'd wash clothes and diapers in the salt water, then rinse them in the fresh, sometimes leaving them there, anchored by a rock, while she wandered in the forest to pick salal berries or huckleberries. She became immune to the swarms of mosquitoes that buzzed around her in the forest. They bit her, but she learned not to scratch the welts and after a while she stopped noticing them. Only on the water, or on the breezy knoll of the island could she be free of the bugs. That was when she first began to consider the knoll as a house site.

The A-frame was on the main part of the island, facing north into Deep Bay. She would leave the cabin and spend long hours on the knoll, letting Hannah kick on the moss, while she gazed at the smooth granite curves and planned out her future home.

People thought she was crazy and tried to talk her out of building on the knoll. "If it doesn't get washed away, it will blow away," they said. But she persisted. Her plans imbued the future with hope and gave her something to work toward. She knew she would use up all the money she had saved, but when Hannah was older, she would be able to work as a deckhand again. She would find work wherever she could. She was capable. And in the meantime she would make the perfect home.

Harry smiles in the dark, remembering the summer of construction—how tired she had been, and how happy. It seems so long ago, her life before this home. It amazes her to think where life's avenues have led her. She could have stayed at home with her mother and her stepfather and married the farmer next door. Instead she moved to the coast and acquired a broken heart, a baby and an island home that glued the breakage of her life together. For a while.

90

Harry's dream house, with its weathered, hand-split cedar shake walls and gently sloping roof, sits squarely above the centre of the rocky wrist, blending into the granite. The house faces south; the rest of the knoll rises and spreads out behind it. Two islets protect the house from the southeasterly, which washes into the cove below. In bad weather, when the moon is full, or new, and the tides are unusually high, the knoll becomes an island. Waves wash across the lowest rocks of the isthmus, into the bay on the north side, splashing ineffectually like the slop from an overfull bath. Here, the waters of Deep Bay are sheltered enough that Harry has built her dock, with a shed containing gas barrels, an ancient cash register and two mouse-proof, mink-proof totes of gas bar essentials: pop and chips.

Still smoking the same cigarette, Harry meanders along the path above the dock and heads to the eastern reach of the trail, where the islets no longer shield the land. One tree has not made it through the last storm, she notes. A fifteen foot shore pine lies on its side, displaying its scabby bark and pitiful root mass, no bigger than Harry's mixing bowl. The island is sparsely treed, making this a noticeable loss.

Harry reaches the garden and wanders through it, pausing to drop her cigarette into the sand-filled garden ash can. In summer, this island is so dry that the lichen is more flammable than tinder. A fire could destroy the place in seconds. The stone chimney she has built for her house is much higher than it needs to be, poking absurdly skywards.

Among the raised wooden beds, little is visible except for a few brave stems of kale. Nothing seems to be amiss, though, so she heads back home, passing the new bathhouse with its tangy smell of cedar and following the covered way back to the mudroom. Kicking off her clogs, she pulls on her shoes and reaches over to turn on the radio. The house fills with the gentle patter of familiar voices. Harry goes into the kitchen to wash her hands and start the day's work: measuring, mixing, kneading, punching, shaping, tasting and watching the ever-fascinating metamorphosis of flour into bread.

From the kitchen window, as her large-knuckled fingers flex and bend in the soft dough, she gazes at a mass of mossy tufts bravely padding the rocks on their slide to the water's edge. Not for the first time, she wonders how many centuries it will take before this rock becomes lush and forested.

BIG MACK

The daughter, Hannah, is pretty stressed. Mack can tell. He recognizes the look about her. One winter he shot a deer and didn't kill it. He tracked it through the bush and snuck up on it near a creek. It wasn't ready to die yet, and he watched it panting and peering around while its dark blood spilled onto loose gravel.

Hannah isn't bleeding to death in his boat, but she seems to blank out for periods. Then, when she talks to him, she's either arrogant or too polite. He wonders if it's a good thing that he's taking her to Fortune Island. He doesn't think Harry knows she's coming. And if it's been five years since Hannah was last there, there might be some crying for him to avoid. Maybe he'll stay down at the dock with the boys and deal with the tank. They could put it on the beach while the tide's high and then go beachcombing in Silent Inlet.

It's awkward having a stressed woman around. Normally, Mack likes taking the boat out. There's something about the feel of the water under him as he holds the wheel and steers the boat. He looks at the shapes of the islands and rocks, like freckles and birthmarks. Two hundred years ago they would have looked the same. But two hundred years ago his people would have been healthy. He can't wish things back, but sometimes he dreams of what it might have been like, his mind lingering on the dark, smoky longhouses filled with families and the warmth of affection.

One of the reasons he likes to go to the fishing hole at Kingfisher Rock is because his grandfather showed it to him, shortly before he died. When he catches a fish there, he feels like holding it up high and yelling: "Hey, Grandpa, I got one for you!"

Mack wonders if Lonny and Sam will feel the same way about him, when he's older. He likes the idea of things continuing. He's pleased with himself for escaping the Christmas stress and doing something smart for a change. He figures this trip can be the boys' Christmas present. It's not wrapped up in paper and it's probably not what they dreamed of, but it'll do. No one ever gave Mack a Christmas present until the first year he was with Sara. She gave him a hunting knife and he cried. Then Sara was mad at him because he didn't get her anything. She sulked the whole day, even through the dinner at her parents' house. That was when Mack realised that Christmas gifts were complicated bargains he would rather avoid.

Hannah gets down from her seat and goes out onto the back deck without saying anything. It doesn't surprise him. They are nearing the island now, although the house is still hidden by a couple of smaller islands. The wind has been picking up steadily and Mack thinks back to what his dad said earlier about the waves on the beach. He hopes the weather won't be too snotty. At least the water's deep around here, so Mack doesn't have to worry about running into any rocks. There's probably quite a bit of current, though, when the tides are big, at new moon, or at full. It would take a lot of current to turn a boat like the *North Wind,* but if Mack and the boys were in the canoe, one of the whirlpools might tip them over.

"I saw it first!" yells Lonny as Harry's house comes into view. They've been watching for a while, with several false alarms.

"I saw it at the same time," protests Sam.

"Why didn't you say anything, then?"

"I'll see the dog before you do."

They are passing the islands now and rounding the corner into Deep Bay. The water here is black and deep and wrinkled with wind. The rocks on Mack's left are bare, except for some moss and a few little pines. Harry is lucky her house is protected by those two islands, Mack thinks. The wind would be nasty here, otherwise.

Continuing around the island, Mack sees the lop-sided fuel dock and the neat white shape of the *Polynesia.*

"I'm gonna tie up on this side, you guys," Mack indicates with his left hand to the boys. "I want one of you to tell Hannah that we're going to stay down here and put the tank on the beach. Then we're going beachcombing for a little bit. We'll come back later to put the tank in place. Got that? Remember to say we're coming back later, okay?"

Mack turns back to the wheel and concentrates on docking the boat, no small skill with a vessel this size. He wants the bow facing out, so that the water tank is closer to shore. He smiles when the boat responds well, drifting against the dock in a perfect parallel glide. The boys jump off in unison, each with a rope, Sam runs forward while Lonny secures the stern. The dog wags its tail and barks, turning circles on the dock and knocking over crates and pieces of lumber. The boat moves gently when Hannah steps off it. Mack eases down from his seat and turns his back to the house and the dock—minding his own business.

He wishes that Hannah had thanked him for the ride.

LONNY

When Lonny tells Hannah what his uncle has said, she just stares at him. "We're coming back later," Lonny repeats, a bit louder in case she hasn't heard him. Uncle said to remember that part and Lonny has a good memory. He remembers everything.

When he jumps off the boat the dog is going bananas on the dock. Lonny's never seen a dog get so excited before. It even knocks over a crate and some pieces of lumber with its tail. He ties up the boat with a clove hitch and watches the dog trying to jump on Hannah. She touches the dog on the head and makes it stop jumping by holding her hand above its nose. She can't make it be quiet, though, and it runs up the ramp in front of her, barking and barking. It remembers her. It would be nice to be remembered like that, Lonny thinks.

He watches Hannah and the dog. Hannah has her bag over her shoulder and she's walking along a trail that has white edges. Beyond her, the path curves around to a wooden house which Lonny can only see part of, but there's a door there and someone is coming out of it. Harry. She's looking down and fiddling with her fingers. Probably making a roll-up cigarette, which she does in a flash—just like that! Lonny and Sam tried to copy her once when she left them on the boat and went uptown. They sat in the cab making imaginary cigarettes, mimicking Harry's one-handed rolling and the deep puffs she takes, closing their eyes and making groaning noises, too. They got the giggles outdoing each other that night.

Lonny screws up his eyes to see better. Harry puts the cigarette in her mouth, but then her mouth hangs open and the cigarette falls right out again. She grabs the door with two hands.

Hannah has put her bag down too, Lonny sees, although she is not at the house yet. She is kneeling on the trail with her hands by her eyes. The dog is dancing around on the path between Harry

96

and Hannah. The two ladies stay where they are, as if someone has put a spell on them.

"Lonny!" calls Big Mack, from the back deck of the boat. "Come here."

Lonny turns around and climbs onto the boat, looking over his shoulder to see if the women have moved yet. They haven't.

"I need you to untie these knots," his uncle points at the ropes on the water tank. Sam is untying knots on the other side of the tank. Lonny turns so that he can untie the knots and still see the trail, but his uncle is watching him. "It's not nice to stare at people, Lon," he says quietly.

Lonny hangs his head and fumbles with the knot. His cheeks feel hot. In the distance, the dog barks and barks and barks.

BIG MACK

Mack is pretty happy to drive away from Fortune Island and go beachcombing. He wonders how he would feel if he saw his mother again after all this time. He's not sure. At this point, he doesn't feel as if he ever really had a mother. He was eight when she left, so his memories are hazy: a tiny body—he was almost as tall as she was when he was eight—and finely-plucked eyebrows, curved like question marks. Her hair was always short, even though his father wanted her to grow it long. "Too old fashioned," she'd laugh. Then, she'd kiss his father's cheek. Mack wishes he could remember some special thing he and his mother had done together, just the two of them.

The worst thing was the way she disappeared. One day they came home from school and she wasn't there. There was no note. No explanation. Mack looked everywhere for her. She could have been playing hide-and-seek so he checked the kitchen cupboards and under the couch. Lila looked for her in Hanson Bay and asked at the bar. Silas and Nelson went around the village, asking at each house. When Old Mack came home from fishing, two days later, they still hadn't found her.

"So she finally left, eh?" was all his dad said. Then he went to Hanson Bay, to the bar. He drank steadily for four months.

Night after night Mack dreamed that he found his mother under his bed. "You just weren't looking hard enough," she would grin. Then all her hair would fall out and she'd become a corpse. He would wake up, sweating, and jump out of bed. He'd take his blanket over to the twins' bed and sleep on the floor near them. Once, he had that dream when he was at the foster home. Afterwards, he crept downstairs and curled up near Sinbad. In the morning, his foster father kicked him in the stomach where he lay, on the floor. After that, Mack was locked in his bedroom at night. If he had to go to the bathroom he rang a little bell until the man eventually came, grumbling and cursing, to let him out.

It was easier to pee from the open window—the same window he escaped through, the night he eventually ran away.

A few years ago Mack asked Lila what she thought might have happened to their mother. Instead of answering him, she lit a cigarette and picked up a magazine, flicking through the pages until he left in disgust.

In a way, even if it hurts, Mack would prefer to know what happened. That way he'll know how to think of his mother—alive, dead, happy, sad. At the moment she's a ghost that floats around the edges of his mind with no place to land.

Mack's not sure that Hannah wanted to see her mother. Maybe she did run away. If she did, she might be sorry now and that's why she's back. He hopes that things will be better between the women by the time he and the boys get back to Harry's this evening. He wants to tie up for the night at the dock and cook the fish on board. Then if Harry or Hannah want to come for dinner, they can.

The *North Wind* moves slowly up Silent Inlet towards the river mouth. Forbidding pillars of rock guard the entrance to the bay, plunging hundreds of feet straight into the water. From a distance, the boat looks like a bright marble rolling through the crack in a door. Beyond the rocky gatekeepers, steep snowy mountains loom close. The temperature seems to drop by five degrees.

When he comes to this bay, Mack feels as though he and the boys are the only human beings in the world. He thinks of wolves and eagles and lets the feeling of wildness sink into him. It's like a song, or a rhythm, that makes him shiver. He carries a memory of it inside him, so that when he feels it in the air, his body vibrates. Part of him likes this feeling, but it saddens him, too. If the winter village site by the river had some inhabitants left, this bay might not feel so lost. The spirits would not call him this way. Smallpox sucked the life from the coast, making it empty. It's as if the people had vapourized, vanishing as mysteriously as his mother, like droplets of water going back to the clouds.

Ahead of the *North Wind* there is a small rocky beach. A long log rests there, held up at one end by its octopus-like root mass. The log looks good. Maybe a few days' work to buck it all up and stack it outside the house. Old Mack will be happy. Mack steers towards the beach.

"Dad?" Sam's voice sounds small, uncertain. "Dad, I'm cold."

"It's colder here, son. We're close to the mountains."

"I don't feel so good."

Mack looks at Sam. His skin is dull, his eyes are overly bright. He's been wearing a t-shirt all day, but Sam is usually tough that way. Mack reaches down and rests the back of his hand against Sam's forehead. Wet heat radiates, but nothing too serious, for now.

"Drink a glass of water, son. Then hop into one of the sleeping bags. A rest will make you feel better. Lonny can help me with the log. We'll have some lunch when we get back."

Sam goes straight down to the bunks, and curls up, a sure sign that he isn't feeling well.

"Where's the log, Uncle?" Lonny asks.

Mack points to the beach ahead.

"If Sam's not coming, will I have to pack the wood out to the boat by myself?"

Mack laughs. "I don't think you'd get very far, Lon." He looks at Lonny's face, all wrinkled with confusion. "We're going to let the boat do the work for us," he explains. "You're going to row me to shore. I'm going to take the roots off. Then we're going to tie a line on the log and tow it to the beach at home. Don't worry, you'll be doing lots of packing once we're home."

"Oh. You're going to cut it up on *that* beach." Lonny's face smoothes over with comprehension. "I thought me and Sam would have to take all the rounds out to the boat in the canoe."

Mack laughs again, as he pictures the boys in the canoe trying

100

to heave the unsplit rounds of wood over their heads onto the *North Wind*, each round outweighing them, the canoe rocking. He squeezes Lonny's shoulder.

"Get your boots on and we'll go."

LONNY

It works out just like Uncle said it would. The log falls down when the saw cuts the roots off. It rolls towards the water, while the roots slam over sideways, like a trap door shutting. Uncle Mack picks up a staple and pounds it into the small end of the log with the back of his axe. Then he ties on a piece of line and motions for Lonny to come and get it. They load the chainsaw and the axe into the canoe and Lonny rows Mack back out to the *North Wind*, the line snaking across the water behind them. It's hard work, with the wind and the weight. When they first came into this bay there wasn't any wind, but now there is.

When Big Mack puts the boat in gear they can feel the tug of the log on the beach. The boat keeps going, though, pulling and pulling, like a horse. All of a sudden, they fly ahead as the log finally floats.

"Aah-ha-haa!" Lonny laughs. It's been a good, long day. First he caught that huge fish and now he's had a whole hour doing stuff with Uncle by himself. He can tell that Mack's real pleased with him. It makes up for the thing earlier, about staring at people.

Sam hasn't woken up yet and it's afternoon. They still haven't eaten lunch and Lonny's stomach is gurgling, but they had to get the log before the tide got too much lower. Now they are driving across the bay to a waterfall Uncle knows. He says it falls right into the salt chuck.

"C'mere Lon," Mack beckons from the driver's seat. Then he gets down and pats the seat.

Lonny stares at his uncle, wondering if he really means it.

"C'mon!" Mack laughs. "Hop up!"

Lonny scrambles over to the seat and climbs up on it. He grabs the steering wheel in both hands, leaning forward to reach.

"Captain Lonny!" Uncle laughs.

Lonny smiles, not looking at his uncle. He has to make sure the boat goes the right way. Steering is hard work; harder than it looks.

"Go faster," Mack tells him, pushing on an imaginary throttle with his hand.

Lonny pushes on the real throttle and the boat leaps forward. The engine whines, loud and high. Lonny can't believe how fast he's going. It's even harder to steer now.

"Slower again," says Mack.

Lonny pulls back on the throttle and the engine hums a more gentle tune. Lonny's heart beats more gently, too. He watches the far side of the inlet and follows the directions of Big Mack's hand. At first the boat takes a zig-zag course, but after a while it goes in a straight line. Lonny imagines an arrow travelling in slow motion across the bay, just a white vee of wake left behind to mark its passing.

After about ten minutes, Big Mack motions for Lonny to get down. Lonny wiggles the steering wheel one more time, for luck, before Mack reaches out an arm, scoops Lonny up and swings him over to the passenger seat. He grins at Lonny, then climbs into the captain's seat and speeds up. The boat goes way faster than it did when Lonny was driving. Lonny watches his uncle. Driving is pretty easy. And fun. No wonder Uncle Mack and Grandpa like it so much.

When they get close to the falls, Lonny can hear the water over the noise of the boat. There is a tall cliff above them and river water topples off the edge in three streams of spray, white as stars. Eventually, Uncle shuts off the boat and it drifts close to the waterfall. The log catches up, then passes them and bounces against the cliff wall. The water is deep here. Lonny wonders how far down in the water the rocks go, but it's hard to tell.

The sky and the cliffs are muddy grey. Against them, the water dances and winks. The noise is so loud that Lonny can hardly hear his uncle's voice. Big Mack squeezes around the cabin and goes up to the bow. He motions for Lonny to come too. Together they sit on the cabin roof, breathing in cool pricks of spray as they eat their lunch.

Gradually, the force of the water pushes the boat away from the falls. The bow spins northwards, facing the estuary. Mack is eating his second sandwich. Lonny is staring at the twisty river valley, wondering where it goes to. A low noise catches his ear. Then he hears it again: *Tunk*. He swivels his head and looks behind him, tugging excitedly on his uncle's sleeve as he sees the source of the sound. A huge white bird, like a goose, is flying towards them. It's bigger than a goose, with a long, long neck. As it gets nearer, he sees another one behind it.

"Swans," says Big Mack in a loud whisper. "Trumpeter swans."

They are flying close to the water, approaching the boat. As they near, Lonny can see more behind them. Like the water, they are bright white, glowing as they flap their long, low wings, their heads so far in front of their bodies. Lonny has never seen such beautiful birds.

As the lead swan passes, its wingbeats strum the air. Lonny catches a glimpse of black around the beak and then the bird is gone, but another arrives. One, two, three, four.... Thirteen swans, floating into the distance. They glide over the estuary, following the river. Then they circle slowly and descend, disappearing, one by one, below the treetops.

Lonny and Mack are silent for a while. Lonny remembers what the priest once told him: that his mother is in heaven. He was only little at the time and he wasn't sure what that meant. The priest said heaven was a beautiful place in the sky and that angels were pure white, with wings. Until today, that hasn't meant a lot to Lonny. Now, after seeing the swans, Lonny can picture his mother as one, drifting through the air, pure white, with wings. Maybe she can fly now; she doesn't fall any more, the way Lonny saw her fall: down, down, down, from the apartment window, where she and his dad were fighting. Maybe she can land safely now, without thudding flat on the ground, all broken and dead. And maybe Lonny's aunt doesn't have to cover his eyes any more and rush him inside, away from the shape on the ground. If his mother is a swan, she might be number twelve—the second last one of the group—because of the way it looked right at him, with a bright and shiny eye.

Lonny bends over. With the edge of his t-shirt, he swipes at a wet spot on his cheek, hoping that Mack won't notice. He pulls his knees up to his chest and hugs them, closes his eyes and lets his head droop. When he slides sideways into a doze, Big Mack puts an arm around him.

They float quietly on the dark water beneath the mountains as a stiff wind builds behind them and the log drifts nearby. Further up the valley, the swans go about their business, their long necks probing the icy water for food. Above the water, their heads swivel and tilt as their wary eyes seek out the ever-present danger that is life.

HANNAH

She curls on her mother's bed and breathes in the smells: bread cooling on the rack; chocolate melting in the oven. Nearby, a stack of firewood mingles red cedar and fir, strong and aromatic, sweet and sharp. The woodstove's draught is a barely-audible whoosh; its constancy soothes her as she presses against a scratchy grey wool blanket. Outside, there are voices, mostly Mother's, that blare and then fade as she moves through the trees, in and out of the wind, orchestrating the placement of the water tank.

It feels so strange to be here. As if she had never left. Maybe that is what home is supposed to be: a place that never changes; a place that you can never change. The clamshells still line the pathways. Rustum still smells and barks. And Harry—just the shape and size and living flesh of her had made a strangling sense of guilt sweep through Hannah when she saw her mother, there on the trail: What have I done? How could I have shut her out for so long?

And then her spoken words: "It's been so awful," again and again, as they embraced. The tears, the feel of her mother's body, the love, the unconditional love, the grief, the loneliness, the loss.

Gone was the firm resolve to remain aloof, to keep her experience a mystery. Nothing has worked out as she had planned. She'd thought that she would tell Jack her secret and yet she wasn't able to. Then here she was, blurting it to Mother in seconds flat—my life is a mess, my boyfriend attacked me, I left my job—while Harry soothed her with silence, stroked her hair.

And when she could speak normally again, the banal: "You dropped your tobacco."

Snuffling laughs. Tears.

"I thought I'd have time for a puff. I didn't know . . . ."

"Jack arranged it."

Harry peered anxiously at the dock. "Is Big Mack leaving?"

"He's coming back later."

Anxiety refocused on Hannah. Sudden awkwardness.

"Come inside. Have coffee. Get warm."

"I'm fine. Smoke your cigarette. I need to walk."

They walked the trail, hearing the waves slap the rocks, louder by far than the wind in the pines. The knoll was the same, but the garden was changed—fuller, more beautiful. Hannah wondered which plants these were that could live here and thrive.

From time to time Harry inhaled sharply, as if to speak.

Hannah feels the wind build to a gust, a slowly gathering assault on the house, pushing like banshee fingers, into every crack and crevice, until it climaxes. These sounds were Hannah's childhood lullaby. She would snuggle in the dark warmth of the loft and drowse to the battering wind while the rain pelted down on the roof.

Downstairs, on her mother's bed, Hannah's breathing slows. Her muscles relax. Images move fluidly behind her closed eyelids.

Harry has changed. White strands frame her face now, softening the look of it. Dark hair still predominates in her bangs and her pony tail. Her skin is more creased, like a mushroom left too long in the bag. Molars dark with amalgam fillings. The rims of her brown irises are ill-defined and tinged with blue. Less. There is less of her. Where once she seemed indomitable, now she is frail, her body stiff and shrinking.

Then she looks at you, thinks Hannah—fixes you with a javelin glance, pinning your thoughts where she can read them—and the impression of fragility flees. So much vitality. So much will. Doing whatever she wants, undaunted by the world.

The smell of chocolate is stronger now. It cloys in Hannah's nostrils. She opens her eyes and sits up; straightens her back and strides over to the oven. With a practiced glance, she examines the cookies. Done, she thinks. She rests the two trays on the stove top and turns off the oven. Prodding at one of the cookies with a spatula, she sees that even the recipes haven't changed around here. These could be the same cookies she pulled out of this oven when she was ten. She breaks off a piece, warm and gooey, and yearns for the innocence of ten. She can see it in the bright eyes and skinny-limbed exuberance of Mack's two boys. They switch easily from project to project, seeming to live only for the moment. It's as if the past and the future don't exist for them.

Thinking about it, Hannah remembers how it felt to live like that. She pictures herself as a little girl, kneeling under the pine trees, playing with sticks and flowers. The pink fawn lilies were like ballet dancers to her—like the heroine in Swan Lake, her impossibly graceful arms behind her, fluttering her tragic last. The lilies, too, would flutter their pink wings, their golden hearts spilling out of them in the breeze. Back then Hannah's entire day could be spent inventing worlds within worlds. Everything she needed was right there on the knoll. Only Mother's voice calling through the wind would remind her of time or hunger.

The summer she turned thirteen everything changed. Her emotions began to dominate her life. Harry became her jailer, imprisoning her in this isolation of feelings and resentments.

"Hannah?"

"What?"

"We can't go to town today. We'll have to go tomorrow, instead."

"What? But we have to go to town, today!"

"I'm sorry, honey, my order won't be in yet."

"I don't care about your order. We've been here for fifteen days and I'm sick of it. I'm dying out here. If you don't take me, I'll go by myself!"

"Well, you can do that when you're older, but right now, you have to wait for me."

"No I don't. I can drive the boat!"

"And what would I do here, without a boat?"
"Swim."

Hannah's adolescent mind could see freedom, out of reach, beyond the water. But once she finally got there, she could still feel the cage she had flown from. The feel of it kept up her sense of past injustice, from which she tried to escape by diving into the future. That didn't work. The cage still pressed in on her. Hannah wonders if she will ever find comfort in the present, be able to shut out the background whine of *if onlys* and *what ifs?*

She scoops up the rest of the hot cookie and takes it over to the window. Up the hill, through the trees, she can see the dance of the workers as they fine-tune the placement of the tank. Big Mack's body moves constantly, fluidly, with a strange kind of grace, despite its huge size. From time to time Hannah sees his face and hair as he turns, a flash of brown and black, that gleams despite the flat grey light. The smaller boy, Lonny, waits for instructions. Harry stumps around the perimeter of the tank with an air of authority, pointing out deficiencies. She's in her element, loves being in charge. At one point she rests her arm on the boy's shoulder and looks at him fondly. Hannah turns away. If they had lived in the city Harry probably would have taken in every stray kitten she could. She's drawn to strays. And they to her.

So here is Hannah, back home, with a storm building rapidly and three strays for Mother to pet. Well, I'm not going to fight for her attention, that's for sure, she thinks. I'll just be here and if she wants to find out what I've been through, she can make the effort.

The first of the rain hits the windows like a handful of gravel. Hannah moves back to the kitchen and lifts the cookies off the tray onto the cooling racks. When she turns on the taps in the sink she is amazed to feel hot water scalding her fingertips. The bath house, the hot water and the new composting toilet were things that Mother used to talk about, but not things that Hannah imagined would ever be put into place. She wonders what heats the water: propane or the woodstove? Whatever it is, the water bites her skin with delicious heat.

More rain, then the sound of running footsteps and the door swings open. It's Lonny.

"We're all coming in now!" he gasps. "It's too stormy."

"Better take your shoes off, then."

"I know," says Lonny, lingering by the door, not moving into the room.

Hannah puts the kettle on. Mother's bound to want tea, or coffee. She can hear more footsteps now, a heavy scraping of boots and the buzz of voices, mostly Mother's, as the door opens.

"I don't think you should risk it, Mack, especially if Sam's not feeling well. Stay for as long as you like. It's going to be a doozie." Harry's favourite word for storms.

"Can we, Uncle?" Lonny pleads.

Mack's voice is low, a murmur.

"For heaven's sake, I've even got a turkey! We won't be short on food. Talking about which, there should be some cookies ready by now. I can smell them."

Harry comes into the kitchen in her socks, her hair all blown about.

"Oh, they're perfect," she beams, looking at the cookies. "Good job!"

"Well, you made them," Hannah shrugs.

"Ah, but it's all in the timing."

"Smells pretty good to me," says Mack from across the room by the woodstove. He smiles, a moon-white glow under prominent, wide cheekbones. So different from the faces Hannah is used to. Her eyes linger on his face after he's turned back towards Harry. Hannah is not very familiar with Native people. Theirs is a different world, one she knows little about and which she hasn't involved herself in, in the past.

Hannah turns back to the kettle.

110

"Do you want tea or coffee?" she asks.

"Coffee," says Mack.

"Tea," says Harry at the same time.

There's a moment of awkwardness, as if it's impossible to make both.

"Whatever you're having," nods Mack.

"No, no, there's lots of coffee," Harry assures him.

"I'm making both," says Hannah, with finality.

"What would you like, Lonny?" Harry asks.

"Cookies!"

"Of course. Anything to drink? I don't have any juice."

"Just a glass of water, I guess."

"What's the matter with Sam?" Hannah asks Mack.

"Um. I'm not really sure."

"What does *that* mean?"

Harry glares at Hannah.

"I think he's got a little cold. He's sleeping it off, down on the boat." Mack mumbles these words slowly, without looking at Hannah.

Harry crosses the room and pulls open the door to the woodstove.

"It's almost out!" she exclaims and rushes to fill it.

Here we go, Hannah thinks. It's my fault, but Mother won't say so directly. She busies herself with the coffee, then slides several cookies onto a plate. She takes them over to the table and plonks them down, not speaking.

"All right!" breathes Lonny, rushing over to get one.

"Pretty good, huh?" Mack nods to him, after they've both devoured their first.

Lonny just raises his eyebrows and looks expectantly at the plate.

"Well, have another," urges Harry, smiling at him.

Déjà vu, Hannah thinks. I might as well not exist. She tries to get over her pique. It seems so petty! Somehow it stays with her, though. She wishes she could go upstairs to the loft without being rude, but it doesn't seem possible. Maybe she'll just read a book. Mack and Harry are laughing at something, now. Low chuckles: Heh-heh-heh. Hannah watches the bubbles in the percolator. She feels as if she has just climbed into a time machine and now she's a teenager again, full of outrage. Her mother pays attention to everyone but her. She watches the way Big Mack falls under Harry's spell. He seems like a different person than the boat driver who brought her here. His broad, hard face has softened around the temples. The crease in his forehead is gone. His whole body seems open, relaxed, even though he barely fits in the chair.

Lonny is sitting on the floor, leaning against Mack's knees with Mack's hand on his shoulder. He seems to need attention, this kid. Too bad for him, Hannah thinks. There won't be a lot of that when he grows up. Better make the most of it now. She vaguely remembers the Native kids she was in school with—a sense of toughness about them. And they got tougher as they got older. She knew they had their own hardships, but she was indifferent to that, absorbed as she was in her own situation, which was stressful enough. She mostly hung out with the other white kids. It was easier. In fact, most of her exposure to Native people has been through her mother, in moments like this. What does that say about her? Should she make more effort?

"Do you take sugar?" she asks, her voice too loud.

The conversation stops and everyone turns to look at Hannah. "I'll come and get it," Mack replies, as he heaves himself out of the chair. In a few steps he crosses the floor and stands beside Hannah. As he takes the mug from the counter, his upper arm brushes her shoulder. He turns and thanks her—*kleco, kleco*—strange words, like raven calls, that form between his tongue and the roof of his mouth.

Another pelt of rain hits the windows. "I guess you're right," he swivels back to Harry. "It'll be pretty nasty out there. We should stay." He steps across the room again and Hannah follows him, pulling a chair from the table over to the sitting area even though there is an empty armchair next to Mack and Lonny.

"Lonny here caught a ling cod at Kingfisher Rock this morning," Mack says to Harry. Lonny looks up, grinning. "We would like to cook it up for you guys for supper."

Harry claps her hands. "Delicious! I haven't had fresh cod for ages. That sounds wonderful, doesn't it Hannah?"

Hannah nods at Mack and Lonny, noticing the matching darkness of their eyes. She wonders how they will cook the fish. Mack doesn't strike her as being very domestic, although, to be fair, he *is* raising his kids, which is a task a lot of men bail out of. She wonders how his other kid is doing.

"Do you want me to check on Sam?" she offers. "I'm a nurse. I would know if it's anything serious."

Mack is quiet for a while, considering.

"I think I'll just let him sleep, for now," he decides. "If he's still feeling rotten by suppertime, I'll send him your way."

Hannah shrugs. She leans forward and takes another cookie, surprising herself with her appetite.

"It's the fresh air," Harry says, as if reading her thoughts. Her aging eyes seek out Hannah's. They suddenly fill, brimming with emotion that takes Hannah by surprise so that tears almost come to her eyes, too. She holds her mother's look and for that moment they connect.

Equilibrium. So easily lost; so erratically found.

"Dad!" whispers Sam, kicking Mack's shin under the table, "we can see your cards."

"Oops." Big Mack lifts his hand closer to his chest. "Maybe that's why I keep losing."

"Nah," says Sam. "You're just not very good at playing Hearts."

They've been stuck at Fortune Island for almost two days dividing their time between Harry's cabin and the boat. Right now they're on the *North Wind*, feeling the full effects of the storm. The windows are completely fogged up and the rain sloshes onto them. It's so dark that Mack has switched on the lights. The rigging whistles and jangles and the boat is in constant motion, jerking and swinging on the lines with every gust. Sam is back to his usual self.

"I've never been away from home on Christmas," Sam states while he waits for his turn.

"Me neither," says Lonny.

"It's an adventure," Mack tells them. He plays his hand and waits to lose. He's not really very interested in cards and he's feeling antsy. He wants to go back home, but he's not sure why. He likes Harry a lot, she's entertaining and a great cook. Christmas will bum him out if he goes home. So why does he want to?

"It's your shot, Dad," Sam prompts him.

Mack plays his turn.

"Hide your cards, Uncle!" Lonny giggles, pushing Mack's hand back up. "You just showed us everything again!"

"Then I guess I have nothing to hide anymore, eh?"

The boys laugh and roll their eyes.

Maybe it's the joint in Mack's pocket that stops him from concentrating. He really wants to smoke it, but so far it's been hard to slip away to somewhere dry and private. He'll have to think up an excuse. Christmas dinner will be ready pretty soon.

Harry has shooed them out of the house, saying that they'll just be in the way. She and Hannah are going to fix the whole meal. The turkey's been cooking since morning, making Mack's stomach rumble.

"Uncle!" Lonny is exasperated. "You keep forgetting to play!"

"You know what?" Mack confesses. "I can't concentrate. I think I'm going to go and split some more wood."

"Aw, do we have to?" Sam groans.

"No. It's okay. You guys stay here. I'll go by myself. Just come and get me when it's dinner time, okay?" He throws down his remaining cards and squeezes out of the booth. His raingear is still dripping from his last trip out of doors, but it's better than nothing.

"Which one of you is going to turn off the lights when you leave?" he asks.

"I will," Lonny volunteers.

"See you in a bit, then."

The boys go straight back to their game. They were reluctant to learn at first, but Harry persisted and now they're right into it. Mack can make out the dark shapes of their heads through the fogged-up windows as he steps off the boat and braces himself against the wind and rain. He bends his head and shoulders as he climbs up the ramp.

Once in the shelter of the woodshed he straightens up again and takes off his dripping coat. The knees of his jeans are soaked, but that's inevitable in winter. It doesn't really bother him anymore. He dries his hands carefully on some fresh sawdust, then wipes them on his shirt.

He sits down on the chopping block and lights up. Funny how such a little thing can make so much difference, he marvels, sucking in smoke. He can feel everything changing, becoming mellower. His blood slows down and moves more thickly to his hands and feet, making his world a dream.

Dreams are better than reality.

Mack's dreams aren't always pleasant, but you can always wake up from a dream. Wake up and leave it behind.

One time he dreamed he was six years old. There was no food in the house, but that was normal. It was winter and there was no firewood, either. That was normal, too. His brothers and sisters were with him as they climbed, shivering, into every cupboard, looking for something, anything to eat. It was warm in the cupboards, so they decided to stay there. They closed the door and in the darkness they all turned into rats.

In the dream Mack knew that it was better to be a rat. His fur coat kept him warm. He could look for food in other people's cupboards, too.

Mack re-lights his joint.

There's no shortage of food on this island; he's seen the garden, and the shelves full of preserves. There's no shortage of firewood, either. This shed is pretty full. He looks around the roomy building, with its double doors and winch for pulling logs up from the shore. Most of the wood is in rounds and he's been making the boys split it for Harry. She's older now. She shouldn't have to do that.

Mack wonders how old she is. At least sixty, he figures. But Hannah isn't that old. Mid-twenties, he guesses. So Harry must've had her late in life.

She's different, Hannah. Awkward.

Sharp.

Beautiful.

A couple of times Mack thought something passed between them. Then it was gone.

He sighs.

White people just don't feel comfortable around him. They only see the differences. It's a rare few that see him as a fellow human being.

Mack grinds the last ashes under his feet and stands up, feeling the delicious rush as he does so. He picks up the biggest round of wood he can find and heaves it onto the chopping block. It's hemlock, heavy as concrete. He examines it for stress cracks before swinging the maul down hard. The crack gives way and the wood splits easily. He loves doing this. He's smashing something to bits, but there's an art to it. It's more than just brute force.

He gets a rhythm going and before he knows it, there's a knee-high pile around him.

"Mack?" Hannah's voice at the door of the shed. "The boys said you were here. Dinner will be ready soon."

Mack wonders if there's still any trace of pot in the air, but it's been a while since he smoked, so he doubts it.

"I'll be right up," he says, letting the axe head fall and bite into the chopping block. "Do I have time to stack this lot?"

"I guess so." Hannah moves into the shed, a stick-like silhouette against the light. "I can help."

"It's okay. It won't take me a minute."

"I used to do this all the time when I was a kid." Hannah picks up some wood.

"I guess we all did."

"I didn't really like doing it," Hannah confesses. "I always got splinters in my fingers. Like I've just done now." She holds out her hands: thin ivory fingers, motionless in the grey light of the shed.

Mack puts down the load he is stacking and moves close to her. He holds out his hands, too: his fingers are branches of yew wood, knotted and rich with colour.

Mack gazes at his outstretched fingers, wanting to move them towards Hannah's. The air between them bars the way. Negative space.

He turns his hands over and flexes his fingers.

"Not too many splinters can bother these," he says. With effort, he draws back and bends to pick up another load of wood.

HANNAH

Mack moves his arms and hands in and out of the soapy water, plunging a plate in, wiping it with a languid, circular motion, then pulling it out and inspecting it, before rinsing it under the tap. Hannah takes the plate from him and dries it, placing it on top of several others. This pile of dishes is all that remains of Christmas dinner, with the exception of a few hunks of turkey. Between Mack and the boys, everything else was devoured. Even Hannah had two helpings of turkey. Her eyes glaze as she stands by the sink with the rag, watching the foamy white bubbles form tidelines on the smooth dark skin of Mack's forearms. Is this a dream? Is she really at home after so long?

"Here." Mack passes her a china gravy boat, white with a blue swan painted on either side.

"I used to love this when I was little," she says, turning it over and holding it up. "I imagined riding on the back of the swan, flying off to magic lands." She trills a high-pitched laugh and puts the gravy boat on the counter.

"We saw some swans today, me and Lonny."

"Where?"

"Behind there," Mack jerks his head in a northeasterly direction.

"In the inlet? Silent Inlet?"

"Mm-hmm." Mack's hands disappear into the water for a while, rubbing the inside of a bowl, round and around.

"When I was in Whitehorse, I dreamed about Silent Inlet."

"How come?"

"I don't know, because I haven't been there very much. But it's a haunting place; frightening, almost."

"What did you dream?"

Hannah's voice is soft and monotone, as if she's fallen back into the dream. "I dreamed that I came home," she says, "but instead of coming here, I ended up at the river mouth, at low tide,

118

and the estuary stretched out for miles around me, so that I was completely alone, in the middle of nowhere. I felt as small as an ant. Then the wind started to blow and I could see it, as if it was in colour. It dived down purple-blue from those high rocky cliffs. It swooped like a bird and knocked me flat on the gravel. It flew up green into the sky, in a circle, then swooped back down on me again."

Mack's hands pause and slowly withdraw from the water, his wrists resting on the edge of the basin, his fingers riffling the foamy white surface. He stands still, staring at his fingers

"The second time, I could hear it coming," Hannah continues. "It had a sound, like the reverberation of a bell after it's been struck. The sound grew louder and louder, so that I put my hands over my ears and I couldn't hold tight to the ground. Then the wind picked me up and all these colours swirled around me, purple, blue, green. The noise was so loud that it woke me up and I wasn't in Silent Inlet at all, I had fallen asleep on night shift in Whitehorse. When I looked at the clock, I realised I'd only been asleep for a couple of minutes, but it seemed like forever. The dream was so real. It took a while to snap out of it."

"Huh," says Mack, still staring at his hands.

"It's funny, I haven't thought about that dream for ages. I never told anyone about it."

"Dreams are private," says Mack. "They're like a little hole that your heart spills through."

"I've never thought of them that way. It was just too bizarre, that dream." Hannah shudders at the memory.

"Not too many people would understand."

"I didn't understand it myself," says Hannah.

"But anyone who's been in Silent Inlet would know how it felt. That place is my connection to the universe. Sometimes when I'm there, I feel I could get sucked right out into the galaxy and I wouldn't be human any more, I'd just be a little piece of something—life, I guess."

"It's a strange place, alright."

Mack turns to Hannah, leaning his hip against the sink, his hands dripping soap onto the counter. "If my ancestors hadn't died from smallpox, Silent Inlet wouldn't be silent. Imagine that river mouth with longhouses, dugout canoes, children running up the beach, laughing and chasing each other, women smoking fish. That's what I think about when I go there. Sometimes I can almost see it, too."

"Was there really a village there?"

"Of course there was! A salmon river like that with no village?"

"I guess so. I don't know too much about the history here."

"Your mother never told you?"

"Maybe she did. If I'd been listening I might have heard something. I was usually too busy arguing with her." Hannah looks over her shoulder, but Harry is still in the bathhouse, unable to hear her.

"How come?"

"I don't know. Teenage stuff, I guess."

"Huh."

"You didn't fight with your parents?"

"My mom disappeared when I was eight. I couldn't argue with my foster parents; they were too mean."

"Oh dear," Hannah wasn't expecting this. "Where did your mother go?"

Mack shrugs, his shoulders rising like a wall above her. He shakes his head; shiny dark hair swings back and forth over his eyes as he turns back to the sink and dumps a pile of cutlery into the basin.

"That's why I have Lonny," he says, not looking at Hannah. "Lonny and me are kind-of alike, that way. I know what it's like to lose a mother."

Hannah's glad she hadn't asked more about Lonny's parents when she was on the boat. It sounds like a saga, one he probably

120

wouldn't want to talk about. She wonders about Mack's mother, where she disappeared to. She almost feels guilty for having a mother and not treating her like gold, the way Mack thinks he would. She watches him scrubbing at the cutlery as if he's trying to grind the dirt away. His infectious aura of calm has vanished.

She turns and begins to put the dishes away. A sudden wash of embarrassment comes over her for admitting to that stupid dream. Mack must think she's a flake, even though it happened that way, with the multi-coloured wind. She hadn't fallen asleep again, that night shift. She'd floated along until breakfast, the feel of the wind ruffling her hair, making her shiver.

LONNY

Lonny pets Rustum until his uncle calls him away. Wet dog hair clings to Lonny's palms and his clothes, but he doesn't care. He wishes Rustum could come with them.

"C'mon, Lon," Uncle calls from the doorway of the *North Wind*. "I need you to get the last line."

Lonny moves to the tie-up line and fights with the knot. The wind has made it tight and the boat is heaving with the swell, pulling on the line, making the knot hard to untie. Lonny wipes some of the dog hair onto the rope and wiggles it as much as he can. The rain makes his fingers slippery, but the rope is more flexible when it's wet. When it finally comes apart Lonny scrambles onto the boat, fast. There's no way he could hold the rope for long in this weather.

He turns around before going into the cabin. Rustum is still standing on the dock, looking as if he wants to come with them. Harry and Hannah are up at the house. Uncle told them not to bother coming out in the storm to say good-bye. It's not as windy as it was before Christmas, but it's still kinda wild.

"Come inside and close the door, Lon!" Uncle calls from inside the cabin.

Lonny waves once more at Rustum, then turns around. Once inside, he can hardly see through the rain and foggy windows. Sam is in the front seat across from Big Mack, reading an Archie and Jughead comic book. After a moment, the boat seems to drag. Lonny knows that the long tow-rope has finally pulled tight and the log is starting to follow behind them. Uncle has said that this will slow them down and make the storm seem worse. He seems to think it will be okay, though. He's whistling under his breath and smiling. Lonny hasn't seen his uncle look so happy for a long time.

Lonny wonders what Christmas had been like at home. Maybe someone bought him a present and it's waiting for him there.

For a moment his mind drifts to an imaginary Christmas tree, with gifts wrapped in shiny paper. He can almost make out the letters of his name on the little white tags. Then the picture fades. He tries to swallow the disappointment he knows he will feel. In reality, Lonny hasn't been given a present for a long time because Uncle says he doesn't believe in Christmas. But at Fortune Island, not having presents was okay. The day was upbeat and fun. And the food . . . there was so much of it! And it wasn't just Lonny who didn't get a present there. Nobody did. There was just food. Food and people. And Rustum. For the second time that day, Lonny wishes Rustum could have come with him.

BIG MACK

Big Mack smiles as he drives back to North Hanson. The rain and wind have eased a little, but the trip is still a challenge. No matter. They'll be home soon enough. Home: Old Mack, Raylene, the baby. For a while Fortune Island had begun to feel like home. Harry was such a comfortable person to be around and the cabin was so cosy in the storm. Christmas has never been like that for him before—fun, easy, no expectations. Nobody fought, nobody hurt themselves and, best of all, there were no stupid presents. He didn't have to feel like a loser dad, just because he didn't have any presents for the boys. The day itself was a gift. Human treasure and food! Mountains of delicious food!

Mack's stomach rumbles quietly as he thinks of the cold turkey sandwiches Harry packed for them. Turkey and mayonnaise and wild cranberry sauce. Too bad its not lunchtime yet. He glances over his shoulder at the boys. They are holding on tight, watching the water and bracing themselves against the lurching of the boat each time a big wave hits. They haven't said much since they left, except to ask when they're going to be home. Sam's asked twice. Lonny's asked once. Each time Big Mack's given the same answer: "When we get there."

The boat is nearing a point, now, and for a moment the waves diminish. The rain and wind will pick up again as soon as they're out of the lee, but for now there's a respite. Mack feels a finger tapping on his shoulder. It's Sam.

"What, son?"

"Dad. Please, can you stop?"

"Stop the boat? Why?"

"No. Not that! Stop whistling!"

"Was I whistling?"

"Me and Lonny are going nuts. You're doing the same three notes, over and over again."

"Gee, son. Sorry. I didn't notice."

"Well, we did."

Big Mack looks over his shoulder at the boys and pulls an exaggerated shrug, palms out. Then he wiggles his ears and crosses his eyes until Lonny and Sam burst out laughing. Mack turns back to the wheel, smiling, and catches himself just as he begins to whistle again. It must have to do with concentrating. He doesn't usually whistle unless he's really happy. But maybe he *is* happy. He's had a great few days and he's coming home with a log. His mind flicks to that moment in the woodshed: he and Hannah; so close and yet so far . . . . She shied away from him for a few hours after that, but by the time he left she seemed less self conscious. He thinks of the dream she'd told him about. Such a strong dream, it must have had an important message. Funny how she was embarrassed by the dream. As if people would think she was crazy. As if you were responsible for your dreams. If that was the case then he was probably certifiable!

He imagines telling Hannah some of his dreams, sees the images fill her eyes until they spill out as tears, his stories sliding down her cheeks. Chaos and darkness against the smooth white surface. His hand reaching out to brush them away. His hand touching her. Her face not moving, not pulling away from him.

The *North Wind* rounds the point and the first wave slaps it with vigour.

"Dad!" yells Sam.

Mack glances over his shoulder, barely taking his eyes off the water.

"You're whistling again!"

Mack laughs out loud and nods his head. The laugh takes him again and he opens his mouth to the rain and the spray and the waves. Somehow, when life is good, it always takes him by surprise.

HARRY

A week after Christmas, Harry checks the latch on the mudroom door and turns back down the path to the dock. Hannah is down there already with her bags, and with Rustum. Polynesia is warming up; the pale wisp of exhaust smoke hangs in still, cold air. It is a clear, frosty morning, after a week of darkness, wind and rain. Harry would rather putter around at home today, but Hannah wants to go to town. She wanted to stay with Jack for a while, she'd said yesterday, to catch up on his news.

"Huh. He's got about as much news as I do," Harry bristled, "which is no news. Café in the morning, Legion at night. Nobody lives out here for the news." She stopped herself.

She's been pretty good so far. Hasn't pried, hasn't criticized. She strides down the ramp to the boat. Hannah is looking healthier now—still too thin, but there's a touch of pink in her cheeks. She's already untied the lines and is holding the boat close to the dock for Harry. Anxious to leave, Harry thinks.

In a way it was lucky that the weather was bad over Christmas. Leaving just wasn't an option. Big Mack was stuck there for a while too, which turned out to be fun. He and the boys installed the new tank, which promptly filled with rainwater. They ate the ling cod and played endless games of Trumps and Hearts, while the rain and wind flailed against the little house, or rocked the *North Wind*, wherever they happened to be at the time. Christmas dinner was truly a feast, with the table sagging under mounds of turkey and potatoes and wild bog cranberries. Harry hasn't celebrated this way for ages.

Hannah had been quiet, re-reading old favourites in the armchair by the woodstove, or sleeping upstairs in the loft. Everyone let her be and from time to time she would make an effort and join in. In between bouts of cards, coffee, snacks, Mack took the boys off down to the woodshed to split firewood for Harry. He said they had to practice because there was some firewood to split when they got home. The boys took turns wielding the axe and stacking the wood. They brought several loads up to the storage box at the cabin, relieving Harry of a chore she had been avoiding. Eventually, the day after Boxing Day, they left.

"Dad will be wanting the boat back," Mack said.

At Christmas, he had radioed home to let them know he was waiting out the weather. It hadn't improved much by the time he left, but the *North Wind* was a big boat and seaworthy.

"I wonder what their trip was like?" Harry ponders out loud as they head out into open water.

"Whose trip?" asks Hannah.

"Big Mack and the boys."

"Oh. Them."

Harry is still getting used to the sound of Hannah's voice. There's a deadened edge to it. Defeated, sort-of. Like her eyes. No more glaring pin-points of light. Harry knows that events have not been good, but she's going on limited information, which has been hard to extract. Hannah only gives out fragments and Harry doesn't want to press, because it's the first time in years that Hannah has confided anything to her, anything at all. Harry's hoping that when she's ready, Hannah will tell her everything. For now, all she knows is that there was a boyfriend who turned out to be no good. There was a violent ending. How violent? Bruises.

Hmmm.

"Hannah . . ."

"Uh-huh."

"Are you planning to go back to Whitehorse?"

Silence.

"Mother. I . . ."

"Okay, okay, I won't ask," Harry rushes to avoid a quarrel.

"No. It's not that. It's just hard to think about it, that's all. But the way things stand, there's no way I can go back there."

Relief floods through Harry. She clicks her heels and rolls forward on the balls of her feet.

"Actually, I was thinking about asking at the clinic, here, for a job."

This time Harry can't keep the joy out of her face. She turns to her daughter and grins.

"I'm sure they can use you. One nurse practitioner. One doctor. Nine hundred people, not including North Hanson. They're going crazy with overwork."

"Well. We'll see," says Hannah. "It's just an idea right now."

Harry steers the boat, humming under her breath. Perhaps she *will* stay in town for the New Year celebrations after all. She hasn't done something like that for ages.

"I suppose I'll have to make another New Year's resolution," Harry says. "I hate those things."

"So why do you do them?"

"Character-building, my mother used to say."

"Did she make resolutions, too?"

"Well, she said she did, but I think she cheated, because I found her secret store of gin one year. I thought it was water and I almost choked on it."

"You never said she was an alcoholic." Hannah turns her head to stare at Harry.

"She wasn't, really," says Harry. "More like a closet swigger. You know? A swig here, a swig there. Especially when her husband was acting out, I bet."

"And what about him? You never talk about him."

Harry's turn to be quiet—reflecting.

"He was my stepfather, Hannah. He wasn't Papa. When Papa died, everything stopped. The flow was interrupted. All my love went to Mother. And once it started going that way, it couldn't seem to go any other route.

"Children don't usually have easy relationships with their step-parents," Harry continues. "It's a rare case that works out. My stepfather never liked me and I never liked him. Mother married him out of necessity. He and I both resented that. I fought to love

Mother; he fought to make Mother love him. The more he drank, the less she loved him. A recipe for disaster."

"Did he take it out on you?" Hannah asks suddenly, as if a revelation is dawning.

"Enough about me. Let's talk about something else."

"Oh."

Polynesia putts along, slicing silky water blue with frigid sky. The two women stare ahead at the route, not speaking.

Once they're in Hanson Bay, Harry and Hannah make a beeline for Jack's house. Behind them, Harry can hear someone yelling: "Auntie, Auntie!!"

When the yelling persists she turns her head. Running up the road is Lonny Stanley. A shiver of pleasure runs through her. She's never been "Auntie" to anyone before. She's touched. Lonny reaches them, then stops, panting.

"Well, hello, Lonny!" Harry gives him a hug.

"Where are you going?" he asks.

"We're going off to Jack's house. What about you?"

"My Auntie Lila brought me and Sam and Boy. We're going back home soon."

Boy is Lonny's relative, somehow. Harry often sees him in town, with his mother. He's only a little taller than Lonny, doesn't speak much and his hearing is poor. A simple soul, helpful when he can be. He's twenty-something now, so hardly a boy any more. Harry hasn't asked what's wrong with him. In a way, it doesn't seem to matter much. He's part of the community. And he's always smiling.

"Where's your uncle?" Harry queries.

"Uhhh. I'm not sure," Lonny hesitates and scuffs the ground with his toe.

"Oh yeah. Drinking, is he?"

"He's with Uncle Silas. Grandpa kicked them out of the house."

129

"That why you're with your auntie?"

"I guess so."

"Hmmm. Well, if you need anything, you just call Jack Stimpson's house, you hear? That's where I'll be for a day or two."

"You're staying in town?" Hannah interrupts, surprised. "I thought you never went to New Year's parties."

"Well. I changed my mind."

"I gotta go now," says Lonny, already moving away from them.

"Don't forget to phone me if you need anything," Harry calls. "Promise?"

Lonny waves over his shoulder and starts running again. The women turn and keep on walking.

"Poor kid!" Harry laments. "I'm going to strangle that Big Mack next time I see him. On the wagon, off the wagon, on the wagon, off the wagon. I guess the holiday season got the best of him."

Hannah is quiet.

"Oh," Harry sobers. "You said something about alcohol and your boyfriend. Was it like that for you, too?"

"No. He hid it from me. I didn't know for ages. But it wasn't just alcohol." Hannah's voice is brusque, forbidding more questions.

"Oh," says Harry again, taking the hint. "I'm sorry."

As they near the steps of Jack's house, goosebumps prickle Harry's arms. Her daughter has responded to a personal question. No matter that it was a guarded response. It was something. Harry dared to ask. Hannah dared to answer.

HANNAH

When they reach Jack's house, Hannah heads straight for the shower, leaving Jack and Harry to discuss the evening's events. The sea air makes her hair and skin sticky. She had never noticed that before. Maybe she'll get used to it, but for now, she wants to wash the salt off. She's relieved to be back in town, away from Fortune Island. Everything is so stilted between her and Harry. Every conversation seems to come up against a bank of past history, where it falters and stops. Hannah isn't sure how long she can keep up the effort, even though she'd like to get past this stage, on to something smoother.

Hannah's got something else on her mind, though. Something other than Harry and Rob. She wants to figure it out today, because she won't be able to think straight until she does. She turns off the taps and reaches for the pale pink towel, with which she pats her face and hair. She wraps the towel around herself then sits on the chipped, enamel edge of the bath and works the comb through her hair, taking care with the damp, dark tangles. The scent of soap and shampoo mingle with the warm steamy air. It's a good smell. Clean. Hannah's plan is to put a load of laundry in the washer, then head back into town, without Jack or Mother. She'll wear a scarf and her brown fur hat, but escaping recognition is still likely to be a challenge.

When she's ready she slips out the back door. She's only going to be a few minutes and the lively conversation filtering from the kitchen assures her that she won't be missed. Yet.

Blue sky! Something she learned to take for granted in Whitehorse. The coastal darkness and rain have already been dragging her down, as if the clouds pile up and rain in her head. Today's sun feels good on her face as she strides down the back alleys, peering into people's gardens: this one is so tidy, everything put away for the winter; that one is rambling, with overgrown trees and vines but well-tended flower beds.

131

At the last minute she slips down a path between two buildings, turns right and enters the drug store. A quick glance tells her it's empty. She's lucky; it could be packed with last-minute shoppers. For that matter, she's lucky it's even open on New Year's Eve in Hanson Bay. In the second aisle she sees the clerk bent over, stocking shelves. Hannah moves towards her, takes a deep breath and taps her on the shoulder.

"Yes, dear?" She's an older woman; white roots sprout in her wiry brown hair. Hannah doesn't recognize her—a plus.

"I'd like to buy a pregnancy test." The words fly out of her mouth and float in the air between them. There. She's spoken them out loud. Somebody else knows. The clerk scrutinizes Hannah, trying to gauge whether this is a fortuitous event. Hannah smiles. Not a big smile. A smile of reassurance, but not of joy.

"Well, this way dear," the woman seems relieved, and leads her to the counter. She takes a rectangular box off the shelf and plunges it into a brown paper bag. The cash transaction is mercifully quick, but still it's hard for Hannah to remain casual.

"Thank you," she says as she walks, slowly, to the door.

"You have a happy New Year," returns the clerk.

"I will," replies Hannah. "You too."

Still floating, Hannah heads back through the alley. The brown paper bag is just for confirmation. She knows she's pregnant, really: the nausea, the tiredness, her tender breasts—not to mention the fact that her period is four weeks late. It's a wonder she hadn't guessed sooner. Crazy that she'd thought it was seasickness, until she felt it daily, in varying degrees. Missing her period wasn't so unusual. As the stress at work and at home had built and built, her bleeding became sparse and irregular. What *was* unusual was that all her precautions had failed. Hannah had been meticulous about birth control.

She opens the back gate and lingers in the garden, trailing her fingers down the silvery trunk of Jack's prized eucalyptus. Would Rob have deliberately tried to get her pregnant? If so, why? Hannah shivers. Any minute now, he could walk around the corner and back into her life. Her child is his child, too. If she chooses to have it. She sidles back into the house, grimacing at a peal of raucous laughter from the kitchen. Mother always laughs hardest at her own, frightful, jokes.

Hannah's room hasn't changed a jot. She lies on the white bedspread, paper bag in hand, and gazes at the nylon lace curtains with their scalloped edges and machine-made flowers.

Mother, I have something to tell you.

Well, Mother, I have to tell you this: I'm pregnant and I'm going to have the baby.

Mother, I'm pregnant, but I can't go through with it. I'm going to have an abortion.

Mother. I was pregnant but I had an abortion.

Mother, I'm so frightened. I'm pregnant and I don't know what to do. I don't want to be a single mother. I don't want Rob to have control over me through this child. I don't have a job. I don't have a life. I don't know how to cope with this. Help me!

The options are dire. Hannah has never believed in abortion, because prevention is so easy. When women came into the hospital wanting abortions, she chastised them for their carelessness. Now that she's pregnant, however, abortion seems sane. She feels the box, through the paper bag. She hasn't even taken the test yet. She could take it and find out she's not pregnant at all. But the tests are most effective in the morning. She'll wait until tomorrow.

BIG MACK

It's New Year's Eve and Big Mack and his brother, Silas, are sitting around the little table in the cabin of the *North Wind* with a case of Budweiser. The diesel stove is going, but the windows are still damp with cold.

Silas lifts his can: "Happy New Year, bro!"

"Happy New Year, Si," replies Mack, with a nod.

It's ritual now. Every time they open a can, they toast the new year.

"Next year's gonna be better, for sure," says Mack after a long gulp.

"For sure," replies Silas.

"Can't get worse," says Mack.

"Sure hope not," says Silas. He laughs momentarily, a kind of moan. Silas is smaller than Mack, but still a big man, lanky and serious, more like Old Mack. He works hard during the week and usually only drinks on the weekends. He often goes out of town—says he's visiting cousins.

When Mack looks at Silas, he finds it hard not to think about Nelson, Silas's twin. It's like looking at a ghost. The two of them are so alike, or were, before Nelson got hauled off to jail. Big Mack wonders what Nelson looks like now.

"Hey Silas."

"What?"

"Let's go visit our brother."

"When?"

"Now. For New Year's."

"Yeah! Let's do it!"

"He'd be so happy to see us."

"I miss my brother." Silas's voice breaks.

"We could take Lonny."

"Nelson's boy. He needs his boy."

"I bet Lila won't let us."

"Nope."

"How do you get there?"

"Er. Hmm. Gee, I'm not so sure."

"We've missed the bus." Mack finishes his beer and crumples the can.

"But we could hitchhike."

"Whereabouts is that jail again?"

Silas takes a long gulp. "I don't remember the name right now."

Big Mack leans back against the bench and looks through the window at the blue sky and winter sunshine. He was starting to think the rain would never stop. The last time he was in this boat the boys had to hold on pretty tight. The storm was still running and the swell was lumpy and foul. The boat got a good saltwater bath that day, for sure. Dumb day to tow a log, but at least he got it home. It's sitting on the beach now, waiting to be cut up. Maybe he'll do that the day before school starts. Or the weekend after that . . . .

"What d'you say?" Silas interrupts Mack's thoughts. "Time for another?"

"Sure thing," says Mack, reaching over behind the seat to the case. As he turns back to Silas, he catches a glimpse of someone coming down the ramp. He takes a second look, blinking like a bear in springtime.

"Shit! It's the old man! Hide the beer!" Mack scrambles out of the chair and throws the case of beer on the floor below the table. He takes off his sweater and throws it over the box. Too late, he sees a handful of empty cans lying by the steps beneath the cabin door. The door opens. Old Mack's bony hands grab the frame and he leans down to peer in.

"Off this boat right now!" he commands, his white hair bristling, his eyes bright with anger. "You're pathetic. Both of you! Grown men and you look like babies. Get out of here!"

Mack goes to pick up his sweater and the case of beer.

"And don't even think about taking that beer with you! Get lost! And sober up!"

Mack and Silas scramble out of the boat, stumbling and sliding, blinking in the light. Neither of them looks at their father. They keep going, up the dock, heading for the road.

"Fuckin' guy," grumbles Silas.

"D'you got any money?" Mack asks.

"Yeah," replies Silas.

"You want to go to the bar?"

"Uh-huh."

"We'll be welcome, there."

"Fuckin' guy."

LONNY

Lonny knows his uncles are going to get in trouble. He's heard his auntie Lila telling Old Mack about it on the phone.

"They're down on the boat now, Dad," she said. "It'll be a pig sty by morning if they stay there."

From the porch steps, Lonny sees his grandpa storm down the dock. Then he sees Uncle Mack and Uncle Silas leave the boat, walking in wiggly lines, their shoulders slumped over, heading for the road.

Uh-oh, Lonny thinks. They're going to walk to town. They'll be on a bender for a while, now. Sometimes it doesn't bother him. Today, it does. He's not sure why. Maybe it's because he's by himself. Sam has gone to see his mom, leaving Lonny at Auntie Lila's. He's got a few cousins there, but it's not the same as having Sam around. Not so much fun. Maybe he'll just go inside and watch TV. But it's a nice day. If Sam were here they might go in the canoe.

Lonny watches his uncles straggling down the road. Uncle Silas trips over a rock and tumbles into the ditch. After a while, Uncle Mack bends down, holds out his hand and pulls Uncle Silas up. But he pulls too hard and Silas goes flying forward and lands on his knees on the road. Big Mack is holding his stomach, now, and Lonny can tell that he's laughing his drinking laugh: wheezy and raspy; dumb-sounding. Lonny hates when his uncle sounds like that. But there's nothing he can do about it. As the men continue along the road, he sees that Uncle Mack has dropped his sweater. He wants to call out to him, but there's no point, they're too far away. He might as well just go and get it himself.

As Lonny walks away from the house he hears a noise behind him. It's his cousin, Boy.

"Hi," says Lonny. "Those guys dropped something on the road. I'm just going to get it."

Boy smiles with one side of his face and ducks his head.

"Wanna come too?" asks Lonny.

Boy clasps his hands together and smiles again. He waits for Lonny to move forward and then he follows. He likes it better that way. When he's following someone, he knows he's doing the right thing. Lonny's used to Boy's ways. He doesn't mind having him along. They walk in single file between the brightly-coloured houses to the road; Boy nods and stoops as he lopes along.

Lonny finds the sweater right away, just where he knew it would be. He gives it to Boy to carry. Boy likes to feel important. Carrying the sweater is the kind of job that Lonny knows will make Boy's day. It's okay, hanging out with Boy. Better than with some of his other cousins, who like to fight and argue. Being with Boy is like being by yourself, only you're not alone.

"Wanna go down the dock and fish?" Lonny asks, when they get back from their mission. There's not a lot of daylight left and Lonny doesn't feel like being inside. He'll go in when it gets dark, but for now the dock is calling. It's too bad he's not still at Fortune Island. It was fun there. The best Christmas he's ever had.

He likes Harry. She makes good food.

He liked the card games. They were fun.

The cousins head down to the docks, Lonny in front, Boy bumping along behind.

Lonny's still thinking about Christmas.

He liked that nobody got drunk.

BIG MACK

Big Mack and Silas have reached the sign that says "Welcome to Hanson Bay." They're less drunk now, on account of the walk. Silas is pouring his heart out.

"They should've picked me," he moans for the umpteenth time.

"They should never of split you guys up, period."

"I'm the one should've gone to the school," Silas continues, "Not my brother."

"We shouldn't have had to leave home in the first place. Fuckin' nosy social workers. Nothing better to do than destroy people's lives."

"It should've been me."

"Those fuckin' priests!" Mack bursts out. "They should be strung up!"

"My brother!" cries Silas. "We should've swapped. Nobody would've known. If they'd laid a finger on me I would've killed them, I swear I would."

Silas's twin brother, Nelson, was sent to residential school, while Silas went to a foster home—a better home than the one Big Mack had.

At residential school, Nelson was one of the unfortunates. Already lost without his twin brother, he became a scapegoat, abused in every way imaginable. But nobody knew about it. The family was split up and none of them had a clue what was happening to the others. By the time the residential school was done with Nelson, he was shockingly transformed. The smiling, impish boy was gone, replaced by a blank and expressionless man, no childish sense of fun, no opinions on anything, a robot, unless he was drinking. When that happened, anger would roll over him like a bank of crimson fog and he would roar and bellow and punch the walls and slash his neck, his wrists, his legs. He'd slash you, too, if you tried to stop him. "Leave me alone! Don't touch me!" he'd cry, repeatedly, even if he was alone.

Big Mack shivers as he walks the road. He looks over at Silas to reassure himself that he's not Nelson. He remembers carrying Nelson to the doctor's house, sticky blood pouring from his arms despite the shirts that were tied around them. Dr Haswell was the one who pointed out Nelson's other scars to Mack, the ones that couldn't have been self-inflicted, on his back, on his scalp, on the soles of his feet. They tied Nelson down that night, gave him drugs to knock him out. Then Mack sat by his brother's head and stroked his hair and cried great hiccoughing sobs, while Dr Haswell stood in the doorway, staring into space, breathing deep and slow.

Mack's always felt close to the doc since then. He knows Doc's seen a lot of shit. Mack knows Doc cares, too. At Nelson's trial, Haswell asked for counselling and treatment for Nelson, instead of jail. He argued that the death of Nelson's wife could have been avoided if these things had been in place. Nelson's wife had tried to stop him committing suicide. Nelson lashed out wildly at her. She fell. Not murder; an accident—a terrible accident. But apparently, the judge didn't understand this, because Nelson went off to maximum security, for at least twenty years.

Huh. Not much counselling there, Mack thinks, as he leans against the sign. Silas is in the bushes, sort-of, taking a leak. The sun's going down and a chill creeps over Mack. He feels around his shoulders for his sweater, but it's not there. Must have dropped it. As Silas scrabbles back up to the road, a pale cargo van speeds out of town. It nears them and accelerates. The horn blares and the van swerves violently towards them, missing them by inches.

"Jesus!" Silas yells, as he grabs onto Mack and the sign, fear in his eyes.

"Assholes gave us the finger, too," Mack growls, watching the van disappear. "Whose van is that, Si?"

"Dunno. White cargo van. Could be anyone."

"Bet it's Kevin McKay. Fuckin' racist. He better stay out of town tonight. That's all I can say," Mack snarls. He's rarely angry, but when he is, his fists curl and his eyes narrow. He seems to grow even bigger. If he had a tail, it would be twitching.

"C'mon, Mack. Let's go!" Silas tugs at Mack's arm. Mack drags his eyes away from the road and turns to walk into town. There's no stumbling now. He feels the blood pushing through his upper arms and thighs. He walks fast hoping the rest of the evening will be okay.

LONNY

It's dark by the time Lonny goes to get his Grandpa. Auntie Lila's been cooking since she got back from town and Lonny can hardly wait for the halibut they're going to eat. It'll be fried all golden brown and when he sticks his fork in it, the shiny white layers will flake apart and melt in his mouth.

He doesn't knock on Grandpa's door. He pushes it open and finds Raylene inside, on the couch with Kenny. Kenny's got one arm around her shoulder and the other one is patting the baby, who's on Kenny's knee. Raylene is smiling and laughing. She looks pretty like that, Lonny thinks.

"Where's Grandpa?" he asks.

Raylene keeps smiling and looking at the baby, so Lonny kicks off his shoes and goes into the kitchen. He finds Old Mack sitting at the table with a cup of black coffee in front of him, long thin fingers touching the rim.

"Auntie says for you to come over now."

Old Mack drains the coffee in one long swallow, then gets up and pulls on his coat. From time to time, he leans on Lonny's shoulder as they negotiate the ups and downs of the path between the houses. It's dark outside now. And cold. The grass feels firm underfoot as the frost begins to settle and the stars seem to wink extra fiercely as Lonny leads his grandpa along.

"Did Boy go with you?" Lila asks, when they arrive.

"No."

"Are you sure?"

"Yup. Why?"

"I can't find him."

"Oh."

Finding Boy can be hard sometimes. It's never obvious where he might be. One time he was under the house, wrapped in a blanket, while people looked everywhere. For some reason, he

142

doesn't always come when he's called. Sometimes he's just in his own little world and nothing gets through to him.

"We were watching TV together," Lonny says, "but he stayed because the show wasn't over yet."

"Oh well," sighs Lila. "He'll show up once dessert's on the table. He always does. C'mon, let's have dinner."

Lonny shuts the door and aims for the table, where his cousins are seated. The food is already out, steaming in pots and bowls. On the counter are two pies—lemon meringue, Lonny's favourite. Not such a bad day after all, Lonny thinks, as he slides onto a chair and pours himself a glass of purple juice.

Maybe things will be normal again soon.

HARRY

Just before sunset Harry takes Rustum out for a walk.

"I think I'll just lock up the boat," she tells Jack. "Since it's New Year's and all. And since I'm staying at your place tonight."

"Sure, sure," Jack agrees.

"See you in about an hour," she calls, as she passes through the gate. The moment she's on the road, she pulls out her pouch of Drum. Seconds later, she's lighting up.

"C'mon Rustum, you big lump!" she calls behind her. He's investigating a scrabbling noise, coming from a fuschia bush. Probably a bird; cats are quieter.

"You should be so lucky," she ruffles his ears. "You'll never catch a cat, Rustum. You're just too big and slow."

Harry watches the blue fade from the sky as she walks. The sun is on the southwest horizon, glowing with orangey-gold light, brilliant, but not gaudy, the way it can be sometimes. It's a mark of the winter solstice to see the sun setting so far south. Low in the sky, a planet is beginning to glimmer. Venus, she thinks.

What a way to end the year. When the weather gets to howling like that, she forgets what sunshine is like. It's as if the storms will go on forever. And then she wakes up one morning and there's silence and a sky. Just like that. Or she walks out her door and there's Hannah, arriving unannounced, after five years' absence. Just like that.

At the dock, Harry climbs onto the boat and sits on the back deck, still watching the sunset and working on her second cigarette. Yup, this place can play tricks on you alright, she thinks. The Natives are right to believe in a trickster. Forget benevolence, omnipotence, forgiveness—forget all those qualities that Christian deities are supposed to possess. Trickiness. There's your answer. Fate is tricky and the rules (what rules?) can be adjusted to suit the day. Yesterday a nobody. Today a mother and even an auntie. Harry smiles remembering Lonny's face as he ran up to her.

144

"What a doll," she says out loud to Rustum. He thumps his tail against the worn deck planks. "Not you," she smiles, "Lonny." His tail thumps harder. "Well, okay, if you insist. Doll."

Harry fusses around the boat until it's too dark to see anymore. There really isn't much to do, but her boat is her own space. She can't help feeling a bit claustrophobic at Jack's. Part of her feels like untying the lines right now and heading for home. The idea of a party—a drunken crush of old folk—doesn't appeal to her. She's promised Jack that she'll go to the Legion with him, where there's a New Year's dance.

"I don't have any fancy clothes," she warned him. "It'll be me and my blue jeans as usual."

"They won't recognize you otherwise," Jack laughed, which wasn't so far from the truth.

Afterwards, there'll be fireworks. That's what she's looking forward to. She loves the whoosh and crack of the rockets and the spangled, falling stars.

She wanders up the hill, but waits until she reaches the flat before rolling another cigarette. Four in a row. But she really didn't smoke much today, so she's making up for it now. She pauses across the street from the bar, to light up.

Through the orange glow of the windows, Harry can see people moving around. Raucous yells and laughter indicate the progress of the evening's celebrations. Two cars squeal around the corner, the deep bass of modern music thumping through the metal, slightly muffled, but still loud. The cars are small and low to the ground. One of them has tinted windows. As the doors open, the music blares and four girls climb out, scantily clad and wearing too much make-up. The other car has four men in it. Men? Or boys? Harry can't really tell any more, now that teenagers seem to disguise themselves as adults. She can hardly distinguish a fifteen-year old from a twenty-five-year old, especially amongst the girls. After childhood, there are only two categories for Harry: young and not so young. This lot are young.

145

Harry wishes her body was young again, but she doesn't want to be part of this particular generation. She can't relate to them at all. They're all about entertainment. They are always bored, or obsessed with their own problems. It's one thing to go to a film or a play, but now there's TV all day long and computers and cars and drugs. People are rude without needing to be and it seems that nobody cares. About anything.

Hannah doesn't appear to be like this. She's a working woman, after all, and Harry can't imagine her socializing with this crowd. Maybe that's why Hannah doesn't want to go out tonight. Over her dead body will she go to the Legion, she says, with the old fogeys. She's agreed to meet them for the fireworks, though: 11:30, down at the dock.

Harry wanders towards Jack's house, lingering over the end of her cigarette. She's picked up some fish and chips for supper— her treat. If she stays tomorrow, she'll do some cooking for Jack. He's such a bachelor! It's pathetic the way he can't cook. Since Ada died he's shrunk by about two clothes sizes, just because he doesn't eat well. She could make a batch of chili, or stew, and put it in the freezer for him. Then all he'd have to do is heat it in the microwave, his prized new possession.

Men!

From the gate Harry can see into the house. Hannah and Jack are in the front room, talking. Jack's face is bright with animation and Hannah is leaning forward, listening. Harry can't help noticing the way Hannah looks at him, her face soft and receptive. That look seems to be reserved for Jack. She tells herself that it's good that Hannah found a father figure. Harry's experience with stepfathers was something she would never wish for anyone else, least of all her own daughter. Hannah got to pick her own "stepfather." Much easier than the other way.

Still, there's the jealousy to cope with. Harry bites it back whenever the taste reaches her mouth, but at moments like this, when she sees the easy flow of love between her daughter and someone else, well . . . it takes a bit of getting used to. Whatever it takes, though, she'll do it.

Harry closes the gate and walks up the new front steps, with their rough-hewn cedar boards.

"I'm back!" she calls, as she steps through the door, out of the now-frigid night. "I'm freezing! I'm starving! Let's eat!"

HANNAH

Hannah is on the couch with her feet up, a crocheted blanket over her legs. She's been watching TV for a while, now, but ask her what's on and she'll be hard pressed to say. It's tough to concentrate when so much is happening. Plus, she fell asleep for an hour after Mother and Jack left to go to the Legion. Amazing how her body has changed. She was never able to nap before. And she used to do fine on six hours of sleep per night. Now she is able to sleep for eight or nine hours straight.

At this moment, she's picking the rough skin around her thumbnail. It drives her crazy, this little thing, like a hangnail, but fiddlier. It never goes away. Even if she trims it, it still sticks out and catches on things like panty hose.

Would Rob come down here? In her mind, she sees him driving up in his yellow Mustang and dragging her back by the collar. He probably won't, but if he's overusing alcohol and cocaine who knows what could happen. He has no one to hide it from now, the way he hid it from Hannah. She'd found him using cocaine once, in July, but he said it was a special occasion; a one-time thing. She never saw him do it again, so she almost forgot about it. His mood swings became more frequent, though, perplexing her, sometimes scaring her. Twice, she found an empty bottle of Silent Sam vodka under the front seat of his car, but he never seemed drunk, so she didn't ask him about it. It wasn't as though he staggered home, weaving down the street, slurring his words and smelling like a brewery. Nothing like that.

She thinks back to that last crazy scene and the face of the woman he was seducing the afternoon that Hannah walked in, after having fallen sick at work.

Two people wound around each other, half naked. Empty wine and scotch bottles on the floor. On the coffee table a tightly-rolled hundred dollar bill, a small mirror and a razorblade. Close by, a spoon and a lighter, a little glass pipe. The man is Rob. Who is the woman? Something is familiar about her.

Hannah can't breathe, cough, speak.

Rob stares back, dark eyes getting darker. "What are you doing here?"

She wants to say "I'm sick. I came to sleep," but no words come out.

"What do you think you're doing?" Rob comes towards her, fast. He grabs her arms, snapping into fury, pinching, shaking.

"Hey! What're you doing?" The woman's voice, from behind. Sharp. Angry. Is she mad at me, too?

"You keep out of it!" Rob turns his face away for a moment. A large vein pops out on his neck.

"Why aren't you at work?" More shaking. Pain from his fingers. Hannah can't speak.

"Answer me!"

Throat constricted. Mouth frozen.

A slap stinging her left cheek. A backhand slamming across the right. Hannah crumples. Rob's face is scarlet, glistening with adrenalin. He kicks her in the ribs, once, twice, three times, four times . . . .

Looking up, Hannah sees a bottle smack into Rob's right ear. Kerplunk. Oh shit. His head flies sideways, like a boxer being punched, then whips back. His eyes swirl, refocus. Dark red liquid everywhere, like blood. The woman is behind him, clawing him, pelting him with cushions, shoes, plant pots. She's on Hannah's side. She's crazy and savage.

Hannah crawls away. Rob lunges for her, breathing hard, punching her, pushing her down. The woman screams, hits him, runs into the kitchen.

Hannah raises her hands to protect her face from Rob's fists. She pulls her knees up to keep her abdomen safe. She inches towards the door.

Whomp! A heavy pan thuds against Rob's head. His body, like a bag of sand, slumps at Hannah's feet.

The woman's voice: "Go! Run! NOW!" Her finger a shaking arrow, pointing to the door.

Hannah cringes a little when she thinks of the red wine flying all over those beautiful furnishings: the sheepskin, the cream woollen rug. Knowing Rob, he'll just throw them out and get more. But where's all his money coming from? If he's sniffing some of it up his nose and drinking the rest, it won't last very long. That's the part she's worried about: when the money runs out and he gets desperate; that's when he'll come for her. For a moment it seems so real. She shudders and pulls the blanket over her, tucking in the edges. Her hands come to rest on her abdomen, tenderly, trying to protect the fragile world within her from the crazy world without.

The phone rings and she's tempted not to answer it. They can call back later, whoever they are. Or tomorrow, for that matter. But it could be Harry, or Jack, so Hannah heaves herself off the couch and picks up the receiver.

"Hello. Jack's house."

"Hi." A small voice, very quiet and faintly familiar.

"Who is it?" Hannah demands.

"It's me."

"Me, who?"

"Me. Lonny."

"Oh."

Silence.

"Lonny, what are you calling for?"

"Well, it's just that—umm—well, it doesn't really matter."

Hannah pictures Lonny at the other end, nervous and childish.

"What doesn't matter, Lonny?" she asks.

"Is your mom there?"

"No, she's not, Lonny. Can I take a message?"

"Um. Is Boy there?"

"Who's Boy? Your dog?"

"My cousin! We lost him again. He might have gone to give my uncle his sweater."

"Which uncle?"

"Uncle Mack."

"And where's your uncle?"

"There. In town."

The picture's getting clearer. Hannah is amazed at how badly this child communicates.

"Lonny, what's your phone number?"

"Five-five-oh-six."

"I'll tell you what: I'm going through town at eleven thirty to find Harry and look at the fireworks. I'll tell her about Boy, then. Does she know what he looks like?"

"Yeah! He's my cousin!"

"Okay, Lonny. If we see him, we'll let you know."

Hannah puts down the phone with a big sigh.

Jesus! Some people!

Then a dim picture floats into her mind. A guy her age, but disabled; hunched-over, silent. Boy. She begins to understand what all the fuss is about. Maybe he needs his meds, or something.

She sits back down on the couch and picks up the remote. There's nothing much on, though, mostly glitzy galas and stupid New Year specials. She zaps the TV off and looks at her watch: ten past eleven. Time to get dressed up. She's going to wear her leather pants tonight. She may not have many more opportunities. Not that anyone will be able to see them in the dark, but she likes the feel of them. And they're warm, especially with her silk long johns on underneath.

Hannah brushes her long dark hair, tossing it back and forth to fluff it out. She picks up a tortoise-shell clip, then puts it back down again. Tonight she'll leave her hair loose. She hasn't done that for ages.

She scrutinizes her belly in the mirror, turning left and right.

151

Nope, nothing showing. And her pants still fit; a little loose, in fact. She leans into the mirror and blinks her eyelashes against the mascara wand. Then she adds some pink lipstick. The effect is subtle but sexy. Her appearance is one thing Hannah hasn't had to worry about. She's lucky. She pulls on her blazer and her hat, then goes to the door. She pulls it shut carefully behind her. Jack has never locked his door and he probably never will.

It's freezing outside, alright. Her breath billows out of her like dragon smoke. Hannah sees a sheen of ice where the puddle is, to the right of the gate. The bushes are already showing signs of frost and the road glitters faintly. Maybe she'll see Dr Haswell tonight and ask him if they need any help at the clinic. She's okay for a while, financially, but since she quit her job in Whitehorse, she can't get employment insurance. She doesn't want to touch her savings, for now.

Two streets later she's at the Legion. She's five minutes early, so she waits under the eaves, against the railing, preferring not to venture in. A small dark car squeals by, stops, then reverses. The window opens and a guy she was in school with rolls down the window and whistles at her.

"Cut it out, Dave!" Hannah snorts, surprising him. "Having some difficulty growing up?"

A shout of laughter comes from inside the car.

"Who is that?" Dave mutters. Then louder: "How come she knows my name?"

"Because I sat behind you in school."

"Huh?" He stares at Hannah, screwing up his eyes. "Really? Christ! It can't be! No way! It's Hannah Farre, you guys!" Dave swings open his door and stumbles out towards her. "Long time no see, woman! Jeez, you look like a million bucks!"

Hannah recognizes some of the others. Jimmy was a couple of grades behind them, a small blonde boy who skipped school a lot. Rebecca was only one year behind. She was plump, with dark frizzy hair and braces. Now she's slim and her smile is neat and even as she greets Hannah: "We thought you ran away to make your fortune."

"No such luck," Hannah smiles back. "I went to school. Can't get rich doing that."

"What're you doing tonight?" Dave asks.

"I'm going to the fireworks with my mother and Jack."

"We're all partying at Mike Hadley's house tonight, after they chuck us out of the bar. You should come. Lots of people there that you'd know."

"I'll see," says Hannah. "I only just got here, you know? But maybe."

"Aw, come on," wheedles Dave. "Come and join us. It'll be fun."

"I'll see," repeats Hannah. Seeing them makes her feel as if she's back in high school again. The door opens behind her and people start leaving. They're all going down to the dock. Hannah turns and sees Harry and Jack walking towards her.

"I've got to go," she shrugs. "I'll catch up with you later."

"Awesome! Let's go fit in another round, you guys!" They all pile back into the car and screech down the road a few more blocks to the bar.

Jack and Harry look happy, companionable. Hannah slips between them and they all link arms. This feels good, Hannah thinks, as they head down the slick slope of the hill together. It's as if something has fallen into place for her, but she's not sure what it is.

"Have you thought of your resolution?" she asks Harry.

"Not exactly," Harry evades.

"What's that supposed to mean?"

"Well, I know what I should do, but I'm not prepared to do it. And that's all I have to say about it."

"You should quit smoking, Mother. I know that's what you're talking about."

"I'll quit smoking when I'm good and ready. Now leave me alone."

"You'll never be ready, Mother. What about you, Jack, any resolutions?"

"Harry says I should eat better. She just wants to see me in an apron."

"It'll be easy. I'll help you," says Hannah.

"S'that mean you're staying?"

"Maybe," says Hannah.

"You could make it your New Year's resolution," says Jack.

"Maybe I will, if Mother quits smoking," bargains Hannah.

"Shylock," mutters Harry crossly, unlinking her arm from Hannah's and digging in her pocket. "I'll have to fit a few in before midnight, then."

BIG MACK

The long red fingernails belong to Shawnee Matthews. She's dragging one of them lightly down the side of Big Mack's face. Shining black hair tickles his arm as she nestles against him in the booth.

"Aren't you going to put your arm around me, strong man?" she asks, almost shouting to be heard above the noise.

Big Mack obliges, but his arm is so large that it forces Shawnee's head forward at an uncomfortable angle, possibly not what she had in mind.

Mack's two cousins, Dennis and Diesel, are sitting across the table with half-empty mugs of beer in front of them. The bar is packed. It's hard to move, or hear anything but noise. Mack can't remember seeing the bar so jammed with people before. He's lost track of Silas, which is a bit of a problem. Silas is the one who has the money, so unless Mack finds him, Mack will have to borrow from someone else.

Dennis and Diesel yell with laughter at something Mack didn't hear. It doesn't matter. He talked to them earlier in the evening when they were talking about clam digging. One of their aunties got stuck in the mud and they had a hard time getting her out. Then they all started getting stuck in the same spot. "The tide was coming in, too," Dennis chuckled as he retold the story. "We were all covered in mud! The house still reeks of it."

"And we left the clams behind!" Diesel chimed in. "Edna says we must be jinxed. She's never coming with us again! "

"She was the jinx!" Dennis shouted. "It was her that got stuck in the first place."

That was the last time Mack was able to hear anything they said. It's possible that he passed out for a while, because he doesn't remember Shawnee arriving. She lives a few houses away from Big Mack and normally she doesn't say much of anything to him

He's not sure why she's so keen on him tonight, but he's not asking any questions, either.

"There's gonna be fireworks, soon," she says, right in his ear. "We could make some of our own, too."

Mack feels his body begin to tingle. It's been a long time.

"You wanna go smoke a joint with me?" he asks her. He doesn't need money for that.

"Sure thing!" she says. "I've gotta go to the can first, though. Wait for me outside."

She stands up and walks away, her sexy black pants disappearing fast into the sea of bodies. Mack slides to the edge of the seat and stands. A wave of dizziness hits him and he grabs onto the table.

"You okay, bud?" Diesels yells.

Mack nods. He stands there for a while, swaying and watching all the people. Then he moves to the door and pushes it open. The motion upsets his balance and he swings back against the outside wall of the bar, his arms out, scrabbling for a hold. A cloud of mist appears in front of him from out of nowhere. Someone must be smoking. Then he sees that it's his breath, freezing in the cold air. He wishes he had a sweater.

Breathe in, breathe out. Mack stands on the kerb, his head tilting back and forth. He can see the green marker light flashing out in the bay: dangerous green, don't go there, the rock will sink your boat.

The boat, Mack thinks. We should go back there. It's cold here. He clutches his arms to his chest and turns around. Through the glass he sees a grey and orange blur. Then he makes out the window booth where he was sitting. Shawnee's there, with Kingston Richards, a rich white logger from Hanson Bay. He's got one hand on her ass and she's smiling, touching his face with her long, red fingernails. Dennis and Diesel don't even notice what Shawnee's doing. Mack stares and stares. Kingston's hand moves higher, while Shawnee's hand moves lower.

"Well, Happy New Year to you too!" Mack grunts, only it

doesn't come out sounding that way. It comes out more like: "Well-pyeartyouu." He reaches in his pocket for his wallet. It still has no cash, but a joint falls out of it, onto the sidewalk. Shit, Mack thinks. He kneels down to grab it before it gets wet. Right now his fingers feel as useless as toes. He chases the joint around for a while before he can actually pick it up. Then he holds onto it tightly and wonders how he's ever going to stand up again. Just then the door of the bar swings open and Kevin McKay wanders out, in his matching jeans and jacket. His brown, collar-length hair is layered and wavy. He's short, like his father, and he walks with his chest puffed out, as if he's pushing his way through a crowd. Was he in there the whole time, Mack wonders? How come I didn't see him?

Kevin reaches into his inside pocket and pulls out a kingsize pack of DuMaurier and a shiny gold lighter. As he leans into his cupped hands, to the flame, he sees Mack and smirks. He blows out a plume of smoke and pockets his lighter again.

"Whatcha doin' down there Hamburger? Lookin' for pennies?"

And Mack is on his feet, anger catapulting him. Now, there is clarity. His only sound is a bellow as he flies towards Kevin. He sees the fear on Kevin's face, the moment of hesitation. But Kevin has protection. He ducks behind the parked vehicles and jumps into a small black car. By the time Mack reaches him, he is squealing out onto the road, horn blaring. Once he gets to a safe distance, he stops the car and winds down the window. He scatters some coins on the road and accelerates away, jerking his forearm and fist down as if he's tugging on a chain.

Big Mack is beside himself. He can't even think. The rage is blinding. He gasps with the effort of the run, then bellows again and again, like a sea lion. The sound hums on in the cold, otherwise-quiet, street.

After a moment, Mack unclenches his fingers and releases the bent, crushed joint. He looks at it with reverence as it lies in his shaking hand: it's his only salvation right now. He needs it to calm him down, make him forget. Just then, there's a crashing noise, like rapid gunfire. Mack ducks, quickly, almost falling over. The noise comes again, followed by cheering. He lifts his head to see white lights gleaming and falling out of the black sky. Another explosion brings a burst of fluorescent green. The lights swirl and dance in front of him, blurring, then sharpening; exploding and then drifting down, each new flowering accompanied by whooping, happy voices. Yeah right! he thinks. He wobbles towards the alley behind the bar, sweating despite the freezing air. Smoke this and go home, he thinks. Tonight is bad. Don't let them tell you any different. It's bad. Bad, bad, bad.

LONNY

Boy doesn't appear in time for the pie, so they eat it without him. Afterwards, Lila delegates people to search for him. He could be hiding in the house, so they check there first. Lonny's older cousin, Elton, gets to go look under the house with the flashlight. Lonny checks the laundry room, picking up piles of clothes, some of them clean and folded, smelling of detergent, others dirty, a messy heap on the linoleum floor.

"Boy!" he calls out. "It's me, Lonny. Do you wanna come and play?"

Lonny looks between the washer and the dryer, then under the big table and all the cases of jarred fish and stacks of extra toilet paper.

"How come you're hiding, Boy?" he asks, hoping for an answer. No chance, the laundry room is not hiding anyone. Just as he heads out the door, Lonny remembers something: he and Boy brought Uncle's sweater here after they came up from the dock. Lonny figured it was probably dirty, so he had put it on the messy pile. Just now, when he was going through the pile, he didn't see the sweater. He opens the door again and switches on the light. He searches the room without finding the black and red sweater, with a picture of a wolf mask on it.

Hmmm. A little thought worms its way into Lonny's head. What if Boy was trying to take the sweater to Big Mack? It's the kind of thing Boy would do. He'd feel important, carrying it all the way to Hanson Bay. And Mack would be so pleased with him. Boy would be proud. But it's cold out tonight, and dark. What if Boy got lost?

"Auntie!" Lonny calls.

"Did you find him?" Lila's voice from one of the back rooms.

"No, I . . . he might have gone to town."

"What?" she screeches.

Lila comes stomping out of the back room down the corridor.

"How come?" she demands.

"Um. Uncle dropped his sweater on the road. We picked it up and brought it back here. It was on the laundry pile before, but now it's gone."

"So?"

"Maybe Boy tried to bring it to Uncle in case he got cold, or something."

"What did you guys have to go picking up after Mack for? Are you his little puppy dogs? Let him wreck his sweater when he's like that! It's his fault. Jeez, I don't know what you see in him, Lonny, I really don't. He doesn't do anything for you. I know he's my brother, but he's no help to anyone."

"Lila!" Grandpa's voice cuts in like a whip. "Leave Lonny alone. It's not his fault Boy's missing."

Lila folds her arms and exhales long and loud, like a whale.

"You're no saint yourself," Grandpa continues. "Don't think I don't know."

Lila's cheeks brighten and she turns away. She goes to the door and calls Elton.

"I want you to go from house to house. Ask people to check around for him, okay?"

Lonny looks at Lila and takes a deep breath. "I could call Harry," he offers. "She said I could call her."

"Who?" Lila's eyebrows shoot right up.

"You know, the white lady we stayed with at Christmas. Harry."

"And just how is she going to help?" Lila folds her arms again.

"She's in Hanson Bay tonight. And she knows what Boy looks like."

Grandpa finds the number and Lonny makes the call. But Harry's not there, just Hannah, who makes Lonny nervous. Nothing comes out like he'd hoped it would and Hannah fires lots of questions at him in a hard voice. Worst of all, she doesn't seem to understand how important it is. But she says she'll pass the message on to Harry as soon as she sees her. And Harry will help.

"She's going to tell Harry," Lonny explains to Old Mack, who nods and stares out the window.

"New Year's Eve," he announces in his deep, gravelly voice. "Bad night to be out."

Lonny fiddles with his sleeve, nervous about where Boy might be. If Boy has really gone to town, it's probably Lonny's fault. He hopes everything is going to be alright.

"Don't worry about it," his grandpa tells him. "Go out and look around. See if you can find him."

"Okay," Lonny nods. He heads to the door and pulls on his shoes.

"I'll check the dock," he says. "We were fishing there, earlier."

Old Mack raises his eyebrows in acknowledgment. As Lonny leaves he realises that his grandpa has probably talked to him more in the last few hours, than he has in the last few months.

"Please let Boy be safe," Lonny whispers to himself as he walks towards the dock. "Please let him be okay." In the distance there's a loud noise, then the sky lights up. Fireworks. Lonny turns to look every time there's another round going off. Maybe the fireworks will bring Boy out of hiding. He sure hopes so.

HARRY

When Harry comes out of the Legion with Jack she sees Hannah standing there, looking suave and polished—immaculately out of place. Her way of dressing hints at aspirations beyond anything that Hanson Bay can fulfill. She's talking to some kids she was in high school with, kids that have never left Hanson Bay. For Harry, it's like looking at different species of birds: they're gene-pools apart. Who will Hannah relate to here? Hannah likes company, and sometimes the wrong company is better than no company at all, but not forever. If she expects to find lasting friendships among her old crowd, she'll be disappointed. The gap is too wide between them. Hannah never had a best friend in school and Harry doubts she's made any lasting friendships since. For all that she wants to fit in, Hannah is a loner. And Harry made her that way. Raised her in the bush and ruined it for her.

Still, Hannah takes Harry's arm with what seems like affection and the three of them walk down the hill looking for all the world like a family.

Individuals, Harry wants to tell her. Crowds are herds. They'll stifle you. Choose your friends from different walks of life. Harry's friends are about as varied a group as you would find anywhere: young, not-so-young; Native, non-Native; conservative, radical— you name it. She doesn't have many close friends, but she has support, good company when she needs it, and the kind of exposure to people that keeps her mind stimulated.

The midnight fireworks are bang-splash with joy and excitement— the sky the ultimate backdrop. A clear night in winter can be almost as uplifting as a sunny day; just seeing it gives you hope, optimism, pleasure. Exhilaration courses through Harry with each new burst of light and after each rocket fades, the sky gleams out again—a reminder that fireworks explode and die, but the universe is forever.

162

Will I be part of the galaxy when I'm dead? Harry ponders, her head upraised. She likes the idea that her spirit will twinkle with the others, out in the faraway darkness, a glimmer of light for someone, somewhere.

"So, are you going to give up smoking?" Hannah asks, startling Harry from her thoughts.

"I know you think I should."

"But are you going to?"

Harry sighs and examines Hannah's face in the flickering light. "I can't," she admits. "It's too much, too soon."

"You're going to have to do it sometime, though," Hannah persists. "You'll get cancer, or emphysema, if you continue."

"I know the risks," Harry insists. "And I'm changing. Or trying to. But I need to do it gently. I can't quit smoking tomorrow. I'd go crazy. Really. Let's call this year the weaning year. I resolve to try and wean myself off cigarettes this year."

"Okay," says Hannah. "You're on."

"And how about you? Will you stay? Will you give it a go?"

"I think I have to."

"And can we break the deadlock?" Harry pushes, with new-found courage.

Hannah doesn't reply, but when she looks up, Harry sees a glistening in Hannah's eyes. It's all she needs for an answer.

After the show, when they're walking back up the hill, Hannah says, "Oh yeah, Mother, Lonny called this evening."

"Why?" Harry and Jack ask in unison.

"Well, it was a bit confusing. The kid just doesn't know how to put a sentence together."

"It's all in the asking," Harry interrupts. "What did he need?"

"Oh, so it's my fault?"

"Forget I said that. What's the message?"

"He said that they've lost Boy."

"Oh dear. And?"

"Well, they think he might have walked here, to find Big Mack, who's maybe in the bar."

"Did Lonny want us to look for Boy?"

"Well, you can phone him yourself if you want to find out. I took his number. I said that if we saw Boy, we'd let his family know."

"We can use the phone at the Legion," says Jack.

"Okay," Harry puffs, walking faster up the hill now. It's a freezing night and Boy's an unpredictable fellow—a sweetheart, but not a logical one.

"Five-five-oh-six," Hannah says when they reach the phone. Harry deposits a quarter and punches in the numbers.

"Hello. Who's that?

"Lila? Lila, this is Harry. What's this about Boy?

"Since about suppertime. Really?

"Huh.

"Well, there's three of us here, we're at the Legion. We'll each take a few blocks on our way home. I'll look in the bar, too.

"Yes, he might. If you still think he's in town later, Jack can come get you in his truck. Can't you Jack?" Harry adds outside of the receiver.

Jack nods.

"Well, you've got Jack's phone number? Call us if you find him. And we'll call you if we do.

"*Choo.*"

Harry puts down the phone and scrutinizes Hannah. "You should have told me sooner."

"I forgot, okay? Besides, what can happen to him? Everyone knows who he is. At the very least the cops will pick him up."

"Let's hope they don't have to. I'm going to the bar. If I don't see him or Big Mack in there, we can each take a gander along the streets on our way home." Harry starts striding towards the bar and the others follow. "Wait for me," she orders, as a crowd of people spills onto the street outside the bar, all of them drunk, screaming and hugging and laughing. She pulls open the door and gasps at the intensity of the crowd. The heat and smoke and general stink make it hard for her to breathe. If Boy is in here, she might never find him. She works her way to the bar and barges in front of some people buying drinks.

"Was Big Mack here tonight?" she shouts, as loud as she can, at the bartender.

He's filling a glass, but he looks up and jerks his thumb towards the window. Harry smiles at him and then elbows her way in that direction. The crowd is a mix of white people and Natives, in little groups. Harry sees someone she recognizes in one of the window seats. He's a mechanic who sometimes fixes her boat for her. One final push and she's close to him.

"Hey Diesel," she yells. "Have you seen Big Mack?"

Diesel smiles and raises his eyebrows. He lifts his glass to toast the New Year for Harry. She tries again:

"Diesel! Can you hear me?"

He nods.

"I'm looking for two people!" She holds up two fingers.

He nods again.

"Big Mack and Boy!"

Diesel gestures across the booth, where a white man and a Native girl are groping each other under their clothes. He leans as close as he can to Harry and grasps her hand.

"He was there." His speech is slurred and his eyes are hazy.

"Who?" Harry yells.

"Mack."

"Where is he now?" Harry persists.

Diesel closes his eyes momentarily, then opens them, shrugs and grins.

"Gone home?"

Harry frees her hand from his grasp and nods a curt thank you. She presses past the throng in the direction of the washrooms and pushes open the door to the men's. A quick glance is all she needs to know that the stalls are vile and that neither Mack nor Boy is there. Back in the meleé, she picks a route, a pattern that should get her past most of the people present. She keeps to her route, gasping and pushing, boldly making her way. At one point she almost gives up when a spiked heel jams down hard on her foot, but she keeps on going until she's completed her circuit. Then she bursts through the exit, wheezing and almost collapses.

"Disgusting!" she pants, as she leans against the wall, trying to get her breath back and gingerly rubbing her foot.

"I should have gone in," says Hannah.

"You don't know what Boy looks like."

"Yeah, but I'm more used to bars than you."

"Well, you're welcome to them," Harry snorts. "Honestly, humans are revolting!"

"You're a tough old hen, Harry," says Jack. "You'll recover! Come on, let's take a look along the roads."

They agree to separate and meet up again at Jack's, in half an hour.

"Then we can say we tried," says Jack. "But if we don't find nothing, then maybe Big Mack's gone home and he took Boy with him. It'll turn out okay. Sure."

"I hope so," agrees Harry, feeling in her pocket for her tobacco. She sees Hannah watching her, makes a face and pulls her hand out empty. She'll wait until she's by herself and then she'll smoke as much as she wants. After all, it's only the beginning of the year.

HANNAH

Hannah opts for the back alleyways, stopping to chat with another old school friend on the street outside the bar. Kathy McKay used to be one of Hannah's closer friends and it's nice to see her, even though she's plastered. Her shoulder-length blonde hair has lost its careful sculpting and there's a smudge of mascara on her cheek.

"Oh my God!" Kathy exclaims, over and over again. "I can't believe it's you!"

"Let's go for coffee sometime," suggests Hannah, unwinding Kathy's limp, heavy arm from her neck. "Catch up on old times."

"You got to meet my kids," Kathy drawls.

"Kids?" Hannah pulls back and stares at Kathy. "Who did you have kids with?"

"My hubby, Brad."

"You guys got married? I thought that was just a high school fling!"

"It was, till I got pregnant," Kathy giggles. "Meet Mrs Kathy Davis, wife of one an' mother of two." She collapses with giggles again.

"Call me next week, okay?" Hannah tells her. "We'll get together."

"Right on!" Kathy shrieks, although Hannah wonders if she'll remember their talk at all. Maybe New Year's Eve wasn't the best time to be re-united with all of Hanson Bay. But she had to start somewhere and now that she's seen everybody drunk, things can only get better. Anyway, everyone drinks at New Year's. Everyone except pregnant women.

Hannah makes her way into the alley behind the bar, squeezing against the wall to let a van go past her. The alley's dimly lit and it reeks of beer. She's not afraid, though. This town is too familiar for her to be frightened.

It would be helpful to know Kathy McKay again, she thinks. *Davis,* she mentally corrects herself. Kathy's okay. And since she has a family, then if Hannah decides to have the baby, maybe they'd have something in common.

If.

Tomorrow she'll do the test as soon as she wakes up, then she'll know for sure. But will she know what to do with her life?

"Boy?" she calls tentatively as she looks into the garden across the street from the bar. It's pretty dark and she has no flashlight. It's up to him to come when she calls, otherwise he probably won't be found. If he's even lost. Hannah has her doubts about that. It's probably just a false alarm. Mother's such a worry-wort, over-reacting and being bossy. So what if Hannah didn't tell her right away? As if an hour was going to make a difference.

BIG MACK

Mack's anger fades with every toke. His head is still spinning and he feels better where he is, propped against a tree a few streets away from the bar. Out of sight. It's quiet in here. No more screaming and yelling. No more Happy New Year.

Mack shivers. He's been cold for a while. The tree has no leaves. It's probably cold, too. Clothes are good when it's freezing out. But so is fire. This joint is warming him up. When he feels better he'll hitch-hike home. For now, maybe he'll close his eyes.

A noise wakes him. A car door shutting. The soft hum of an engine fades into the distance.

Mack lifts his head and lets his eyes adjust to the darkness. A few feet away there's a strange shape, lumpy on the grass. Curious, he tries to stand, heaving himself up by pulling on the alder branches. Snap! One of them breaks and he falls forward onto his shoulder.

Sore. Hurting.

He pushes his head up and pulls his knees forward. Then he crawls. Brambles bite his right arm, tearing skin. He inches forward.

The shape is a person, lying on the grass, asleep in an uncomfortable position. *Kuu-us*, Mack thinks. Native. He's doing like me. Then he makes out a little plastic bracelet around the person's wrist. Where has he seen that before? There's something nearby, too, by the guy's hand. Clothes. A sweater. Mack clutches his chilled arms. It would fit me, he thinks as he holds it up. It's dark, with a hood and a design on it.

"Hey!" he snorts out loud. "S'mine. Where'd you get it?"

The guy doesn't reply. Mack studies his face, flicking his lighter near it, so he can see. That's where he's seen the bracelet before. It's Boy's. Please call this number if I am lost, or something.

Mack pauses.

Why's Boy passed out?

169

"Boy!" he calls, shaking him. "Boy!"

But Boy doesn't move. He lies there as still as a dead person. What if he is dead? Mack suddenly panics.

"Boy!" he calls again. He pulls Boy over onto his back and pushes up his sweater. Then he leans his ear down onto Boy's heart. His eyes close as he tries to listen. All he can hear is his own blood rushing through his ears.

And then, all of a sudden he is sure that Boy is dead.

But why is Boy here? He should be at Lila's.

Mack's brain fades. He slumps on Boy's chest, trying to think. There was a noise. A car. Someone gave Boy a ride. They left him here. Someone found him and left him here. No. Someone killed him and left him here.

Maybe he was hitch-hiking, Mack thinks. Some weirdo killed him. Why was he hitching?

Mack starts to cry. Boy is dead! he realises, Boy is dead! With all his strength Mack pulls Boy into the bushes, away from the road where a car might hit him. He leans back against the alder tree and heaves Boy against his chest, making an armchair of himself. His chin rests on Boy's head and his tears trickle down, wetting Boy's hair. Mack's vision blurs as he hugs Boy to him, hoping he's wrong and that Boy will wake up soon. Mack's sweater is by his right knee, but he doesn't want it anymore. Boy's clothes are warming him up.

I'm too drunk, Mack realises. I'm too drunk. I can't even walk. I'm a failure. I can't do anything.

HANNAH

"Boy, where are you?" Hannah calls again, not so loudly that she'd wake anyone. Two of the yards are fenced with chain-link metal. She doesn't bother looking into those. If Boy was searching for somewhere to hide, there are easier places. She wanders down the alley, swinging from side to side, calling out occasionally.

It's amazing how little has changed since she's been gone. The Mendezes still haven't finished their addition, which they've been working on for at least ten years. The tree fort is still in the Greens' apple tree, although their children left home years ago. The vacant lot is still vacant, just a winter straggling of alder trees and blackberry bushes. The trees are taller, that's true, but alders grow fast around here, like scar tissue over a wound.

"Come on out, Boy!" Hannah calls. "Everybody's looking for you."

Suddenly the hairs stand up on Hannah's neck and she turns around in a flash. A strange groaning noise is coming from one of the bushes in the vacant lot.

"Who's there?" she shouts, not moving, but the groaning continues, rising and falling, oblivious to her shout.

Hannah takes a deep breath and moves towards the noise. She wishes she had a flashlight.

The noise gets louder: "Nnnnnnnnnnnoooooooooooo. . ." It might be someone weeping because Hannah can hear a snuffling noise, too. This is it, she thinks. Boy made it to town and now he's cold and tired and lost.

"Hey!" she calls. "Boy! Is that you?" The noise stops for a moment. It must be him.

"It's Hannah. I've come to take you home!"

"NNNNNNNNNNOOOOOOOOOOOOOOO!!" The wailing is terrible, a heart-stopping scream.

Shit, Hannah thinks. He must be freaked about something. She pulls back the leafless branch of an alder and peers at the strange shape on the ground. She can't make it out. It doesn't look like a person. It's too big and there are too many pieces, or maybe those are limbs. She bends down closer and feels around with her hands. Feet. Four feet.

"Who's here?" she demands, as a wall of beer fumes assaults her face. She takes a deep breath and walks around to the other side of the shape. Against the residual light from the street, she can see the outline of the faces. One she doesn't recognize, the other one she does.

"Big Mack!" she shouts. "What the hell is going on?"

The crying starts again, worse this time. It's Mack and he's hysterical.

"Shut up!" she yells and slaps the side of his face.

The crying stops.

"Quit bawling and tell me what happened! Now!"

She wishes she had a flashlight to shine in his face. She stares at him and she can see that he's turned to face her, too.

"Dead." He says, clearly, without crying.

"Who's dead?" Hannah demands. "This guy? Is this Boy?"

Mack squeezes his arms around the human body, hugging it. He nods his head. Hannah leans over and pinches Boy's shoulders, hard, just below the collar bone.

"BOY! HEY BOY! WAKE UP!"

"Are you sure he's not just drunk?" she asks Big Mack. She leans forward to smell Boy's face. Just the smell of a person, nothing else.

BIG MACK

Dimly, through his torrent of thoughts and tears, Mack hears a noise. It's someone walking by. He freezes. Is this Boy's killer coming back? Nah! It's a girl's voice. But why's she calling Boy? he wonders. He wants to call back to her, but nothing comes out, just crying. He's blubbering like men aren't supposed to do, but he just can't stop. A sea of faces floats in front of his eyes: his mother, Silas, Nelson, Old Mack, Lonny, Diesel, Shawnee, Nelson again. Kevin McKay! Asshole!

Something touches his feet. His feet and Boy's feet. The girl is moving around asking him questions. He can't answer. Saliva clogs his mouth and his tongue is swollen. Messages from his brain are forgotten before they reach his limbs. His chest is shaking. Boy is dead! Boy is dead!

WHAM!

A smack on the face! Mack's eyes fly open. That hurt! He can see the girl now. It's Harry's girl, Hannah. She's being a bitch. She's mad at him for something—yelling at him. She wants to know what happened.

What happened? Mack wonders. Then he feels Boy's weight against his chest. Oh, yeah, she's a nurse. She can help.

"Dead."

She asks more questions. Words in the dark. Too many words. Then she takes Boy away, so that Mack can't hold him anymore. Mack feels cold again then. He grabs his sweater and clutches it to his empty chest.

HANNAH

"Help me!" Hannah orders. "I've got to get him flat on the ground." She pulls Boy by the feet and he slides down Mack's body, between his legs. Boy's not heavy, but Mack isn't being any help.

"Jesus Christ, Mack, help me!"

Mack lifts Boy's shoulders enough so that Hannah can pull him clear onto the grass. Then he falls back against the alder. Hannah squeezes Boy's shoulders and tries to wake him again.

"HELP!" she shouts at the top of her voice. "SOMEONE CALL THE DOCTOR! HELP! HELP! HEEELLLLPPPP!" Somewhere down the road she hears a window open and a door slam. "CALL THE AMBULANCE!" she shouts again. She kneels down knowing she's going to ruin her leather pants. Then she tilts Boy's head back and rests her cheek near his mouth, to feel for breathing. She's breathing so hard herself that it's almost impossible to feel anything. Calm down, she thinks, as the blood rushes through her, making her hands shake.

She tries again, counting the seconds, to make sure she waits for long enough. Still no breath. She pinches Boy's nose, leans over and blows into his cold, clammy mouth. His chest rises. She does it again. No resistance, she thinks, as she feels her breath slip into him. He's not breathing on his own.

Mack is crying quietly, now. "Ooo-hoo-hoo. . . ."

Her fingers travel down Boy's neck to his Adam's apple, then slide over sideways to search for the carotid pulse. At first Hannah can't feel anything. She may have got the position wrong, so she tries again. She hasn't done this kind of first aid for a long time. At work there are monitors, machines, lights to see by, helpers. There's less urgency there. She counts, slowly: "one steamboat, two steamboats," until she gets to ten. No pulse in ten seconds is bad news. She's about to pull her fingers off when she feels

174

something, a little flicker, like a puff of wind. She keeps her hand in position. Sure enough, she feels it again. Life!

HARRY

Rustum comes thumping down Jack's stairs barking loudly when Harry arrives.

"Shush! You'll wake the neighbourhood!" she stage-whispers, as she opens the gate. He pushes against her legs, nearly knocking her over, and his tail flaps back and forth in a frenzy.

"Well, I'm glad to see you too," Harry says. "Now, where are the others?"

She climbs up the stairs to the porch and leans against the railing. Everywhere she looks, old strands of honeysuckle twist and turn. It's like standing inside a giant wicker basket. In the distance, Harry can hear a reveller still screaming and yelling. Rustum pricks his ears in the direction of the sound. He sits up and moves to the top of the steps.

"Wuf," he grunts.

"It's okay," Harry pacifies him, "they'll be too hoarse to say anything for the next few days. It'll be really peaceful."

But Rustum is not convinced. He sits rigid, growling softly, even after the noise has stopped.

"Oh come on, you two!" Harry sighs, wondering where Jack and Hannah are. It's been a long day and she'd like to go to bed. She decides to go inside and wait in the warmth, but on opening the door she finds the house is cool. She switches on a light and moves over to the stove. It's almost out, she can tell by looking through the soot-darkened glass. Hannah must have forgotten to fill it up before she left. Honestly! It's not as if she had anything else to do!

Harry lays a mat of cedar kindling on top of the coals. Then she adds some bigger chunks and turns up the draught. She goes outside to look through the woodpile on the porch. Maybe Jack has some Douglas fir saved up, something hot-burning for such a cold night.

"Well, I didn't find nothing," Jack's voice floats up from the street. "You?"

Harry looks up from her search. "Don't you dare bark, Rustum!" she hisses. "Nope, nothing on my route," she replies to Jack. "All I found was an empty wood stove and a stone cold house."

"Oh Jeez," Jack reaches the steps. "Tonight of all nights."

"I know," Harry frowns. "You got anything hot-burning?"

He lifts a sheet of plastic and hands Harry an armful of sweet-smelling wood. "See if that'll do the trick." He takes a load himself and together they manage to sidle through the front door without dropping any. The cedar has caught now and orange flames twirl and leap behind the glass.

"That's better already!" Harry sighs.

"Nothing like a fire."

HANNAH

Footsteps clap up the road towards the vacant lot, music to Hannah's ears. It seems as if hours have passed since she first called for help, even though it has only been minutes.

"Over here!" she yells again as she moves back to Boy's head to give him some more air.

"He came for me," sobs Mack. "It's all my fault."

There's a rustling noise close by and a flashlight beam swings from side to side, not resting on Hannah. They'll see me, though, Hannah thinks, as she concentrates on giving air. Her fingers don't leave Boy's neck, pressing down firmly to keep track of the pulse.

"Oh-oh-oh-oh-oh," quavers a female voice as the flashlight finally rests on Hannah and Boy. "Who is it?" Then, when nobody answers: "I live there. I call ambulance and doctor when I hear you. My husband be right over."

Hannah wants to say Hey, Mrs Mendez, I'm Hannah Farre. I know you, but she can't let go of the rhythm: inhale, blow, inhale, blow and keep on checking the pulse. The flashlight moves away from Hannah, onto the collapsed, weeping body of Big Mack.

"Oh-oh-oh-oh-oh!" the voice says again. "What's going on? You fixing up a dead one? What about this other one? This big one? He beat him up? He kill him? Maybe I call the police, too."

Hannah's about to say no, but she stops. Boy is unconscious. Something made him that way.

Hannah crawling away. Rob lunging for her. Another woman saving Hannah from this man she thought she could trust.

Mack is crying and saying that it's his fault. He is also piss drunk and the largest man Hannah's met. A tap on the head from one of those meaty hands could easily knock out a featherweight like Boy. She's liked Mack, up until now. She liked Rob, too, before he assaulted her.

178

When the flashlight swings away and the shoes tap back down the street, Hannah does not protest.

"Jorge!" she hears the woman cry. "Bring shotgun and call police!"

BIG MACK

As he falls back against the tree Mack's head clears for a moment. He's holding his sweater. He lost this sweater on his way to town. Somehow, Boy must've found it. Boy was coming for him. Boy was bringing Mack his sweater!

But why is he dead? Mack feels the tears flooding back. Boy is dead! "He was coming for me. It's all my fault!" The blackness gets stronger now, fighting with Mack's mind. He feels his body going limp. He needs to tell Hannah, though, before he falls asleep. In case he forgets what happened.

"He was coming for me," he explains. "It's all my fault."

Even as he says the words, the edges of his brain crowd in, forcing out a harsh, bright light. He sobs, leaning against a tree, as his eyes close on the darkness. The cold, cold darkness.

HANNAH

Through the scrub, the alley becomes brighter as house lights are switched on. More feet come down the alley, critch-CRUNCH, critch-CRUNCH. Mr Mendez's hip acting up, Hannah thinks. Blow, inhale. He should have it replaced.

Swinging band of light over long grass, glittery with frost. Back and forth, then in Hannah's eyes. Blow, inhale. Look up. Then the light on Big Mack's face, shiny with tears, wet eyes closed against the brightness, grown man all broken, like Humpty Dumpty after his fall. Blow, inhale.

Click. Hannah tenses. The barrels of a gun pointing at Big Mack. It seems ridiculous, since he's passed out now.

"Don't move a muscle." Mr Mendez like a little John Wayne, no ten gallon hat, just the edges of the light glowing over his balding head. "The cops are on their way here. They're coming for you!"

And then the sirens, on and on, the ambulance, the police, the noise, the confusion. More lights, lights everywhere and the vacant lot so naked, stripped of night. Blow, inhale. People talking. Mrs Mendez telling the whole story: "Yes officer, I hear her scream for help. Oh-oh-oh-oh-oh. I come down here right away. I t'ink he is maybe dead. And the other, he one did it. He dangerous. Look at the size of him! My husband, he was guarding him for you."

A tap on her shoulder. The ambulance attendant bends down, rigs the oxygen mask, Hannah lifts her head and body from Boy's, her fingers still on his neck.

"He has a pulse," she breathes as the mask slips over Boy's face. "He has a pulse. He's alive." And finally the stretcher. Boy strapped down, moving away. Hannah's fingers slipping from his neck. Boy on a tray, sliding in behind doors that close and lights that fade to pinpricks in the distance. And Hannah, on her knees, mute, staring.

HARRY

"I wonder if Hannah's been sidetracked off to a party," says Harry. "I know those kids outside the Legion were trying to talk her into going."

"Oh, she'll be along soon enough. Especially when she smells the hot chocolate I'm going to make."

Harry rubs her palms together. "Now that will warm me up!"

As they walk to the kitchen a siren starts up, distant at first, then closer. RCMP. Harry stops. Goose bumps prickle her arms and her throat feels cold.

"I don't like the sound of that," she says, slowly.

Jack doesn't reply. They stand there, in the hallway, listening.

A second siren starts.

"Ambulance," Jack states after a moment.

Harry moves to the front door and reaches her coat down from the hook. "I don't like it," she repeats. "I'm going out there."

"Me too."

"What if Hannah comes back? You should be here, just in case."

"Dammit." Jack's hand pauses at the coat hook. "Okay," he agrees. "I'll stay. But phone me, y'hear, or come back as soon as you know anything."

Harry doesn't answer. She hurries out the door, down the steps, through the gate, up the road. A small, bustling shape, covering ground, heading towards the noise. Too much noise, she thinks to herself. Humans are so noisy. The noise seems to be centred in one place now and Harry takes the back alley that Hannah had opted for earlier. People are out and about, seeking the source of the trouble. In a small town, when you hear the ambulance, there's a good chance it's for someone you know. That siren means someone is suffering. And their family is suffering, too. Harry tries not to think of names and faces as she stomps towards the lights. The noise has stopped, except for a general babble. Now, she looks to a glow of light, occasionally swiped by beams of blue and red. The night of lights, she thinks. The night of sky.

At the vacant lot she sees the ambulance parked on the grass, facing the alley. On the roadway crouches the police cruiser. Sgt. LeClerk is leaning against it, listening to Cecil and Violet Mendez as the lights twirl round and round. Stanley Meeker, the auxiliary, is doing something in the back of the car. Occasionally, the radio blurts loud exclamations of static. Harry moves around the side of the ambulance, but Sgt. LeClerk sees her and motions her back with his hand. The ambulance attendants are bending over a shape in the bushes, but that's all Harry can see.

Where is Hannah? Harry wants to cry out as she looks around wildly, turning in circles. Just then she catches a glimpse of the face in the back of the police cruiser.

"It can't be," she breathes, but it sure looks like Big Mack. If it is him, then he's drunker than she's ever seen him, passed out against the window, his mouth hanging open, his cheek pushed flat against the glass. Would Mack have taken Boy drinking with him? she wonders. Sure, Boy's old enough, but it's a matter of ethics. Mack's unlikely to lead Boy astray.

But, if he did, would that explain the ambulance? Does Boy need to have his stomach pumped? Harry wrings her hands and stands on tiptoe, trying to get a better view. They're bringing the stretcher over now, but the shape under the blanket is just that—a shape with straps criss-crossing it. At one point, Harry can see a face, but it's covered by a mask. She looks as hard as she can but the stretcher disappears behind the van and the driver comes around to the front.

"I'm leaving," he nods to Harry, so she stands back across the road, against a cedar hedge, pressing her body into the soft fronds so that the ambulance can squeeze past. As they accelerate down the alley, the sirens come on again and Harry stares after them. She's come here and found out nothing. She turns slowly back to the police car, but something snags her attention. There, kneeling on the grass, is Hannah. Her mouth and eyes are open, unmoving. She's staring in Harry's direction, but she doesn't seem to see Harry.

"Hannah!" Harry yells, stumbling over the grass. "Hannah!" She tumbles down in front of Hannah and holds her face with both hands. "Hannah! Darling, are you okay?"

Hannah's eyes move onto Harry's face and seem to focus. "He has a pulse," she says softly. "His heart is beating." Her voice is muffled, toneless. Her lips are bright red, sore-looking, but her cheeks are white.

"Who is it?" Harry asks her, quieter now, but still breathing hard.

"Boy." Hannah's voice is empty.

"What happened to him?"

"He was here, in the bushes, he wasn't breathing."

"But why?"

"I've been breathing for him since I got here."

"Hannah, what happened to Boy?"

"Mack says it's all his fault. He says Boy was coming for him." Hannah's eyes regain expression.

"But Mack would never hurt Boy. Mack loves Boy."

"People hurt people all the time. People they love."

"But Mack wouldn't do that."

"Oh, so all the other people here did it?" Hannah glares at Harry. She seems angry and she's starting to shake. Harry says nothing, but holds her tight. The auxiliary comes over and squats down near them. He looks at Harry, since Hannah's face is buried.

"Is this the woman who found them?"

"Yes."

"Could I have her name please?"

"Hannah. Hannah Farre. My daughter."

"We'd like to ask some questions. Get some information."

"You can do that," Harry allows, "in the morning. When she's feeling better." She glares at the auxiliary, daring him to push her further.

"Um," he ignores the look, "we usually prefer to get some answers right away, while it's fresh."

Harry wrinkles up with anger. She takes a breath and opens her mouth, ready to let fly.

"But let me check with Don, just to make sure," the auxiliary rushes to add. He straightens his knees with caution, stands up and walks away. Hannah is still slumped in Harry's arms. She seems to have stopped shaking now, which Harry hopes is a good sign.

"We need to get you out of the cold," Harry decides for her. "Into a hot bath and bed." She can feel Hannah's head nodding in agreement.

"Can you get up?" she asks, shifting her weight and preparing to help Hannah stand. "Here, give us a hand," she tells the officers as they approach. "We need to get her warmed up," she says to LeClerk firmly. "She's shaking like a leaf."

Hannah looks over at the police car.

"Just two questions," LeClerk bargains, looking at Hannah, not Harry.

Hannah turns and nods.

He takes her arms and leads her over to the cruiser.

"Was this man with the victim when you found him?"

Mack's face is against the window, limp and expressionless, still smeared with tears.

"Yes, he was."

"Did he assault the victim?"

"I don't know."

"Do you think he did?"

"That's three questions, officer," Harry interjects crossly.

"He said it was all his fault," Hannah states, overriding Harry. "He said Boy was coming for him and that it was all his fault."

"Hannah! How can you say that? He didn't mean that he hurt

185

him! He would never hurt anyone!" Harry contradicts, her voice rising. But LeClerk holds up his hand against her.

"Thank you for your time," he nods to Hannah. "Thank you for your good work, too. Will you come and give us a statement tomorrow?"

"Yes."

The police officers climb into the cruiser and drive down the alley. Suddenly it is dark again. And quiet. Harry wants to explode with questions, but now is not the right time. She picks up a pebble and pelts it into the brambles. Hannah turns away from her and takes one last look at the grass where she had knelt. Then they turn for Jack's house. The sky rises darkly above them, still cloudless and full of stars. The space between them is dark, too. Starless.

HANNAH

The nausea wakes Hannah. A subtle reminder. Enough to keep her from sleeping, but not enough to make her throw up.

"Oh God," she groans into her pillow. It's still dark. The day hasn't even started yet and already her mind is full. Images of last night build a strange collage in her mind, pasted together at random. Faces. Lights. Her mouth against Boy's. Why was that so hard? She's a nurse. It's part of her job. Perhaps because she wasn't in a hospital, was out of context.

She wonders how Boy is doing, what his injuries are. She never went beyond the rescue breathing, so she didn't find out. It would be good to know if she had helped save his life, though. She remembers the stretcher disappearing into the ambulance, the doors closing. Then she sees Mother's face, Mother asking her questions, saying Big Mack wouldn't hurt anyone. Ha! Just like Rob wouldn't have hurt Hannah. How would Mother know? Mack said himself that it was his fault and he was there! Harry just wants to believe that the Indians are the good guys. Well, sometimes the cowboys are the good guys.

Hannah pulls the blankets up around her neck. The house is absolutely quiet. If she's going to do the stupid pregnancy test, she should do it now. What's the point, though? she wonders. Leave my warm bed to go and get cold and confirm some bad news? It's more than a little obvious that there's a baby inside me. She stops. Until now she's been thinking of pregnancy, gestation, foetus—clinical words. Baby sounds different. She pictures the tiny infants she's seen, newborn and scrunched up, their little tongues wavering as they bleat for comfort. There's something magical about witnessing such new life and people's reactions to it. Beyond exhaustion and bewilderment, there's a look that comes over a new mother when she holds her baby.

I wonder what Mother looked like when she first held me? She's tough, but she must have been a little frightened. It was harder to be a single mother back then and Hannah's father had left before Harry knew she was pregnant. Mother's never romanticized that part—always told it straight out: your father was a handsome drifter, not looking to get hitched, but whenever she tried to say more, Hannah would hold up her hand:

"I don't want to know, Mother."

"But your father was—"

"Quit it! He's a non-person as far as I'm concerned!"

"That's not fair, Hannah. He was a—"

"Mother! Shut up! I don't want to know, okay?"

For some reason, being fatherless doesn't upset Hannah. She never knew her father, so she can't miss him. Why bother imagining someone who'll never be real? As far as she's concerned, her father was a sperm donor. End of conversation.

But would this baby want to know about Rob? What could she say to her, or him? Your father was possessive and angry and he slept with other women and he drank too much scotch and took too much cocaine and he used to be a successful accountant but now he's a tramp and he's still out there somewhere and he could come for you any day.

Of course, Hannah might find a new boyfriend, someday, although right now men are out. She can't imagine herself trusting someone ever again. How can a person possibly tell if a man is who he seems to be? Which brings her back to Mack.

Hannah has known Mack for about three days. In that time she has seen a rugged, easy-going man who seems well-intentioned. A little lacking in communication skills, but otherwise he's been quiet, respectful, helpful, nice to his boys, amusing and knowledgeable about the ocean. Last night this same man was a blubbering wreck, reeking of beer, helpless. What does she really know about him? Nothing.

What does Mother really know about him? Nothing! She only knows what he shows her. She only sees what she wants to see. Oh God! Only one week at home and already there's a row brewing between her and Mother. But Hannah's going to stand her ground. She'll tell the truth. They can interpret her words as they please, but she will have done her duty. After all, she's a professional. Nurses are trained to write down everything they see, without making judgements. Judgements are for someone else to make.

Hannah starts slowly counting down from ten, her way of getting out of bed when she doesn't want to. From the corridor comes a squeak of floorboards. She stops counting. Someone else is awake, too. The last thing she wants at 5:30 am is a well meaning heart-to-heart, a deconstruction of the night's events. The noise moves away to the kitchen. Hannah stays in bed, listening. The test will have to wait.

The noises continue for about half an hour, muffled sounds with long intervals between them. Someone tiptoeing, trying to be quiet. Eventually Hannah hears the front door open and close. There is more noise then, as Rustum gets up from his bed on the porch and whumps his tail around, claws skittering on the wooden boards.

Mother, Hannah thinks. I wonder what she's doing? She hears the faint clink of the gate closing, then throws back the covers. In the dim light from the street, she wraps herself in her robe, opens the top drawer and pulls out the box. Her fingers jitter as she takes it out of the paper bag and she finds herself overcome by nerves— what if? what if?—even though she already knows the outcome. Later, shivering in the bathroom, she waits for the answer to materialize, like a polaroid photo, with pee for ink. Hannah feels like flinging the whole thing out of the window. Instead she picks up the wrappings and jams them back into the box. A glance is all it takes to confirm the pink plus sign of pregnancy. She goes back to bed and lies there, waiting for signs of daylight, wondering what the hell she should do.

BIG MACK

He's crawling over an asphalt road. It's melting under intense heat, worse than summer sun. The tar sticks to his fingers and his knees. He has to get across the road because a van is coming fast towards him. The closer the van gets, the more the tar binds him. The heat sears through the knees of his pants. Over the road is a wild river, cool and sweet, with salmon running home to spawn and die. Mack cries out with longing as he sees the river. He doesn't care about the van now, he just wants to get to the river. He wants to crawl in and drink, right there among the fish.

Sickness, sickness. Mack's body spews poison. He has to get rid of the poison. It's like a snake coiled around his gut and his head, squeezing his brain, so that his pulse beats hard, like a fist in soft flesh, driving the poison deeper.

Someone pours him a glass of water. "Drink this" they say, but he can't reach it. His arms won't move, even though he tells them to.

He's out on a fish boat. Not one with a name. Smoke wafts from the exhaust, turning his stomach, making him puke, right there on the deck, over and over. Stop! He wants to cry out. That's my blood running out of me, overboard. Instead he watches it flow like red water, on and on, until he shrivels up like an old balloon.

And then Lonny touches his shoulder and points and suddenly there are swans floating through the clouds, heading for the river, where they fade into the haze, promising to return one day and bring good medicine in their feathers. The haze turns into bright light, so bright it hurts Mack's eyes. He can hear the talk of the swan people, loud and honking, close by, behind the bright light. He turns and turns, trying to see them, but the light is too strong and he gets dizzy from all the motion. He falls forward to vomit and his head slams downwards and pulses with pain. He wants the swans to take him to the river. He wants to lap the water like an animal, face right down in it, drinking as much as he likes, no cups or glasses, no limits, just cold, fresh water flowing through him, purifying him.

"Wake up!" someone yells at Mack. "Look at yourself, you're disgusting!"

The snake is back around Mack's head, squeezing in bursts, painful bursts. Every time it tightens its coils, strange stars or fireworks shoot through the blackness where his eyes are.

"Wake up!" the voice yells again. "Pull yourself together!"

What does he mean, Mack wonders. Why doesn't he do something about the snake? The bright light hasn't flown away with the swans. He wishes it would. It's stronger now, torture. Mack's no longer on the boat. He wishes he were because now he doesn't know where he is. He's lost somewhere, on a beach, or a road. Watch out for roads. Roads are dangerous. Pull Boy away from the road. Hold Boy tightly. Keep him safe.

Whoooosh! A huge wave breaks right on Big Mack's face. How come he didn't see it building? Oh, it's so cold! Oh, it feels good! Maybe he's back in the river again.

Smack! Another wave, right in the face, hurting Mack's eyes, making them open, open onto bright light, light that hurts. A face close to his, staring, angry. Whose face is that?

"Time to get up, Mack. You've made enough mess. You're gross, disgusting, pathetic."

Who is that? Who's talking to him that way? Maybe it's his foster parents, the ones he ran away from. Mack closes his eyes again, but this time, the man pulls him by the shoulder. It hurts! His shoulder hurts! His eyes open again onto a plain room, no furniture, no pictures, hard floor. Mack's never been here before.

Suddenly he's going to be sick. He can't stop it. Out it goes, wrenching through his body. It's tearing his guts apart. An arc of spray.

"Jesus Christ, that's disgusting!" The man is yelling again.

Mack's eyes blink open. Pink puke like stars on shiny black boots. Oh, he thinks and slumps against the wall.

LONNY

Lonny sits on the couch, wrapped in a blanket. The house is dark and quiet. He's not sure how long he's been there, but it feels like forever. It's hard to do anything on a night like this, except remember all the things you should have done. Like stopping Boy from going to town.

The longer it took to look for Boy, the more Lonny worried. He wanted to go to Hanson Bay and find him. He could've walked along the road. They all could've walked along the road, with flashlights and clam lanterns. Lonny looked in the laundry room, at the dock, along the beach and under the upturned wooden boat near Lila's house. It was hard work without a flashlight, but Lonny has good eyes. He can see better than most people. He knows where Boy likes to go, too. He's often found him hiding out. That's why he checked under the boat.

He was just heading back to his auntie's when he heard her scream. The sound came out of the door like a cloud. It filled him up, scaring him, so that he rushed up the stairs, tumbling into the house.

Auntie was sitting by the phone with Alice Matthews in front of her. Alice was holding Auntie while she cried. Grandpa was sitting across the room on a grey metal chair with his arms folded. Some of Lonny's cousins were in the room, others were still out looking. Lonny crossed over to his grandpa and sat down on the floor. Grandpa's mouth was a thin, hard line. It didn't change when Lonny looked up at him. Grandpa usually only looked like this when serious things happened; like two months ago, when Lonny's cousin, Fergus, hung himself. Lonny hoped that Boy hadn't hung himself. He hoped that Boy wasn't dead, but he'd find out soon. He imagined Boy dangling from a rope, like a puppet, saw Boy's face all green and puffy, his mouth in an o. Suddenly, the face in Lonny's mind became his own. He stared at himself, not wanting to see, not able to stop looking. Finally, he jerked out of his thoughts.

Then Alice held Lila away from her and stroked her hair, looking in her face.

"What did they say?"

"They're taking him to Victoria."

"Is he going to make it?"

"He's not conscious."

"Did they say what happened?"

This must've been a bad question because Auntie started crying a lot—long noises—so Alice hugged her again and patted her back. Auntie tried saying something, but the words disappeared into Alice's pink shiny shirt and they turned into crying anyway. Whatever happened, Lonny had found out something: Boy wasn't dead. Yet. He crossed his fingers.

"Nah!" breathed Alice, who must've heard the words. "They can't be saying that!"

"What?" called Grandpa. "What are they saying?"

Alice turned to look at him, but Lila looked up, too, her eyes all red and puffy. "They're trying to say it was Mack!" she bawled, breaking down again.

"NO!" Grandpa's voice was so loud, it made Lonny jump. "No," he said again, quieter, but just as strong. "Mack doesn't hurt people!" He shifts in his chair. "Who's saying that about him?"

This time it's Alice who replied.

"The cops."

"They've arrested him," Lila added, sniffing hard. "They said he admitted it was his fault."

"No." Grandpa said again, getting up. "That's wrong. I'm going to tell them."

"They won't be there now," Alice told him. "They'll just lock him up and go home."

"Then I'll be there when they open in the morning." Grandpa got up and went for his coat. "Come with me, Lonny," he said. "We're going home."

Lonny crossed over the room, looking at Auntie Lila. He didn't feel very good and he suddenly missed Big Mack. He wanted to cry, but he couldn't with so many people around.

"I want to know what happens," Grandpa said gruffly. "To both of them. I want to know."

Lila took a deep, quavery breath.

"As soon as I hear anything," she said. "But I'm going to look for a ride. I'm going to go be with my Boy."

Grandpa nodded and pulled open the door.

"I'll pray," he said, "the Lord will keep him safe."

Lonny followed him outside

"I will, too," he told Lila, through the closing door. "I promise."

Back at Grandpa's, Lonny finds out that praying is hard.

I pray that I never went to get Uncle's sweater with Boy.

I pray that Boy never went to town.

I pray that Uncle didn't start drinking.

Praying never seems to change the things that have already happened, otherwise Lonny would have a mother and father and a regular home. So praying has to be about what's going to happen. Lonny wishes he knew what was going to happen so that he can pray everything right before it goes wrong. He pulls the blanket tighter around his neck. It sure doesn't take long for things to go wrong, he thinks.

HARRY

There's something rotten in the state of Denmark. The quote goes round and round in Harry's head as she lies in bed waiting for daybreak. Her eyes are closed but she hasn't dozed off once tonight. She's just lying there, letting her mind spin, wishing she were at home.

How could Hannah implicate Big Mack like that? And what really happened to Boy, anyway? That's the missing piece of information. Maybe he just had a seizure, or something. One part of Harry is full of pride that Hannah saved Boy's life. Her daughter had the guts to find Boy and save him. Another part of Harry is furious. It would have been so easy for Hannah to get Mack off the hook. All this nonsense about not trusting people. It's not as if Mack would ever hurt anyone. Harry rubs her toes against each other and wriggles her feet. The house is cool. She imagines the frost outside, thick and sharp, piercing the trees, the plants, the earth.

It's so frustrating to be awake in the dark. In summer she could be out doing things at this hour, but in mid-winter it's just not practical. She'll have to fumble around in the dark, looking for lights, trying to be quiet and will probably wake the household anyway.

Harry opens her eyes and looks at the red numbers that tease her from across the room. She should have thrown a blanket over that nasty digital clock before she went to bed. From time to time during the night her curiosity got the better of her and she'd check the clock, but it just showed her how slowly the time was passing. Now the clock shows it's five fifteen, so the bulk of the night is behind her. It won't be light until at least seven thirty, more like eight, but she'll be able to start doing things soon. Jack will wake punctually at six, but he'll be quiet because of Hannah. Maybe he'll even go to the Seagull for coffee.

Suddenly Harry realises that she doesn't want to talk to Jack or Hannah. She wants to be alone. This house is penning her in when she wants to be free. She thinks of the dawn breaking over the frosty land and the calm water swirling with the tide, empty of colour, waiting to be filled with sun and sky.

She fumbles with the switch on her bedside lamp and sits up, shivering as the chill touches her shoulders. Hurriedly she crosses the room and pulls on some warm clothes, then brushes her hair, pulling it into a clip at the back of her neck. She'll make some coffee here, but after that she's heading down to the boat, where at least she'll be able to think.

She's as careful as she can be, but it's an old house and the floorboards squeak. Still she's pretty quiet. No noises come from either of the bedrooms, thank goodness. She scribbles a note and leaves it on the kitchen table.

Gone for a boat ride. Back later.

They'll understand, she thinks.

It's harder keeping Rustum quiet, but as soon as they're out of the gate it doesn't matter. The early morning sky is still black and starry. Harry can see stars reflected in the ocean as she walks along the road, curving around the bay to the dock. She pulls her toque down over her ears and wraps her scarf around her nose and mouth to stop the cold air from burning her nasal passages. She doesn't have any gloves so she jams her hands deep into her pockets.

The road to the dock is slippery and silent. It doesn't seem like the same road they'd walked down earlier for the fireworks, arms linked, joking. No, this is the sweep of Raven's wing. He showed Harry a moment of joy, a glimpse of light through his feathers. But that was all. In that glimpse she saw goodness in her daughter and Mack. Now the feathers confuse it all. She can't see anything, doesn't know which way to look.

The padlock on *Polynesia* is stiff with cold. Harry warms it up with her hands and her breath before she can fiddle it open. The boat is as cold as a vault and the windows are frosted over. She lights the diesel stove first. It won't take long to warm the space. Then she goes back outside to sit on the deck and smoke.

"Come here, Rustum," she calls. "Come sit on my feet and keep me warm."

Harry wonders how Lonny and Sam are doing. They live with Mack. They obviously love him. If Mack goes to jail, his boys will have to find different homes. For an orphan like Lonny, that's one more change in life that he doesn't need. Harry's seen how delicate children are, how easily they're affected by their upbringing. She's seen how it affected Big Mack. His mother was a fly-by-night and left all the kids behind when she took off. His father drank like a fish for a while after that, but then he did get his act together. That's probably why Mack can function at all. A father. An island of normality. A thread of continuity.

Where's the continuity for Lonny if Mack's not there? Harry wonders. He's such a great kid. A beam of light. She can't bear to think of him sliding away, out of reach. That's what happens to so many kids. You can't see into their eyes anymore, as if there's a bank of fog between you and them. Well, Lonny might have other family connections that Harry doesn't know about. Maybe he's close to his grandfather.

The grandfather! she thinks. Old Mack. That's who I should talk to. She's met him a few times, remembers his arrow-straight posture and white hair. She's not sure which house is his, but that doesn't matter. She'll go to North Hanson and someone will know. She could walk, but she'll take the boat and drift awhile, let the water pull away all the clutter so that she can see clearly again. She stands up stiffly and steps back into the boat. The cabin is much warmer now, but she's going to have to scrape the windows if she wants to see anything through them. She finds the scraper for the hull and takes it outside, squeezing alongside the cabin and up to the bow. It's slippery and dangerous, but she's careful. The frost is tenacious, and the work warms Harry up. When she looks up, the sky is lighter. She can feel the world awakening and it excites her. She moves carefully back into the cabin and starts the motor. It takes a few tries, but eventually it turns over, chug-chug-chugging the way it should. Harry lets it hum along for a while before struggling with the tie-up lines, which are also frozen stiff. She fills the deck bucket with salt water and splashes the ropes several times before she is able to work them loose.

Finally, she is free, puttering out of the harbour and turning towards the eastern sky, which glows with the promise of light. Five minutes out of the harbour, she puts the boat in neutral. She hunkers down on the back deck, faces the dawn and lights a cigarette.

BIG MACK

Mack wishes this were all a dream. He's locked in the clink, accused of aggravated assault. He knows he wouldn't have done what they're accusing him of, but much of the night is a blur. He wishes he could remember more details. His head still hurts and any movement makes him feel sick. LeClerk The Jerk has given up trying to get anything out of him since last night's "talk." This "talk" runs through Mack's head as he sits on his bunk, picking at his pants, which are filthy.

"So, you're trying to tell me that the boy just appeared out of nowhere and passed out on the grass right next to you?" LeClerk had scoffed, thick lips showing beneath his short brown moustache.

Silence.

"What makes you think I'd believe such a stupid lie?"

More silence.

"Why did you beat him up, Mack?"

"I never did anything!"

"So why were you crying that it was all your fault?"

"I wasn't!"

"Well, the young lady says you were."

Hannah. What has she said about him? Mack remembers her slapping his face. Why was she so mad at him? Why has she said this about him?

Mack stares at his feet in their grey wool socks. LeClerk must have taken his shoes. He wishes he could go back to sleep, but he can't. Hannah's face comes and goes behind his eyes—friend, enemy—changing with every blink.

Suddenly he punches the wall with his fist. "Fuck!!"

"Hey! Calm down in dere, or we'll handcuff you!" LeClerk's French accent pops out, his voice sounding muffled, faraway.

"Fuck you!" Mack bellows, but the effort hurts his head and

200

his stomach begins to churn. He lies on his back and closes his eyes, trying to remember what happened.

Nothing comes into his head.

He tries again.

He's with Silas on the boat, drinking. The Old Man comes down and kicks them off. Silas is crawling out of a ditch.

Long black hair. Red fingernails. Shawnee snuggling up against him.

Dennis and Diesel.

People. Lots of people.

What's going to happen to the boys? Mack wonders. They'll be so ashamed of me. He squirms as he thinks of people's reactions. Some people will be happy that he's in jail. There're guys in the village that don't like Mack. Mack hears their voices: I always said he was no good; just like his brother, Nelson.

It takes a while for Mack to realise that LeClerk is talking to someone out there. It's impossible to make out what he's saying, but Mack hears the ping-pong of voices. One of the voices is definitely LeClerk's, he can tell by the nasal whine. Another is female. It's possible that there's a third voice, but whoever it is doesn't say much. Like Boy. Boy never usually says much, either, but he can when he wants to. Well, not now, since LeClerk says he's in a coma somewhere, maybe even dying.

Jesus! Mack sits up. If Boy dies, will I be charged with murder?

Sweat pearls on the back of his neck. His heart hammers in his ribcage. Blood flies through his body, missing some parts of him, filling up other parts too much. His hands and arms tremble violently. The sweat creeps up his scalp along his hairline, prickling and beading. In seconds he feels damp all over. His chest seems cold and empty.

He clutches his hands to his chest and tries to tune out what he's feeling. His breath comes in little gasps, short and fast. Gone are all the symptoms of his hangover. All he can think of now is Boy. Boy's got to live! Whatever happened to him, he's got to keep breathing. Assault is a bad enough charge, but murder—that's in a different league!

The voices are still battling outside: louder, softer, rumble, rumble. Mack rocks his body and listens. Suddenly the voices get clearer and he hears footsteps echoing down the hall, towards Mack's cell. The voices stop, while the feet approach. Sliding noise—the little window panel in the door.

Mack raises his eyes slowly, unsure of what he'll see. And then, at the sight of his father's white hair, tears claim his vision. He can't see LeClerk, he can't see his dad. He can't see his way out of here.

"It's okay, Mack," the woman's voice—Harry. "We're going to get you out of here."

A snort from behind: The Jerk.

Harry's voice again. "We are."

Something in the calm, firm way she says that makes Mack stop shaking. His eyes begin to clear, so that he can see the stern look on his father's face. Old Mack says nothing, just looks at his son, no pity in his eyes, just belief, understanding.

"Lonny's with me," Old Mack says, his voice flat and quiet. "Sam's with Sara."

Mack nods, wishing the boys weren't split up, but feeling too grateful to complain.

"We're calling a lawyer," states Harry. "They can't keep you here. And they know it," she adds turning sideways to eyeball LeClerk.

Mack nods at them both and sits on his hands. He likes hearing their voices but it's hard to look at their faces.

"Bye, son," his father says gruffly.

"We'll see you soon," says Harry. "Real soon."

The window slides shut.

LONNY

It's another beautiful day, but Lonny doesn't care. He sits on the back of the *Polynesia* next to Rustum and watches the water swirl past. It's warm where he is, in the sun. His grandpa and Harry let him come as far as Hanson Bay, but they wouldn't take him to see Big Mack. They went to the police station by themselves.

Harry showed up at their house this morning, early. She hugged Lonny and shook Old Mack's hand.

"I want to help," she said.

Grandpa didn't say too much, but he made her some coffee and they sat at the table together.

"Does he have a criminal record?" she asked, meaning Uncle.

Grandpa shook his head. "Nope."

"Does Lila want to press charges?"

"Pfft!" Grandpa snorted. "No!"

"The cops will still press charges, but if the family's against it, then it's better for Mack. Have you heard how Boy's doing?"

Grandpa stirred his coffee and took a long slurp. "They said he's bleeding in his brain. He could live or die. He's breathing on his own, though."

"Is he black and blue all over?"

"A bump on the head, near his eye."

"What do you think happened?"

Grandpa just shrugged, not looking at Harry.

Lonny drapes one of the tie-up lines in the water and watches it curl in the tide. He tries to picture Boy in a hospital bed, with a bump on his head. In his mind's eye, Boy looks like an Egyptian mummy, all wrapped up in bandages. Lonny flips the rope and slaps it against the water. He likes the way rope changes shape. It's a straight line, then a snake, then it curls into a loop. The loop makes him think of his daydream yesterday. He wonders why his mind did that yesterday, pictured himself and Boy hanging from

203

a rope, dead. Maybe he's just worried about what will happen if Boy dies.

From what he can tell, Uncle Mack might go to jail. Lonny's dad has been in jail for a long time. Lonny doesn't even remember much about his dad, except that he looks like Uncle Silas. It's different with Big Mack. Lonny's been attached to him for a long time. When he's with Mack, he doesn't feel lonely or sad. So who will he live with now? Grandpa, maybe. Living with Grandpa's not so good, but maybe it'll get better. Old Mack's spoken to Lonny a lot more lately, as if he's singled Lonny out for some reason. Perhaps it's his job to watch out for Grandpa. Keep him safe.

Lonny wonders where Uncle Silas is. Nobody's seen him since he went to the bar with Uncle Mack on New Year's Eve. It seems so long ago since Lonny saw them wobbling down the road, it's hard to believe it was only last night. That's probably why nobody's looking for Silas. If he was drinking, they won't expect him to appear until later today, or tomorrow, even.

But what if he saw something? Maybe Uncle Silas has the answer that will get Big Mack out of jail. Lonny sure hopes so. He must remember to ask Grandpa about it later. They might as well ask around for Silas while they're in Hanson Bay.

Rustum rolls back against Lonny's legs, begging to be stroked. He's so big, this dog, but so gentle. In a way, he's kind-of like Uncle. Lonny runs his hands through the dog's thick, long fur, looking at all the different colours: black, brown, white. He wishes he could take Rustum home with him, to Grandpa's. Then his room wouldn't feel so empty. It used to have Uncle and Sam in it. Now it's just Lonny. Maybe he should ask Grandpa if Sam can come for the night.

Rustum jumps up with a bark, then leaps off the boat, wagging his tail. Lonny looks up at the main wharf. Sure enough, his grandpa and Harry are there, Rustum must have pretty good ears. Or maybe he smelled the smoke. Harry and Grandpa are both smoking. They stop and talk. They stare out towards Bailey's Rock as if they can't see Lonny. Their faces are serious. Maybe the cops aren't going to let Uncle go.

Lonny starts slapping the rope against the water again, harder and harder and harder. He doesn't move from his place, even when the water splashes him.

HANNAH

"The heroine herself!" Jack exclaims, as Hannah comes into the kitchen for breakfast. She smiles back at him and gives him a hug.

"At least someone's proud of me," she says.

"Not just me. Lots of people. You saved a life, there, girl!"

"Lots of people except Mother, apparently."

"She's proud of you, too, sweetheart."

"Jack, my Mother doesn't believe me! She tried to stop me from talking to the police last night. She's made me feel like some kind of outcast."

"Maybe she just thinks there's an explanation for what you heard Mack say—you know?—a different meaning."

"An explanation for 'It's all my fault'? She was butting in last night, totally undermining me."

Hannah looks out of the window where a shaft of sun glows across the garden, its yellow warmth teasing swirls of mist from the frosty grass. She turns to Jack.

"Do you think he did it?"

Jack pulls out two chairs and presses Hannah into one of them with gentle hands. He takes the other chair and faces her.

"Anything could've happened last night, Hannah. It was dark—eh?—and the road was icy. Everyone was celebrating, drinking, excited—Big Mack included. Lila's family told us Boy was coming to find Big Mack. He was bringing him something. Who knows what happened to Boy between North Hanson and here? We can only hope that somebody actually saw something."

"He was coming for me," Hannah says slowly. "Of course."

"What do you mean?"

"When Mack said: 'He was coming for me,' I thought he meant that Boy was trying to attack him. Huh. I knew that Boy was coming to find Mack. That's why we were looking for him in the first place."

"Well. It's two-edged, that's for sure."

"Huh."

Hannah crawling away. Rob lunging for her. Another woman saving Hannah from this man she thought she could trust.

Hannah is quiet, she stares without seeing anything and rubs her forefinger against her upper lip. The kitchen clock ticks its rhythm into the silence. A minute passes and still she sits there. Jack slurps coffee, breaking the quietness. Interrupted, Hannah sits up in her chair, shoulders back, arms folded.

"You know, Jack," she says, pewter eyes flashing suddenly silver, "I've seen a lot in the last few years. Learned some lessons from life. Working at a hospital shows you a grim world. I discovered that nice people are capable of terrible things. If it seems as if I'm being rough on Mack, it's because I've learned not to trust anyone. Appearances are deceptive."

"Don't you go through life not trusting anyone, Hannah Farre!" Jack exclaims, reaching out and grasping her hand. "There's a good side to trusting and it's way better than the bad side. Believe me; I know!"

"Well I don't know anything, Jack. I really don't." Hannah's voice is shrill, breaking. "I just heard what I heard. And that's what I'm going to tell the police, after breakfast. Then it will be over with. It won't be my responsibility any more."

"Hannah, sweetheart, relax, everything's okay. You're a grown woman now. You know right from wrong. Do what you have to do. Just remember that you're loved, eh? You'll always be loved."

Hannah looks at Jack's face, creased like a tightly-woven fishnet.

She looks down at her fingers and picks at a hangnail.

Hannah nibbles at some dry toast over breakfast, avoiding the leftover bacon. If she were to throw up in this thin-walled house, it would just be a matter of time before the questions started. That's the last thing she wants. Which reminds her that she should make an appointment to see Dr Haswell at the clinic. She picks up her glass of water and walks into the living room where the phone is. She's just reaching for the directory when she remembers that today is New Year's Day. The doctor will only see emergencies today. He probably would have been called in to help with Boy last night, too.

Hmm. Hannah wonders whether she should call him at home. It's 9:30 now. It might be good to know what happened to Boy before she goes to make her statement, but Haswell could have been up as late as three or four in the morning. She decides to wait and call him in when she gets back.

Just as she puts the directory back, the phone rings, making her jump.

"Hello?"

"Is that Hannah?" It's a woman's voice, scratchy and sleepy, definitely hungover.

"Yes, it is. Who's that?"

"Hannah, it's Kathy Davis, we ran into each other last night." Hannah is amazed that Kathy has remembered anything about last night. She seemed so drunk at the time.

"Well hi, Kathy. Happy New Year!"

"Oh, I'm not quite ready for that yet," Kathy groans. "My kids were screaming at six this morning, with no sympathy for the size of my hangover."

"You poor thing," Hannah commiserates, wondering why Kathy is calling her.

"Just you wait till you have kids, girl. You'll find out what it's like." Her laugh turns into a coughing fit and Hannah has to wait a while before their conversation can resume.

"So anyway," Kathy says, "Apparently you saved someone's life last night and I was just phoning to see if it was true."

The grapevine. Hannah is always amazed at how efficient it is in Hanson Bay.

"You know what, Kathy?" Hannah plays it safe. "I don't know if I did, or not. I haven't heard anything about it. The guy could be walking and talking or stone cold dead for all I know."

"My dad heard that it was that retarded kid from North Hanson and that Big Mack Stanley beat him to a pulp."

Kathy's dad is Cutter McKay, a heavy drinker. Hannah pauses before answering.

"Well, he wasn't pulp, Kathy. As a matter of fact, I don't remember seeing any obvious marks on him. It was dark, though. I can't be sure."

"Huh," says Kathy. "Hey, what're you doing today?"

"Not too much," Hannah allows. "Why?"

"We're having a few people over for a late lunch. You know? Hair of the dog and all that. You're welcome to come. It'll be at around one. All leftovers, nothing elaborate."

"Where do you live now?" Hannah asks.

"We're two doors down from the Fyffe's."

"No kidding. That big house?"

"That's us. Fancy, huh?"

"Well thanks for the invitation, Kathy. I'd love to come. We can catch up on all the good stuff. Can I bring anything?"

"Just yourself." In the background Hannah hears a kid begin to scream.

"I gotta go," Kathy sighs, then hangs up.

Hannah listens to the dial tone and wonders how she feels about the lunch party. On the one hand, it's a great opportunity for her to get back into the social life around here. On the other hand, she doesn't want to feel pressured to discuss last night's events. She feels funny having said as much as she did, but she was a bystander last night, so confidentiality isn't essential.

She gets up and heads to her room, feeling the old floorboards give under her feet as she treads down the hallway. The house is starting to need the kind of attention that Jack probably can't afford. Hannah guesses he'll just patch it up from time to time, as he's done with the front stairs. It's the mould that bothers her. She's seen it in so many west coast houses. Jack's healthy for his age, but if his house gets damp, he might start having chest problems.

She takes last night's outfit off the back of the chair in her bedroom and examines the damage to her pants. It isn't as bad as she expected; dark patches mottle the pale brown leather below the knees. She might still be able to wear them if she takes them to a professional cleaner. She takes a hanger out of the closet and puts the pants away. For now, she's going to stick with clean pressed jeans and a sweater. They'll be tidy enough for the police and for lunch, which sounds pretty informal. Her hair needs attention, though; maybe a French braid. She usually reserves that for nursing, because it's so tidy, but it'll be good for today. It'll make her seem professional, give her an air of authority.

Hannah thinks about what she's going to say as her fingers twist and tuck her hair, tying the end of the braid with a black ribbon. There's not really a lot she *can* say. She found Boy and breathed for him. Mack was pretty incidental. She'll have to tell them why she was looking for Boy in the first place. That will ease her conscience. She's been feeling a little uncomfortable since her conversation with Jack this morning. Maybe she *is* misinterpreting Mack's words, but it's not her fault. It's Mack's responsibility to give the right information.

She thinks of his face, flattened against the window of the police car, and squirms, remembering the moments over Christmas when he seemed strangely attractive. She wonders if she'll ever encounter a man who will earn her trust. It'll be harder to meet a man, anyway, once she has a baby.

Hannah's fingers stop where they are, near the bottom of the braid.

It's as if her sub-conscious has decided for her: you are going to have the baby.

She pinches the braid with one hand and re-ties the ribbon with the other. Me, a mother? It just doesn't seem right, no matter how she thinks about it. Maybe she should try not to think about it.

Outside on the street, the world seems gentle. The low winter sun throws lustrous shadows, dappling the town. The water floats out to sea like a shiny blue skin, with a path of light up the middle. There are times when this land takes Hannah's breath away. Harry has always nattered on about nature and beauty, but it wasn't until Hannah was older that she began to see these things for herself.

She turns a corner and strides down the empty streets, her breath lingering behind her. Ten minutes after stepping out of Jack's front door, she sees the police station sitting squarely on its plot of grass, the Canadian flag hanging down stiffly in the cold air. As she walks up the concrete path, the door opens, surprising her. It's a Native man, old and gaunt, his face expressionless. And right behind him is Harry. Hannah takes a step back.

"What are you doing?" she demands of her mother.

"Oh, Hannah, there you are," Harry turns to the Native man. "This is Mack Stanley, Big Mack's father."

Hannah stares at this man whose son her testimony may condemn. He stares right back at her with steely eyes that pick out every jot of weakness in her. White hair rises back from his face like a halo, making his dark eye sockets even more prominent. Has everything about her just been revealed to this stranger? Hannah takes another step back.

"Hannah," prompts her mother, looking downwards.

Following Harry's glance she sees that the man's hand is outstretched. He's waiting for her to shake it.

"Thank you," he says, as she holds out her own hand and presses it against his dark, bony fingers.

"I . . . I don't understand."

"For saving my grandson's life."

HARRY

Harry stands on the dock with Old Mack, taking in the beauty of the day. It's incongruous to have such good weather. A storm would be more suited to her mood.

"Is Mack on good terms with the doctor?" she asks.

"He works for him, sometimes."

"But does the doctor have a good sense of Mack's character?"

Old Mack pinches his smoke between thumb and forefinger and takes a measured puff, squinting down at the boat.

"That decking will need re-doing pretty soon," he says, jerking his chin in the direction of the boat.

"Summertime." Harry dreads re-doing the decking; it's such a chore.

"Those guys are friends," Old Mack states.

"Who?" Harry asks, still looking at the boat. "Lonny and Rustum?"

"My son and the doctor."

"Well that's good. Haswell's a helpful man to have on your side."

"For some people."

"What do you mean?"

Old Mack smokes and stares out to sea. Harry doesn't press him. She's watching Lonny, who's slapping one of her tie-up lines against the water with an angry look on his face.

"My other son went to jail anyway," Old Mack resumes. "The doctor tried to help. He stood up and told what the residential school done to Nelson. He said it made my son crazy. It was true. He said Nelson needed help, not jail. But he needn't have bothered. If a Native only makes one mistake in his whole life, that's what a judge will see. Nothing else."

"The whole system is screwed!" Harry exhales loudly. "Is Nelson still in jail?"

Old Mack nods his head. "I'll be dead when they let him go."

Harry feels a pang of sadness sweep over her.

"That's his father," Old Mack says, gesturing toward Lonny.

"Poor kid," Harry sighs. "He must be frightened he's going to lose his uncle, too."

Old Mack grunts and drops his cigarette under his boot. "He's going to stay with me until this is over, whatever happens."

"Well, I'm glad to hear it. He needs someone special in his life."

They start to walk down to the dock, holding tight to the scarlet railings because of the slippery ramp.

"I'll talk to the doctor if you like," she offers. "And I'm going to call that lawyer, too. I'm sure there's a way to get Mack released before there's a trial. Heck, I'd even bail him out."

Old Mack turns around sharply, dark eyes glaring.

"If there's money to be spent, then my family will raise it!"

Harry stumbles on the ramp and grasps the rail. "You're right," she says. She drops her gaze from his. "I'm sorry. Sometimes I get carried away."

Mack turns back, apparently satisfied and continues down the ramp to the dock, where Rustum is barking, happy to see them. Harry ducks into the boat and turns the key. She'll take these two back home and then drift away for a while. People's boundaries are like eddy lines, constantly changing with the direction and strength of the tide. She's lived by herself for so long that she doesn't always feel the push of water warning her of a change in current. She obviously needs to pay more attention.

She goes outside to untie the lines, but Old Mack and Lonny have beaten her to it. She nods her head and they hop onto the boat, pushing it away from the dock. For the second time today, *Polynesia* turns out of Hanson Bay. Harry stifles a yawn. It's been a long morning.

Once she has dropped off Old Mack and Lonny, she decides to check in with Jack and Hannah. It was awkward meeting Hannah at the police station this morning, the kind of thing that will cause friction between them. Harry wishes it didn't have to be this way, but she's never been able to talk Hannah out of anything before.

I've got to let go, Harry thinks. Hannah is a grown woman with a mind of her own. She has to make her own choices. And her own mistakes.

Harry locks up the boat again and heads back into town. This is a record for her. She can't remember the last time she spent so many days in Hanson Bay, but it's a small sacrifice, really.

She thinks back to their meeting with LeClerk. They must have spent half an hour trying to explain what happened last night. It should have taken half a minute! Boy went to Hanson Bay to give Mack his sweater because it was cold. Boy is Mack's nephew; Mack would never beat him up. Mack has no prior history of assault or criminal behaviour. Boy's mother does not want to charge Mack for the assault. Mack's family want him out of jail. So easy. Unless you're talking to Sgt. LeClerk on New Year's Day, when he makes double time and a half. "Who is Boy?" he'd actually asked! "How old is he? Where does he live?" On and on, writing notes to himself in French that Harry couldn't read, even though she tried. And all the while, his moustache hairs stuck out like so many fibre-optic lie-detectors, bristling importantly with each new piece of information.

It was the sight of Big Mack that has stuck with her the most, though. All day she has seen his face in her mind, lost and lonely, frightened. She wishes she knew what happened last night. She's sure he's innocent. She has always been one to trust her instincts and this is no exception. Whatever happened, it wasn't Mack's fault.

"Hello!" she calls, opening the door to Jack's house.

"C'mon in," his voice floats out from the kitchen.

When she enters the little kitchen, Harry finds Jack slicing the rest of the bread. On the counter there is a tomato, a half-eaten package of cheese, a jar of mayonnaise, some ham and two plates.

"We've been abandoned," he explains, pointing to the two plates with the bread knife.

"What do you mean?"

"Hannah has been invited out for lunch. D'you want your sandwich grilled?" Jack reaches for the frying pan.

"Of course. Who invited her?"

"Her old classmate, Kathy."

"Cutter's daughter? Really? I wonder what *she* wants."

"Whoa, there, Harry! Don't make Kathy a monster just because of Cutter. Those two girls were in school together. Hannah invited her over here a few times as I recall."

"Well, I guess you'd know more about her social life than me," Harry sighs, pulling out a chair. "I just can't imagine Cutter passing on a single nice piece of genetic material. He doesn't have any."

"Well, aren't genetics supposed to skip a generation anyway? Old Stewart McKay wasn't so bad."

"Cutter's father? I guess not," Harry concedes. "And maybe Kathy's mother is okay. I don't really know her."

"Oh, Aileen's a sweetheart. How she wound up with Cutter, there, I can't imagine."

"It's not what brings people together that interests me, so much as what keeps them together. I mean, if you live with a self-centred little tyrant and your life is miserable, then walk out the door. That's what it's there for."

Jack raises his eyebrows. "Harry . . . " he begins, butchering the tomato because the knife is so dull.

"Yes, Jack."

"Did something bad happen to Hannah in Whitehorse?"

"Why do you ask?"

"Well, this morning, I was talking to her—eh?—and she got so bitter-sounding, it kinda took me by surprise. She was getting

215

worked up, so I left it, but I wondered if she told you anything over Christmas."

"Amazingly, she did."

Jack passes Harry her grilled cheese sandwich and fixes his eyes on hers.

"I only know the tip of the iceberg, Jack. As far as I can make out it's one of those monster-boyfriend stories. She left when things got violent."

"No! Is she okay?"

"Physically, I think she's all in one piece. A few bruises, maybe."

"Is she going to press charges on this goon?"

"I think she just wants to escape from him. Make a clean break. A lawsuit would tangle her up, make things worse."

"My God, I had no idea," Jack stares at Harry across their untouched sandwiches. "You're calm about this."

"Should I scream and stamp and tell the world? I was hoping she would talk to both of us about it, but then this thing happened with Big Mack. We've hit a little stumbling block. If history's anything to go by, she might stop talking to me. That's why I'm telling you."

"So you're *planning* to argue over this little thing? Handing over to me? Giving up responsibility?"

"What do you mean?"

"Well, you're being stubborn, siding against her about Mack, right when she needs you most. She's been through hell, been beat up, fer crying out loud!"

"Are you saying that I don't love my daughter enough?"

Jack slaps the palm of his hand on the table, making the plates jump. "Well, hell, Harry. Maybe I am!"

Harry picks up her sandwich and snaps off a big bite. "Then we disagree," she says, mouth full, eyes glowering.

LONNY

"Grandpa," says Lonny, as they eat their soup, "where's Uncle Silas?"

Grandpa finishes his spoonful, then takes another one. It's hamburger soup, with carrots and potatoes—Raylene left it for them.

"Probably passed out somewhere," he says gruffly.

"Oh." Lonny crumbles some more crackers into his soup.

"Don't you ever start drinking, Grandson." Grandpa's voice suddenly gets loud. "You see what it does? It ruins everything. I lost my kids because of drinking. That's why I quit. Now they've lost themselves because of it. It has to stop. I want it to stop with you."

Grandpa stares hard at Lonny, making him forget his soup. He fiddles with his spoon.

"I'm going to talk to your cousin, too," Grandpa continues. "You and Sam will be the ones to make this family forget drinking. Whatever it takes. Even those counsellors. I've said nothing for too long. I don't have a lot of years left in me, Grandson, but I'm going to make sure those years count."

Lonny wants to be excused, but there's no way Grandpa will let him go yet. He's on a roll. He won't be finished with Lonny for a while. Lonny sprinkles some more salt into his bowl, stirs it in and takes another spoonful.

"If someone cuts up that log on the beach, I can pack it up to the house and split it," he offers.

This seems to please Grandpa. He puts his spoon down. "Hard work is good," he says. "It's when people get bored or lazy that they start drinking. People used to say that I worked too much. I didn't. I worked just enough to keep myself sober. People think hard work makes you a slave or stops you from enjoying yourself. They don't know how to enjoy work. Work is good. You'll see."

"Grandpa," Lonny says quickly. "I've got to go to the

217

washroom." He puts down his spoon and squeezes out from the bench. He walks fast down the hallway to make it seem as if he really has to go. Once he's in the bathroom he sits on the edge of the tub and wonders how to find Uncle Silas. He should have asked about him when they were all in Hanson Bay. With Harry there, Grandpa might not have gotten started on this thing about work. But Grandpa said something to Harry when they were on the ramp. He turned on her the way a dog snaps at a fly. Lonny didn't feel comfortable saying anything after that. Nobody said very much on the way home, either.

Lonny wonders what Harry is doing right now. Maybe she's outside with the dog, smoking. She does that a lot.

The smell of dirty diapers is strong in the bathroom. Raylene hasn't dumped the bag and now it's full. Lonny would do it, but he doesn't like to touch those things. He gets up and runs some water in the sink. Then he flushes the toilet and opens the door. When he gets back to the kitchen he sees that Grandpa has cleared away his bowl, even though he wasn't finished yet.

"I'm going to go to Auntie's," Lonny announces.

"What for?" Grandpa asks.

"In case they've heard anything."

Grandpa nods. "They would of phoned here if they'd heard anything, but go anyway. It's good to show your support. Tell them I'll be over later."

Auntie is still in Victoria, but there're lots of people at her house. Lonny doesn't really want to go there, but he doesn't want to be at Grandpa's either. Maybe he'll go by Sam's house, first. As he walks, a dog starts to follow him. It's a big black one, called Muscles. It's supposed to belong to Uncle Silas and it's friendly as long as you don't run away from it. Soon another dog appears, then another one. They're so curious. If anyone's going anywhere, they want to come along. Lonny takes a detour around Edna's house because she's got one that's part pitbull. It lives on a chain and it growls and snaps its teeth, and never takes its evil eyes off you. It's better to avoid a dog fight. Lonny hates dog fights. If they're bad enough, the dogs end up getting shot.

He sees Sam before he even gets to the house. Sam's out front with a small red car that's remote controlled. His mom must have given it to him for Christmas, but Lonny's hardly seen Sam since then.

"Hey, Sam!" he calls. He wants to run over there, but the dogs might chase him, so he doesn't.

Sam waves and keeps on playing with the car. By the time Lonny gets there Sam's got the car stuck under the house.

"There's nowhere flat to do this," he complains.

"How about the beach?" Lonny suggests.

"Mom told me I can only play with the car if I don't get it sandy."

"Huh."

"What are you doing right now?" Sam asks, bending down to crawl under the house.

"Nothing. What about you?"

Sam makes a grunting noise as he squeezes back out, his car in hand. "I was trying to play with this, but the grass is too bumpy. I tried the road, but the rocks are too big and it gets stuck in the potholes. Now the wheel's come off."

Lonny looks at the car and wishes he had one like it. Then they could race their cars together somewhere. He didn't get any presents at Christmas, though. "Hey Sam," he says, changing the subject, "d'you know where Uncle Silas is?"

"Um, maybe my mom does. Why?"

"Because maybe he doesn't know about Uncle being in jail. But he was with Uncle last night. He might know what happened."

Sam is quiet. A dark look comes over his eyes and forehead. "Ask my mom," he says, motioning towards the door. When Lonny goes up the crooked steps, Sam stays on the grass, fiddling with his car.

Lonny taps on the door as he opens it.

219

"Auntie?" he calls.

"Yeah?"

"It's Lonny. Can I come in?"

"No, Lonny, you have to stay by the door." A deep chuckle rasps across the room from the kitchen. Sara moves into view, still laughing. "Of course you can come in! Since when did you start being so polite?"

Lonny's not sure why he felt he had to knock. Maybe it's because Sam always comes into the house first when they're here, but today Lonny's coming in by himself. Sara freaked out one time when Lonny walked across the pale blue carpet in his shoes, so he kicks them off and goes over to give her a hug. Her nice long hair has been cut short around her face, leaving a thin pony tail at the back. She's wearing some beaded earrings that dangle almost to her shoulders.

"Happy New Year, Lon," she says ruffling his hair. "Now, what do you want?"

"Um," Lonny hesitates. "I'm looking for Uncle Silas."

"I think he's passed out somewhere in town," she says. "Why?"

"I want to go tell him about Uncle."

Sara's forehead wrinkles up. "You shouldn't bother with Silas until he's sober, Lonny."

"What if he wants to keep drinking?"

"He won't," Sara shakes her head. "He's probably broke by now."

Nobody wants to help Lonny with this!

"Whereabouts in town is he?"

"Nephew, I just told you not to bother!" Sara's voice is stern.

"But I have to!" Lonny bursts out. "He was with Uncle last night. He might know something that can get Uncle out of jail!"

Sara looks at Lonny and puts her hand on his shoulder. "It's okay, Lonny," she says, quietly. "Sam's scared, too. We're all scared. But Silas can't help anyone right now. Can you imagine what it would be like? The cops would treat him bad if he went there drunk."

Lonny curls his fingernails into his palms so that he won't cry in front of Sara. He's relieved when she takes her hand off his shoulder and goes over to the phone.

"What's your grandpa's number?" she asks.

Lonny looks at the floor, afraid of what she's going to tell Grandpa about this.

"Mack?" she says, after dialing. She doesn't say "How are you doing?" or anything like that. Instead, she says "Sam's lonely and he's missing his dad. Can Lonny stay the night?"

There's a long pause. It could be one of Grandpa's silences, or he could be talking real quiet, Lonny's not sure which. Sara says nothing and the moment drags out.

"Tomorrow?" Sara asks.

The next pause is not so long.

"I'll send them over right after breakfast."

She puts down the phone and looks over at Lonny. "He's a hard one, your grandpa," she says. Then she grins. "The trick is to wait him out. If you interrupt him, you lose."

Lonny has never seen Sara being this nice to him. Not that she's mean or anything. It's just that most times she says everything to Sam, as if she doesn't notice Lonny. Today is different. Today, she's on Lonny's side.

"You get to stay over," she tells him. "But tomorrow you and Sam have to split firewood at your grandpa's. Someone's cutting up a log for him."

"Thanks, Auntie," Lonny says.

"Now forget about Silas for a while," she shakes her finger at him. "He'll be back this evening, I bet."

Lonny lifts his eyebrows and moves towards the door. He wants to be outside. Maybe he and Sam can take the car over to the baseball field and try it there.

HANNAH

By the time Hannah nears Kathy's house, she's feeling a lot better. After her shock at meeting Mack's father had subsided, the rest of her time at the police station had gone well. The French-Canadian RCMP officer was courteous and polite. He thanked her several times for saving a life. He said she was a real asset to the community. Are you planning to stay on? he asked with sincere interest.

Like her, LeClerk was only interested in the facts, which made things so much easier. She remembered the events in clear, chronological order, which he obviously appreciated, taking his time to write careful notes. It gave her confidence, the way he paid attention to the slightest details.

At one point a wave of nausea had risen in her chest and throat. LeClerk did not ask any questions, merely showed her to the washroom.

Hannah remembers this as she walks up the painted wooden steps to Kathy's front door. She hopes that she will be able to get through lunch without throwing up. She rings the bell. A squealing scrabble of small children rushes to open the door.

"Not so loud, you guys!" Hannah hears the wince in Kathy's voice before she appears at the top of a short flight of white carpeted steps.

"You made it!" she smiles, holding out both hands. "I'm so glad!"

"Of course," Hannah smiles back. "Now which of these are yours?" She inspects the four kids—one redhead, two blonde ones and the littlest with a wild brown mop of uncombed hair. "Hello," she says to them. "I'm Hannah."

The kids look back at her, fidgeting and nudging each other.

Kathy points to the blonde boy and girl. "That's Eric, he's five, and Katy's three. They're mine, the scamps. The little Rastafarian is Emily, she's two. She and Megan, here, are my cousin Sandra's

222

kids. Her husband, Reg, is a redhead, too. Do you remember Sandra? She was three years ahead of us in school."

Hannah finishes taking off her shoes and moves through the small mob towards the stairs, smiling at the upturned faces.

"Is she here right now? I remember faces much better than names."

"No, actually, she and Reg had a big row last night and they're trying to patch things up." Kathy reaches forward to give Hannah a hug. "They called this morning to excuse themselves and I offered to take the kids."

"Well that was nice of you," says Hannah looking around the living room. The carpet is white and the couch, with its back to the picture window, is beige leather. A huge television screen takes up one corner of the room and flickers with Walt Disney cartoons. The carpet is littered with toys and streamers and articles of children's clothing. Kathy's dad, Cutter, is reclining in a brown velvet chair. His small round face is stubbled and puffy, heavily lined. A strong smell of booze wafts from him. He looks at Hannah without getting up. "Happy New Year!" he grunts.

Hannah wonders if he's been to sleep yet. "Happy New Year to you," she answers. She turns around as someone comes out of the kitchen behind her. It's Kathy's mother, Aileen, wearing a blue apron. She's small and thin, with grey-blonde hair back-combed to look fuller and puffier than it is. Her arms are outstretched and she greets Hannah with a warm hug.

"We thought you'd gone for good," she fusses, looking Hannah up and down, as if she's inspecting a dress for flaws. Her scrutiny done, she declares: "You look wonderful! Doesn't she, Kathy?"

"Sure thing," says Kathy.

"Well, what can we fix you to eat and drink?" Aileen asks.

"Nothing alcoholic, that's for sure," Hannah states, engineering a pained look.

"I sympathize with you," clucks Aileen, taking the bait, "although, my daughter, here, is hoping that she can drink her

223

hangover away." She looks at Kathy, mouth pursed, hands on hips.

"Oh, give up, Mom!" Kathy groans, rolling her eyes and picking up an open can of Blue.

"Where's Brad?" Hannah asks.

"He'll be back in a sec. He's visiting Pete and Angie, two houses over. You probably don't know them. They just moved here a couple of years ago. Nice people, though. She's a hairstylist and he's a fisherman. They came from Port Hardy."

"Sit down, sit down," Aileen interrupts, guiding Hannah to the leather couch. She hands her a tall glass of coke, with ice and lemon. "This will fix you up," she says.

Kathy brings her beer over and joins Hannah on the couch. Her eyes are tired and her face looks pale, but her appearance is neat and tidy. Kathy's always been proud of her hair, which is naturally blonde, with platinum streaks. The shape of it changes from time to time, but it usually falls in careful layers to her shoulders. Today is no exception.

Kathy holds up her beer: "Here's to old friends!"

"Happy New Year!" Hannah adds.

"Are you going to stay?"

"I think so," Hannah says slowly. "Things were going okay with Mother when I first got back, but now I'm not so sure."

"Chermothersanoldcow," Cutter rasps under his breath. "Thas why."

Hannah's guts freeze. Did she hear right? She stares at Cutter, but he doesn't look back at her. His eyes are closed, his head's tilted back. Hannah looks at Kathy, to see if she heard what her father said, but Kathy's bent over, putting her beer bottle on the floor.

"What are you fighting about?" she asks, straightening up.

"Oh," says Hannah, still frozen. "It's nothing."

"Yeah, it's always the small stuff that sets people at each other. I'm like that with Brad sometimes. Our last fight was about peanut shells in the couch. But I guess it was really about the mess he makes in general. I have enough to do as it is without having to pick up after a grown man all the time.

"So what's your beef with your mom?" Kathy asks again, picking up her beer and draining it. "It was almost empty," she explains, then gets up and takes another one out of the box.

"Hey!" calls Cutter from across the room.

"Catch!" Kathy tosses a can at him—an easy, accurate underhand. Despite his lethargy, Cutter stretches out an arm and swipes the can out of the air. "Jesus Christ! How many times I gotta tell you not to do that! Fuckin' foam bath now."

"Well, keep it for next time."

"Makin' me get up when you know I'm sick."

"Ah, shush, Dad!"

"Oh here, honey. Here." Aileen appears out of nowhere and rushes across the room with a can of beer and a glass. Cutter takes the can and waves away the glass. Aileen pulls a beer mat from the coffee table and places it on the arm of Cutter's chair. He grunts at her and she smiles, touching his forehead. He pulls away. As she walks back to the kitchen, he grabs the beer mat and flings it across the room. The kids turn and stare at him, but he waves his hand and grunts at them, too.

Hannah wonders what Cutter is sick with. She doesn't remember him being so ornery before.

"Dad's not feeling so good these days," says Kathy.

"Has he been to the doctor?" asks Hannah, feeling weird, talking about Cutter as if he isn't there.

"Won't go. He's too stubborn."

"But it might be something simple."

"I think it's just too much of this," Kathy mouths the words and lifts her can.

Hannah looks at Cutter's profile. The smell, the bulgy nose, the bags under his eyes. "Oh," she says.

"So he doesn't want people gossiping," Kathy tells her. "Sure you won't have one?" She holds up a can of beer.

Hannah shakes her head. Kathy's right. Rumours fly faster than the wind in Hanson Bay. Hannah imagines the rumour that will spread once she is visibly pregnant.

Across the room, a cartoon stallion races across an open plain, his dark mane and tail tossing in the wind. The four children gaze at the screen, half-eaten bags of potato chips strewn around them.

"Your kids are sweet," Hannah says.

"Aren't they?" Kathy beams, her face relaxing. "But they're monsters, really. They've got us wrapped around their little fingers. Isn't that right, Mom?"

Aileen reappears from the kitchen, wiping her fingers on her apron. "What's that?" she asks. "I was loading the dishwasher."

"I was telling Hannah that the kids have got us where they want us."

"The darlings!" Aileen gushes. "I tell you, being a grandmother is so much better than being a parent. I mean, I can just take them or leave them, whatever I feel like."

"As if you ever turn down a chance to see them," Kathy grins at her mother. "It's great for me," she tells Hannah. "I've got a baby-sitter, a mom and an advisor, all in one."

"I can see," says Hannah, wishing that life could be that way for her. Just seeing these little ones has made her feel calmer and more confident about her own situation. In a small town like this, a single mother could have a lot of support. It might not be so bad. She sips her coke and wonders if she'll be able to pour it down the drain, unnoticed. She shouldn't have caffeine.

HARRY

By the time the lunch plates have been washed and put away, Harry's ready to go outdoors again. It's a crime to be inside when the winter sun is shining. The daylight hours are so short and precious.

"I'm going for a walk," she says to Jack. "I have to digest."

"I have to digest, too," says Jack, "but I think I'm going to do that in an armchair."

"See you in a bit, then." Harry closes the door.

"I saved you some ham," she whispers to Rustum, sliding her hand out of her pocket. "Let's go for a walk."

Harry turns right at the gate and walks away from town, thinking about her conversation with Jack. Is she really so selfish? That's a hard pill to swallow. She thinks about Hannah, wondering how best to approach her. Harry's intent on helping Big Mack, so her actions will inevitably be misinterpreted by Hannah. She can't sacrifice her principles over this, however, and she feels trapped by the circumstances. Jack doesn't appreciate quite how complicated the situation is.

Right now, Harry is walking towards Dr Haswell's house, hoping he's in. It's afternoon, so he should have had time to recover from the events of last night, whatever they turned out to be. She wonders how much work was required to keep Boy alive until he got to intensive care. If he was bleeding in his brain, as Old Mack said, then things must have been dicey. Poor Boy! Harry thinks. That's another person who needs some compassion.

Harry sees Dr Haswell's weathered cedar fence, with its decrepit hand-split pickets leaning against each other for support. Harry imagines pushing a single picket and watching them all topple like dominos, in a fluid, gratifying *whoosh*! Dr Haswell's house, once blue, is now tinged with green algae and in places the paint is peeling. It's ironic, really. He's the hardest-working person in the town, yet he never seems to have enough money to fix his house. Maybe he doesn't care, or maybe he just doesn't have time to organize a work crew. Harry sees that the curtains are open and wonders if that means that the doctor's awake. She skirts the frozen puddles in the path and knocks on the door.

There's a loud clattering of dishes in the kitchen and then rapid footsteps. The door is thrown open.

"Harry Farre!" the doctor peers at her over half-moon lenses, wiping his hands on a towel. "Come in! How unusual to see you."

He leads her into the kitchen, where a pile of coffee mugs has fallen over in a heap on the draining board.

"I took the wrong one," he says gesturing at the mess. "The house of cards collapsed."

"Are they broken?" Harry asks, wondering if he ever eats.

"I haven't checked. If they aren't, I can pour you some tea. I was just having a cup myself."

Harry picks up a thick brown mug and inspects it for cracks. She presents it to the doctor. "I'd love some, Doc."

"Oh, James, please, James," he waves his hand. "I'm almost sick of being a doctor. Thirty-five years, if you can believe that!"

"Well, you've been here as long as I have," replies Harry, looking at his long, smooth fingers as he pours the tea. His hair is thick and blackish-grey, with patches of white. His dark eyebrow hairs are almost an inch long in places, giving him a look of permanent surprise.

"Milk? Sugar?"

"Just milk."

"Well, I haven't seen you for a dog's age," his voice ranges from high to low, then back again. "Must be healthy."

"Just age to complain about, I guess," says Harry.

"Nuisance, isn't it?" He hands her the mug. "Well, happy New Year!"

"Not really," Harry begins. "Not entirely happy, that is."

"Oh."

228

"It's because of last night. My daughter, Hannah, found Boy and Big Mack."

"Well, she helped save a life, you can tell her that from me."

"I will. She did a great job. She's a nurse, you know."

"Oh really? Does she need a job?"

"Well, she's thinking about it, I know. She's been working at the Whitehorse hospital the last few years."

"I'd kill for an extra hand around here."

"I'll let the two of you discuss work, James. That's not why I came."

"Well then, don't keep me in suspense."

"We need someone to advocate for Big Mack."

"Why?"

"He's being charged with aggravated assault."

"But that's ridiculous!" the doctor scoffs. "Mack wouldn't hurt a fly. How can they blame him?"

"He was there," Harry says grimly, "and somehow in his drunkenness he managed to blame himself. He said that it was all his fault."

"Oh dear." He takes off his glasses and fiddles with the arms, opening them and closing them several times.

"Old Mack said that Boy was bleeding in his brain and could die. I can't bear the idea of Mack being on trial for murder."

"Oh no. Oh dear." The doctor replaces his glasses.

"Do you think he was beaten up?"

"I'm afraid I can't really say, Harry. Not allowed to gossip about my cases. The doctors who are looking after Boy now are better equipped to answer that question, anyway. Boy's family could ask them. But what exactly did Mack confess to?"

Harry sighs. She's starting to know this story too well. She begins at the beginning. The doctor doesn't interrupt and the story comes out smoothly. Harry breathes out and takes a sip of tea. The doctor stares out of the window.

"My concern," Harry says, "is that they'll keep Mack in jail, he'll never get proper representation, his name will be mud and his family will be devastated. Then racial tensions will heat up—which doesn't take much around here—and everything will be a muddle."

The doctor drags his eyes away from the window and looks at Harry. His eyebrows have sagged and his face seems slack. He heaves a huge sigh and leans forward.

"Do you have a plan?" he asks.

"Old Mack and I want to get him released until his court date. And we've got to do it before they send him elsewhere. He has no prior history of assault or criminal behaviour, so I think it's possible, especially if we have someone like you to say that he's not a threat to society. They may impose some conditions on him, but I think it's vital to get him away from the RCMP, for everyone's sanity. Then we might be able to find out the real story. I asked about bail. Old Mack said that he would raise the money if necessary. I still have to call the lawyer to see what he says, but I needed to find out if you'd be a willing advocate first." Harry bunches her eyebrows together and tilts her head on one side, inspecting the doctor for his reaction. She's not sure what he's going to say.

"This is why I have to retire," he gets up and walks around the table. "These things are too distressing. I'm reaching the end of my rope." Sitting down again, he sees Harry's worried look. "Of course I'll speak on Mack's behalf," he reassures her. "I just wish I could prescribe a solution. We will never learn what happened to Boy unless he can tell us himself."

"I know you spoke for Mack's brother, Nelson," Harry says quietly. "Old Mack told me about it."

"It was awful." The doctor seems to be daydreaming. "He pushed his wife out of a window. But he was hysterical, suicidal. She tried to stop him from hanging himself. He lost control and pushed her. He was pushing her away from him, not murdering her. He was the most damaged man I've ever treated. I hope those

230

priests are proud of themselves, because I'm sure God isn't. And the justice system, too. It's a travesty. It's our duty as humans to help other humans—show them how to help themselves. But we're too mean for that, apparently. We seem to want people to suffer. Well, Nelson's suffering all right."

Harry drinks her tea, wondering why she has never been better friends with James.

The doctor gets up again and goes over to the sink. One by one, he inspects the fallen mugs. "No casualties," he pronounces. "Yet."

"That's a lot of mugs," Harry comments, putting hers down.

"It's because I can never finish anything I start," he frowns. "If I make a cup of tea, then the phone's guaranteed to ring. It never fails, even at six in the morning."

"But the phone hasn't rung all the time I've been here," Harry points to his still-full mug.

"It might as well have," he sighs, his shoulders drooping.

Harry wonders if she should apologize for disturbing him. She gets up and rinses out her mug, turning it upside down on the now-empty draining board.

"It's not your fault," the doctor reassures her, putting his hand on her shoulder. "I'm just tired. I think I'll have a nap."

"I'll see myself out," Harry tells him, "but I'll keep you informed."

As she reaches the door, Harry remembers something she meant to say.

"James," she calls, "there's one other thing." She moves back towards the kitchen. "Hannah and I don't see eye to eye on this. I'm hoping we can resolve our differences, but in the meantime, I don't want you to feel embroiled in a family dispute."

The doctor looks up: "Of course," he says. "Circles within circles."

Harry's not sure she understands what he means. She nods her head and turns to leave again. As she pulls the door shut she hears a long, drawn-out sigh float down the passage from the kitchen.

LONNY

"You guys get your shoes on!" Sara yells down the hall. "We're going to your grandpa's for a meeting!"

Lonny looks up from the Nintendo game he is playing. Uh-oh, he thinks. Family meetings are usually serious and Lonny seldom understands what's going on. Sometimes the elders come to the meetings and talk Indian or sing a prayer. Meetings are often held when there's a funeral.

He looks at Sam. "Do you think Boy died?" he asks.

Sam shrugs. "Dunno." He looks at the Nintendo game. "You did better that time."

"Can I play it when we get back?"

"When I'm not on it."

"Smarten up and get your asses out of there!" Sara yells from the front room.

"We better go," says Sam, getting up quickly.

The boys scramble to the front door and pull on their shoes. It's getting dark outside and Sara is fiddling with a flashlight, shaking it.

"Stupid thing was working fine last night," she mutters.

"Give it to me," Sam tells her. She passes it over and he smacks it with his shoe. The light comes on right away. Sam grins and passes it back to her. Sara grins too.

"Old Indian trick," she giggles, and they all burst out laughing.

It's not really dark enough to need the flashlight. Lonny can see most things fine. It's going to be another clear night, but there's just a little breeze starting. Maybe the weather will change.

At Grandpa's house the front room is packed. Somebody has brought some folding chairs so that most of the people can sit down. The younger ones are milling around in the kitchen with hopeful eyes. Melina Roberts passes out Styrofoam cups full of coffee, while her little girl, Stacy, follows her with a bowl of sugar and a bowl of milk powder. Stacy is about five, so she looks pretty cute and everyone makes a fuss over her.

Lonny and Sam head for the hallway. From there they can peek into the front room, or go play in the bedroom. They're also close to the kitchen, in case there's any *cha-mas*, like the cherry pie Lonny saw in the fridge at lunchtime. There was only one pie, though, and there are lots of people.

When Lonny turns around he sees Uncle Silas, sitting right in the middle of the front row of chairs. He looks as if he's just had a shower, but his eyes are droopy and he's staring across the room without blinking. Lonny feels happy all of a sudden. Maybe Silas can tell everyone what happened.

Right then, Madison James Senior stands up with his drum. He says he's going to sing a prayer song to start the meeting. When the stick hits the drum for the first time, everyone stops talking. Lonny shivers. He feels as if his skin has become the skin of the drum, vibrating with every beat. Then Madison's voice wavers out across the room, rising and falling like water rushing up and down the beach. The drum goes on and on until there's a silence.

Madison waits for a while, then he talks. At first he talks in Indian and Lonny doesn't understand what he's saying—just *kleco-kleco* and *choo*! Then he switches to English. He explains a bit of what he's just said.

"I am talking on behalf of my cousin, Mack Stanley. He has asked me to thank you for coming here tonight, to his house, to show your support.

"Some of you may know what has happened to his family lately. His grandson, Lila's son, is in hospital with a . . . " he leans over and Grandpa whispers in his ear " . . . a sub dural hema toma," he says each word slowly. "He is bleeding in his brain, which means he could die. Mack would like you to know that Boy is doing a little better today. His mother Lila is by his side. She is praying for him. We all need to pray for him." Madison picks up a glass of water and takes a sip.

234

"This injury hurts us all," he carries on. "It hurts us because we might lose our loved one. It hurts us, too, because Mack Junior," Lonny has never heard Uncle being called this before, "is being accused of causing this injury. However, information that has come to light this evening tells a different story." Madison looks down at Silas as if to check that it's okay to go on, but Silas is still staring across the room at the wall.

"Silas, here," Madison gestures, "was with his brother on New Year's Eve. They walked to Hanson Bay together. That night a cargo van swerved at them, on purpose, almost knocking them into the ditch. This van was going fast and trying to scare them. The driver did this intentionally." He glances down at Silas again.

This time Silas looks up and his eyes open wide.

"The driver gave us the finger," he says, then drops his head again.

The room breaks out with a buzzing noise as everyone murmurs at once. Madison's voice isn't strong enough to be heard, so he sits down for a few minutes. Lonny looks at Sam with his eyebrows raised.

"QUIET!" somebody yells.

Madison stands up again.

"Silas believes that whoever was driving that van did the same thing to Boy, but he hit him. He took Boy to town so that nobody would connect the accident to the van."

The room is instantly noisy again and Madison sits down. This time the noise gets louder and louder, like the waves and the wind at Harry's house when the storm was going on. Lonny closes his eyes for a minute. When he opens them again he sees Uncle Silas, still sitting in the middle of all the people, staring at the wall, as if he's in a dream.

After several minutes of noise, another elder—Daisy Roberts, Melina's grandmother—stands up. She is very short and plump, with an old, wrinkled face. Lonny has always liked Daisy. She's comfortable to be around.

She holds up her hands, which are strangely shaped from the pains she gets. Her voice is quiet as she sings, but like a magic trick the song makes everyone stop talking until her voice is the only sound in the room.

When the song fades, she nods at Grandpa and turns around, looking at everyone in the room.

"This family is hurting," she says. "It is our duty to show respect for this family. Without family, we are nothing. But," she raises a knobby forefinger, "if we only see our closest family, then we are like the bear, or the mouse. Our vision is poor. We do not see the world that we live in. Without vision, our actions can ruin our lives. Our lives depend on this whole village. They also depend on our neighbours. They are family too."

Lonny thinks of Harry. Even though she's a white lady, she feels like family. He looks at his grandpa, sitting up so straight, facing Daisy, his eyes downcast. He hopes Grandpa will give up the lectures about drinking and then home will be an okay place again.

"Family!" Daisy says, gesturing to all the people in the room. "We must not jump to conclusions. We must not make divisions where none exist. We have a duty, here. That duty is to help our cousin find the truth. Pointing fingers is the easy way. Finding truth is the hard way. I trust you all to do the right thing. I pray for your son and your grandson," she looks at Grandpa again. "*Choo!*"

She sits down fast.

After Daisy has spoken a lot of other people get up and take their turn. Lonny stops listening, because his mind is full of thoughts. Sam snuck off into the bedroom a while ago and Lonny figures that's not a bad idea. There's a crowd of people blocking his way though, so he decides to stay where he is. Daisy's words float back into his head and he wonders what she meant about pointing fingers and finding truth. He looks around the room but he can't see her anymore. Maybe she went home right after she spoke.

Lonny wonders about the van that swerved at his uncles. He pictures a van swerving at Boy—Boy all bent over as usual, probably not even seeing the van, then getting a bump on the head. It helps to think about this. Lonny was upset whenever he thought about Uncle beating up Boy. It seemed too weird. Uncle has never lifted a finger to Lonny or Sam, ever. Not even when he's been drunk. Other guys get mean when they're drunk, but not Uncle.

There's a lot of movement in the kitchen and Lonny sees Raylene and Melina passing out bowls of red jello and strawberry icecream. It's just as well he didn't go into the bedroom, he's in a good position to get dessert. Raylene offers some to Grandpa and Uncle Silas, but neither of them want any. Lonny grins at Melina and she passes him a bowl. It's a big helping, too. The servings will get smaller towards the end. All around him people are talking about this and that. Everyone seems to have forgotten the meeting already.

HANNAH

The way things turn out, only a few people come over to Kathy's house for lunch. The others are all too tired or hungover. Kathy's brother, Kevin, arrives late, looking haggard. He says little and eventually disappears into one of the bedrooms. Hannah talks with Brad, who hasn't changed much since high school. Still tall and muscular, with brown hockey-hair. He's clean shaven, but his face is dark with shadow. He's working at a heli-logging site, making lots of money. It sounds pretty dangerous, the way he describes it. He has to be alert and quick on his feet. Accidents happen frequently and some people get badly hurt. He shows her a scar along the back of his arm, where a cable grazed him. The scar snakes across his flesh, bumpy and pink. "I got lucky," he tells her. "I had my foot trapped between two branches and I couldn't get out of the way in time. I might have ended up on compo for the rest of my life."

"Or dead," Hannah suggests.

"That too," Brad agrees.

"Sounds like a hazardous career. You wouldn't catch me doing that."

"I hear you're a nurse. That sounds hazardous to me. Think of all the diseases you could catch."

The expression on Brad's face makes Hannah laugh. He looks truly frightened at the idea of treating a sick person.

"I rarely get sick," she explains. "And I take a lot of precautions. I can't think of an occasion when I've felt truly at risk."

"How about last night?" he asks her.

She pauses.

"How do you mean?"

"Well, you had your mouth against a stranger's mouth for a long time. That's pretty risky, if you ask me."

"Only if there's a lot of blood, which there wasn't. Even then the risks are pretty small."

"I thought there was plenty of blood," Brad presses her. "Kathy's dad said the kid was beat up pretty bad."

"Well, I don't know where he got his information," she replies, "but I didn't see any blood."

"Really?" Brad muses. "Mind you, it was night time. You probably didn't see much."

Hannah's eyes swing over Brad's shoulder, then blaze back at him. "It was dark, I'll give you that," she says, her lips tightening, "but I know for a fact that I saw a whole lot more than anybody else could have, including Cutter's informant."

Brad smiles briefly and scuffs his toe on the carpet. "Point taken," he says. "Listen, can I get you anything to drink?"

Hannah holds out her glass. "If there's some soda water in this house, it would make my day."

Later, Hannah looks around at all the familiar but changed faces, casual folk in jeans and sweatshirts and slippers. In some strange way, it feels like home, except for one thing: Hannah can't see herself in the picture. Yet. It'll just take time, she thinks. She'll file down the square edges, round herself out, so she fits in. Something about that idea doesn't feel right, but she doesn't pursue it.

"It's been wonderful to see you and Kathy," Hannah tells Aileen as she gets ready to leave.

"Well, we're delighted to have you back in the community," Aileen says with a beaming smile. "Don't pay attention to Cutter, though," she lowers her voice. "His head is hurting today, you know what I mean? He'll be back to normal tomorrow, you'll see."

Hannah nods and smiles. "I should be getting back soon. Jack will be wondering where I've gone."

"You be sure to say hello to him from me. Cutter usually sees him at the café in the mornings, but they weren't open today because of the holiday."

By the time Hannah actually leaves, another forty minutes have

239

elapsed. It's hard to leave when you haven't seen people for a long time. They're so curious about your life. There's so much to say, too. When she finally closes the door and walks down the steps, it's getting dark. There's a faint glow of light in the southwest, but a few stars are out. She hums a little tune as she heads home. She's almost forgotten about Mother and Rob and being pregnant.

Hannah wonders if Harry will be at Jack's house when she returns. She doesn't want to talk to her mother; doesn't want to think about Big Mack any more. She wishes she could rise above her petty responses to Harry, but she's found a stubborn streak in herself that's hard to control.

As she crosses the road, she sees Lonny on the far side.

"Lonny," she calls. "Lonny."

The boy looks up at her, but doesn't say anything.

"Is that you, Lonny?" she asks, squinting in the fading light.

"Uh-uh," says the boy.

"Oh. I'm sorry. I mistook you for someone else." She sees that this boy is bigger than Lonny, with longer hair.

"How come you know Lonny?" he asks, kicking up gravel.

"Oh, just because."

"Lonny's at his grandpa's. His uncle's in jail."

"Oh."

"What's your name?"

"Hannah."

"I'm Lonny's cousin."

"Oh. Well, you have a nice night now."

"Uh-huh," says the boy, kicking up more gravel.

It's only when she's a block away that Hannah realises she didn't ask the boy's name. He asked hers and she didn't ask his. She was too busy picturing Lonny at his grandfather's, without his uncle. She can still see herself quailing at the power in his grandfather's face, the all-seeing, cave-like eyes. She wonders if Lonny is afraid of those eyes, too.

She takes a deep breath of the cool, darkening air. It feels good in her chest, pumping through her lungs into her bloodstream. She wonders if Lonny is lonely.

Hannah has often felt lonely. As a girl, at Fortune Island, the days crept by with a chronic sameness, only offset by the arrival of visitors. She wasn't alone, because Harry was there; instead, her loneliness was really a need for stimulation, a desire to do something different.

The first year she went to school in Hanson Bay was lonely in a different way. She had Jack and Ada, so she wasn't by herself. There was a lot to do, but it took time to learn the ropes, to fit in and make friends, especially since she was a kid with an eccentric mother who chose to live in the bush. That was such a stigma in school. Eventually she created a screen that veiled her background. People began to see her as the rebel she was. They were impressed by the way she stuck up for herself and left the bush behind. Still, even though she made a niche for herself, in any group she always hovered near the edge.

It was the same in Whitehorse. It took time to get to know people, even in the hospital. For the first time in her life she lived alone and felt alone. She found it hard to blend in. In her time off, she would sit near the window observing people in the street and the way they related to each other. She never heard the words they spoke, but from these strangers she taught herself mannerisms that seemed natural: how to greet others with an easy smile, relaxed face, artless gesture. Bit by bit, she ironed out the creases in herself. Her awkwardness became less visible from the outside, but still it lingers. She feels it often, especially on nights like tonight.

Was it life with Rob that finally sealed her into this strange existence, the one that keeps her apart from other people? Whatever it is, Hannah feels as if she's lived in a bubble, separated from the world by a thin wall.

When she set foot back on Fortune Island the bubble burst.

Her body reacted to Harry with a fierce tug of animal love. Part of Hannah wanted to fly with this feeling, to let go and see where it would take her. Then, gradually, the bubble of isolation formed again. Trapped inside it are the experiences she has been unable to share: the details of her relationship; her pregnancy; her fears of being alone.

Hannah doesn't want to be alone. She knows that, but being secretive is so easy for her now. Too bad pregnancy is not something that can be kept secret.

She pushes open the gate to Jack's house and looks up in surprise. Is she here already? She'd rather not be. She's had enough of Mother and Jack for the day. She climbs the stairs while Rustum flounders across the deck to meet her with a woof. The lights are on and Hannah can see shapes in the front room, through the mesh curtains. She takes a deep breath and pushes open the door.

HARRY

Instead of going back to Jack's, Harry finds herself walking down to the dock. *Polynesia* is still in the sunlight, but the heat has vanished and the cabin is cool. The route to Fortune Island beckons her with silky blue fingers, curving out and away from the harbour. She should be out on her knoll, planning next year's garden in her head. Instead, she's vibrating with other people's troubles, which are fast becoming her own.

In her pocket is the little slip of paper with the lawyer's number on it. Harry could phone the woman right now, but it's New Year's Day. On the other hand, Mack will probably be transferred tomorrow, unless they can get him released. Part of her hesitation is due to Old Mack. His experiences with the law have obviously left him bitter. She's pretty sure he wouldn't call up a stranger and ask for help. If she does it, will she be interfering?

She thinks of Big Mack's face, and Lonny, all angry and quiet. Old Mack will have to stuff it, she decides and searches through her wallet for her phone card. Leaving her things on the boat, she climbs the ramp and crosses over to the phone, which is on the main wharf. The cramped little booth stinks of alcohol. A suspicious splash of yellow lingers down one of the walls. Harry stands on the other side and picks up the receiver, inspecting its condition. Taking her glasses out of their cloth case, she squints at the numbers on the card. It's a complicated procedure: dial here, enter a code, dial there. It takes her a few attempts before she hears the sound of a phone ringing.

The lawyer's name is Frances Everleigh. She lives in Nanaimo, but she travels to the coast often, where she's known for representing Natives. Harry has a dim impression of a tall, squarely built woman, with straight, short hair and black glasses.

"Hello," says a male voice at the end of the phone.

"Frances, please," Harry asks.

"Who's this?" demands the voice.

243

"My name is Harriet Farre. I'm a client. It's important that I speak to Frances."

"Have you heard of business hours, Ms Farre?" inquires the voice, in a belligerent tone.

"Tomorrow will be too late," persists Harry.

There's a pause, the sound of the receiver shuffling. "Can I tell her why you're calling?"

"No," says Harry. "It's too complicated. I have to talk to her myself."

A longer pause. More shuffling. Static on the line. Harry waits, rehearsing what she will say.

"Harriet, did you say?" a female voice asks.

"Well, Harry, actually. And you're Frances?"

"Yes. What's your trouble?"

The story rolls off Harry's tongue, with occasional pauses for breath, or effect. From time to time, Frances interrupts to slow her down, or ask a question. She's scribbling notes to herself, Harry can tell.

"Are you sure he doesn't have a criminal record?" she presses Harry. "There might be something he didn't tell his father."

"I can't guarantee it, but I believe it. And when we mentioned it to LeClerk, he didn't contradict us."

"What makes you believe it? How do you know this man?"

Harry explains her connection to Big Mack. She elaborates on his visit over Christmas, suggesting a long-standing friendship. In fact, Harry and Mack have only known each other on a casual basis until now.

"So where exactly do you live, again?" Frances asks.

Harry obliges her with a description of the island.

"This is good." Frances sounds positive for the first time in the interview. "And he's stayed with you before?"

"Yes, he has."

"And can he stay with you if he's released from jail?"

"Why would he have to do that?" Harry wonders out loud.

244

"Well, they won't release him just like that. There are bound to be conditions. Sometimes they ask for bail. In this case there are no witnesses. The doctor can say that Mack has no history of aggression and is unlikely to harm anyone in the future, either. That leaves alcohol. The situation may have been exacerbated by it. He was drunk at the time. If you live in the middle of nowhere, and you agree to have him stay with you, he won't have access to alcohol. He'll be high and dry and removed from society. That will be attractive to the police. They'll be more inclined to release him themselves, instead of letting a judge release him. If he goes before a judge, you'll have to come to Nanaimo for court; it will take a while and he'll be in jail for longer."

Jack's voice hums through Harry's mind: So you're handing over to me now . . . Then she sees herself scrambling through the dark night to Hannah, where she knelt in the grass after saving Boy's life. She thinks of Lonny, slapping the tie-up rope against the water, scowling.

"Are you still there?" Frances voice is sounding impatient now.

"I'm here," says Harry. "I'll do it."

"Do what?"

"Have Mack to stay."

"Right, then. Leave this with me. Where can I call you?"

Harry dithers for a while, not wanting to give out Jack's number. But she's going to have to explain herself to Jack, anyway, so transparency is best. She speaks the digits slowly. "If I'm not there, just leave a time when I can call you back," she says. "Don't leave any other message."

"I'm not in the habit of giving out private information."

"Right."

She hangs up the phone, noticing how much light has fled the sky. It's chillier now, but less so than last night. Harry looks again at the water and sees a ruffle of wind that she hadn't noticed before. Maybe the weather will change tonight, she thinks.

245

Harry doesn't bother with the padlock this time. The day's been too quiet. Everyone's in hiding. She bundles her belongings into a bag and beckons to Rustum. Together they leave the dock, their backs to the sinking sun as they climb the hill.

When she gets back, Jack's absorbed in a television program, something that seldom interests her. She heads into the kitchen and starts going through the cupboards looking for supper ingredients. She wonders what Jack would be eating tonight, if he were by himself. There's some store-bought bread, some tins of soup and beans. In the fridge there are the remains of lunch, a carton of milk, half a dozen eggs, some potatoes and carrots. Useless! Harry thinks. She goes through the drawers until she finds an unopened bag of green split peas. Probably been here since Ada's time, she imagines. But the bag is sealed, so she decides to use them. The ham will help flavour the soup.

Under the tap, she rinses the peas and picks through them with meticulous care. From the front room she can hear bursts of sitcom laughter and the occasional guffaw from Jack. Hannah is not back yet and Harry's gut tightens thinking about their next encounter. She feels stuck, not wanting to undo the progress they have made. She finds a small stone among the peas and puts it to one side. Always a few in every package. Teeth breakers.

When the peas have started cooking, she puts on the kettle and goes into the front room.

"Can I make you a hot drink?" she asks Jack. "I was thinking of some tea."

He glances up at her. "Sure, sure," he agrees, his eyes sliding back to the screen as soon as politely possible.

Right, Harry thinks. I'll wait until the show's over. She glances at the kitchen clock: ten to five. She turns the peas down to a simmer and rummages around for the teapot and a tray.

How can I have Mack to stay without putting Hannah's nose

246

out of joint? she wonders. It might be a month or more before there's a trial date. Harry questions how much of that month she and Hannah would naturally spend together. Even over Christmas, she could sense Hannah's restlessness, as if she were just biding her time—waiting, not living.

Well, living has a different meaning for everyone, Harry supposes. Maybe Hannah needs an up-beat, fast-paced life, filled with work and friends and parties. Maybe Hannah was never the little girl she knew, lying on the moss, playing make-believe for as long as time allowed.

The kettle boils, startling Harry with a sudden shriek. She warms the pot and adds the tea. There's no tea-cosy, so she wraps the pot with a clean dish towel. As she carries the tray into the front room she hears Rustum moving around outside, which might mean that Hannah's back. She goes back into the kitchen to find a third mug just as the front door opens.

"I'm just getting you a cup, Hannah," Harry explains. "We're having some tea."

"I don't want any."

Harry stops in the kitchen doorway.

"Okay, then," she says. "How was your lunch?"

"Fine."

Harry stares at Hannah as she hangs up her coat and takes off her boots.

"Is that you, Hannah?" Jack calls from the front room.

"Yes, it is."

"Come on in by the woodstove and get yourself warm."

Hannah stops by Jack's chair and kisses his balding head. "In a minute," she says. "I've got some stuff to do first."

"You what?" Jack asks, swivelling his head to stare after Hannah. She passes Harry in the hallway, and, without looking up, disappears in the dimness of the corridor, as she heads for her room.

Harry holds the cup in her hand, rubbing the rim with her fingertips and gazing into the darkness of the corridor.

She goes back into the kitchen and stirs the soup. Then she turns it down low and goes to Hannah's room. She knocks—two gentle taps.

No sound comes from the room.

"Hannah. It's just me. There's some soup ready if you want."

Without warning, the door swings open. Hannah stands there, tall, looking down at Harry. "I had plenty to eat at the party, Mother," she says. "I'm tired. I'd like to be alone."

She closes the door and Harry turns away, back down the hall to the front door. She lifts down her coat and checks for her lighter. Then she slips outside, onto the porch, into the night. She's never thought of it before, but suddenly she hates doors.

BIG MACK

By the time the tall woman enters his cell, Mack has already consigned himself to life in jail. His dreams have been full of dead ends. He knows that nothing he can say will convince anyone of his innocence.

"That's why you won't say anything," says Frances. "Since you can't remember anything, I'll go out of my way to avoid putting you on the stand."

Big Mack just stares at her. She's the kind of person he least understands. No small talk. No attempt to get to know him; just business—the details. Answering her questions is like trying to fill in an application form. Whatever he says is bound to be wrong. He stares at her dark lipsticked mouth.

"At least we'll have you out of here soon," she says.

"What?"

"I'm going to get you out of here."

"How?"

"Conditional release."

Her mouth is a straight line. No curves anywhere. Mack wonders how come he's not guilty all of a sudden.

"Did they find the person who did it, then?" he asks.

"No."

"So why can I go?"

"The RCMP don't have enough to hold you for too long, especially if there's a good offer for your release. Dr Haswell is vouching for your character and your friend, Harriet Farre, has agreed that you can stay with her until your trial. That way you'll be away from society, and alcohol, and the police are willing to accept that."

Until your trial. Huh. So he's not free. He's still guilty.

"What's that about Harry?" he asks.

"Ms Farre lives twelve miles away from the nearest town. If you agree to stay with her until your trial, you'll be released."

249

Big Mack imagines himself staying on Fortune Island for a month. He'd go crazy. There's nothing to do there.

"How did she get into all this?" he asks.

"She's the person who contacted me. She's concerned for your welfare. When I found out where she lived I realised that it was a perfect set-up for a conditional release."

"So this was your idea?"

The red lips widen slightly.

"And she agreed?"

"She said that the two of you were friends and that you'd stayed there before. She agreed, yes. She's signed an undertaking."

"Huh."

Mack's mind reels, threatens to shut down.

"You seem surprised. Are you against the idea? Would you prefer to stay in jail?"

"Uh. No."

"Well, good. I can get on with it, then." She fluffs the papers into a pile then fiddles with her briefcase. Mack wonders if she ever gets dirty. Every bit of her seems clean and untouched. No wrinkles in her clothes; not a hair out of place. A bit like Hannah. He steers his thoughts away from Hannah.

"One last thing, Mack." Frances says, staring right at him. "If you do this, you can't mess up. This is your opportunity to prove that you're a responsible citizen. If you take one wrong step, you will jeopardize the only chance you have for staying free. I can't emphasize how important this trial period is. You cannot— *cannot*—mess up."

Mack listens to the words with a sense of doom. It's that reverse psychology again. The woman has no idea what she's just done to him. Condemned him to failure. He closes his eyes. Things are going to get worse.

LONNY

Lonny sweats as he pushes the wheelbarrow up from the beach. Sam was supposed to be helping, but he disappeared a little while ago. He said he was going to the bathroom, but he was probably just trying to get out of working.

The log is down on the beach in front of Grandpa's house, so the distance isn't too bad. The problem is getting up the concrete ramp from the beach. The storms and wind have pounded the ramp to bits, so that big slabs of concrete stick up all over the place. The wheelbarrow gets stuck there every time. Twice, it's fallen over and spilled all the firewood.

Part of Lonny likes doing the firewood. He feels so mad today and wood is good to throw around. Bam! Bam! Splitting it feels good, too, but Lonny can't get all the cuts. Sometimes, there're knots and no matter how hard he swings, the maul just bounces off. Then, old Leo comes over to help him. Leo looks ancient, with a big tummy and pants that fall off his bum, but he can still swing an axe a lot harder than Lonny. Lonny doesn't stick around to watch him. He starts picking up the pieces and heading back to the house with the wheelbarrow.

On this trip he sees Sam in the distance, playing with his stupid car. Lonny gets to the woodpile and throws the pieces extra hard. One piece hits the house and puts a ding in a board.

"HEY!" yells Raylene from inside. She stomps across the floor and swings the door wide open.

"What are you doing?"

Lonny doesn't answer her. He doesn't look at her either. Raylene is always in a bad mood, so there's no point in saying anything. He throws another chunk of wood onto the pile, hard.

"Aahh, you!" Raylene growls and slams the door. She stomps back across to the kitchen.

Lonny flings all the other pieces onto the pile and turns to go back to the beach. How come Sam can get away without working?

Sam always slides right out of trouble while Lonny gets yelled at for even the littlest stuff. He turns the wheelbarrow and heads back down to the beach. Leo is sitting on a stump, surrounded by wood, sipping coffee from a thermos.

"Lots to do, boy," he chuckles when he sees Lonny looking at the pile.

Lonny scowls and doesn't look up. He throws more wood into the barrow.

"Hey!" says Leo.

"What?"

"*Chu-quah.*"

Lonny stares at him, trying to figure him out.

"*Chu-quah,*" Leo repeats, beckoning Lonny over.

Lonny comes over slowly. He doesn't like Leo much and he wants to get this stupid job over with.

"Just because life doesn't go right, doesn't mean you can act up, young man. As far as I can tell, life never goes right. You just have to get used to it."

Leo slurps his coffee loudly, then burps.

"You see that dog down there, shaking off water? You gotta be like that. When bad stuff happens, shake it off. Don't let it get to you. Getting mad makes everything worse."

Lonny stares at Leo. What does he know about Lonny's life?

Leo looks right back at Lonny and shrugs. Then he puts down his cup and picks up his thermos. He pours himself another coffee, humming quietly under his breath. "O-bla-di, o-bla-da, life goes on, oh! la la how the life goes on."

He doesn't say anything else, so Lonny gets up and starts collecting wood. He goes slower this time, though, and stacks the wheelbarrow neatly. When he gets close to the ramp, he picks out a route through the cracked concrete so that he doesn't get stuck. By the time he gets to the house, he's humming the same little tune that Leo was humming. He's not sure where it comes from, but he's heard it before somewhere.

The sound of the chainsaw interrupts his humming. Leo is finishing up the last of the log. It's pretty big at the butt end and the saw is screaming on and on. When Lonny looks at all that wood the job seems impossible. He's been here since breakfast and now it's almost lunchtime. The pile on the beach has grown bigger, not smaller. He could be here forever. The thought of it makes Lonny want to cry. It's just so lonely doing this, especially since Sam's taken off. At least when he was here they could joke around and have fun.

Lonny sits down for a moment and stares over at the docks. He can see the *North Wind* tied up there and he wishes he were on it. When he's on the boat he can be away from all the stuff that goes on at home. He can float on the water and travel and fish. He's happy out there; the water feels like a place where bad things can't happen to him. It's not safe for everyone, though. Sara's father drowned when he was out fishing. His little troller went down at night. It hit some rocks after the anchor dragged. A while later some divers found him, still stuck in the cabin.

Other people from the village have drowned, too, like Old Man Solly. He used to sell his fish in Hanson Bay and then go out on the town. One night he stumbled back from the bar and fell off the dock. There was no one around to help him, so he was stuck between his boat and the dock and he couldn't get out. They found him the next afternoon, all tangled up in seaweed.

Some people like to warn kids away from the water by talking about the drownings. Lonny doesn't listen to them. He knows the water. He has a feeling about it. He never says anything about this, in case people laugh at him, but it's true. The water's on his side. If things get bad, that's where he'll go. Out there.

Lonny realises he's staring, but his eyes are locked and it's hard to pull them away from the boat. For an instant, as he tries to make himself look somewhere else, he sees the *North Wind* leaving the dock in a storm. He blinks. It's another clear day, no wind or waves anywhere. The *North Wind* hasn't moved. He must be imagining things, or remembering the trip back from Fortune Island, with Uncle and Sam.

That doesn't explain the feeling in Lonny's chest, though. It's the same feeling he gets when the water seems to talk to him. He rubs the goosebumps on his arms and gets up. All of a sudden, he has lots of energy. Soon it will be lunchtime and, before long, it will be dark. He sets his mind to the firewood.

HANNAH

By breakfast, Jack has gone to the Seagull, so it's just Hannah and Harry in the house. Hannah puts on her nursing persona, so she's calm and untouchable despite the morning sickness. Mother is not Mother, she's just another patient. Good morning. Coffee? Orange juice?

But Mother looks about a thousand years old. The wrinkles have tripled overnight, as if stress has fractured her face. One look at Harry makes Hannah's heart pull painfully at her ribs. Guilt for her childish behaviour last night. Guilt and love and fear and pity and anger, all bundled into one feeling.

"I'm going to go home, today," Harry announces. "The weather's still fine, but there's a southeaster in the works. I don't want to be caught out."

"I can't believe we've had *this* much sunshine."

"It happens. I wish it happened more, though."

"Whitehorse was usually sunny all winter. The most amazing blue skies."

"Lucky you."

Later, when Harry is washing the dishes, the phone rings. Hannah listens to a brisk-sounding woman who wants to talk to "Harriet" and doesn't give her name.

Hannah walks into the kitchen.

"It's for you."

It surprises her that Harry doesn't ask who it is. She just dries her hands and heads for the front room.

"Perhaps you can finish those up," she tells Hannah, looking over her shoulder at the dishes.

Hannah moves slowly to the sink, listening hard for fragments of conversation. It's a brief talk, though. Harry just says "yes," or "all right." After she puts the phone down, she goes out onto the front porch and talks to Rustum. Eventually Hannah ventures out onto the porch, too. Harry is smoking, of course, sitting on the steps with Rustum by her side. What would she ever do without that dog?

Hannah clears her throat and Harry looks up expectantly.

"Nothing," says Hannah, wishing she could say everything.

Harry flicks the end of her roll-up into an ashtray, exhales and turns around.

"When I go home today, I'm taking someone with me," she says.

Hannah's mind races through all the possibilities.

"The woman on the phone?" she asks.

"No. But it's her idea."

"What do you mean?"

"She's Mack's lawyer. She's got him released on the condition that he stays with me until his trial."

Hannah's mouth drops open and she stares at Harry.

"You're joking!"

"I wish I was."

"You won't be safe!"

"Do you really think I'd agree to this if I thought it was unsafe? I wish you'd be honest with yourself."

"I am being honest! I told the police exactly what I heard. You would have given false testimony. Lied."

"Just be honest with yourself," Harry repeats, staring out at the garden as if she's in a trance. "I love you. I'm not taking sides. I'm just trying to do the right thing."

Hannah breathes deeply and counts to ten. Then she walks through the door, through the house, to her room and her bed. She doesn't want to see Harry's tired old face any more. Love and hate undulate through her body, threatening to make her vomit. She stays on her bed, hoping that Harry will leave. Perhaps all her problems will disappear then, too. After a while she goes into the bathroom and turns on the taps. She adds some bubble bath and watches the water froth, like the wake of a boat.

Slowly, the bath fills up, while Hannah sits on the edge gazing at the swirling water. She stands up and strips, noticing that her breasts are definitely swollen, poking outwards in an awkward way. She's amazed her belly isn't larger, because she feels the pressure of the baby, just above her pubic bone. Her abdomen seems solid now. If she presses it, there is resistance.

Is this what I'm concealing? she wonders as Harry's words float back to her. Or is there something more?

Gradually, Hannah slides into the bath. The heat creeps into her, relaxing her all over. She tries to imagine how people see her, but she can't. She can't even picture what she must look like walking down the street. So who am I, then? she wonders. Do I exist?

Steam rises around her in wisps and curls. It would be so easy to slip into the water and disappear. Be truly invisible. Vanish into the ether. Hannah wonders if all her problems would vanish, too, or if they would follow her into the next world like an old sea anchor, slowing her down, taking her in a direction she wouldn't want to go.

She thinks of the baby again, wondering what sex it is, seeing herself breastfeeding. Perhaps that's who I am, she thinks. Somebody's lifegiver. Somebody's mother. A lifetime role to play. If I want it.

Beyond the bathroom, Hannah's mother, her lifegiver, moves around, tidying up the house. As she dresses, Hannah thinks about what Harry's planning to do. It's a slap in the face, as if she has to protect Big Mack against her own daughter. But, despite herself, Hannah senses a tone of guilt vibrating in her chest. In a way, she knows that this is a lot more complicated than just giving evidence. She remembers the Big Mack she got to know over Christmas. She remembers the two boys and the way they looked at him, depended on him, loved him. She thinks of Lonny at his grandfather's. Then she thinks of the scene with Boy. She shudders and picks up her towel, then opens the bathroom door. Harry is by the front door, pulling on her boots.

"I have to go and stock up on supplies," she explains. "Those bush bachelors will be desperate for bread by the time I get home. They'll think I've abandoned them."

"Do you need a hand?"

"It's okay. I'll get a delivery, right down to the dock."

Silence.

"When are you planning to leave?"

"About two. That'll give me time to get the house warm and in order before dark."

"I'll make lunch."

"Sure."

"One o'clock?"

"Sure."

Hannah watches Harry go, Rustum shambling along beside her, making her seem small. She wonders if Big Mack will be leaving with Mother at two, down at the dock, for all the world to see. It'll be best to say goodbye to Harry from here. She breathes deeply, enjoying the sudden freedom of the empty house.

Jack returns just as Hannah is getting ready to leave the house.

"I'm going down to the clinic, to talk to Dr Haswell," she tells him. "I told Mother I'd have lunch made by one. Is that okay?"

"I'll be here, with bells on."

Hannah pauses. "Mother's going home today."

"I expected as much."

"Did she tell you that Big Mack will be staying with her, until his trial?"

Jack's eyebrows shoot up towards his receding hairline.

"Apparently some lawyer planned it and she agreed. I'm concerned about her safety."

"Oh, I shouldn't worry about that," Jack mutters moving past

Hannah, towards the front room. "Your mother can take care of herself."

"She's bitten off more than she can chew," Hannah persists, following him.

Jack is quiet for a while, looking at Hannah. "Let's talk about something else, eh?"

Hannah drops her eyes and turns back to the door. Jack has always taken her side, until now. She hears a rustling behind her and sees that he's come back to her, his eyes round and serious.

"It's just that you have to work it out with Harry, eh?" he says, slowly. "I've stopped you guys from talking to each other. That was my mistake. She's your mother—your blood. I'm just in the way."

"You're not in the way! I love you."

"Ah, but that's different. No shortage of love here." Jack holds out his arms.

Hannah stares at him, a wrinkle deepening in her forehead. She hugs him briefly. "I really should go. I'll be late for my appointment."

"Lunchtime, then."

"Lunchtime."

HARRY

Harry stows the groceries on board with a gathering sense of urgency. The southeaster is gentle, but it's there—ruffling the water and warming the air. It's only a matter of time before the clouds creep into the sky. This wind is a reliable warning, no different from the fog horn. It's time to go home.

Even without the wind, it's time for Harry to go home. She feels so disembodied, here in town. It's hard to think clearly; it's hard to think at all. She wonders what will happen the day she is forced to leave her island for good. That time will come, she knows. Some kind person will drop by and find her lying on the floor with a broken hip, or wandering the knoll without her mind. They will whisk her away and park her in a home. She won't have any say in the matter, because she will be old.

She squeezes a bulky grocery bag into a cupboard. It's a calm day, so it's not as though she has to prepare for rough, rolling seas, but stowing gear is a habit with her. She likes to be methodical: flour here, candles there, everything in its place.

What about Big Mack, though? Where will he fit into this picture? Harry sighs. She likes Mack, but she feels as though this month will be a challenge. Sharing will be a challenge. At least she'll have tonight to herself. Old Mack is going to drive up tomorrow with the *North Wind*. He'll drop Big Mack off and continue on a freight delivery, weather permitting. Harry has yet to see father and son together. She wonders how they relate to one another. Not a lot of talking, that's for sure! Old Mack likes the spaces between words. His mind is sharp and careful. Big Mack listens for the speaker's tone. Words matter less to him. If Harry woke up one morning in a bad mood, Mack would sense it from the loft. That's where he'll be sleeping. He'll have to crouch down to avoid cracking his head on the beams, but it will be his own space. Harry will have to get used to the heavy thud of his feet above her bed. Hannah used to slide around like a mouse, hardly making any noise.

Harry winces as she thinks of her talk with Hannah this morning. For the life of her she can't understand why Hannah is persisting in her ideas about Big Mack. It seems senseless—racist, even. She opens a drawer and takes out a block of writing paper. Since their relationship seems to be unravelling anyway, she can't lose much by sharing some history with Hannah.

She puts down the paper and picks up her tobacco. This will require some serious consideration. She takes her smoke outside and lights up.

"What shall I tell her, Rustum?" she asks aloud, needing an audience.

Rustum eyes her from the dock, reluctant to move from his place in the sun.

"I wish I had more time to think this through."

Harry gets up and ducks into the cabin, to check the time. It's eleven. She has time. After lunch there will be no time. She will be taking up her bags and leaving. If she's going to do this, she should do it now.

Later, on her way back to Jack's, Harry stops at the post office.

"One regular stamp, please."

"Do you want a Christmas edition?"

"Not really."

"How are you keeping, anyway?"

"Oh, fine."

"I hear your daughter's back in town. That must be nice for you. Is she going to stay?"

"Only if the sun keeps shining like this all winter."

"Can't say I blame her. The rain we get in these parts! We better hope it stays sunny then; we could do with another nurse around here, especially such a pretty one. The men will be getting sick like . . ."

"How much for the stamp?"

"Sorry?"

261

"The stamp. How much?"

"Oh. Ha ha. It's still the same, just the GST to add."

Harry puts the exact change on the counter and posts her letter through the slot. As she leans her shoulder against the door, she sighs loudly.

Outside, the street is busy. People re-stocking after the holiday; work continuing; the brightness that goes with a new year. As if anything has changed, or will change. For Harry, the first of January is not endowed with great significance. Instead, what she enjoys is the feeling of hope that goes along with the returning of the sun. The seasonal change so celebrated by ancient cultures. When the clouds allow, she notices where the sun rises and where it sets. On clear days, she gazes at the shadows on the old sundial in the garden. Candlelit mornings lose their gloom because, suddenly, they are finite—diminishing. In January, Harry feels like a seed underground, still surrounded by darkness but sensing the light, ready to burst into the excitement of spring, savouring the anticipation of the moment. That is what makes sense to her, more than fireworks or drunken parties. She thinks it a shame that the old ways have been discarded.

At least the Natives have kept their potlatches. They travel around from celebration to celebration, making the most of being indoors. Harry likes their lehal—the gambling bone game—where two sides sit facing one another in rows, singing. The teams takes turns to conceal the two thumb-sized pieces of bone in their hands. They pass them back and forth and flash tantalizing glimpses, singing and drumming and teasing, drumming and singing and teasing. The other team must guess who has the bones. Amid swirls of smoke, they nod their heads and confer. At their feet, packets of cigarettes and bottles of Buckley's cough syrup—complementary medicine.

She pauses in front of the corner store. Mack smokes the occasional cigarette. She wonders if two tins of tobacco will be enough for both of them. What about her resolve to quit smoking?

262

It's not a very strong resolve yet. Harry has a year. It's a lot of time. She does not need to move quickly. She will use cigarettes to help her through the long, dark winter hours and then, when summer comes, the warmth and sunlight will give her the strength she'll need to cut down.

She nods her head and walks into the store. Two more pouches ought to do it. If she can afford them! She stashes the pouches deep in her pockets and hopes that Hannah won't notice. Actually, in the last twenty-four hours, Hannah seems to have noticed little that doesn't concern her directly. Harry frowns. She can't force her daughter to tell her anything. As a teenager, Hannah would just set her mouth and refuse to speak. And what can you do with a person who won't speak?

Perhaps Hannah will talk to Jack after Harry leaves. Jack doesn't want to be stuck in the middle of a family row, he's made that clear, but he would be happy to share any personal problem Hannah is struggling with.

Harry checks her watch. Once she'd started writing, the letter flowed out of her. Writing it only took her half an hour, so now she has time for a walk. She retrieves Rustum from the litter bin he is decorating and bustles along the road, lifting her face to the precious winter sun.

BIG MACK

The fresh air smells so good! Even though his life has become some kind of hell, Mack wants to kick up his heels and run all the way home, whooping. Instead, he sits on the bench outside the police station and waits for his taxi. The open highway doesn't appeal to him. He is branded, now. A criminal. His innocence isn't something he even thinks about any more. It doesn't matter. What matters is that he went to jail. And he could go there again, if things don't start looking up. He wonders how Boy is doing. Nobody's told him anything, just the basics: Sign here. These are your belongings. You can go.

As he squeezes through the door of the taxi, he wonders how people will treat him at home. He's longing to see his family, but what if they don't want to see him? Well, his dad wants to see him; he knows that. He knows by the way Old Mack looked at him at the police station.

The cab driver looks at him in the rearview mirror. Her eyelashes are caked in blue mascara and her permed hair is dyed blonde. She looks forty, going on sixty. When she opens her mouth, her voice has the painful wheeze of a whiskey drinker.

"Had a good New Year, then?"

"Not really."

"Must of been all right, for you to be in the clink."

"Naah."

"Still hungover?"

"Maybe."

"Which house am I taking you to, then?"

"My dad's. It's the yellow one, near the water, with blue windows."

"You'll have to show me."

A few minutes later she pulls up in front of the house. Thankfully, no one seems to be around.

"I'll go inside and get you some money."

"Oh no, you won't!" She turns around and fixes him with a vicious stare. "Don't think I haven't heard that one before! And you, just fresh from the police station. You'll just go inside and never come out again is what you'll do. I know the routine."

Mack is speechless, staring at her bobbing yellow curls.

"My dad has some money."

"Well, let your dad come and pay me, then!" she snaps, then jams her fist on the horn and leaves it there. It wails out, real loud, just so everyone in the village will know he's home. People start appearing everywhere, coming onto their porches and looking out of their windows. Raylene throws the door open and stands, scowling, on the porch.

Mack taps on his window and beckons her over. She squints at him and doesn't move. The horn keeps going, on and on.

"Hey, lady! How can I tell anyone anything when you're making all this racket?"

She glares at him, then takes her fist off the horn. Mack rolls down his window.

"Ray! You got ten bucks you can lend me?"

"Maybe."

"Please!"

"Why?"

"Because this lady's going to honk her horn all night if you don't get me out of here."

"Damn right," the driver wheezes.

Raylene shoves her fingers into the back pocket of her jeans and brings out a crumpled wad of notes, all fives. She unravels two of them and puts the rest away again. She moves slowly down the steps, before coming to a standstill at the bottom. She's in her slippers. She stares at the cab driver and holds out the money.

"Oh, for crying out loud!" The driver heaves open the door and shifts her body to the edge of the seat. It's an effort for her to get out, Mack can tell. He picks up his plastic bag of belongings and leaves the cab. People are still watching, so he heads straight for the open door, past a pile of newly-cut firewood. He doesn't wait around to see the cab leave. For the second time in ten minutes, he's free. That's plenty good enough for him.

LONNY

Lonny hears the honking horn from down on the beach. He heaves the wheelbarrow up the ramp just in time to see the cab driving off. What was a cab doing at Grandpa's house? he wonders. Raylene is stalking up the stairs, looking cranky. Kenny's taken off again.

Lonny stares at the big front window of the house. A large shape is moving around in the house. Could it be Uncle? Lonny is so busy looking through the window that he pushes the wheelbarrow into a rut. The handles twist through his fingers and the cart turns on its side, spilling all the wood. Lonny looks at the pile of wood, then he looks back at the window. He leaves the wood where it is and runs over to the house, pelting up the stairs to the front door.

"Uncle!" he yells. "Uncle!"

"Jesus!" snaps Raylene. "You don't have to yell. I just put the baby to sleep and that stupid woman started honking. Now you're screaming your head off. Shush! Uncle is in his room. He wants to get clean before he sees anyone."

Lonny stands at the door, looking at his feet. Uncle's not in jail any more! That means he and Sam can live here again, the way they used to. Relief floods through Lonny. Life can get back to normal again.

"Hey, Lon." Big Mack's voice is deep and gravelly. Lonny looks up and sees Uncle peering out from the hallway. "I'm all horrible and dirty right now. I'll see you when I'm clean, okay?"

Lonny nods, smiling. Even though his boots are on, he runs across the room and wraps his arms around his uncle. Then he turns and runs outside before Raylene can say anything about his shoes. He skips down the stairs, sprints over to the wheelbarrow, piles all the wood back in and makes it to the house in record time. One more load, then he'll go in and wait for Uncle.

As he heads back down to the beach, Lonny wonders if he

should go and tell Sam. If Sam had been working as he was supposed to, he would have been there when Uncle arrived. Perhaps it will be Lonny's reward for doing all the work, to have Uncle to himself for a while. But even if Sam doesn't know, pretty soon someone will tell him. Lots of people saw the taxi, or heard the honking horn.

"I'm going to go home after this," Lonny tells Leo. "Uncle Mack is home."

"Huh."

"I'll come back down tomorrow. Maybe Uncle will want to do some wood, too."

"Feel that breeze? Gonna rain soon. Maybe even tomorrow."

Lonny pauses. Does that mean Leo wants him to finish all the wood today? The pile is huge. He could never finish it today, even if he tried.

"Tomorrow, you bring that cousin of yours. Make sure he doesn't run off. You'll finish it before it rains."

Lonny nods, then starts on his last load, piling the wood as high as it can go. It's a lot harder to control this way, but Lonny weaves along through all the driftwood on the beach to the ramp. Then he pauses to gather his strength and gets the whole works to the top in one go. When the last piece of wood is on the pile, he upends the wheelbarrow and leaves it there. He takes his shoes off outside the house and brushes the bark and sawdust off his t-shirt. He leans over and shakes his head to get any stuff out of his hair. Raylene has her hands in a bowl, covered in flour.

"What are you making?" Lonny asks.

"*Cha-mas.*"

"What kind?"

"Blueberry pie."

Lonny grins, then laughs. Raylene even smiles. The sound of chuckling comes from the bedroom as well. Lonny wonders what Uncle is laughing at. He taps on the door.

"Can I come in?"

"Haa-ah."

When he pushes the door gently open, Lonny sees Uncle Mack sitting on the bed, his hair still wet from the shower, his arm around Sam. Sam is showing Uncle the car he got for Christmas, explaining why it doesn't work. He doesn't look at Lonny.

Lonny stands in the doorway, staring. How did Sam get here so fast? Sam doesn't deserve to be here after sneaking away from the firewood like that.

"Are you coming in?" Mack asks him.

"Uh, it's okay. I better wash up."

Before he can change his mind he heads down the hallway to the bathroom. He slams the door behind him, then flings the shower curtain aside. It rips away from the rail, but Lonny doesn't care. As he takes his shirt off he catches a glimpse of himself in the mirror. A runt. A skinny ugly runt. No wonder nobody loves him.

BIG MACK

A shower and clean clothes have done wonders for Big Mack. On top of that, his boys are here and they're happy to see him. At least, Sam is. He thought Lonny was happy to see him, too, the way he came crashing into the house, yelling. But the second time, when he knocked on the bedroom door his face was all twisted up and dark. Mack wonders if some kids have been teasing him. Kids can be pretty cruel. He'll have to talk to Lonny about it later. Meanwhile, he's catching up with Sam.

"So what've you been doing, the last few days, son?"

"Living with Mom."

"And?"

"Playing Nintendo. Helping Grandpa with firewood."

"Did you and Lonny make the big pile by the house?"

"It's from that log you got before Christmas."

"Huh. I should go away more often. Get everything done for me, just like that. Who was bucking it up?"

"Old Leo. I don't like him. He's gross."

"Leo? He's a good person, he just looks funny. Don't judge people by how they look, son."

"I still don't like him."

"He's okay."

Sam pushes the wheel of his car with his forefinger. "Dad?"

"Uh huh."

"Did you beat up Boy?"

Mack takes a deep breath. "No, son. I didn't beat him up."

"Then why did you go to jail?"

"Because they couldn't find the person who did."

"Do you know who did it?"

"No, son, I don't."

Sam keeps fiddling with the wheel of his car.

"Some boys were saying that you're nothing but an old drunk."

Mack sucks in his breath. He stays absolutely still.

"Who said that to you?"

"Just some boys."

"So what did you say?"

"Nothing. I just picked up some rocks."

Mack hears the floorboards creak outside his door. "Lonny?" he calls. "Lonny!"

The door squeezes open. "What?"

"Are you clean?"

"Yeah."

"Well, get in here! I want to say hi to you."

Lonny comes slowly into the room, not looking at Mack or Sam.

"What's up, Lon?"

"Nothing."

"Oh."

Mack decides not to press Lonny. He'll come around in his own time.

"Lonny, has anybody said bad things to you about me?"

"Nope."

"Huh. Well, they've been saying stuff to Sam, so I was just checking. They've been saying that I beat up Boy and that I'm nothing but a drunk, stuff like that."

Lonny sits on the floor, looking up at Mack and Sam on the bed.

"I'm telling both of you, right now, that I'm not guilty. So if anyone says anything to you, you just ask them if they'd like to say that to my face, okay?"

Sam giggles. Even Lonny cracks a smile.

"That's better," says Mack. "No more long faces. I came home to a bunch of long faces."

"It was lonely without you," says Lonny.

"It was lonely for me, too."

"But now you're back," says Lonny.

271

"Uh. Yeah. Well, sort of."

"What do you mean?" asks Sam.

"Well, I guess I'm not really back. I have to go away again tomorrow."

Big Mack watches Lonny's face change again. His eyebrows pull together in the middle. His mouth turns down and he fiddles with his fingers.

"Where to?" asks Sam.

"To Fortune Island. To Harry's place. For about a month."

"How come?" asks Sam.

"Can we come, too?" asks Lonny.

Mack stops to think for a minute. Lonny's face is open again—eager.

"I think you're allowed to visit me, but you can't stay over. I don't really understand it myself, to tell you the truth. This woman—she's a lawyer—she got me out of jail by saying I would go to Harry's place. I have to stay there until my trial. Grandpa's going to take me there tomorrow."

"Tomorrow?" cries Lonny, his eyes full of disbelief.

Mack nods his head and lifts his hands in apology.

HANNAH

At the clinic, Hannah speaks to the nurse, Louise, who's also the receptionist. She's a little older than Hannah, with a thick brown ponytail and lively green eyes.

"I'm Hannah Farre. I called this morning."

"That's right. Isn't that lucky we were able to squeeze you in?"

"You must be pretty busy."

Louise just rolls her eyes.

"I'm a nurse," Hannah says.

"No. Really? You need a job?"

"Do you need a nurse?"

"Oh my God, I'd give my eye teeth for some time off."

"Well, I'm considering staying in Hanson Bay, if there's work for me."

"Is that why you came to see the doctor?"

"Not entirely. I need some medical advice, too."

"You have no idea how happy this makes me. I could go on holiday, go shopping, get a love life." She frowns. "Well, maybe not a love life. Slim pickings around here. I know the entire medical history of everyone. Not that I breach confidentiality of course, but it's hard to date someone when you've just treated them for hemorrhoids or something. You know what I mean?"

Hannah laughs. It's hard not to like Louise.

"Hey!" exclaims Louise. "Are you the woman that did CPR on that boy?"

"Well, yes."

"That's so brave! I mean, doing CPR is hard enough, but out there, in the dark, all alone, must have been brutal. I can't imagine."

Hannah's arms prickle with goosebumps. It feels so good to have someone understand what she went through. Louise comes out from the office and reaches for Hannah's hand.

"Have you talked to anyone about it yet?"

273

Hannah shakes her head, afraid to speak, in case she loses her composure.

"Where are you staying?"

"Just down the road at Jack Stimpson's place."

"Oh, Jack! He lives in the little honeysuckle house, doesn't he? You know, if you'd like, I could come over this evening, after supper. Bring us some Scotch. You could tell me the whole story."

Hannah looks around the room, checking to make sure they're alone.

"I can't drink," she whispers. "I think I'm pregnant." She giggles out loud at her audacity. She's just told her secret to a virtual stranger. She claps a hand over her mouth, but tears pop into her eyes.

Louise stands in front of Hannah, examining her face. Then she reaches out and gives Hannah a warm hug. It makes Hannah want to sob, but she holds it in. They are standing like this when they hear the doctor ushering his patient out. Louise releases Hannah and goes back to the office.

It's been years since Hannah's seen Dr Haswell. He hasn't changed much, just aged. If possible, his eyebrows have grown even longer, sticking up in straggly hedges above his eyes.

"James," Louise begins. "This is Hannah, she's a nurse."

"Ah, yes. Harry's girl. Your mother told me you were here. I was hoping you'd drop by."

"She told you already?"

"Your mother is Harry?" Louise marvels. "Harry from Fortune Island? But she's legendary around here!"

Hannah looks at Louise, then at the doctor. He turns to put away a file.

"Good job on Boy, by the way," he says, his back still turned. "Since you're a nurse, I don't mind telling you that he's opened his eyes a couple of times." He turns back to Hannah. "He wouldn't have had a hope without you."

Hannah smiles and blushes.

"Do you think he'll come around?"

"Could do. Subdural hematoma. Not a lot of exterior damage, but that doesn't mean much. Hard to know what's happening under the skull—you know? Hope it doesn't damage Boy further. Sweet fellow. Happy. Used to get along just fine before this happened."

Louise looks pointedly at the clock.

"Hannah's your next patient, James."

"Oh. Oh, right. Got to be punctual. Doesn't pay to keep people waiting, especially not prospective employees. Come on in." He extends his arm in a gracious sweep, knocking the tissues off the reception desk. "You *are* a prospective employee, I hope?" he asks as he shows her into his office and shuts the door.

"Well, I would like to work here. But I need to see a doctor, too."

"Of course, of course. What is it you need to see me about?"

"I'm pregnant."

"Are you sure?"

"The signs are all there. I've done a test. Yes, I'm sure."

"Well, you're a woman *and* a nurse, so I'm sure you're right. Is this why you're moving back home?"

"I didn't know about this until after I got here."

"And the father?"

"He doesn't know."

"Are you planning to have the baby?"

"Er. Yes. I think so."

"Tell me about your circumstances."

Hannah looks at him, not knowing where to start, or how much to say. Her circumstances are difficult to describe, even to herself. Dr Haswell raises his bushy eyebrows expectantly.

"It's a long story and I haven't told it before."

"Why don't you start now?"

Hannah examines his comfortable old face. She can tell him, she decides. She can tell him everything.

When she finally leaves the clinic, Hannah feels light. She had no idea that her life story could weigh so much; could push her down like that. She wants to go back tomorrow and talk to the doctor some more. She's shy, though. She shouldn't take up his valuable time when he could be treating sick people.

Hannah swings her arms as she strides down the sidewalk. The air is warm and damp, different than yesterday. Mother must be right about the weather changing.

Louise seemed to think Hannah's upbringing must have been idyllic. Tonight she'll drop some hints that life with Harry was not all sweetness and roses. Louise probably grew up in a city and thinks that the wilderness is romantic.

The doctor seems to be on Mother's side, too, though. Not that he said much about her. It's just that whenever Hannah mentioned her battles with Harry, his eyes seemed to get this look, as if the problems were minor. At one point he said: "Ah, but you love her because she's your mother. We like to think that our umbilical cords are severed at birth, but they aren't, really. Mothers are mothers. You'll find this out soon. In fact, I expect that once your baby is born, your relationship with your mother will improve."

Hannah didn't respond to him, then. She just changed the subject to her relationship with Rob. The doctor was definitely concerned about that. He asked her several questions about the nature of the violence she had experienced. Twice, he asked her if she felt safe in Hanson Bay.

"There's two ways to look at it," she told him. "Since he didn't come to find me right away, he's unlikely to come at all. But there's a small chance that he'll lose all his money and get crazy. If that happens, he might want to find me, but he probably won't have the money to get here. So, I'm not too worried. It feels so far away. It's as if that chapter of my life barely exists any more. The

276

present is so strong—being pregnant and making new friends. Dealing with Boy and Big Mack. . . ."

"Ah, Big Mack!" the doctor said in a fond, indulgent tone. He didn't say anything else, though, for which Hannah was glad. She didn't want to get onto that topic. She was the only person who saw Big Mack with Boy that night. She was the only person who was there. So what if Mack wasn't normally a violent person? Booze and drugs make people behave out of character. Mack could be one person when he's sober and another person when he's drinking. Dr Jekyll and Mr Hyde. Just ask all those women who come into the hospital because they've been raped. Alcohol and drugs are always a factor. Then, when everyone's sober and normal, the women drop the charges, as if nothing had happened—anything to maintain their precarious domestic stability. Hannah's seen it happen over and over.

Well, she's said her piece. She told the cop everything in her statement. They can make what they like out of it. At least Boy seems to be showing signs of life. If Boy died, then Mack would be on trial for murder and that thought makes Hannah uncomfortable.

HARRY

As *Polynesia* rounds Bailey's rock and points homewards, Harry feels her spine straighten and her shoulders arch. Air enters her lungs more freely now. She is re-entering her element and her body can relax. It's not that she resents the time spent in town. There were matters to attend to and she would have been remiss had she not dealt with them. It would have been nice to leave on better terms with Hannah, but staying on might not have achieved that. In fact, Hannah already seemed happier at lunch time, just before Harry left; remarkably happy, in fact. There were no traces of anger visible in her face; instead she'd chatted about her new friend, Louise, at the clinic and the fact that she might have a part-time job.

Jack seemed happy, too. Harry is grateful for this. If the situation had deteriorated, she would have stayed on her boat. Happily, things didn't reach that point. Harry wouldn't want to hurt Jack's feelings, or to take advantage of his hospitality.

The first hints of ocean swell swing under the boat in a slow, steady rhythm, barely disturbing the calm, blue surface. The conditions are so good that Harry doesn't want to rush home. She should make use of the day, do something exciting, or different. But what? She can't just land somewhere and go for a hike. It's too difficult with *Polynesia*. Shallow water and an ebbing tide are not a good combination for the boat. Imagine if she got stranded on shore somewhere, unable to get floating again! The alternative is to anchor out in deep water and row ashore with the dinghy. Ten years ago, she wouldn't have thought twice about doing that. Today, the idea seems a bit much. She'd have to get the dinghy down from its place on the back deck, which is above head height. In an emergency, she would just cut the ropes and let it fall down. But rope is precious and Harry hates to cut it unless she has to. Then she'd have to get the dinghy back in place again, which would require help. So that idea is out.

Her eyes pick out a curl of smoke from one of the bachelors' shacks. Perhaps she should go visiting—do the rounds. People may have been wondering why the gas station had been closed for so long, even though most of her neighbours can operate it without her, which they sometimes do, leaving the money in a tote. But few of the people who live out around here have docks for her to land at. They mostly use small boats that they leave on the beach and launch at high tide. San and Clarissa have a dock, though. Well, it's not much of a dock, just a couple of long logs, chained together, but Harry's landed there before. Swan Bay is behind Fortune Island, but it's not too far out of her way.

The more she thinks about this idea, the happier she feels. San usually has a lot of projects on the go. If he is open to it, he might even be able to share his boat-building skills with Big Mack. That would expand Mack's repertoire, give him more opportunities in life. He's already familiar with wood, so he'd have a head start. Mack probably knows Clarissa pretty well, too. They grew up in the same place, around the same time. Yes, if Mack had somewhere to escape to, this situation might end up suiting them both.

Harry rubs her hands, then shuffles her feet. She can hardly wait to get to Swan Bay now. It will be fun. She hasn't been there since the early summer and it was raining the day she went. It had been raining for about two weeks and she had a bit of cabin fever. She hasn't seen San and Clarissa's place on a clear day for ages.

Soon, Fortune Island grows more distinct. Harry smiles at the sight of it, this amazing spiral of land, with water swirling all around it. The first time she ever saw the island, she was deckhanding on a fishboat. It was love at first sight. Right away she looked it up on the chart. Harry pushes away her homing instinct and steers past the island. It feels odd to bypass Deep Bay, but her excursion will be fun.

When she rounds the point into Swan Bay she can see some kids on the beach. One of them sees the *Polynesia* and waves and points. Then all four of them scramble out to the tie-up logs, still pointing and waving. As she manoeuvres the boat into place, the two boys grab her tie-up lines. The girls waste no time jumping on board to pet Rustum.

"Well, hello you lot!" Harry hugs each child in order of their age—oldest first.

"Did you bring us any cookies?" asks Sonny.

"Oh dear," Harry realises too late. "I just came from town."

"Aw," says Bear.

"Next time you come over," Harry promises. "Double rations!"

The children help Harry negotiate the slippery logs to the beach, where San is waiting.

Even though he didn't grow up among Japanese people, San has cultivated some of his traditional heritage. On the beach there are seven striking boulders placed along a wide curve. They guide people from the dock to an opening in the trees.

Harry walks up the beach with San, while the children throw sticks into the water for Rustum.

"Good to have sunshine," San comments.

"Feels like our world tripled in size," Harry agrees.

They meander up the stone pathway to San's cabin. The path is carefully designed, flat rocks placed vertically within triangular wooden frames. The rocks in each triangle face a different direction. Harry's feet tread from one pattern to the next.

The house is raised up off the ground, sided in hand-split cedar shakes. Clarissa is waiting on the porch, smiling. She hugs Harry tightly and wishes her a happy new year. Inside the house little has changed since the last time Harry was there. There are still very few chairs, but there are piles of cushions and some low tables. Harry picks up one of the cushions and admires the design. It's a patchwork window, with four faces looking out—the kids. She steps down into the centre of the room, which is sunk below the rest of the floor level. The woodstove sits there, heat rising up from it in waves, warming Harry's knees. The split level makes a square border, perfect for sitting around the stove and getting warm. It's a practical design. The family gathers here in the evenings and listens to San read out loud.

"Tea?" Clarissa asks. "Coffee?"

Harry opts for coffee and a cushion by the window in the sun. She catches up on the family's developments. Midori and Naomi are "A" students in their correspondence courses; Sonny is a challenge: rain or shine, he just wants to play on the beach all day; Bear is learning to read and write.

After a while, Harry shares the story of Big Mack and Boy.

"What did Mack tell the police?" San asks.

"That he didn't do it," Harry replies. "The problem is, he can't remember what he did do. He was so drunk."

"He wouldn't hit Boy, no matter how drunk he was."

"That's what I think. I just don't know how to persuade Hannah of that."

"Don't try."

"She has to see it," Clarissa agrees, "but maybe she doesn't want to right now. She may have reasons."

"What kinds of reasons?"

"Well," Clarissa hesitates. "I don't mean to be rude, or anything, but Hannah hasn't been around men much. Growing up, she didn't have a father. She probably hasn't been around Native people much, either. Not that it's your fault. You live out here where there's nobody. But it's hard to trust what you don't know."

"But she had Jack," says Harry. "And you guys. And there were Native kids at school once she got there."

"I'm sorry, Harry," Clarissa shrugs, "but school's the worst place to learn things. School teaches the bad things, and the stereotypes. I should know; I went to school in Hanson Bay."

Harry's shoulders droop. "I wanted her to take correspondence, but she begged to go to school."

"Then you did the right thing by sending her." Clarissa hands Harry her coffee and smiles, before continuing. "But it doesn't mean that she sees people the way you or I do. Life in my home village would be like life on another planet to Hannah. Some of the differences are obvious, but others aren't. It's like me teaching Bear about right and write." She mimes writing. "A person won't know the difference, unless they see the way the words are spelled. You have to learn these things."

Harry stares at the woodstove seeing only a jumble of past events as Clarissa's voice leads her along.

"Until Hannah feels safe around men or Natives, she won't be able to learn about them. She won't see any of the landmarks—the things that tell you whether a person is trustworthy, or not. You, for instance, I bet you think a person is honest if they look you straight in the eyes. In my family, we don't do that. It's aggressive; not polite. So right away you think we're being shifty and we think you're being rude. Simple things like that."

Harry sips her coffee and tries not to stare at Clarissa. She has never heard her say so much before. This is obviously a subject that is close to her heart.

"Your daughter needs time," Clarissa finishes up. "Time and the right people. She'll come around."

"I guess her time with Jack just wasn't enough," Harry says, slowly. "Or maybe it was just wrong to raise her out here."

"No. No," says San. "Children will struggle wherever you raise them. Hard times can help our children to find themselves."

"Well, thanks for that," Harry says. "We'll have to wait and see, I guess. Meanwhile, I'm not really sure that Mack will be able to manage a month at Fortune Island. I thought a woodworking project of some kind would give him something to focus on. D'you have anything on the go, San? I know Mack will feel frustrated otherwise."

Clarissa laughs.

"San was just saying, 'If I had some help, I could build a big boat shed!' He's got the logs, he just needs to mill them into beams and planks."

"You could do that in my woodshed," Harry offers. "The boards would be dry in there. You'd be dry, too, of course!"

All three of them start laughing. The noise brings the children running in from the beach. Harry is amazed at the tidy way they hang up their coats and take off their shoes.

"What's so funny?" asks Sonny.

"It's a long story," Clarissa tells him.

"I want to hear it," Sonny persists.

"Oh, you'll hear about it. Later. Right now it's time for you to bring me some firewood."

"Aw, Mom!"

"Get going!"

"Do I have to?"

Clarissa smiles at Harry. "They give me hassle, I make them work. They'll thank me for it later."

"My own words," Harry agrees. She stands up slowly, giving her body a chance to unbend. "I wish I didn't have to go, but I do. My house will be freezing and there's a lot to unpack."

"When's Mack arriving?" San asks.

"Tomorrow."

"I'll come over in the afternoon then, if the weather's not too bad."

"You'll be welcome whenever you come. I can't thank you enough for all your advice. You'll get sore teeth from chewing all the bread I'm going to make you!"

"You don't owe us anything, Harry," says Clarissa, as she hugs her goodbye. "Don't think like that."

"Mack's visit will be good for all of us," San says as he walks with her down the path to the water. "You'll see."

BIG MACK

It's hard to make the boys go to bed when they all have so little time together. They're tired, though. Mack can see Lonny yawning and blinking. Finally, at about ten o'clock, he sends them off, telling them he'll join them soon. It's a little white lie. Mack needs to talk to Silas, but Silas seems to have disappeared again. No one is really sure where he is. Mack pulls on his coat and opens the front door.

"I'll be back in a few," he tells his dad.

Old Mack just nods his head and continues watching the TV.

The grass outside is damp, not frosty, and a thin haze veils the stars. Mack walks in the light from the houses, occasionally dipping into pools of darkness, his feet steady on the path, feeling their way with confidence. How many times has he walked this path? Even though the houses are modern in this village, Mack feels sure that the path is ancient. White shards of clam shells speckle the black earth, a reminder of all the people who lived here, whose feet walked this path, too. Once he even found a blue bead along this trail. His ancestors traded furs with the Russians for metal and glass beads. A lot of people dig around in the middens for blue beads, now. They're a rarity. The artists like to use them, so they're still an item of trade.

Mack found one that was about the size of a small marble. The glass was worn and pitted, so that the bead was almost round. He could tell that it had once been angular, though, cut with many faces. Sometimes he carries that bead around in his pants pocket for luck. He's not sure why it should be lucky, though. It wasn't lucky for the sea otters. They got wiped out because of the trade. And blue beads represent the beginning of contact, which wasn't lucky for Native people at all. Maybe it was just the way that the bead shone out from the path, like the shiny eye of a crow or a raven winking at him on a rainy evening.

Soon Mack finds himself at the top of the wharf. He steps

carefully down the slippery ramp and along the float, until he reaches the *North Wind*. A great blue heron screeches its rasping prehistoric cry and flaps away from its perch at the end of the float, startling him, just like he has startled it. These birds seem to take pleasure in screeching as much as possible, especially at night, when everything else is quiet. Mack takes a deep breath and steps up onto the *North Wind*. The door is unlocked and he climbs down into the cabin.

"Silas!" he calls. "Silas. Wake up!"

There's a grumbling noise from the front berth. Mack finds the light and switches it on.

"Silas, it's me, Mack. I've got to talk to you."

Slowly a shape unwinds itself from a tangle of blankets. Silas's head sticks out, tousled and sleepy.

"How did you know I was here?" he asks.

"You always come here when something's wrong. So do I."

"You too?"

"Uh-huh."

"Huh."

Silas blinks his eyes in the dim light. He sits up and reaches around for his jeans, pulling them on in one swift, practised motion. He climbs out of his bunk and up into the cabin, grabbing Mack in a fierce hug.

"It wasn't you!"

"What do you mean?"

"You got set up."

"How?"

"You remember how that van almost drove us into the ditch?"

Mack closes his eyes. His mind is a blank, but there's a sense of something.

"You remember," Silas prods, "that white van. It swerved right at us when we were going into Hanson Bay. It made you real mad. He gave us the finger, too."

285

Slowly a picture forms in Mack's mind. He doesn't see the van, but he sees Silas's face and his hands clinging to the signpost.

"Don't you get it? That guy was driving around terrorizing people all night. It was freezing out and the road got icy. I bet he skidded and got too close to Boy. He probably hit him, then dumped him in town, just in case anybody'd seen him on the road."

"So I was right," breathes Mack. "There *was* a car that dumped him there. I remember hearing one. That was how I found Boy. The noise woke me up."

"You see! We just have to find the owner of that van and we're laughing. They'll never be able to say you done anything."

"Holy shit. So whose van was it, d'you think?"

"Well, at the time you said it was Kevin McKay's."

"How come you remember all this?"

Silas ruffles his hair and looks beyond Mack's shoulder.

"How come?"

"I left the bar because I met someone. I was pretty sober by the time we got to town, then I had one or two more drinks. I met this girl and we rented a room, so I didn't have time to do too much more drinking."

"Oh yeah, who'd you meet?"

"It doesn't matter, okay?"

"Alright, alright, never mind," Mack backs down. "It must be serious," he can't resist adding.

Silas ruffles his hair again. "It doesn't matter. What matters is that there was an asshole out there that night. And because of him, you're in deep shit."

Mack sighs. "Dad says that Boy's opened his eyes a few times. Maybe he'll live. I was praying that he'd live."

"You and everyone else around here. They even had a meeting about it the other night. I told everyone about that van."

"You did?"

286

"Well, yeah. I didn't want everyone to think that *you* done it, even if that lady said you admitted it. What'd you do *that* for?"

"You know what, Silas? I have no clue what I said that night. I barely remember a thing that happened. But I know that someone left Boy there. I remember finding him and panicking. I just kept wishing he would breathe, or make a noise." Mack's voice falters a little and Silas looks away.

"I should've been there with you," he says. "If I'd of been there, none of this would've happened."

"Jesus, Silas, anyone would think it was your fault! It's not even your fault. It's my fault. I'm quitting drinking forever."

"That's what I should do, too."

"Well, don't quit because of me. Quit because you want to. I don't even know if I *can* quit, although if I go to jail, I'll have to. Listen, Silas, did the old man tell you I'm going away tomorrow?"

"I haven't seen him."

"How long you been hiding out for?"

"A few days."

"How come?"

"I dunno."

"Look, I've gotta go away for a while. I need you to keep an eye on the boys for me. Lonny especially, you know how he is?"

Silas doesn't reply.

"Can you do that for me, Silas?" Mack persists.

"I guess so."

"What's wrong?"

"Nothing."

"How come you don't want to keep an eye on them?"

"It's not *them*. It's Lonny. I just can't look at that boy without seeing Nelson. It's hard. It's like looking at my own face, but he's not my kid. And every time I see him I think how I should have been the one to go to residential school. Then Lonny would have a father."

287

"Jeez, Silas, you make me mad, you really do! How long are you going to go on crying about this? We can't change our past. There's no point thinking like that when there's a boy here that needs us. Do you think he's going to get any younger while you sit here feeling sorry for yourself? He's a kid! He needs somebody to make him feel special. If you want to feel better about Nelson, then the least you can do is pay attention to Lonny."

"You don't know how it feels to share a face with someone! Every time Lonny sees me he thinks of his dad. I'm not his dad. I don't want him thinking like that. I don't want a kid in this life."

"Well you don't have a choice. There's kids all over who nobody wants. The least we can do is take care of our own. You want them to grow up like we did? You want to make them suffer too?"

"No."

"Well, act like a man and stop snivelling about it! You're my brother. I need you right now. Your nephews need you. It's not forever. It's just for a while."

"I'm not snivelling!"

"Well, whatever."

"Why are you freaking on me all of a sudden?"

"Because I'm up shit creek and I need your help! I need to know I can rely on you while I'm gone. Raylene told me that Lonny's been acting out. He's frightened. His whole world just turned upside down. At least go stay at the old man's with him. Please?"

"All right! I'll keep an eye on the boys while you're gone! Now can you let me go back to bed?"

"No, because we need to figure out what to do about that van. You need to tell my lawyer about it."

"You got a lawyer?"

"Yeah, I do. How do you think I got out?"

"I don't know."

"I've got her name and phone number at Dad's. I'll write it in the front of the phone book. You'll have to call her and tell her what happened, okay?"

"Uh huh."

"Will you really?"

"Yes! Now leave me alone and let me go back to sleep."

"How come you're so tired, anyway?"

"Didn't get much sleep the last few days."

"Oh yeah. The woman. Kept you awake, eh?"

"Ah, shaddup and go away."

"Okay, okay, I'm going. Maybe I'll see you in the morning before I leave. By the way, Dad's going to be taking me in the boat, so he'll probably be down here fussing around in the morning."

"Great."

"Sweet dreams."

"Huh!"

LONNY

Lonny is so tired, but he can't fall asleep. There's a whole 'nother day of firewood tomorrow and he knows it won't be fun if he's tired, but he can't help it. Part of him is waiting for Uncle to come in. He said he'd only be a while, but it's been a long time now. Even Grandpa's gone to his room and Sam fell asleep ages ago, but Uncle's bed is still empty.

When Lonny found out that Mack had to go away again, he nearly cried. He's getting good at holding it in, though. It's part of growing up and being tough. The last few days have shown him that he's pretty grown up already. Doing the wood is making him strong and that's a good thing because he might have to defend himself one of these days. When he hangs out with Sam the other boys leave them alone, partly because there's two of them, but also because they're afraid of Big Mack. But if Lonny has to be by himself a lot, he might get picked on. When Uncle goes, maybe he'll make a punching bag in the bedroom. He could use some of the pillows.

Tonight he was hoping he would be able to chat to Uncle in the quiet darkness, one of those talks where both people have their eyes closed and the words flow out real gentle. Lonny likes talking like that. It's easy to say what's on your mind when it's like that. But can Lonny say what's really on his mind? Maybe growing up means that you don't ask questions any more. You just figure things out for yourself.

Lonny hears the neighbours' dog bark. Shortly after, there are footsteps on the stairs. Oh good. Uncle's back. The footsteps go down the hall to the bathroom, Lonny squirms among the covers, trying to get comfortable. When the door opens he sits up in bed.

"How come you're awake?" Uncle whispers.

"I can't sleep," Lonny whispers back.

"It helps if you're lying down."

290

Lonny lies back down again, then sits back up.

"Uncle?"

"Haa-ah."

Fabric rustles as Big Mack undresses and climbs into bed. It's the only noise in the darkness.

"Never mind." Lonny lies back down.

"What's on your mind, Lonny?"

"It doesn't matter."

"Sure it does."

"No, really, it's not important."

"It's not important, but you waited up this long to tell me?"

"I didn't wait up. I just couldn't sleep."

"And you couldn't sleep because something's on your mind."

"No. I just couldn't sleep."

"Huh."

Lonny squeezes his eyes shut and tries to feel sleepy, but he's wide awake now. "I missed you," he finally whispers.

"I missed you, too, Lon," Mack whispers back.

"Will you ever come back?"

Mack pauses, then whispers slowly. "Things are looking good, Lonny. I just have to be on my best behaviour for a while, that's all."

"Are you sure I can't come, too?"

Silence is real noticeable when someone is supposed to answer, but they don't. Uncle takes forever and it makes the room seem empty.

"Lon, if there's a way for you to come there, I'll fix it," he says, after a while. "But I can't make any promises, okay? You hear me? No promises. Now go to sleep."

"Okay."

HANNAH

Louise shows up at the front door about an hour after Hannah and Jack have eaten supper. She already knows Jack from the clinic, so Hannah doesn't have to introduce them.

"Is Harry here?" Louise asks.

"No. She's gone back out to the island."

"Oh. Too bad I missed her."

Hannah grabs her coat. "Do you feel up to a stroll around town?

"Oh sure, sure. It's good to make the most of the dry times. They're rare enough. Besides, I've been stuck in the clinic all day."

"Would you ladies like some hot chocolate when you get back?" Jack asks.

"Well, sure!" says Louise.

"You and your hot chocolate," Hannah laughs, then kisses him lightly on the cheek. "That sounds lovely. See you soon."

As they walk through the gate, Louise asks, "Does he know that you're pregnant?"

"No, I haven't told him. I haven't told anyone except you and Dr Haswell."

"I'm honoured."

"It's easier to tell a stranger, although, for some reason, I feel like I've known you for ages."

"I think I have one of those faces. People are always mistaking me for their long-lost relative, or the girl next door in their home town."

"Well, it's more than your face, but I don't know what, exactly. My instincts made me tell you and maybe they're right, for once. I feel as if I'm floating around in somebody else's dream. The fact that I'm pregnant is so bizarre, it's taken me until now to figure out what I'm going to do. I mean, I've never believed in abortion, because I believe in prevention. So when I realised that somehow, prevention had failed, it was like coming up against a ten-foot wall. I kept looking at this wall, thinking 'Well, I can't get over it, so I'll have to turn back.' And the only way to turn back was to have an abortion."

"But, you've decided against that now?"

"Well, I never decided *for* it. It seems like I'm just going to do nothing. Which means I'm going to have a kid."

"Your mother will help you, won't she?"

"My mother and I don't always get along."

"Oh. Sorry."

"No, it's not your fault. I wish we could get our act together, but it's a struggle."

Night walks around Hanson Bay are easy with the street lights. Hannah and Louise barely notice the houses they pass. They don't discuss a route, just flow along, letting their legs take them from one place to the next.

"I guess it's like that in a lot of families," Louise says. "For years I thought that other people had wonderful relationships with their parents. I had this picture in my head, of what things could have been like if I had a real mom—whatever that is—but there don't seem to be so many of those around."

"What's your mother like?"

"She's an artist. She does all this experimental stuff with textiles and metals. She's often completely wasted on some kind of drug, doesn't seem to matter which. She moves around from place to place, lives with the worst kind of men and occasionally sells a piece of work."

"Was she around when you were growing up?"

"Not really. I got in the way, so I often went to stay with my aunt, who ran a farm in the interior. By the time I was sixteen I was living on my own. Life got a lot better then. Mom forgot about me and I didn't have to deal with her habits or her men. Once in a while I get news of her through my aunt. Apparently she always says to tell me she loves me."

"I left home, too. I moved in with Jack and Ada. Anything to get away from the island."

"Really? For me, it would have been paradise. I loved my aunt's farm. I wished I could stay there forever, hiding out in one of the stables. Going back to whatever city my mother was in was always hell. I hated it."

"I guess we always seem to want what we can't have."

"I don't think we can help our desires," Louise says. "That doesn't mean we should always give in to them, though. There's a strong part of me that would love to be a hermit, living in the bush like your mother."

"That's why you're so intrigued by her."

"Well, partly. She's been living out there for a long time, yet she never seems to get 'bushed.' Some people just can't handle the loneliness. They come to town looking over their shoulders, as if they're mice being chased by hawks. They duck their heads when they see you, so that they won't have to say hello. They're happier talking to themselves."

Without choosing a route, Hannah and Louise have wound up on the government dock. The water is inky black, slightly rippled by the wind. Louise sits down on one of the railings, but Hannah stays standing, clutching her arms around herself even though she's not cold.

"I hated the loneliness," she says. "I always had Mother around for company and sometimes there were visitors, or people coming for gas, but that was it, really. I wanted friends, company, people my own age to relate to. In the end I came to live in town. Mother has never understood it."

"We probably both moved out at around the same age," says Louise.

"Sixteen?"

"Uh huh."

"What made you decide on nursing?"

"It's ironic. I wanted to be in charge of my life."

294

"And you're not?"

Hannah pats her stomach and shrugs.

"Oh," says Louise, sitting down on a tie-up rail. "Who is?"

The two women stare down at the water, watching the undulation of light and shadow. Their voices are a quiet ebb and flow, mimicking the shush of water as it meets the dock and the beach. When Hannah tells Louise about rescuing Boy, she sees the darkness again, the confusion, Mack crying, Harry bursting across the grass towards her. It was so good to be held by Harry. Why did it all have to change? She tells Louise everything, until her voice dies away and the story comes to an end.

Louise gets up from her perch on the railing and stretches. Hannah is still staring at the water.

"The weird thing about this was how lonely I felt afterwards," she says quietly. "It was as if I was Boy's mother and they had taken him away from me. For twenty minutes I gave him life and then he was gone."

"Have you thought of going to see him in hospital?"

Hannah joins Louise and they head back up the wharf, towards the road.

"I haven't thought about it—no. To tell you the truth, I don't feel much like travelling. The bus ride here was bad enough."

"That road . . . . "

"Try sitting in a bus on that road and having morning sickness!"

"Oh dear! No wonder you want to stay put."

"Other than the travelling, I haven't thrown up. The feeling is just so persistent, though. It's hard to think straight when the nausea is there, taking all your attention."

"The joys of motherhood."

"Oh God. Right now, I'll settle for the joys of hot chocolate. Jack will be so happy to make it for us."

"Have you thought about how he'll react to your pregnancy?"

"Jack? He's pretty old-fashioned so he'll stumble over the single-mother thing. His precious girl, knocked-up and single. You know? But when he realises that he's going to be a grandfather, he might be excited."

"So you're planning to be a single mother? There's no man on the scene?"

Hannah stops walking and looks at Louise. "Um. No," she says. "Oh look, we're here already."

She pushes open the gate and ushers Louise into the garden. They walk up the steps, kicking dirt off their feet onto the mat and opening the door to warmth and light.

HARRY

Harry wakes up in the dark as a scattering of rain dances over the roof. There's no hint of light in the sky, so there's not much point in getting up, but she's restless. Her cosy bed suddenly feels uncomfortable and she throws off the blankets, reaching around for the matches to light her bedside candle. The wick flares for a moment before settling and she sees the clock: six a.m. It will be dark for a while.

She pulls on her dressing gown and slippers and opens the draught on the woodstove, then adds a chunk of cedar. She turns on one of the lights that are hooked into her solar electricity system and the cabin grows around her as the light spreads outwards.

Well, she thinks to herself. I can bake and I can clean the house.

Last night, when she unloaded *Polynesia,* she piled the wheelbarrow high with paper sacks of flour and clear plastic bags of soft dark sugar, raisins, cranberries, pecans, dates. The flour has been tidily put away, but the other ingredients are sitting out on the kitchen counter, waiting to be used. She admires their rich colours and textures while she adds freshly ground coffee to the percolator and breathes in the smell. She leans against the counter, picks up one of her best-loved cook books and thumbs through it. From time to time she stops at a page—date loaf, cinnamon buns, gingerbread cookies . . . .

She is over by the fireplace, enjoying her coffee, when she realises that she hasn't even thought of smoking yet. Perhaps she woke too early. Whatever the reason, she'll wait a while before she smokes. She decides to hold off until the first batch of bread has been set to rise. And even then, she thinks, if I'm not desperate, I won't bother.

Harry wonders if Big Mack will actually show up today. It's a big step and she can picture him at his dad's, not wanting to leave, dreaming up excuses. Old Mack will bring him, though.

He's rigid, that man. Harry wonders how Old Mack and Lonny get along. Old Mack is aloof and reserved, where Lonny thirsts for affection.

Oh well, this fiasco may only last a month. Perhaps they will discover that they can't pin anything on Mack after all. Or perhaps they will find the person who did attack Boy—the real culprit. Harry wonders how the poor kid is doing. In all the fuss of the police and the lawyer and Big Mack, Boy—the person in the most serious trouble—seems to have faded out of view. She should have phoned Dr Haswell before she left, to see if he'd heard anything. Mind you, Hannah was at the clinic that day. She would have mentioned if there had been any developments . . . .

Hannah. How happy she seemed at the prospect of work and friends. Harry can understand the need to work—to do something!—but the need for other people has always been peripheral in her life. Still, seeing her daughter's face glow with excitement was a reminder that Hannah's needs should not be taken lightly. They are as real as Harry's yearning for solitude.

Is that what all Hannah's years away were supposed to illustrate? That her "teenage" fuss was genuine, after all; that she needed to be taken seriously? It seemed so much greater than that at the time.

It's just that the change was so rapid—so dramatic. One minute Harry had a peaceful, contented young daughter; the next, she had a bitter, silent teenager, full of tears and accusations. The hardest thing for Harry has been coming to terms with the fact that her only child does not share her values. She tried so hard to fill Hannah with love for the water and the wild. For the first ten years she thought she was succeeding. She was constantly touched by Hannah's easy delight: Look! Look! There's another starfish. That makes eleven!

The first time Harry noticed the change in Hannah was in late spring, one year, when the daylight hours were long and the weeds were growing a yard a minute. Hannah was helping her

298

with the vegetable beds, something they often did together. On this occasion, every few minutes Hannah would get up from her task and disappear. It took Harry a while to realise that she was going to the water butt to wash her hands.

"Why don't you save up and do it when you're finished, honey?" she'd asked.

"I can't wait that long," Hannah had replied. "The dirt feels horrible."

That was the last time Hannah ever helped with the weeding.

Later that year, in the fall, a mouse had scuttled across the kitchen floor in broad daylight. Hannah had shuddered and drawn her feet up onto the chair she was sitting in.

"Eew," she had squirmed. "How disgusting!"

Mouse traps are a fact of life at Fortune Island. They always have been. There would be a mouse problem without them, but, in general, the mice are healthy little forest mice, with bright, beady eyes and pink noses—cute, even. At the age of seven Hannah had wanted one as a pet. Back then, it had taken quite a bit of effort to talk her out of it.

"But sweetie, if you have one mouse in here, all the other mice will want to come and join it," Harry had said. "Then our house will be overrun by mice."

"Then we would need the Pied Piper," Hannah said, clapping her hands. "And I could go into the mountain with the other children."

As if it would be a great adventure . . . . Harry remembers how she'd felt her heart constrict and she wanted to cry out: "But what about me? You would leave me behind forever!" Perhaps that was what had happened. Hannah had danced away to the melody in her head, away into the mountain where her mother could no longer reach her.

Harry sighs. It's amazing how much can go on inside a person's head: new likes and dislikes hiding in the folds of the cortex, visible only by accident. Too bad people don't have tails, like dogs, to show off their feelings.

"Eh, Rustum?" she says.

From Rustum's corner there comes a single thump.

"Only one?" Harry presses.

Another lone thump.

"It's okay," Harry says. "I'm not going to make you get up. It won't be light for at least another hour."

She eases out of her chair and moves back to the kitchen. She measures out the oatmeal for her breakfast, then sets it on the stove and turns on the flame. While the oats are cooking she dresses for the day: jeans, warm shirt, wool vest. The house is warm enough, although there is a lingering feeling of dampness. By this evening that will have vanished. It takes forty-eight hours of wood heat to warm her house right through after it has lost its residual heat.

I abandoned you for several days, she says to the house. How did I manage that?

She breathes in the steam from the warm oatmeal, adds a pinch of cinnamon and some cranberries. She opens one of the bags on the counter—demerara sugar, the softest, darkest sugar, just perfect for swirling into a steaming bowl of porridge. Harry assembles her breakfast while mixing the yeast with water and leaving it to sit. Then she flips on the radio, smiling at the voices that she's missed the last few days. She doesn't listen to the radio all the time. Some programs annoy her and besides, too much noise is distracting, it takes away from the rhythm of her breathing, the rhythm of the island's breathing. But, for now, the chatter of soft voices livens up the dark morning and will quicken the long minutes of kneading, once she begins to make bread.

"Always knead for at least a quarter of an hour," Harry's mother used to advise. "And knead with gusto, but never with anger." Harry smiles as she measures out flour. She pulls the dough apart, feeling the elasticity, the perfection of it.

I bet Mother's dough never once looked like this! Did she really knead it for fifteen minutes each time? Unlikely!

She looks at the clock. She's only been kneading for twelve

minutes—three more to go. She loves the discipline of the fifteen-minute rule. It makes it impossible to rush this precious time when she remembers Ruth. Papa can be remembered when cutting firewood, or tending the garden, but Mother comes to her mostly when she makes bread. Harry settles the dough in the bowl and takes it over to the woodstove, where she'll leave it to rise.

Will Hannah take up bread-making? she wonders.

BIG MACK

Raylene makes a big breakfast, as if this is the last time Mack will ever eat. Probably the last meat I'll eat for a while, he thinks, adding another slice of bacon to his plate. He's sure Harry doesn't eat a lot of meat: her wiry little body and the amount of time she spends out there, without a freezer, makes it unlikely. She liked the fish he caught before Christmas, though. Maybe he should bring his shotgun and hunt for ducks while he's up there. Or would he get in trouble for bringing his gun? He can't remember the lawyer saying anything to him about guns, so it's not as though he's been specifically told not to bring one. Maybe they just don't know he has one, because his isn't registered. Registered—ha! It isn't even legal. He got it from one of his cousins a long time ago and it wasn't the kind of deal where you ask questions.

Hmmm. How can he pack a shotgun along, without looking as if he's packing a shotgun? Maybe he can stuff his big green duffel bag with clothes and the gun won't be too obvious. It would be good to have it. Harry probably doesn't have one. He can throw his raincoat over the top of the bag when he's carrying it around, then no one will notice anything.

"Did you listen to the weather this morning, Dad?" he asks.

"Nah. It'll be okay."

Big Mack stares at his father, who is cutting up a piece of bacon with his fork. So far, Old Mack has eaten half a piece of toast and a piece of bacon. The current piece of bacon looks set to become leftovers. Sure enough, Old Mack soon gets tired of fussing with it and pushes it to one side of his plate. He puts his fork down and reaches for his cup. The coffee goes down easily.

"How come you don't eat so much these days, Dad?"

"Not hungry."

"Does your stomach feel bad?"

"Nope."

"Huh."

302

Mack stares at the skeletal fingers gripping the coffee cup. He wonders if his father will just keep on shrinking until, one morning, he really will be a skeleton, sitting at the table, grimacing and drinking coffee. The thought makes Mack shudder and he gets up from the table. There's still some breakfast left and he picks at it, standing in the kitchen. Raylene has gone back to her room. He must remember to thank her before he leaves.

"Dad?"

Old Mack raises his eyebrows.

"Can I borrow ten bucks off you?"

"What for?"

"To pay back Raylene for the taxi ride. I don't have any money right now."

"I'm getting a cheque on Wednesday. It'll have to wait till then."

"I'll tell her. Thanks."

Old Mack shrugs and takes another slurp of coffee. "You better get that boy out of bed."

"Who?"

"Lonny."

"Oh?" Big Mack eyes the last piece of bacon and eats half of it. "I want him to come with us."

"Why don't we take both of them?"

"Sam is packing wood today."

"I thought they did that yesterday."

"Just Lonny."

"Huh. What about Sam?"

"Took off somewhere."

"Huh."

Just in time, Big Mack remembers to leave some hashbrowns for the boys. He'll fry up a couple more eggs when the time comes, but both of them love hashbrowns, covered in salt and ketchup. He washes his hands under the tap and goes off to the bedroom.

LONNY

Even though Uncle is going away today, Lonny is pretty happy. There're hashbrowns for breakfast and on top of that, he gets to go with Grandpa and Uncle to Fortune Island.

"Tattletale," Sam whispers loudly.

"I never!" says Lonny.

"Did!"

"No way!"

"Sam!" says Uncle in a stern voice. "Grandpa was at home most of the day. If you were doing what you were supposed to do, he would've seen you. You should apologize to Lonny for making him do all the work. That wasn't fair. And you weren't real honest with me, either, were you?"

"I never told you I did wood!" Sam bursts out.

"No. But you didn't say you didn't, either."

Lonny stops trying to figure out what they're talking about. As long as nobody's mad at him, it's okay. And he gets to go on the boat!

"It's not fair that Lonny gets to go on the boat!" Sam yells. "You're my dad, not his. I should be the one who goes with you!"

Lonny stops eating his breakfast. He feels full, or sick, or something.

"SAM!" Uncle yells. Uncle never normally yells. Lonny stares in front of him, not looking at anyone.

"Sam! That's not a nice thing to say and you know it! You're acting like a spoiled brat. When did you start acting like this?"

Sam doesn't say anything. Lonny doesn't blame him, either. It's pretty scary to hear Uncle yell.

"Listen up! Both of you. Just because I won't be here doesn't mean that everything has to fall apart. As far as I'm concerned, you guys are brothers, okay? You don't say bad things about each other! You don't take things out on each other. I know what's happening isn't good. It's not fun for me and it's not fun for you.

That doesn't mean you should act up. It means you should stick together more. Be closer. You need each other. I'll wring your necks if I hear that you guys aren't getting along while I'm gone. Do you hear me?"

Sam shoots a look at Lonny, but Lonny is still staring across the room at the fridge and the photo of Raylene and Kenny and the baby. It's stuck to the fridge with a magnet, but the edges have curled up a bit. They're all smiling—even the baby seems to be smiling.

"And I'm not going anywhere until you apologize to Lonny," Mack adds.

Oh good, Lonny thinks. Maybe we could stay here. Sam could refuse to say he's sorry and then Uncle wouldn't be able to go anywhere. But Lonny is dreading Sam's apology. It's going to make Sam hate him and that's the last thing he wants. "It's okay," he blurts out. "It wasn't Sam's fault. His mom called him."

"Nice try, Lonny," Uncle says in an angry way. "If you're going to think up excuses, you should think a little quicker."

"It's true!"

"And what does Sam think about that?" Uncle glares at Sam, his huge arms folded over his chest.

Sam looks at the floor. "I just didn't feel like doing it," he says, in a voice that Lonny can barely hear. "And anyway, I don't like Old Leo."

"Well, that's better," says Uncle Mack. "But life is full of things we don't like and people we don't like. Lonny probably didn't like doing it either. Today you get to spend time with Leo, Sam."

Lonny takes a breath and then sticks his fork into his hashbrowns again. He reaches for the ketchup bottle, turns it upside down and shakes it. Then he leaves it upside down on the table. He'll wait until all the ketchup has dribbled down before he squirts some more onto his plate.

"Can I have yours?" he asks Sam, who has pushed half his portion to one side.

Uncle hears him and looks over. "Sam needs to eat," he says. "He's got a whole day of work ahead of him. Eh, Sam?"

Sam looks up at Big Mack and then back down at his plate. He picks up his fork and pushes some potatoes onto it. Uncle watches Sam eat for a moment, then gets up from the table. As soon as his back is turned, Sam pushes the rest of the food onto Lonny's plate. Lonny grins and tries not to laugh. Sam grins, too, but he puts his finger to his lips.

BIG MACK

Big Mack has to smile when he reaches the *North Wind*. Silas has left everything exactly as it should be. There's nothing to show that he was sleeping here last night. Mack wonders where Silas is right now. This morning, he wrote the lawyer's name and phone number in the front of the phone book, but he's not convinced that Silas will phone. Silas is shy about some things, especially dealing with people in authority. Mack understands. He doesn't like stuff like that, either. He gets tongue-tied.

Mack stashes his duffle bag in the front berth. Part of the reason he came down early was so that his dad wouldn't notice the way the shotgun makes such a rigid shape under the green canvas. It's a bit obvious, if that's what you're looking for. Harry probably won't notice, he figures, but his dad might.

He turns the key in the ignition and the engine coughs to life. It doesn't sound its usual smooth self this morning, although a good long warm-up will change that. Mack leaves the engine running and then ducks back out of the cabin and heads towards his sister's house. She's still in Vancouver, but there're people there who will have the most recent news of Boy. He feels funny walking up the steps, like a criminal. When Elton opens the door, Mack feels as though he's being looked-down on, even though he towers over Elton.

"Uncle," says Elton, nodding his head slightly.

"Elton," says Mack, doing the same.

When Mack continues to stand in the doorway, Elton slowly opens the door. Mack walks into the hallway and stops. The house is a mess and there are small children running around everywhere, screaming.

"Who's looking after all these kids?" he asks.

"I am," says Elton.

"They should be at their own homes. You shouldn't be letting people take advantage of you."

"I'm baby sitting," says Elton.

"Oh. And I suppose everyone is going to pay you next week?"

Elton swallows audibly and looks around him.

"And anyway," Mack continues, "aren't you supposed to be going back to school?"

"My mom wants me here. She wants to be able to call if anything happens."

"So what is happening?"

"She's still in Vancouver."

"I know that. I mean how's Boy doing?"

"He's still in a coma."

"I heard he might've opened his eyes."

"Couple of times."

"What do they expect to happen?"

"Dunno."

"Huh." Mack looks around the room at all the mess. "If you're baby sitting you should keep this place clean, or the kids will all get sick."

Elton doesn't answer.

"Well. When Lila calls, I want you to tell her I came," Mack says staring at Elton hard. "Tell her I'm thinking of her and Boy. Tell her I miss them."

Elton nods.

"You be sure to tell her that," Mack says as he heads back out the door.

As he walks back down to the dock he can see Old Mack and Lonny on the deck of the boat. The rain has been coming in little showers and the wind is steady southeast. It's not bad yet, but it will be by evening. Mack hopes his dad will have a manageable trip. He's got a delivery to make at the logging camp up Dagger Inlet after he drops Mack off. It'll be a long day, so he'll be returning when the weather has worsened. Mack never used to worry about his dad, but he seems so frail now. And Lonny's eager, but he wouldn't be much help in a crisis. He's too small.

Mack watches Lonny as he stands on the back deck, looking around. He's paying attention to everything. One of these days he'll be a good deckhand. Perhaps Mack should start to show him some tricks, to give him a head start. He's already shown the boys how to tie clove hitches and they're good at it. Maybe on this trip he'll show Lonny how to tie a bowline with his eyes closed. There's a trick to it, but once you've learned it, you'll have it for life. He can start teaching him about landmarks, too. How to know where the rocks are; how to find home. He walks down the ramp, part of him wanting to turn back and stay home, but he's committed now. It's best for everyone if he goes to Fortune Island.

At the tie-up rails, he bends over and unties a line. The motor sounds better now. He tosses the line onto the back deck, then moves up to the bow.

"Hey, Uncle! Let me do it!" cries Lonny, hopping off the boat.

"Don't forget to give us a real good push."

"I know!"

Big Mack watches Lonny's matchstick arms straining against the huge weight of the boat. He pushes the boat out as far as he can, then jumps right at the last minute, almost slipping overboard. He catches himself, though, and pulls his foot up. When he looks up, he is smiling—triumphant. Mack grins and gives him the thumbs up. The *North Wind* moves out into the warm bite of the wind.

HANNAH

Hannah feels as if her mind and body are awakening from a deep sleep. For the first time in ages there is clarity—of movement, of thought. She slept well, not waking until eight in the morning. Jack was gone by the time she wandered into the kitchen, so she didn't have to explain why she wouldn't be having coffee. She's going to have to explain it at some point, though. Maybe she'll tell him today.

Hannah rinses her dishes in the kitchen sink, then rummages in the cupboards for a rag. She'll dust all the surfaces of the house today. In some places the soft grey accretion is thick.

By the time she has worked her way through all the bedrooms to the front room, she sees Jack walking back up the street. He ducks his head as a sudden sprinkle of rain flutters at him. He turns sideways to the wind and opens the gate, then walks quickly up the path and the stairs, into the house.

"Just in time!" he exclaims as he sees Hannah.

"Is it getting stormy?"

"Well, not really, but by tonight it will be nasty. I'm glad I got back without getting wet. I was tempting fate. No raincoat!" Jack is smiling as he hangs up his jacket and stamps his feet. "Oh yes, I picked up the mail and there's a letter for you."

Hannah stands dead still. "It must be from someone in Whitehorse," she says quietly.

"Here you go!" Jack hands over the envelope, a small yellowed one, instantly recognizable to her. Thank God it's not from Rob! Harry has used the same stationery for years. She bought a huge box of the stuff in a sale when Hannah was a baby, but she seldom writes letters, so the box sits at the cabin, getting older each year. Most of the envelopes have lost their adhesiveness by now. Hannah turns the letter over and, sure enough, there is a line of tape sealing it shut. So Mother has written her a letter. A feeling of dread seeps into Hannah: what now?

"Thanks," she says to Jack.

"I just got bills. Since you're not far away any more, I don't have much hope of getting a real letter! Say, have you been cleaning my house?"

"Oh, just a little dusting. Nothing much."

"You don't have to do that, you know."

"Oh, I know. But I'm almost finished. It'll only take me a minute."

"I'm going to get spoiled, with you living here. Home-cooked meals and house cleaning. Whatever next?"

Hannah takes a big breath, then plunges.

"How about a baby?"

"Sorry?"

"I said, how about a baby?"

"Well, whatever do you mean?"

"Jack, I'm going to have a baby!" Hannah grips the cleaning rag in both hands as she watches Jack struggle for comprehension. His face goes pale, then blank, then the creases rise upwards into a tremulous, questioning point.

"You are?"

Hannah nods, smiling. She reaches out her hands, grasping his, letting the rag fall to the floor.

"I never thought . . . ." says Jack.

"Well, no. Neither did I."

"Oh my. Oh my. When did you find out?"

"The doctor confirmed it yesterday."

"Well, er, d'you want some coffee?"

Hannah smiles and shakes her head.

"I suppose you're not allowed, or something."

"Or something," Hannah agrees, settling herself into a comfy chair. She sees Jack rubbing his knuckles and suspects he's struggling with a thought. "To be honest, I haven't been too cheery about this."

He looks up at her, into her eyes. "I think I need to know something—eh?—about this baby's father."

"Well," Hannah pauses, "he's not someone I want to be involved with, that's what makes this difficult."

"So you're not going to tell him?"

"No."

"Don't he have the right to know?"

"Maybe."

"What will you do if he finds out?"

"I don't know."

"Did he hurt you? Physically?"

Hannah takes a deep breath and the word yes comes out trembling, but clear.

"Then he don't deserve to know. Nobody should get away with that. There's too many bastards out there that do!"

"It wasn't entirely his fault. He . . . "

"Don't go excusing him! If a man's arm swings, it's because he swung it!"

"He had some, er, dependencies," Hannah finishes.

"And that's not his fault?" Jack is bristling, red-faced.

"Oh, I suppose so. I don't know. He changed. He used to treat me well."

"Just you saying that makes me suspicious. 'Treat you.' As if he was your owner, petting you on the head."

Those words make Hannah see herself back in the relationship—an object, an acquisition. Oh God, it's so true! What could she have been thinking? Why didn't she see that herself?

"Why would you blame yourself for anything?" he continues. "You eat yourself up doing that."

"You're right," Hannah agrees. "But I don't really want to talk about this any more. I can't change it, so I have to deal with the consequences."

"But what if he comes here?" Jack persists. "You should get a restraining order."

"That would be disastrous!" Hannah grips the arms of the chair. "It would incite him—maybe even bring him here!"

"I'm sorry, sweetheart. I don't mean to upset you. I'm just an anxious old man, madder than a bunch of bees."

"I know, Jack, I know. But I need to forget about the past for a while, so that I can go forward. Otherwise I'll be paralyzed."

Jack nods his head and stares out the window. Hannah can tell he's unhappy about something, but he won't press it now. He'll wait until some opportune moment to bring it up again. He's good that way, sensitive. He doesn't forget things, either.

"So, I'm wondering how you'd feel about me living here, if I had a baby?"

He turns his head quickly. "It'd make me so happy. You've no idea how lonely it's been since Ada died. To have voices in this house is joy for me—truly."

"You don't mind that I'll be a single mother?"

"I'd make a stink if you were with *him*."

"Do you want to be Grandad, or Grandpa?"

"Oh, sheesh!" Jack cries openly now, tears streaming down his wrinkled cheeks.

"I think Grandpa," says Hannah getting up to give him a hug. They laugh together as her hands link across his back and his gnarled fingers grasp the backs of her arms.

It's not until late afternoon that Hannah remembers the letter from Harry. After lunch she had gone for a walk in the showery wind. The sky was completely clouded over, making the world seem dim and confined. She'd bought some groceries for a slap-up dinner—steak and salad and baked potatoes!—then wondered if she'd be able to eat any of it. It didn't matter, she decided. The point was that they would be celebrating. She would be treating her pregnancy as something positive, something to look forward to, even!

Then, as she comes into the house, warm after her exertions, she remembers the letter.

She stands in the hall fingering the envelope, looking at the smooth sloping letters of her name, wondering if this is a letter she wants to read. What more does Mother have to say? The organs under her ribcage constrict as she stands there. But, despite the dread, she knows that she will open it. She unpacks the groceries, wondering with what clever words Harry will have exonerated herself. Harry's letters always have the guise of motherly caring, but between the lines, there's usually a message, some kind of criticism.

Jack is in his chair, reading the paper, so Hannah takes the letter to her room and sits on the bed to read it. She leans sideways into the yellow light of the bedside lamp as a story unfolds, one which Hannah would never have expected to hear. It seems to be about a man that Harry loved, the man who fathered Hannah.

Hannah puts the letter down for a moment and stares into space. She always thought that she was the result of a sordid one-night stand, between Harry and some no-good man. For that reason she didn't want to know about her father. She looks down at the letter on her lap, wondering if she wants to continue reading. Is it better to know?

And then: Does Mother know I'm pregnant? How can she know?

She picks up the letter again, kicks off her shoes and lies back against the pillows. Her eyes flash over the words, going too fast, having to go back and start again. Sentences get disjointed, phrases swim out at her, then disappear.

I think you should know . . . a good man . . . too far from home . . . It's hard to explain . . . I was in love . . . .

Hannah stops right there. Her mother? In love? Harry's always been such a loner. It seems impossible to link her to someone else. She tries to picture it, but fails. She tries again and sees the shape of a man embracing a woman, sees all the years of isolation flowing

314

out of the woman. She sees a woman transformed by love, with a curve to her cheek and an absence of worry lines. But that woman is not the mother Hannah knows. That woman is somebody else.

Hannah has never considered that Harry's life might have been beset by disappointments. Has she been lonely all this time? Pining for my father?

She reads on, more slowly now, anxious to get the story right.

He told me right away that he was a prairie boy, out to see the world. I heard him. I just believed that he could be happy here, too. Believed what I wanted to believe, the way you do when you're in love. I didn't see how important his family was to him. He said he felt lost without them. Not a real person. That was the difficulty of being Métis. He was half-and-half to begin with, so it was hard for him to know which half to be. Only his family could give him a sense of security in the world.

I was too flippant. I told him that we're all half-and-half: half our mother's family and half our father's. He said it was different when race and culture were involved. I didn't understand. I didn't want to. If I had let myself understand, I'd have had to turn him out, make him go back to his family. He went anyway and it was harder for me that way.

Hannah's hand flops to her knees, taking the letter with it. Her father, a Métis? She must have missed that part at the beginning of the letter. But she doesn't look Native . . . . She rushes over to the mirror and peers into it. Her skin is so pale. It doesn't have a hint of darkness. Her eyes are brown, but they are like her mother's. She grasps a hank of her hair. It's dark and long, but it has a wave to it. It's not a sleek, impossibly-straight curtain of blackness. She stares at her reflection. I'm like Mother, but taller. I'm not Métis!

Hannah turns around and looks at her bed, at the letter. For a moment she cannot move. Her feet seem to be stuck to the floor.

Well, why should this matter? I've been myself for my whole

315

life, I'm not likely to change, just because I've read some stupid letter.

Is that what it is? Stupid? Or is it important—precious? A gift that Harry has been saving for me?

Hannah raises her hands to her cheeks and stands, staring blankly. She remains there for some time, while the southeast builds and the rain falls steadily in the darkening afternoon.

HARRY

By the time the *North Wind* arrives there is a mound of baked goods cooling on the kitchen counter. Harry feels one of the loaves of bread—hmm, still hot—then pulls on a cardigan. Rustum is barking up a storm outside, even though the boat hasn't reached the dock yet. It's raining quite a bit now, so Harry lifts down her raincoat, throws it over her shoulders and hurries off to the dock. In a way, she's amazed that this is happening. It feels like a dream, or someone else's life. The circumstances are certainly strange enough.

The sight of the boat steaming into Deep Bay makes her stop in appreciation. Such a sleek boat! So well cared for! The scarlet planking is cheery against the grey sea and lowering clouds. The lines of the boat sweep elegantly from bow to stern, like an artist's brush stroke. And there, hanging off the stays with one hand, is Lonny, grinning and waving with his other hand. Is he coming too? she wonders, suddenly. No. He can't be. Mack would have said something. It's too bad in a way. Harry's developed a soft spot for Lonny. He makes her smile, as he leaps onto the dock, all legs and arms and energy. He ties the line before he falls on Rustum, ruffling his fur and letting that long doggy tongue slobber all over his face.

Harry picks her way carefully down the ramp as Big Mack steps onto the dock and makes the stern fast. His hands barely move as he slides the rope through them, twisting it into a perfect knot while his eyes are elsewhere, not even looking. Harry is amazed at what people can do when they've been brought up to a thing.

The motor is still going when Old Mack appears in the cabin doorway and casts a critical eye over the tie-up job. It must be adequate because he disappears back inside—white hair glowing in the dimness—and shuts off the motor. Big Mack smiles at Harry as she reaches the bottom of the ramp. She nods at him and smiles back.

"Auntie!" yells Lonny, getting up from his place beside Rustum and rushing over to her. He doesn't open his arms, though, which surprises Harry.

"Where's my hug?" she demands.

"Oh!" he laughs.

Just as he is hugging her, Old Mack comes out of the cabin. Harry sees a flicker of disapproval crease his forehead, as if he thinks hugs are bad. Or is it Lonny hugging Harry that's a problem?

"Come on up to the house!" she invites, watching Old Mack. He hesitates. "I've just baked a mound of goodies," she continues. "I can't possibly let you leave without some."

"Did you make cookies?" Lonny asks.

"Maybe," says Harry, smiling. When she looks at Old Mack again he is stepping off the boat, examining the lop-sided dock.

"You lose some floatation?" he asks.

"It's all the fuel barrels. I'm getting lazy about moving them around. I always used to make sure the whole thing was balanced. Lately, I've just been piling everything on the same side."

"Should use your davit to place them."

"Oh, I do. Couldn't get them anywhere without that!"

"I'll catch up to you," interrupts Big Mack. "Just gotta get my things."

"D'you need a hand?" Harry asks.

"Er, no, no. I just got the one bag."

Harry turns back to Old Mack and Lonny and ushers them up the ramp. Lonny scrambles ahead, pleased to show that he knows the way, the white border of shells framing his feet in their too-large running shoes. When they near the house, Harry takes a moment to show Old Mack the new bath house and privy.

"Where did you get the shakes?" he asks, touching the wood with a bony forefinger.

"Oh, I've got a froe," she says, "so I split them myself. The blocks came from my neighbour, San. You know him?"

"Mmm."

"He comes over here quite often. He'll be pleased to know that Mack is here—male companionship and all that."

Once inside, Old Mack stands in the centre of the cabin, looking around. His gaunt appearance and aura of stillness make him seem like a scarecrow.

"Have a seat," Harry suggests. "Make yourself comfortable."

He continues to stand.

"Coffee?" she asks.

This gets a response. A nod.

"Where shall I put my gear?" asks Mack as he comes through the door.

"You get the penthouse suite on the top floor."

"Oh yeah. The attic," says Mack, smiling. He kicks off his gum boots and heads for the ladder, holding his bag behind his back.

"The loft," she corrects as he disappears upwards. "I've made your bed."

"Oh, I brought a sleeping bag." He peers down at her.

"Well, use it if you want, but it's pretty cosy the way it's set up."

The floorboards creak loudly as Mack makes his way around the loft.

"You *did* make cookies!" Lonny says, grinning and pointing to the racks on the counter.

"Well, look at that. So I did. Would you like a cookie young man?" asks Harry, looking at Old Mack and smiling.

"Uh-huh!" says Lonny.

"Well hang on a minute. I was asking your grandfather."

Old Mack actually smiles for a moment.

"But you said 'young man!'" Lonny protests.

"I did. But all of us here are young. Some of us are just younger than others. It's a trick of the light. But I guess I better give you something, before you keel over."

Old Mack declines food, although when Harry gives him a loaf of bread to take home, he doesn't protest. She makes the coffee strong and watches him swallow it down. Two gulps. She refills his cup without asking.

Mack takes his cup and a fistful of cookies and squeezes himself into a chair.

"Too bad the weather changed," he comments.

"It was bound to happen," says Harry. "Sunny weather in winter is like money from the government. They give it sometimes, but they're quick to take it back."

Old Mack smiles and nods. "Like the fishing quotas, too."

"Do you still go for herrings?" she asks.

"Nah. No point."

"All that waiting," Mack says. "They keep you in suspense until the last minute. Then they tell you it'll be tomorrow for two hours and by the way the opening's a hundred miles up the coast. So you go up there and they put it off till the next day, or the day after. Dad's right. It's too crazy. Besides, it's like that because there's so few herrings left."

"Ach, it's their own fault," says Old Mack. "Greedy fishermen, filling their boats too full and then they sink." He bends over to put down his cup. Harry can see the stiffness in his spine and the way he moves with care.

"Lonny," he says. "Time to go."

Big Mack stuffs the last bite of a cookie into his mouth and drains his cup. "I'll come down with you," he says.

"We'll all go," says Harry.

"You don't need to come out," Old Mack looks at her. "It's raining."

"Okay," Harry speaks the word slowly.

"Dad's going on up to Dagger Inlet," Big Mack explains. "He's got a drop-off to make at the camp there, so he needs to get going."

"Oh, maybe you'll see some swans." Harry sees Lonny's head jerk upwards and his face light up.

"We saw some of those, eh, Uncle?"

320

"There were a few up Silent Inlet when we got that log."

"Thirteen," says Lonny, smiling. "They went into the river."

"Get your shoes on, Grandson."

"Do you think we'll see some today?" Lonny asks Harry, as he bends over to pull on a shoe.

"You never know." Harry slips a couple more cookies into Lonny's pocket. "Well, have a safe trip, you guys. I hope the weather's not too bad on the way back. And don't forget your bread." She picks up the loaf from the table where Old Mack had set it down. "Rustum will escort you."

"Bye Auntie!" Lonny's face is bright, but there's a crease in his brow that has been growing deeper since he arrived.

Harry shuts the door and peers out of the window at them as they disappear down the trail into the greyness.

"Best to let them say their goodbyes in private," she mutters as she rinses out the coffee cups and scoops the cookies off the wire racks into a big round tin. She thinks of Lonny's big dark eyes and wonders how this month will go for him. Big Mack is obviously his guiding star. She wipes the crumbs off the counter, into the sink. The cloth slides over the smooth wood, following the grain and leaving a sheen of dampness behind.

When Mack comes in again, he doesn't say anything, just sits at the kitchen table, watching the window. Eventually, the *North Wind* steams past and Harry can make out Lonny on the back deck, waving.

"He's going to miss you," she says.

Mack doesn't reply. His chin is in his hands now and he is still staring at the rapidly-vanishing boat.

Harry starts to speak, then stops. The boat has disappeared around the corner and only its wake remains, a swirl of turbulence in the gathering waves. She pulls out a chair and sits down, too.

"You're doing a great job with him," she says.

Mack looks up, spell broken.

"Except for this minor fuck-up."

"It's not your fault."

"It's my fault."

"But they love you. They want to be with you. That's called doing it right. I wish I could say the same."

"Don't say that. You don't even know how bad things can be! Your daughter is grown up. She's alive. She's past most of the hurdles. The boys are already up against so much and now they're coming to the hardest part—their teen years, when the world throws everything at them. If they survive—and I mean *survive*—and come out alive and halfway straight, I'll be happy. Until then, they'll be fighting for their lives. And every time I let them down, it'll be a point against them."

Harry braces herself for a run-down of Mack's family problems, but it doesn't come. Instead he says, "I can't kid myself that they won't drink or do drugs. And sometimes it's the bright ones that kill themselves. No real reason. Suicide's like a disease—another epidemic—as if we don't have enough shit to deal with already."

Harry thinks of the waving, smiling boy and the jagged transition into manhood. "How did you make it?" she asks.

"I don't know," he says, finally holding her gaze. "I really don't know. Sometimes I think I keep going because of the boys. Other times I think it's something else. My dad can be pretty quiet, but I know how he feels. He wasn't always there when we were growing up, but he loved us. I know he loved us. It makes a difference."

"So maybe your love will make a difference to your boys," Harry suggests.

"Sam will be okay, I think. He's got his mom's love, too. Lonny's different. He's got that thing about being an orphan, always living on the edge, feeling worthless."

"Can you officially adopt him?"

Mack stops picking at his fingernails. "I hadn't thought of that. They probably wouldn't let me. And anyway, what good is that going to do Lonny if I go to jail? It's being with him that counts."

"Can you talk your dad into bringing them to visit?"

"Maybe. It's unlikely, though. My dad has his own ideas about things. Its hard to change his mind."

Harry laughs. "You can say that again!"

Mack grins for a moment. "He's tough, eh?"

"What a character!"

"He believes in me—you know? Like, I can do something dumb, but I know he thinks I'll do better next time. He hates me drinking, though. I know he does."

"Can you quit drinking?"

"Sure. I quit drinking all the time," Mack grins.

"Oooo-kay," says Harry. "Can you quit starting again?"

"Now that's harder. That depends."

"Depends on what?" Harry asks.

"What happens each day. You have *no* idea how fucked up life gets for me. When shit happens, drink helps."

"Uh-huh," says Harry. "That's what they all say."

"Who's they?" demands Mack.

"Alcoholics." Harry sees a bitter shock of recognition come over Mack's face. Then his expression dulls.

Enough.

BIG MACK

Mack has only been at Harry's for a few hours when a small aluminum boat comes dipping and ploughing through the whitecaps. He can just make out an ancient-looking Johnson outboard motor, but the driver, wearing regulation green rubber raingear, is impossible to identify. Could be anyone, but who would come out here when the weather's bad?

Harry doesn't seem too curious. "Murphy's law," she says. "This place doesn't see people for weeks, then everyone arrives on the same day. D'you want to go and see who that is?"

"Sure." Mack gets up from his chair, glad for the chance to do something. He's beginning to feel this might be a long month. He can't even watch TV.

"Take that stinker with you," Harry points at the dog who is curled in a big messy ball. "He's pretending he hasn't heard anything. He does that, when it's raining out."

"Hey, stinker," Mack says in a quiet voice, as he pulls on his boots, "*chu-quah!*"

Rustum sits up immediately, tripping over his feet as he does so.

"So graceful," Harry says, then adds, "He listens to you."

It's true, the dog does seem to pay attention to Mack. It's not just this dog, though. Mack has a way with dogs. He doesn't have to say very much, but they do what he says. Too bad he doesn't have that way with people.

He hauls on his raincoat and opens the door. "What if they want gas?"

"Call me and I'll come down. Otherwise, invite them up here. I'm putting the kettle on."

Mack pulls down the brim of his red baseball cap and slouches out into the rain. The tree tops are starting to whip around and he wonders how this place survives. He remembers the way the house shook in the storm when he was here at Christmas.

By the time he gets down to the dock, the little riveted boat is tied up. The driver is bailing it out with an old oil container.

"Get a few waves?" Mack asks when he's close enough to be heard.

"Just out there." A hand gestures to the entrance of the bay and a pair of dark eyes shine out from under the hood of the raincoat. It's San, the Japanese Indian. San continues bailing, but as soon as he is finished, he turns back to Mack, smiling.

Mack smiles back. "Long time no see!"

"For sure, for sure!" San agrees as he clambers out of the boat, onto the dock.

"Harry says for you to come up to the house," Mack says, but San is already heading for the ramp. Mack picks up his pace. San's only about five foot four, but quick, like a mink, or a pine marten.

At the house, Mack sees that San is soaked, a dark wet stain seeping over his chest and down his back. One of the waves must have made its way into his raincoat. Amazingly, his hair is fairly dry under the thick wool toque.

San laughs. "My mother's knitting is more waterproof than my raingear!"

"San? Are you soaked?" Harry asks, coming around the corner. "Oh yes, you're drenched! Here, let me get you a towel and some clothes." She bustles off while San peels off his gear.

Mack smiles at Harry's fussing. If she were fussing over him, Mack would have told her not to bother. San's probably going to get wet again on his way out, so there's not much point trying to dry off. A little dampness never hurt anybody. Mack's used to being wet all day.

San moves into the room, rubbing his hands and perching himself on the edge of a wooden chair. "I wanted to talk to you about your woodshed," he says to Harry. "I have a project in mind."

"Uh-huh?"

"What are you up to?" Mack asks.

"Milling." San turns to him. "All the time I've lived out here, I've wanted to build a boat shed. If I had a shed I could do so much. I've got the wood now, I just have to mill it up into beams."

"You'd need some pretty big beams for a building like that," Mack says.

"Sure would."

"How are you going to do that by yourself?"

"Well, I thought I could use Harry's winch and maybe set up some kind of hand crane."

"You don't need to do that. I'm here for a while. I can help you."

"It's okay, I can manage," says San, looking away from Big Mack.

Mack knows that San is proud of his work. He doesn't like to ask for help. Maybe he thinks he would have to pay Mack. He wouldn't! It would be great to have something to do. "I could help you," he says again. "I owe Harry for letting me stay here . . . "

"No, you don't!" Harry interjects. Mack had forgotten she was there until she said that.

"But seriously," Mack continues, "you can repay the favour to Harry after I'm gone." This seems like such a great idea! Mack's conscience is already feeling lighter. He hates feeling he owes people. "I'm here for a month. It's not as if I have anything to do."

"I could pay you," San says, as if he's starting to agree with Mack, now.

"Don't bother," says Mack. "It will be good for me."

"Oh—and it wouldn't be good for me, too?" says San, grinning.

"Sounds like you guys have it all figured out," says Harry, passing out cups of herbal tea. "When do you start?"

"Is it okay for me to use your shed?"

"Of course."

San's grin widens. "Then tomorrow, weather permitting, I'll tow the logs over."

"With that little boat?" Mack asks.

"I've got a slightly bigger one, with a bigger motor."

"What if the weather's like this?"

"We can do it with *Polynesia*," offers Harry.

"No, I can't let you do that." San is firm.

"You put the gas in," says Harry.

For a moment none of them says anything. Mack looks pointedly out of the window at the weather, then over to the woodstove at San's wet clothes.

"Okay, okay, I give in!" says San. "I feel like I'm outnumbered!"

"You are," says Harry. Just then, some kind of knowing look passes between Harry and San. Mack sees it and wonders what it means, but it doesn't matter because things are looking up. His month may turn out to be a little more fun than he expected.

LONNY

As the boat heads up to Dagger Inlet, Lonny sits outside against the cabin, facing the stern. He already feels lonely without Uncle. He's not sure how he's going to survive for a month, or maybe longer. His grandpa doesn't joke around, the way Uncle does, or even Harry. Harry always has a little joke for him. She teases him in a nice way.

Lonny dreads the start of school. He does okay at some of the stuff, but reading is hard and it takes him a long time. That makes him slow at understanding things, so someone always has the answer by the time he understands the question. Not that he would offer to answer, anyway! Those kids that do all the talking are just showing off. They think they're so smart! It's better not to be too smart. Kids get beaten up for that.

Sam and Lonny skip school sometimes, but it's hard to hide for a whole day. In the fall, they hung out in the forest, climbing trees, but then Old Leo saw a Sasquatch near the village and the elders told the kids to play inside. Sam isn't afraid of the Sasquatch but Lonny is. They're big, hairy and smelly, with red eyes and sharp teeth. They make a funny noise that's supposed to give you goosebumps.

Lonny wonders how things will be between himself and Sam when he gets back. They were getting along alright this morning, but if Sam's been hauling firewood all day, he might not be so nice to Lonny when he gets back. Lonny hopes that doesn't happen. He wishes he could stay at Sara's house, too, but no one's suggested that. He doesn't want to invite himself.

Even though they're moving away from the wind, some of the gusts are pretty strong. Lonny shivers in his sweatshirt. Grandpa told him to put on a raincoat, but he didn't feel like it. He doesn't like those things. He doesn't mind being wet. He looks around at the grey water and the whitecaps chasing after the boat. The inlet is getting more and more narrow. The sides of the mountains go straight upwards, like walls, and disappear into the clouds. The boat must be near the camp by now.

He gets up and peers around the side of the boat. There's a dock up ahead. He can just make it out in the grey haze. He wonders if there are any swans, like Harry said there would be. It's hard to tell in this weather. The waves are white and the air is misty grey. He screws up his eyes to see as far as he can, but there are no swans. He goes to the other side of the boat and tries again. Still no swans. Maybe he'll see them on the way back. Lonny's not sure why he likes the swans so much. Maybe it's because they make him think of that great day he spent with Uncle. He kicks at the decking, but there's a hole in the tip of his shoe and he hurts his toe. He turns his eyes back to the dock and watches as they draw closer to it.

HANNAH

"Jack?" Hannah begins when they are half way into their supper. "What do you know about my father?"

Jack slices off a morsel of steak and pops it in his mouth. He chews for a while. "Not much," he says, finally.

"Has Harry ever mentioned him to you?"

"Only in passing."

"Like what?"

"Well, when you turned into a young woman, there, she said something about you having your father's features."

"But I look like Harry, don't I?"

"Have you ever seen a picture of your father?"

"No. Well, yes. There's a picture that Mother has, but he's so far away that it's like looking at a blob of ink."

"What has Harry told you about him?"

"Nothing, until recently. To be honest, I haven't asked. I wasn't curious before."

"Me and Ada noticed that. What makes you interested now, then?"

"Well, for one thing, I never knew he was Métis."

"He was, eh? I guess I never knew that either."

"I never knew how much she loved him, either."

"Oh, she loved him all right." Jack balances a chunk of potato on top of a forkful of steak.

"Really?"

"Lost her heart to him."

Hannah puts down her fork and leans back into her chair. "I can't imagine that. I don't see her as having a heart."

"That's not fair! She's got a big heart!"

"Oh, I don't mean it like that. I mean in the romantic sense. She's so—er—single. So strong in herself. I can't see her accepting someone into her life."

"Well maybe you can't, now, but your mother was quite

sought-after in her day, y'know. That's the reason there's bad blood between her and Cutter. He was sweet on her, eh."

"You're kidding!"

"No, I'm not. He wanted her so bad and she threw him over for this stranger."

"I can't believe this!" Hannah thinks of Cutter's small red face and tight pot belly. She sees him throwing the beer mat across the room. She hears his whispered words: chermothersanoldcow. She could have had him for a father.

"It's funny the way time goes. You forget these things, only see the way they are now. If your mother don't seem to have a romantic side, it's 'cause your father took it, eh? It wasn't long after he left her that she moved out to Fortune Island."

"She's never told me any of this!" Hannah pushes her plate to one side and leans forward, resting her elbows on the table.

"She's probably been waiting for you to ask her." Jack looks at Hannah, raising an eyebrow.

"But how can she have kept it inside for all these years?"

"You tell me, there, Hannah. You've been pretty quiet about your baby's father. None of your letters mentioned him. You still haven't said anything about him. And you were quiet about your, um . . . " Jack gestures at Hannah's belly with his napkin.

"Pregnancy?"

"Mmm."

"That's different, though. That's one of those things that you have to come to terms with in yourself before you can say it out loud. It's overwhelming."

"I'll bet it is."

Hannah pulls her plate back in front of her and starts eating again. "I don't feel too nauseous tonight, so I might as well fill up on calories while I can," she explains.

Jack pushes the potatoes and salad towards her. "Eat," he tells her, with a serious look on his face. "You're pretty thin these days. You never used to be."

"Oh, that was puppy fat," Hannah laughs.

"Whatever it was, you used to look healthier. What made you so thin?"

"Oh," Hannah slices up a potato, "I don't know. Work, I guess. Stress, maybe."

"On account of him! What's his name anyway?"

"Rob. Rob Gilbert. He's an accountant in Whitehorse—or used to be. I don't know how long he'll be able to hold it together."

"Because of drugs?"

"That and alcohol. I was working so many long shifts that I didn't notice what was happening."

Hannah can hardly believe that she's talking about this in a rational way to someone. The words float out gently, as if she is recounting another person's troubles, not her own. In truth, she feels as if the life she led in Whitehorse was a dream—as though she has never left the coast.

Jack's wrinkled old eyes scrutinize her face as she pushes more food onto her fork. He doesn't speak for some time. Finally he blurts out her name, then stops; his mouth opens, but no words come out. Hannah lays down her fork and reaches her hand across the table. She needs to put him out of his misery.

"Jack. I'm okay," she says. "He didn't rape me . . . " she sees Jack shudder at the word. "He *did* hurt me, physically, but I left right after that happened. I didn't give him the chance to do it again. I'm not some battered woman who got stuck in a violent relationship. It's over. It was a mistake. I have no plans to go back."

Jack lets go a trembling sigh. "My God, I was so afraid! You're really okay? You're not just fobbing me off?"

"I'm fine. I promise."

"Well, I'm still mad about it. But thank you for telling me. It's hard to know whether to ask those questions. I don't want to pry."

"But, you're right. Without realising it, I'm being like Mother, not telling anyone anything. I should have told you more. I don't think I was concealing things, so much as I didn't know what to say, or how to say it."

"We never did do the birds and the bees, did we? Or talk about boyfriends . . . ." Jack blushes as he says this and doesn't look her full in the face.

"Well, *you* didn't. Ada did."

"She did, eh? Really? Never told me that."

"She probably thought you didn't need to know. She did a good job, though." Hannah sees Jack's face change at the mention of Ada's name. She realises that she hasn't said much about Ada's absence. How thoughtless of her. "She was a lovely person, Jack. She did so much for me. I think about her a lot, especially when I'm here. Things just aren't the same without her."

Jack looks at Hannah with a sad, small smile on his face. His eyes are dull, no light reflecting in them, just shadows pressing deep into the hollows.

"I miss her now as much as when she first went. I'll never stop missing her," he says.

Hannah is suddenly overcome by the way sadness can be everywhere and nowhere; present, yet invisible. All a person has to do is peel back the layers and there it is—in Mother, in Jack, in Louise, in herself. It makes her feel connected on a different level, as if this thread of sadness binds them together, renders them the same. For someone who has always been a loner, the feeling is strange, but she welcomes it.

She thinks back to all the time she has spent as a nurse, witnessing people's pain. She has always been a distant observer, a robot performing a task. The anguish of others has never touched her before because she has always translated it into physical pain— a treatable symptom—blind to any other type of pain.

Since leaving Whitehorse, Hannah has turned upside down! She pictures the baby inside her as the manifestation of her new upside-down self, created and born in this dawn of understanding. It's almost as if all these years she has been sleep-walking, existing in a void. When the past runs in front of her eyes, she sees everything in black and white.

But all those years of existence must have some value, don't they? she thinks. Or was I just biding my time, waiting to reach the starting line?

Hannah becomes aware of Jack, who is still sitting there in front of her. He has the same small smile, but the sadness seems to have ebbed from him, and now there is only love gentling the creases of his face.

For the second time that night, Hannah reaches her hand across the table.

"This is how I should have felt—how we should have talked—the day I arrived," she says, rubbing her thumb over his palm. "Is it possible to start again, fresh?"

"Don't see why not," Jack replies.

"Then I'd like to."

HARRY

In Harry's dream Hannah is talking to her over the VHF radio. Hannah is trying to explain that something's wrong, but there is too much noise. The squelch dial has been set too high, causing a storm of static. "I can't hear you," Harry is saying, "I can't hear you," louder and louder, as if her shouting will dispel the noise. Eventually there is too much noise, making Harry wince and turn off the radio. As she does so, she sees Hannah striding past the window.

"Hannah!" Harry yells, tapping on the window. "Hannah!" This catches Hannah's attention and she bends over to peer in at her mother. Harry looks at the long legs and the smart city shoes on the slippery boardwalk. "Don't walk too fast," she tells her, "you'll slip on the boards." Hannah smiles and waves and strides away as briskly as before, not paying her any heed. Then, as she disappears into the forest, Harry remembers that something is supposed to be wrong.

"What were you going to tell me?" she moans, knowing that her question is futile, that Hannah is gone again.

Harry wakes from the dream with damp patches of sweat on her chest and the back of her neck. The house is too hot, she thinks. Perhaps she was over zealous with the woodstove now that the warm southeasterly has arrived and the clear, cold Arctic high pressure system is gone.

She sits up and turns sideways on her bed, feet dangling. The wind and rain batter the house in a steady roar that crescendoes, from time to time, into peaks of screaming. Harry can imagine the shorepines twisting and bobbing their heads and arms, unable to escape the onslaught. It amazes her that they can survive the storms at all.

The dream is still with her and she closes her eyes, trying to probe the meaning of it. Some of Harry's dreams are mildly prophetic, especially those that wake her with a pounding heart, like this one has. She wonders what the dream is about. It might reflect her inability to reach Hannah, or it could be that Hannah is truly unwell. She must have received Harry's letter by now and the thought of this makes Harry feel naked, stripped of her most intimate secrets.

Often, Harry's dreams tell the right story about the wrong person, so she'll get her knickers in a twist about, say, Jack, when in fact the dream is meant for San.

Harry flaps the neckline of her flannel nightie hoping that it will dry, but it remains stubbornly limp and moist. She doesn't want to seek out another shirt; any light will be too bright for her night eyes, waking her from the in-between world she is in. She pulls the nightie over her head and reaches her dressing gown down from its hook, a place she knows the feel of by heart. Then she shuffles across the floor to the woodstove and drapes the nightie over the edge of the chair, where it will dry in the heat. It feels strange for her to be nude under her robe. She feels daring, vulnerable, young. Harry has never been one for nudity. She is private by nature. She remembers sharing her body with Hannah's father—how strange it felt! So overwhelming and yet so natural. She remembers him striding around their bedroom without a care for clothes or curious eyes, striding, proud, with his smooth skin and long sinewy limbs.

An only child, Harry had grown up without a brother. Books portraying classical sculpture made up her only knowledge of the male physique. Until she met Alain, that is. He found her innocence amusing and humoured her with funny stories about the functions of his body parts. Harry smiles into the darkness as she sits in the chair, remembering. She had been so shy! After a while the shyness fell away, replaced by a bold yearning for this man she had let into her life. In the early morning she would open her eyes and stare, unblinking, at the jutting cheekbones that shaped his face and told of his heritage. Who is this? she would ask herself. Why is he here?

For the first time in her adult life, Harry had been frightened, uncertain. She felt as if she hardly knew herself. She was only aware of her longing to be with this man, all day, every day, no matter what. She never paused to wonder how he felt about her. She presumed he was caught in the same swirl as she. Surely this wave of emotion was mutual . . . it couldn't exist otherwise, could it?

In the chair next to the woodstove, she brings her feet up, tucking them under her legs to keep warm. That year had been so tumultuous and unhinging. As if she had been catapulted into space, spinning until she was lost in the eerie inky silence, out of reach of anything normal.

Then Alain left—calmly, as if it had been discussed. "I'm going today," he said. "Going home."

"But you are home!" Harry had giggled. "You're here." And he had smiled at her with love and hugged her tightly, repeating his words, "I'm going home," softly into her hair, then released her, picked up his bag and walked away. Just like that. Out the door, down the road, away from Harry as if he was only going to work; as if he would be back later. Despite her confusion Harry understood that he wasn't going to come back. The sick feeling in her stomach told her so. But that night, and every night for the next month, she'd imagined she heard his footstep on the creaky stair, as real as if he were there. She'd lie in bed, not sleeping in case she missed his arrival. Or she would wake from a light doze, listening for further noises, straining her ears but not daring to move, in case she scared him away.

Write to me, Alain, she pleaded silently. Tell me where you are and who you're with . . . . Tell me you're alive; that I didn't imagine you; that I'm not crazy.

It took Harry three months to realise she was pregnant. Her appetite had fled and the feeling of sickness was with her from the moment the door closed behind Alain. Years before, when she first reached puberty, her mother had told her to count the days between her periods, a task that she found tedious. She never

337

fully grasped the significance of the counting. She mentioned her periods in her diary, because it seemed natural. Troublesome days often co-incided with the onset of bleeding and she would remark on this. But in the crater of Alain's leaving, Harry stopped keeping a diary, or turning the pages of the calendar. September was warm and tranquil that year and she scarcely noticed the change in seasons, or the change in her body. When the first big storm arrived, she was surprised by it, astonished to find that winter had arrived. After that she began to pay more attention to herself and her surroundings.

At the end of October, she picked up one of her old diaries and began flipping through it. Occasionally she found references to her menses, but it was only after she put the diary down that it hit her: I haven't bled since he left . . . .

Even then, the implications escaped her. It must be because of the grief, she thought; then, later, maybe I am unwell. I should go for a check up. When young Dr Haswell asked her if, perhaps, she could be pregnant, she'd stared at him in disbelief. Well, no! she'd breathed. And then, after a lightning-strike moment, Well, maybe.

James Haswell, the young, energetic doctor, with his fancy new ways, who all the old-timers complained about. Strange to think of him like that. The description certainly doesn't apply any more. He looks old and tired, as if his batteries are wearing out. They must be, by now! Serving this community for all those years, with never a break. People's secrets must be enough to weigh him down, let alone their ailments. Harry had been so grateful to James, the way he treated her when she was pregnant. He never made her feel guilty or ashamed, the way some people in town did. He never chastized her for being a "loose woman." Nor did he romanticize child rearing. He warned her to be prepared for exhaustion, pain, depression and loneliness. But he tempered that by saying that she might be carried through those things by an underlying feeling of wonder and elation.

For someone who was not a parent, he was surprisingly accurate.

Harry rubs her hands down her bony thighs, to her knees, remembering the way her baby rested on her lap, as she gazed at the tiny face, and felt the grip of love. But just as James had predicted, those moments of euphoria had been matched by moments of desperation. They still are.

Harry sighs and reaches for her nightie. She pulls it onto her lap and rubs her thumbs over the cloth, feeling for dampness. The flannel is warm and soft, with only a trace of moisture. She puts the nightie on and climbs back into bed as another tremendous gust screams around the windows. The storm must be reaching its climax, she thinks, as she pulls the blankets around her. She thinks of *Polynesia*, heaving and yawing on her lines down at the dock. She thinks of Big Mack, lying silently in the loft. She thinks of Hannah, striding past the window of her dream. Come back to me, she whispers into the silence. Come back.

BIG MACK

Despite the howling wind and shuddering cabin, Mack sleeps heavily, the best rest he's had in ages.

"It's the island," says Harry, as she hands him a mug of coffee. "It does that to all my visitors."

Harry looks older this morning. Her grey hair looks straggly and her eyes don't have any smiles in them, the way they usually do. Mack wonders again how old she is.

"High tide was at six this morning, so I think the storm is on its way out," she tells him. "But if it doesn't improve much in the next while, we won't be going over to San's."

Mack peers through the misty windows, trying to make out the water, but he can't see a thing. "It's calming down already," he says.

Harry smiles, but doesn't comment. They drink their coffee in silence and he notices how relaxed he feels. Yesterday he was all nerves, anxious about how things would turn out. Today he has a happy glow inside, as if his body is telling him that everything will be okay. Maybe it's because he slept so well.

"I eat oatmeal for breakfast," Harry says, breaking into his thoughts. "Do you like that, or would you prefer some toast?"

Mack laughs quietly. "Mush!" he says. "We call it mush. We have it sometimes."

"So will you have some?"

"Oh, sure. It's good."

"It's the best! Stays with you all day."

"I know. Well, nothing stays with me all day. There's too much of me."

"You're not kidding," Harry says, in a nice way.

"It's my curse. Clothes don't fit me. People are either scared of me or they laugh at me. I'm hungry a lot. I break things all the time, without even noticing."

"Thanks for the warning!" The smiles are back in her eyes again, despite the tired look.

"No, seriously, my shoulders catch on things and knock them over. I spend my life bending down, so I don't hit my head, and trying to suck my shoulders in so that I don't break things. Like I said, it's a curse."

"Ah, but you have no idea what a blessing your size is going to be for me. Imagine what it's like when everything is always just out of your reach . . . ."

"Then you get a ladder."

"Which is a pain in the arse!"

Mack looks at Harry's small figure, bending over the stove. She turns and looks back at him with a wide grin. "Today I am going to sit down and make a list of things that overly-tall people can do around here. That would be you, of course. The list will start with cleaning the eaves troughs. You'll be able to reach your hand up and empty all the leaves out, just like that!" She twirls the mush spoon above her head and a blob of oatmeal splashes down onto her shoulder. They both burst out laughing.

"Serves me right," she says, dabbing at her shoulder. "I shouldn't tease."

Mack rolls his eyes. "Believe me, I'm used to it."

"I believe you." Then she brings his bowl over and he sees that she's stuck a serving spoon in it, not a regular spoon. As if he really is a giant.

"Jeez, you!" he growls in mock anger, flinging the spoon into the sink. "No respect!" He gets up and strides over to the cutlery drawer and picks out a dessert spoon. If Harry were younger, he would gently swat the back of her head with his spoon as he walked by, but he's aware of her age and her frailty, so he resists. They sit facing each other, Harry grinning, smug, like a cat.

"No respect," he says again, then digs his spoon into the mush.

"Aging has got to have some rewards; that's what I say."

Mack doesn't answer. His mouth is full of the most delicious warmth. He's never tasted oatmeal like this before. He savours the feel of it until it slides down his throat and the warmth spreads to his belly.

"What did you put in this?" he asks.

"Oh, a bit of this, a bit of that."

"No seriously. I've never eaten mush like this. I'm not sure if I can even call it mush. It's too good for that."

"It is good, isn't it?"

"I'm going to watch you make it next time."

"Well, you'll have to, if you want to learn how, because I don't have a recipe."

"I wouldn't be able to learn from a recipe anyway. I like to see things being done. I have a good memory that way."

"Everyone has their own way of learning. I like to read about things first, then see them being done. That way I understand the theory and I'm prepared for what I will be seeing."

"Not me. My dad always showed me everything when I was little. 'Pay attention, son,' he would say. Then, one day he would make me do it. No warning or anything. I got real good at watching him and practicing in my head."

"Oh well, maybe you'll be able to pick up some tricks from San. He's a talented shipwright."

"He fixed a plank on the *North Wind* once. My brother and I came out to get him when the plank popped, because it was the middle of fishing season. I watched him fix it that time, but I wasn't really paying attention. The fish were biting and we were in a hurry to get back on the water."

"He's usually quick."

"He was." Mack scrapes the bottom of his bowl with his spoon and looks up at Harry.

"There's more on the stove," she says. "Finish it."

"We're only going to be Alaska milling, though," he says as he empties the pot. "I've done that before. It won't be new to me."

"Well, what always amazes me about San is the way he works. He's so efficient. He's got all his systems down pat. There's always an order and he always follows it."

"Huh. I guess I'll find that out."

"Oh, you will, if this wind ever dies down."

Mack takes his bowl over to the window and stands there, eating, staring at the roiling water, half-expecting to see San's little aluminum boat tossing through the chaos as it had the day before. Instead, rain pelts the windows, obscuring everything. Mack sighs and sits back down at the table with his bowl.

LONNY

School is the pits and Lonny wonders why he bothered coming, except that it's stormy today and he would have been underfoot at home. He sits at a desk while the teacher goes on about history. To liven things up he tears little pieces of paper off his book and rolls them into balls. Then he flicks them across the room when Mr Hassles isn't looking. That isn't the teacher's real name. His real name is Mr Casçals, with a funny little squiggle under the C. You can tell he likes this squiggle. He always adds it when he writes his name on the board.

Sam is sitting a few desks away, next to Matilda Brown. Lonny wonders if he can get a ball of paper into Sam's ear without the teacher seeing. He makes a bigger ball than last time, pressing it hard to make it heavy.

Last night Lonny got back home around dark. Sam was already at his mom's house. Lonny could see that most of the wood was up from the beach and under a big blue tarp. The wind was playing with the corners of the tarp, flapping them around like crazy bird wings.

This morning Sam was late for the bus—without Lonny to wake him up, he probably slept in—so he sat near the front of the bus. Lonny caught up to him at school, but the bell rang right away and then it was Mr. Hassles and history: how Canada became one big place instead of lots of little ones. Lonny likes the idea of the little places better. His grandpa knows the name of all the beaches and points and rocks and reefs, but sometimes he doesn't know the name of a whole island. "It doesn't need a name," he says. "It's got all the names it needs."

Lonny rolls the ball of paper under his forefinger, back and forth along the desk. It's not getting round, the way he wants it to. He wonders if he should spit on it. Uncle Silas likes to spit on things. He spits when he's talking to people outside, or when he's just walking along—big, pale gobs that go a long way. Lonny's tried to spit that far, but he's not so good at it. Maybe he should ask Uncle Silas to teach him. He could've asked Uncle Silas last night, because he came over to Grandpa's house. He even talked to Lonny for a little while, which he doesn't usually do.

Uncle Silas and Grandpa were talking about Boy. Grandpa said that Lila phoned and she seemed hopeful that Boy might wake up. Silas said that he had to speak to a lawyer about the drunk driver. Actually, he said "that asshole driver" and Grandpa told him to mind his language. Silas didn't stay long after that. He went off to Sara's house, in the storm, without a raincoat. Lonny watched him through the window.

Lonny concentrates hard on his paper bullet. It's getting better now. He rolls it with the heel of his hand, round and round on the desk. Too bad he doesn't have a ruler to flick it with. It might not reach Sam.

"Lonny!" says the teacher's voice.

Lonny looks up and sees that the whole class is staring at him. "I asked you a question," Mr Hassles says in a slow, hard voice.

Lonny puts one hand over the other and stares at his desk. He doesn't look up, even when Mr Hassles tells him to.

"Lonny, if you aren't learning anything in class, you'll have to learn after class."

Oh no. Detention. But that's not fair. He was only daydreaming!

"I know what you were talking about," he says.

"Oh, you do?"

Lonny looks at the teacher and nods.

"So what question did I ask you?"

Lonny hangs his head again. That's not fair. He was going to say that they were talking about Canada. He pulls his hands off the desk and grips the little paper ball tightly, without looking up.

"Lonny," the teacher says in a tired way. "I know this is the first day of school, but you need to pay attention. And you need to look at me when I'm talking to you!"

But it's comfortable like this, not looking up. Lonny can't see all those other eyes when his head is down.

"LONNY!" yells Mr Hassles.

Lonny's head jerks up and he looks straight at the teacher.

"I'll talk to you after class," Mr Hassles tells him. "And in the meantime, pay attention!"

When he turns back to the board, Lonny looks over at Sam. Sam is grinning as if Lonny just did something good. Lonny grins back and almost gets the giggles. He rolls the paper ball onto the ball of his thumb and flicks it with his middle finger, right at Sam. Then he turns to face the board and tries to concentrate on the teacher's words. The lesson drags on and on, as the rain pelts down outside and the world disappears behind the foggy windows. Lonny stares at Mr Hassles and tries not to think about all the days of school that lie ahead.

HANNAH

Hannah is sitting at her dressing table, holding a hank of hair in her left hand and a brush in her right. Mother's letter is in front of her and she reads the words slowly as she brushes her split ends over and over. The disagreement about Big Mack has faded into the recesses of Hannah's mind. There is so much else they should be talking about.

Talking! That doesn't sound like Harry and Hannah.

Hannah looks up as the rain rattles the windows. Jack didn't go to the Seagull Café this morning. It was too wet. She wonders if the library is open. She wants to see if they have any books about the Métis. The library is pretty small, though, just a few shelves and only open when the volunteers can make it. She can probably order something in, but it might take a while. She's not sure if she can wait.

She drops the brush and picks up the letter. Alain Savard. Harry had told her her father's name early on, when she was still tiny. Then it was just a name, but now it is significant. Métis. A lot of them have French names, don't they?

Don't *we*?

Part of Hannah trembles at the thought of having Native blood. In general, it has been her way to stick with the white people; people her own age, people she resembles. She's never questioned that choice before. Only now does she think of it, as she stares in the mirror at her features, wondering what stories they have to tell—stories they have never told her before.

What if I have some kind of Métis status? What if I have sisters and brothers, uncles and aunts, grandparents? Who are they all? Where do they live?

Hannah's interest in her extended family matches her newfound curiosity about her father. Her maternal grandmother, Ruth, died around the time Hannah was born. Her maternal grandfather died before that. There have never been siblings, or uncles or aunts, or big family get-togethers. There has never been a sense of family. When she lived with Jack and Ada, she had a tiny taste of what "family" could feel like, but then she moved away and Ada died.

Does Mother even know where he lives? She said he was a prairie boy.

If Alain left Harry, it's likely that they never corresponded. She would have been too proud to chase him down. Hannah vaguely remembers her mother mentioning that Alain was out there, somewhere in the universe. "Unreachable" was the word she'd used. Was she being dramatic? Or had she tried and failed to contact him about his baby daughter.

In Hannah's room at Jack's there is a picture of herself and Harry. Ada took the photo and insisted that it be hung on the wall. It's not a good photo, by any means, but it shows how much Harry has changed in the last ten years. Roll the clock back another ten years and what would she have looked like then? Hannah tries to imagine her mother's face without the lines slicing down her cheeks and the crease in her forehead. Even when Harry is laughing and joking, she has a cast of seriousness about her, a proud stony centre. It's worked well for Harry. Perhaps she cultivated it to ward off slurs about being an unmarried mother. Whatever the reason, people always take her seriously. The years have shown her to be hardworking and self reliant. But for Hannah, coming up against that stone core has always resulted in battle. She cannot get beyond it and nothing can flow out of it. Except this letter.

Is this a white flag?

Hannah runs her palm over the aged yellow paper. What would you have written when this paper was first new, Mother?

Communication. It doesn't have to happen face-to-face. It can take place on paper, too. This letter has filled Hannah with questions. She needs to ask Harry to fill in the gaps. She needs to write her own letter.

Hannah tries to picture the letter she would write, but all she sees is an empty page with an army of words jostling around the white edges, none of them in order, none of them making it onto the page. The idea seems too complicated. What if she asks only one question at a time? Her eyes fall to the little yellow envelope and she imagines another envelope, her own this time, drifting with the tide, washing up on the shores of Deep Bay. And Harry opening up her vault of secrets, taking one out and sending it back. A slow sweet time of learning and understanding, unfettered by quarrels.

What shall I ask her? Will she answer me?

Hannah's mind races with all the thoughts and questions she has been incubating over the last day. She has so many questions of herself, too; like, why has it taken so long to reach this point? Mostly, she wants to know who she is—the recipe from which she was made. That should be the question, then: who am I? She gets up and rummages in her purse for her notebook. It's the only writing paper she has, but it will do. Especially if she only has one question to ask. She unscrews the lid of the pen, sits down again and writes the date on the top right hand corner of the page.

She is about to write the question out, when suddenly it seems stupid. She is starting at the end, not the beginning. She should ask more about her father. Who is he? She pauses, staring into space. That doesn't seem right, either. She lifts the pen again.

Dear Mother,
Thank you for your letter. There is so much about you that I want to know. Who are you really?

She hesitates before signing the note. The traditional phrases seem awkward and inappropriate, but what else can she say?

Your daughter,
Hannah

She doesn't write your loving daughter. The word *love* is too singular and simplistic. Surely all her emotions and reactions can't be gathered up in the skirts of this one word? She doesn't *love* Harry the way she *loves* Jack. With Harry there are questions, fights, wounds. And then there is the electric sea of feeling that washes over her occasionally when she sees Harry, or thinks about her.

Hannah puts down the notepad and considers the words as they sit on the paper. Absent-mindedly, she raises a hand to her right breast which is swollen and sore, a low-grade pain and one she is getting accustomed to. Only then does it occur to her that she has revealed nothing of herself in this letter. Harry has no idea that she is going to be a grandmother. Is that fair? Hannah ponders. But how can she tell Harry that in a letter, when, with a bit of effort she could tell her in person?

We wouldn't be able to reach that point. Something would get in the way.

Realistically, the pair are doomed to repeat their patterns. If she tries to have this discussion with Harry, Love will shake out her skirts, throwing a mess of emotions in the air, scattering even their best intentions. And communication will fail.

No, Harry has sent a letter. She has chosen her method. By writing back to ask about Harry's life Hannah is revealing her interest, reciprocating. The pregnancy can wait. It won't be visible for the next six weeks or so, anyway. There's no hurry. Jack knows about it and he has promised to keep it secret. Harry can find out later, after she and Hannah have started on their twisty path to truth. For now, the only hurdle is finding someone who can deliver this letter to Fortune Island. She'll ask Jack. He's usually up on all the gossip. It's unlikely that anyone will be going on a stormy day like today, but maybe tomorrow there will be a fisherman heading out, who could be persuaded to take a little detour from his route.

HARRY

By lunchtime the rain has eased and the wind has swung around to the southwest, dappling the sky with swatches of light and dark. Gusts still slap the water, but they come in squalls now, more manageable than the unrelenting southeasterly. If we take *Polynesia* around the north side of the island we should be able to sneak into Swan Bay without too much difficulty, thinks Harry.

She lays out slices of bread and covers them with cheese. Then she presses them together and places them in the gleaming cast-iron frying pan that Mack has reached down from its hook on the beam above her head. She has decided that, unless it pleases her, she is not going to make a lot of effort with the cooking. Mack's appetite is so great that she could use up all her precious spices and condiments without him really noticing. Soup and bread and fish and potatoes. These things will feed her and her guest quite adequately. People have existed on these simple staples for centuries.

Harry's hoping that Mack might feel inclined to catch another fish, or some crabs. She has an old crab trap in the wood shed, but it's a commercial trap, much too heavy for her to heave around. She can use the davit on her boat to winch the trap up from the depths, but it's too much work to justify feeding one person. Picking oysters, or digging clams is more manageable for her.

After breakfast, Mack had taken up the gauntlet and gone outside to clean the eaves, despite the wind and the rain.

"You'll get soaked," Harry protested.

"That's okay," he shrugged.

"Why don't you wait until the wind dies down?" she said.

"Because I don't feel like it."

As Harry presses down on the sandwiches, she thinks about what Mack told her last night. He said that Boy could have been hit by a cargo van and dumped in the alley later. He told her this casually, as if it was of no importance.

351

"Have you told the lawyer this?" she asked.

"My brother told me he would."

"But you don't know if he has?"

A shrug.

"Well, we need to write this down. The police need to know about this. There may have been other reports about that van."

"The police don't want to look for a van. They want me!" Mack's fingers curl into his fists, then release; curl, then release. "You think LeClerk will tiptoe out among the white people saying, 'Excuse me, I don't want to bother anybody, but did one of you run down a Native on New Year's?' Yeah, right!"

"But what if there was a report? What if someone did complain about a driver in a van like that? They can't ignore it then."

"No, but they can cover it up. Don't you get it? I saw what they did to my brother, Nelson. They made his life even more miserable than it already was. They just want to get someone. The easier it is for them, the better. The bigger the punishment, the happier they are."

Harry can understand Mack's distrust of the RCMP, but in this case she's afraid it will work against him. A person can't just produce this kind of information at the last minute. It doesn't look good. There will be questions about the validity of it.

She flips over one of the sandwiches and wonders if she should write to the lawyer about it. Or call her. She can go through the marine radio operator to use the VHF as a radio-telephone. That way she can actually converse with Frances about this. Harry has a sneaking feeling that Mack's brother won't have made the call.

She turns the remaining sandwiches and goes to the door to call Mack in for lunch. In her mind's eye she sees Old Mack's face and his angry response to her offer of bail. He took that as interfering, taking control away from his family. Maybe she was, but now she's involved, so much so that she should be allowed some say in what happens. Mack's with her, isn't he? He's not in jail.

She hears the echoing screech of the aluminum ladder as Mack takes it down. But it's his life, she thinks as she moves back over to the stove. Not his family's life, not mine. She decides against going behind his back. She'll bring up the subject again tonight over dinner.

By the time they leave the dock, the water has calmed down. There's still some wind and rain, but they should be able to tow logs without too much difficulty. Harry is hoping that they'll be invited for tea with San and Clarissa first. She wants Mack to see how happy they are, living off the land and the sea, removed—but not divorced—from the problems of society.

Mack is out on deck, after complaining about the cramped quarters inside *Polynesia*. What surprises her is the way he seems immune to the cold or the wet. "It's bred into me," he said when she commented on it. "You think it didn't rain here when my ancestors were alive?"

She looks through the glass at the tree-clad slopes and the mist that lingers around the cedar spires, threading in and out of the forest like wool. Then she looks at the deep grooves carved into the hills by the rain. There is no doubt that rain has shaped this coast. It's only natural that it would have shaped the inhabitants too.

She seldom goes this direction with *Polynesia*, so it always takes her breath away when she sees the granite gateway into Silent Inlet. It's so grand, this landform, and so forbidding. She can stare at those stark cliffs for hours, but she rarely wants to go beyond them, into the heart of the inlet. She's only been up there half a dozen times in all the years she's lived here and each time she has felt an unbearable weight of loneliness. If ghosts exist, then Silent Inlet is crowded with them. How else can she explain the feeling of both absence and presence that overwhelms her when she is there? She wonders if San and Clarissa ever go there. She would be interested to know if they feel the same way.

Harry decides to break her resolution about smoking on the

boat. She has resisted cigarettes often today, mostly because of the stormy weather, but now she is out on the water and the rain has eased. She makes her way to the cabin door and pokes her head through. Mack is sitting on a crate, with Rustum's head on his lap.

"What a suck!' she says, looking at the dog, then back to Mack, who is grinning. "D'you feel like driving for a while? I need a smoke."

He gets up. "As long as I can do it from here," he says nodding at the outdoor steering station.

"No throttle," she says, "but the wheel works."

"What happened to the throttle?"

"The cable snapped, I think. I haven't got around to investigating."

"I'll have a look for you sometime, if you want."

"Mmm," says Harry, preoccupied with her tobacco.

"You're real *quishnuk*," says Mack, smiling at her.

"I smoke a lot?"

"Haa-ah."

"I know. Hannah says I have to stop."

"I wish my dad would stop. He's starting to frighten me."

"What do you mean?"

"Well, he's got no appetite and no skin on his bones. He drinks about two pots of coffee a day and goes through about a pack of smokes. I don't say anything to him, but I know it's not healthy."

"I noticed that he can swig back the coffee," says Harry, exhaling.

"Well, so can I," says Mack. "But at least I eat. I can't get him interested in food. Sometimes I think he's going to disappear in front of my eyes."

"People do eat less as they age."

"Yeah, but not like this. I'm afraid he's sick—cancer or something."

"Will he go to the doctor?"

354

"Not unless it's really bad."

"Have you asked him?"

"I can't."

"Why not?"

"Because it's like saying out loud that he could die. I can't think about him dying. He's the one who's always been there for me."

"I know what you mean. When my father died I thought the world had come to an end. It was the loneliest feeling. But he died suddenly. My mother had some kind of degenerative illness and she died slowly. I tiptoed around it, pretending she was okay. I didn't go and see her when I should have. I've always regretted it. There's so much I should have told her."

Mack peers ahead, looking for objects in the water. "I can't say anything to my dad. He's quiet enough as it is. He doesn't like to talk about his feelings."

"But it's okay for you to tell him how you feel."

"I don't think he'd like that."

"Well, how will you know, unless you try it? I always wish I'd told my mother how important she was to me. But I skirted around things, making oblique references to this and that, all because I couldn't bring myself to talk about her in the past tense. I couldn't say 'you've been wonderful,' because that would mean that it was all over—the end was in sight. So I said nothing and every year it eats away a little more of me."

"Huh," says Mack.

"I remember having a row with Hannah, when she was about fifteen. She kept saying, 'You know what I mean; you know what I'm going through,' but I didn't have a clue. How could I? She never told me anything when she was that age, and I couldn't read her mind. I still can't. Later, I realised that I did the same thing to my mother. I used to presume she knew how I felt about her and so I didn't tell her. But she wasn't a mind reader, either. I should have spelled it out for her, just once, so that it was clear and we both knew."

"Oh, I think my dad knows how I feel."

"You think so, but do you know?"

"In my family we do a lot without using words."

"I've seen that. And that's wonderful. I'm just telling you that saying you love him only takes about two seconds of your life and it makes you feel a whole lot better. You can practise on Rustum if you like. He's a good guinea pig, aren't you, boy?"

"Huh." Mack is looking ahead with a small smile on his face.

Harry finishes her smoke and rubs her hands. "Well, I'm going back in," she says. "It's too blustery out here. My fingers are going numb."

As she re-enters the warm cabin, she feels Big Mack's weight shift out on deck. He's given up his position at the wheel and gone to sit back down on the crate. If she looks out the door in a minute or two, Harry is sure that she'll see Rustum's head back in his lap.

She hums a little tune as she takes the wheel again.

BIG MACK

Landing at Swan Bay is tricky. The wind is blowing across the bay, pushing the boat away from the dock. Harry backs off and takes another run at it, while Big Mack readies the lines, so that he can jump off quickly and pull them in. By the time the boat nears the dock again, the kids have swarmed out along the slippery logs and are grabbing at the boat.

Mack waits to give Harry a hand getting onto the log dock. Together, they pick their way to shore, the kids jostling along after them.

"What a crew!" Mack says as San meets them on the beach.

San smiles and rolls his eyes. Harry is behind them, producing cookies, one at a time. The kids are guessing where she has them.

"In your sleeve!"

"In your hat!"

"In your socks!"

"Yuuuukkk!"

"Not in her socks, silly! That's gross!"

San leads Mack up the beach to the house. "Clarissa will be happy to see you," he says.

Mack looks down to see the smallest boy, grinning up at him.

"Can I go on your shoulders?" the boy asks.

"Which one are you?"

"I'm Bear."

"I'm Mack. I'm your cousin."

"Harry says you're Big Mack."

Mack bends down and picks Bear up, throwing him into the air, before settling him on his shoulders. Bear giggles and sings, throwing his body from side to side as they move up the path.

Mack hasn't seen Clarissa for many years, but she hasn't changed much.

"Hey, there, cuz!" she says. "I see you got yourself an admirer."

"Is that what this is?" Mack swivels his head to look up at his burden. "I thought it was a sack of potatoes."

"Gee, Big Mack! I'm not potatoes!" shouts Bear and they all burst out laughing.

Mack admires the work that has gone into San's house. Everything has been built by hand, using wood from the beaches. The place is neat and tidy.

Mack puts Bear down so that he can fit through the doorway.

"We can't stay long," says Harry as Clarissa pours coffee. "The daylight hours are so short."

"Getting longer, though," says Mack from the cushions where Bear has crawled onto his lap. Mack tries to imagine what his life would have been like if he had grown up the way this boy is being raised. He gives up. It means imagining a mother and he doesn't know how to do that.

"I anchored the logs out in the bay," says San, pointing out the window. "They shouldn't take you long to tow."

"What do you want us to do with them when we get them to Harry's place?" asks Mack.

"Oh, just tie them near the woodshed. We can winch them up as we need them."

"I'll see if I can get one up at high tide tonight."

"You don't need to do that."

"I know." Mack turns his attention back to Bear, tickling him under his arms, thinking: he *is* like a little bear cub. He looks up and sees Sonny, standing near the door. This must be all the excitement these kids get. Life could be dull out here after a while. Mack already feels antsy at Harry's. He needs to find things to fill the time, otherwise he'll go crazy. He doesn't even have any pot to smoke, which was dumb of him. He should have got Silas to get him some. Then at least he'd be able to relax when he feels bored.

"We should go." Harry's voice cuts into his thoughts.

"I'll go out in the little boat and pass the line to you," says San.

"Can I come with you, Dad?" asks Sonny.

San nods and they all get up.

"Thanks for the coffee," Mack tells Clarissa.

"Anytime. It was good to see you. We don't see enough people out here."

"I can tell," says Mack, looking down at Bear, who is still clinging onto his leg.

"Oh, that's different. He likes you. He doesn't do that to everyone, you know. He's usually kinda shy."

Mack raises his eyebrows and bends to pull on his boots.

"I have to go now," he tells Bear, while he's down low. Bear nods and sticks a finger in his mouth. He moves over and grabs his mother's hand, staring at Mack as he leaves.

"I'll be over after breakfast tomorrow," says San.

"Alright," says Mack. "I'll be there." He steps onto the slippery log float and picks his way carefully out to the boat. Before long they are underway, chugging slowly back the way they came, the skein of logs following obediently.

Mack watches as the figures on the beach become smaller and fade into the grey afternoon. Something about this visit has touched him, but he can't say why. There are times he wishes he could put names to his feelings. Then he would understand himself better. Maybe he's just sad. Sad that it's possible to live in harmony as long as you separate yourself from the rest of the world. It shouldn't be that way. People should be able to live like that all together.

LONNY

From the school bus, Lonny sees Hannah walking along the street, her hair bouncing in a ponytail down her back. He turns to Sam who is in the seat behind him, but Sam is joking with Greg Sellier about something. He hasn't seen Hannah and Lonny decides not to bother pointing her out.

Lonny gets a funny feeling looking at Hannah. She's the one who saved Boy, but she's also the one that said Uncle beat up Boy. He's heard them talking about it. Maybe it's Lonny's fault. He should never have asked her to go looking for Boy in the first place. But then Boy might have died. It's weird that she's Harry's daughter and Harry is so nice. Hannah was real quiet over Christmas. She mostly talked to the grown-ups, as if Lonny and Sam weren't there.

Hannah must be staying with Eagle Jack, because she wasn't at Fortune Island when Lonny went there with Uncle and Grandpa. Big Mack said that she's a nurse so maybe she has a job in Hanson Bay.

The school bus picks up speed as it turns onto the main road to North Hanson. It's a dirt road, so it's bumpy, but the bus can still go pretty fast. The roadside trees start to blur and Lonny gets a case of the stares, his eyes fixed on the window. He's thinking about his last trip on the *North Wind*. He asked Uncle lots of questions about boats and maps and knots. Uncle taught him a bowline, which he still knows how to tie. He's practised every night with the neck tie that Grandpa keeps for church. He can almost do it with his eyes closed now, the way Uncle showed him. He hasn't told Grandpa that he has borrowed his tie, but he'll put it back before Sunday.

That trip, Lonny really paid attention to the route they took. He's been out in the sound before, but he wanted to know the way to Fortune Island. Maybe one day he could row there in the canoe to visit Uncle. It's a long way, but he could probably do it.

Then maybe he'd be allowed to stay the night and go back the next day. That would be fun. Lonny wonders if he should ask Sam to go with him. But if Sam doesn't want to go, he might try to talk Lonny out of it. Sam is stronger than Lonny and faster, but he's kind of lazy. He might not want to go all that way, especially if he can stay at his mother's house and play Nintendo.

Lonny stops staring out the window and turns back to Sam.

"What are you doing this afternoon?"

"Dunno. "

"Can I come over?"

"Sure."

"We could go in the canoe sometime."

"It's full of water."

"So, we can bail it."

"We're always bailing that thing. It's no fun anymore. Anyway, my mom says we're not allowed to go in it again until it has life jackets."

Lonny can't believe what he's hearing. Sam has always been so scornful of lifejackets.

"But she knows we can swim," he says.

"She says that nobody can swim when they have hyp-a-dermia."

"What's that?"

"It's when you're too cold and then you die."

"Oh," says Lonny.

The bus turns into the parking space and stops. Everyone piles out, the bigger kids pushing the little ones aside. Lonny waits until Sam gets up, then he follows him. The high school bus isn't here yet and he's glad about that. The older boys are pretty rough and teasing, especially Rufus Brown, who yells at Lonny all the time. Hey Lonesome! he'll shout, holding up a cigarette. Let's see you smoke like a man! He says it because one time Lonny and Sam tried smoking cigarettes and Lonny got sick. He couldn't believe how much it made him cough! Sam coughed a bit, but he didn't throw up like Lonny. Lonny is dreading the time when he has to be on the high school bus with Rufus. Maybe he'll have to practice smoking before then.

When Sam gets off the bus, Greg Sellier is waiting for him.

"Do you want to come to my house?" he asks Sam.

"Okay," says Sam. Then he turns around and looks at Lonny. "I'm going to Greg's. Are you coming?"

Lonny looks at Greg. He's never been good friends with him. They say Hi to each other, but that's about it.

"It's okay," he says. "You go." Then he turns and trudges along the path to his grandpa's house. A stripy brown dog comes growling out at him from the Roberts' house, nasty little teeth snapping together in the front of its mouth. Lonny picks up a big rock and heaves it at the dog. There is a thud as it hits the dog's ribs, then a high-pitched yelping noise as the dog runs away, its tail between its legs. Lonny thinks about hitting it again, but it's too far away now. He picks up a rock anyway and pelts it into a telephone pole.

"Fuckin' dog!" he yells, just like he's heard other people do.

HANNAH

It's after hours at the clinic. Hannah, Louise and Dr Haswell are sitting in the waiting room, hashing out a work plan for Hannah.

"Well, since Hannah's pregnant, I'd like all the time off I can get before she's unable to work," says Louise.

"I can probably work up until the last couple of weeks," says Hannah.

"Tell me that again after you've tried this place," says Louise. "It's hard work being a nurse and a receptionist *and* getting called in after hours. But you can be the judge of that. The first week will be training. Following me around, learning where everything is, wrestling with the computer, that sort of stuff. Then I'll take a back seat and play catch-up with the filing. You can take over, but I'll be right there in case you need me."

"Sounds like you gals have got it all figured out," says James. "How about a glass of sherry?"

Louise makes a face. "Too sweet for me."

"I can't," says Hannah.

"Oh, cha!" James grumbles. "What a boring crew." He smiles, then disappears into his office.

"He keeps the sherry in with all the medical supplies," Louise tells Hannah.

Hannah smiles at his retreating back. The meeting has assured her that everything will be okay. In coming back to Hanson Bay, Hannah Farre has fallen on her feet.

After leaving the clinic, she heads for the library. She climbs the porch steps and pushes open the heavy door . The gloomy, brown-carpeted hallway is the same. It even smells the same, a damp, old-house smell. She hangs up her coat and scarf and wanders across the room to the reference section, glancing around for the librarian, Brian Phillips. He's not at the desk, so he's probably organizing the shelves. She pulls out the *Canadian Encyclopaedia*, Volume M. Then she hunts around until she comes across *A Precise History of Canada*.

Hannah sits at the long wooden table, still scarred with pencil pokings and many years of graffiti. An oppressive greyness seeps in from the skylight, reinforced by a pale fluorescent glare. She runs her hands across the red leather cover of the encyclopaedia. M is for Métis. She pauses, both hands resting on the book, eyes lost in a blind gaze.

She is thinking again about her letter to Harry. How can she send it? Jack was delighted to phone up all his friends for her, but no boats are going to Fortune Island. Chartering one would be expensive. If she is going to do that, she might as well go to Fortune Island herself. Can she do that, though? She pictures Harry and Big Mack sitting around the wood stove, talking and laughing, happy in each other's company. Would that be too much for her to cope with? She'd felt a few twinges of jealousy at Christmas. This would be worse.

No, that's not the way it has to be. She could wait a few more days for a boat to deliver her letter. If there's still no boat by then, she will have to reconsider. She thinks again of the words in her letter. She wants her mother to read them. She wants to understand. And be understood. She feels the leather book under her palms, suddenly realising that being here is futile. These books will not tell her what she wants to know.

She wants to know about a person, not necessarily a people. She wants to know the history of her mother and her father, their lives together and apart. She is taken by the idea that her existence was born of love, real love, at least on her mother's part. Her father's feelings lie across the mountains, out of reach. This frustrates her. She wants to march into his home, wherever that is. She wants to see his eyes light up in recognition: I have a daughter! She wants the story to come tumbling out, too long choked back, now lined with tears.

She knows it won't be like this. She is reliant on Harry, who will give her snippets of information, hiding the important details the way she used to hide the chocolate chips behind the raisins, so that Hannah wouldn't see them. Hannah ate them anyway, but she was discreet, never giving herself away. This time she will not be so shy. This time she will poke and pry using the techniques she has learned to extract a medical history from a patient: what drugs they have taken, how much alcohol they have drunk. She is better armed now. Harry will have to tell her everything.

Or will she? Harry has always been stubborn and she has had years of practice at keeping quiet. Perhaps she has hidden the details for so long that she has forgotten them.

At least she will know which province Alain came from. Once Hannah has that information she can begin the lengthy process of tracking him down. She can ask the telephone operators in that province; they would help . . . . She stops. Her mind is spiralling ahead, losing the facts. It's all very well to imagine a warm new father, but the reality could be vastly different. He could be dead. Or he could be a toothless old tramp, lying in a tarpaper shack, yelling obscenities at the world. Hannah has lived for many years without a father. She may be better off this way. Instead of wasting her dreams, she should start slowly, peeling back the layers of her mother's life, bit by bit. The letter is a good start. Now, Harry just has to receive it . . . .

HARRY

It rains that night, a steady drenching rain, the wettest rain in the world, Harry likes to call it. It comes from the south and swaddles the coast in gloom. It is relentless, an intense drumming all around them.

"Maybe it will stop by tomorrow," says Big Mack moving a pawn on the chessboard.

"You can't do that," Harry tells him.

"I can't do *anything* in this game," Mack grumbles. He has agreed to learn about chess, but his heart isn't in it.

"You'll get it soon," she says. "I wonder how Boy is doing?"

"I keep thinking about him, wondering what it's like to be unconscious for so long."

"I hope he's having good dreams. That would make it a pleasure. Why don't you put that pawn here?"

Mack moves the chess piece with his thumb and middle finger. "What if he's having nightmares? What if he's dreaming about being hit by a van and left in an alley to die?"

"Don't think like that. Boy needs all the positive thoughts he can get."

"I can't help it. I see his face all the time, with a pile of tubes coming out of him, my sister on one side and a police officer on the other. It bugs me that I keep seeing this cop."

"It's natural. Your position changes quite a lot if Boy dies."

Mack cringes visibly. "Everyone is forgetting that this is my nephew!" he says. "I love him. It would be punishment enough if he dies."

"Punishment for what?"

"For being such a fucked-up failure."

"Don't think like that, either."

"It's true. I can't even help myself."

"What makes you think you can't change?"

"I don't know."

Harry watches Mack intently. He's brooding, face in hands, absolutely still. Finally he looks up.

"It's all the shit." He waves his hand, vaguely. "It's there. It'll never go away."

"Like what?"

"The things my family has been through, you wouldn't believe, the things we've done to one another, too, and yet we stick together because we have to. Family is all we've got."

Harry sees the heaviness pulling at Mack's features, pulling him into the deep.

"I remember your mother," she says.

Mack's eyes suddenly focus.

"What do you remember?"

"She was a live wire, this tiny electric force, whirling around, doing, doing, doing. You kids were like the tail of the comet, always running to keep up with her."

"And in the end we couldn't keep up."

"I don't know what happened in the end. Does you father ever talk about it?"

"Not a word."

"How about your mother's family?"

"I don't know them. They're Heiltsuk, not from here. They never offered to take any of us when she disappeared. In my head, I wrote them off as a bad lot. They showed no interest in us kids, their own nephews! Someone said that they blamed my father for being a drinker and beating Mom up, but he never did that."

"Don't you think she would have contacted them?"

"I don't know. One of the rumours I heard was that she ran away to California with a guy who sold drugs. If she's in California, there's no point."

"But she wasn't into drugs, was she?"

"My sister might know. I was too young to remember much about her, except her smile."

"You should take a little trip to Bella Bella. Go see her family."

367

"You don't understand! They didn't want anything to do with us!"

"If your mother was too ashamed to come back to your father, where else would she have gone? She's a human being. Family are like food—eventually you get hungry enough and you go back to them."

"But *we* were her kids! *We* were her family! She never contacted us."

"Well, let's say, hypothetically, that you got tempted away by a woman—don't scoff, it could happen—and you went to visit her in Nanaimo. That's not very far away from here. You think to yourself, well, it's just for the weekend. But something happens, you go crazy for this woman, she's all you can think about. You lose perspective and think that if you leave her, even for a minute, she'll lose interest in you. So you stay. You know that your wife is looking after your kids and anyway, you'll be back soon. You miss them, but all you can think about is this woman."

Harry pauses to consider the chessboard. She moves, taking one of Mack's pawns.

"But there's a big problem in this situation," she continues. "You're married. You've just deceived your wife. You're ashamed of yourself, too ashamed to face the music. Going home means confronting her. It means fights, humiliation, tears. It's easier to stay away, to live this crazy attraction which feels so good—better than anything you've ever experienced before. And the longer you live it, the further away your family seems, until they become a guilty blur in the back of your mind. And the longer you stay away, the harder it will be to go back. Your children will resent you, your wife will despise you and nobody—nobody—will understand you."

"And *you* would stay away from *your* daughter? I don't think so. I know I wouldn't do that to my boys."

"I'm not saying you would. I'm creating a scenario. I've seen it happen. There was only one child involved, but it happened."

368

Harry gives up on chess. She is looking at Mack's face. "Tell me about the day she didn't come home."

Mack shakes his head and looks down. His hands are wedged between his thighs and he is very still. He starts to speak, but his voice cracks, so he clears his throat and tries again.

"I've never told anyone before. It's hard. I thought she was lost. We looked for her everywhere. I could never understand why my dad didn't look for her. He just sat in his chair, drinking."

The cabin is peaceful, just the thrum of straight-down rain and the quiet whoosh of air passing through the woodstove. A kerosene lamp burns on either side of the chessboard, throwing orange light onto the black and white squares and out into the winter darkness. Harry stays motionless in her chair. Mack looks up at her, through the pillars of light. "I used to think she was dead and it was my fault because I didn't look for her hard enough. I asked the old man if she was dead and he said, 'She's dead to me.' But that's all he said. He knows something about where she went, I'm positive he does. Another time when I mentioned her, he yelled at me. Not long after that they took us away from him. I didn't see him again until I was a teenager."

"So in fact you lost both your parents."

"I lost my whole family, because none of us kids got placed in homes together. I had no idea where my sister or brothers were, if they were even alive. I never saw anyone from home. When my mother disappeared, love stopped for all of us, right then. Some of us have found it again. For me, it's in Sam and Lonny."

"And in your father?" Harry watches Mack roll a chess piece in his hand.

"And in him," Mack agrees. "He always loved us, but the drinking made him crazy."

"And the loss of his wife."

"I guess. I often wonder what he goes through when he thinks about that. He says his religion helps him, but it wouldn't help me. When I think of Catholics, I think of the residential school

369

and my brother Nelson. How many other innocent children had their lives wrecked in the name of the Lord?" Mack's voice is hard. Harry cannot see the chess piece.

"Have you tried to forgive your mother?"

Mack looks up sharply, eyes narrowed. "Forgive her?"

Harry nods.

"How can I forgive her? Everything bad that happened to my family is because of her! She ruined us! I can't forgive that."

"But she gave birth to you. She loved you. What if it wasn't her fault? You don't actually know what happened to her. She could have been killed. Until you talk to her family in Bella Bella, you don't know."

"They would have contacted us if they knew she was dead. Even the cops would have called us."

"You're probably right," Harry says. "I'm just saying that there are always circumstances that we don't know about. People have their reasons and until we know what those are, we can't judge them."

"Well, don't judge me for being angry at her, because you don't know what I've been through!"

"And I will never know, because I am not you. Just as you will never know your mother. But you loved her, you remember her smile. She loved you. She was a good person. Good people don't turn bad overnight. If you're brave, you'll try to find her."

"Are you telling me I don't have the balls to do it?"

"I'm saying that it will take courage. Whether you choose to do it is up to you. Start by asking your father again."

"I'll start by going to bed!" Mack pushes back his chair and rises, chucking the chess piece onto the board where it falls on its side, rolling back and forth in an arc.

"I can't let you do that," says Harry, in a stern voice.

"What?" Mack turns to stare at her.

"Going to bed angry is bad for your health. Run a bath. Soak until you feel better. *Then* come back and tell me you're going to bed."

Mack continues to stare at Harry, his dark eyes flickering in the lamplight. Harry stares right back at him. It feels as if they will stay like this forever, neither one of them looking away. Then, without warning, her right cheek twitches and she giggles. The sound ripples through the air, disturbing the deadlock, breaking Mack's gaze. His mouth opens and a guttural half-laugh forms in his throat. His eyebrows are near his hairline. He shakes his head, turns and heads for the door. "Whatever you say, cap'n," he mutters as he reaches for his rain gear.

Harry doesn't reply, but she stretches her grin across the room, making him smile as he picks up the flashlight and opens the door.

BIG MACK

Mack lies in bed listening to the rain. It's the kind of rain that fills small boats quickly, sinking them where they're tied. It's a known fact that bilge pumps always fail the moment you learn to trust them. Just like people. Mack tries not to think about how many people he has failed. The image of Boy is still there, in his head—Lila on one side, the cop on the other, both of them staring at Mack. No smiles. The tubes climb out of Boy's face like an octopus, smothering his features.

Mack turns on his side and tries to escape the sensation of the rafters pressing in on his face. The loft is roomy enough, but right now the ceiling seems too close, making Mack feel claustrophobic. Perhaps it is the rain, so loud it sounds as if it will come through, onto his face. He half expects to feel a few drops, the way the condensation falls onto his face when he sleeps in the *North Wind*. He wonders where the boat is now and whether Silas is still sleeping there at night. He hasn't figured out why Silas was hiding in the first place. Maybe he didn't want the whole village gossiping about his new girlfriend.

The bath has done wonders for Mack. He made it really hot, filling the bathhouse with steam. Harry's tub is an old one, full length, with lion's feet. He can actually lie in it! The water coming out of the tap was scalding, from passing through a coil in the woodstove. It's been a long time since Mack has soaked like that. His skin pulses with warmth and smoothness and his limbs feel limp, sagging into the cotton sheet.

She was right, he thinks, seeing Harry's saucy old grin behind his closed eyes. This is a better way to go to bed. It's funny how things can change. He was mad at her and it felt good. He wanted to hang onto the feeling—stay mad at her—but when she giggled it all fell apart and he felt silly. He could see, then, that she wasn't trying to insult him. She was just speaking her mind, which is what he's always liked about her. Perhaps she doesn't understand how much it hurts him to talk of his mother. She can't see through his body, to his heart and the way it screams and throbs whenever he relives his childhood nightmares. She can't feel the way his body gasps and tightens. Normally, if Mack had reached this stage of feeling, he would have gone to the bar, or if the bar was closed, he would have rolled a joint. Then gone to the bar the next day. Instead, he had a bath. The difference is that the feelings are still there, but they don't hurt so much. His mother's smile is a beautiful, slightly sad image that flits through his head without causing an upheaval. He even reaches for it, to see if he can get it, but it travels back into his mind and although he can feel it, it won't return.

Maybe Harry is right about trying to reach his mother, or forgive her. She might not have left them on purpose. Anything could have happened to her. She could be dead. He's often wondered about that. How would he feel if all this time she were dead? Would it be easier than finding her alive in Bella Bella, with a new crew of kids? I didn't write, 'cos I thought you'd be mad at me for leaving . . . .

Mack turns onto his back again, tugging the pillow out from under his head and laying it over his face to muffle the sound of the rain. He could torment himself for weeks with thoughts like this. Maybe Harry is right. If he knew what actually happened to his mother, he wouldn't have to waste his emotions on a bunch of what-ifs. But he *would* have to be prepared for the worst. Maybe that's why he has to forgive her before he looks for her, so that, whatever has happens, he can cope. From a faraway corner of his brain, he feels his mother's smile creeping out at him again. It beams at him for a few seconds and then vanishes. Mack feels his own mouth lift at the corners, returning the smile. He smiles harder as a sense of joy and love run into him.

He is on the *North Wind* with his mother. She is on the back deck running the gear, while his father is inside. Mack is waving to her and shouting, "Mom, Mom, I'm here, I'm here," but she doesn't respond. She moves from one side of the boat to the other and Mack is struck by how beautiful she is, how graceful, how strong, how small. The sight of her fills him with longing. He sees her face exactly, even the small mole on her left cheek. He feels the adrenaline pump through him as he reaches out to her, determined not to lose her this time. But his father comes through the door and calls him inside and she doesn't look up, or respond to Old Mack, either. And Mack obeys his father, stepping down into the boat, leaving her behind, wondering why he is doing this, why he is behaving so stupidly. And when his father closes the door, Mack's face is wet with tears and the ache in his chest hurts him so sweetly and he mourns her loss all over again, but this time, instead of anger, there is the pleasure of having seen her, the thrill of knowing that she was once his mother and he loved her.

LONNY

The phone rings early in the morning. It's dark, but it must be morning because Grandpa is already awake and he answers it. Lonny sits up in bed. When the phone rings late at night it is usually bad news. Early morning is the same. He jumps up and switches on the light, then pulls a sweater over his head. He opens the door and sneaks out into the front room. Grandpa is holding the phone with care, nodding and listening. Lonny gets a nasty feeling about this call. Then, all of a sudden, his grandpa is chuckling and saying "*Choo!*" He puts the phone down and smiles to himself. ·

"Grandpa?" Lonny asks.

"He's awake," Old Mack says, blinking. "Boy's eyes are open!"

Lonny wants to jump up and down, but he feels shy in front of Grandpa.

"Can Uncle come home now?" he asks.

Old Mack gets out of his chair and walks across the room. Lonny is surprised to see that his eyes are wet. He is even more surprised when Grandpa hugs him, a big happy hug. It feels kind-of nice and Lonny squeezes back, but not too hard, because Grandpa's ribs stick out.

"Not yet," Grandpa says into Lonny's hair. "Boy's awake, but he's not speaking. It may take him a while to get better, if he's going to get better than this."

"Was that Auntie Lila?"

"Mmm."

"Is she happy now?"

Grandpa smiles and lets go of Lonny. "She sounds pretty happy."

Lonny wonders if Auntie Lila was crying. He's seen her cry and laugh at the same time, wailing and giggling in turns, big tears plopping onto her cheeks, and her nose running. He can picture her on the phone to Grandpa, pulling wads of tissues out of a box on her lap, pressing them up under her fogged-up glasses and blowing her nose.

Grandpa shuffles into the kitchen and pulls the tin of coffee out. Lonny looks at the kitchen clock: 6:30. It's not that early. He normally gets up around seven anyway, but it's dark and he has nothing to do. He goes back to his room and climbs into bed. He's too excited to go to sleep, but his bed is warm and he doesn't mind lying in the dark, thinking.

His main thought is that someone has to tell Uncle about Boy. That means a boat ride. And if there's going to be a boat ride, then Lonny wants to be there, even if he's supposed to be in school. He wonders if he could hide in the boat, then jump out at Fortune Island when it would be too late to send him back. He wouldn't mind getting in trouble for that. It would be worth it! It would be fun, too. Maybe a little scary, but definitely better than the school bus and school. Lonny is dreading school more each day. It wasn't so bad when he used to sit next to Sam in class and on the bus, but lately Sam has been hanging out with other boys and it makes Lonny feel lonely. Everyone in Lonny's family seems to have left him. His dad is in jail, his mother is dead, Lila is in Victoria, Uncle is on Fortune Island and Sam is with Sara. That leaves Grandpa, Raylene and Uncle Silas. Uncle Silas has been coming over in the evenings, chatting to Grandpa and sometimes even saying a few words to Lonny. No hugs, though. Uncle Silas never touches Lonny, just stares at him with a funny look on his face. Raylene doesn't touch Lonny either, but that's because she's always carrying the baby, or cooking, or doing laundry and when her arms aren't full of stuff, then she's smoking a cigarette. And when she's not doing any of those things then she's in her room sleeping or watching her little TV with the fuzzy picture in black and white.

Since Uncle went away Lonny's life has gone haywire. Lonny hopes that Boy will be completely well soon and Uncle can come back. Then everything will get better. Even Raylene is sadder without Uncle around. He teases her and makes her laugh, if you can call it a laugh. It's more like a growl, but that's just Raylene.

Lonny gets out of bed and switches on the light to look for some socks. Then he remembers that he forgot to put all the dirty ones in the laundry, so he'll have to wear the same ones as yesterday. He finds them in a ball on the floor, still wet from the walk home. He listens to the rain pouring down outside. There's no point wearing dry socks, they're going to get wet again today anyway. He shakes them out and starts to pull them on.

HANNAH

Hannah takes her cup of herbal tea into the front room. Outside, the rain is driving down. There is no wind, just a steady pour, saturating the land, overflowing the deep grassy ditch across the road. She adds some wood to the stove and leaves the door ajar, standing nearby to soak up the rush of heat. The weather has warmed up, but all those raindrops make the morning seem cold. And dreary. Hannah remembers getting out of bed on mornings like this, dreading the walk to school. She had an umbrella, which helped, but she would always arrive drenched and spend the day shivering in her damp clothes. Ada tried so hard to make her wear gumboots, but no self-respecting teenager would be caught dead wearing those!

The rain has dampened her elation of the previous few days. Hannah no longer feels excited about her job, curious about her mother and father, or nervous about her pregnancy. Instead, she feels sick and tired. She could sit on the couch all day, wrapped in a blanket, watching television. The idea is tempting, but the professional in her objects. There's so much to do! She'll be working full time soon, so the fridge needs to be well stocked and she doesn't trust Jack to pick up the right supplies. Her clothes need washing and ironing. She must phone the storage depot in Whitehorse and ask them to send the rest of her belongings. The list goes on rattling through her head, forming itself into a timetable for the day: first the telephone, then groceries, then lunch. Laundry can be done in the afternoon. She sits down and blows onto the hot liquid in her cup. But for now, everything can wait until she's had her tea.

As she feels the warmth spreading through her body, Hannah tries to imagine her child. Instead of a fetus, she pictures a miniature baby cuddled in her womb, sleeping away the days until its birth, the warmth of the tea just a passing dream. Her hands rest on her abdomen, feeling for clues but finding nothing. Her pregnancy is still at such a mysterious stage. Until she feels movement, she won't be convinced that anything is there.

When the time comes, she drags herself up off the couch with a sigh. She dresses for the day in the usual jeans and sweater, but no amount of brushing can stop her hair from hanging in limp strands. Her mood is echoed in her appearance, it seems. Even her face looks pale and puffy, lacking animation. She pulls her hair into a French braid, hiding it away behind her, but this exposes her face and she would like to hide that today, too. She needs a hat and scarf and waterproofs. Then she will blend in with everyone else, a dark green shape in the rain. Maybe the rain is a good thing, after all.

At the kitchen table she makes a list of groceries, then she looks up the number of the place in Whitehorse and makes the call. The shipping will be expensive, but it's her only option. She has no plans to return to Whitehorse right now—or ever. She might even end up selling some of her possessions to help pay for the shipping. Jack's house is full and her own furniture is unexceptional. It's the bedding she wants—her down pillows and comforter—and her clothes.

Even as she ties her running shoes, Hannah knows that she must buy some waterproof boots and start to wear them. She's an adult now and she's chosen to live in the rainforest. Some things are unavoidable.

She pulls on her raincoat and digs around under the coatrack for her old umbrella. It's still there, with its black, fake-leather handle and its blue and white sections wrapped on a diagonal, fixed in place with a rusty old snap. Outside, as she opens the umbrella, she sees the orange spots, stained by the rusty metal joints. She hopes there are no holes and the umbrella will get her through today's deluge. She steps carefully along the path, dodging the deepest sections of water. There are no puddles today—every surface is awash, even the road, which is now receiving the overflow from the ditches. By the time Hannah reaches the end of the block, her shoes are soaked through and her feet are squelching. She ignores the noise and keeps on walking. She won't be the only wet person today.

She manages to get through the Co-op without attracting attention. There are only a couple of other shoppers, nobody she recognizes. The cashier looks familiar, but Hannah can't remember her name. She can tell that the woman recognizes her, too, but neither of them says anything, they just stare at each other, their curiosity partially concealed.

The clinic will be the perfect place for Hannah to meet old friends and acquaintances. Their names will be written next to the time of their appointments, which will prompt her memory. She will be able to chat for a few minutes, but then her work will claim her and she'll escape the telling of details. Word will get out that she's back and soon any interest there might be in her will fade. But there will always be interest in this town. Too little happens here, so people's personal lives are thrown on stage for all to examine. Her baby will be one such item. It—she?—can't be zipped into Hannah's mind and hidden forever. Pregnancy falls into a category all its own and there's nothing that Hannah can do about it.

As she steps out into the rain again, Hannah puts down her bags and opens the umbrella. Just then, a car door slams and a tall, dark-haired man runs across the road away from her, shrugging his neck into his coat as if this will keep him dry. Hannah freezes, her bags still on the ground at her feet. She stares at the man, gasps out loud and pulls the umbrella down over her head. Slowly she raises an edge of the umbrella and peers back across the street. Through the rain she can't see much, but she is sure that the man is Rob. It looks as if he is heading for the post office. Could he be looking for her? Asking around?

"Excuse me," says a voice behind her and she jumps, gasping again, and turns to see a woman with a grocery cart, trying to exit the building. Hannah tugs her bags out of the way, dragging them on the concrete sidewalk and ripping the bottom of one of them. She does not speak to the woman, or give her a second glance. Her eyes are glued to the disappearing figure on the other side of the street. A bottle of olive oil tumbles out of the plastic bag. She bends down to pick the bottle up, not caring if it is broken, her fingers and hands shaking so that it takes several attempts to right it. The man disappears behind the post office door. She picks up her bags, clutches them to her chest and runs back into the store, dropping the umbrella in her hurry to get through the door. A trip to the post office won't take long. He'll be coming back to his car soon.

"Can I leave these here for a minute?" she asks the cashier as she dumps them beside the door, just out of the way.

The woman stares at her and Hannah doesn't wait for a reply, just backs out of the door, retrieving her umbrella and dashing down the street. She pauses alongside the man's car, bends down and peers through the window, looking over her shoulder every so often to make sure she hasn't been seen. It's no good, the windows are fogged up from all the rain. She can't see a thing. She is tempted to open the door, but what if there is an alarm? It's unlikely, here in Hanson Bay, but Rob had an alarm for his car in Whitehorse. This is a different car. Maybe it's a rental. She scurries back to check the license plate. No sticker. It's a BC plate, too; not the Yukon.

Hannah straightens up and whisks down the street. Everywhere is open. There is no way she can hide herself and still be able to see the man's face. She scurries to the corner, looks left and right, then stops and comes back. She starts to cross the road, then turns back, looking over her shoulder. She still can't see the man. He could be anywhere. She is panting—shallow, uneven breaths that seem to feed the violent shaking of her hands. She goes back down to the corner of the road, turning right, until her body is almost concealed. Deep breath. Breathe out slowly. An elderly man is limping along the sidewalk towards her, probably Mr Mendez. Hannah pulls the umbrella over her face and turns her back, giving the impression that she is going to cross the road. The last thing she needs is to rehash the events of New Year's Eve, here in the rain, just feet away from her ex-boyfriend. Imagine if Mr Mendez said her name out loud! Rob would hear it and come to investigate. Then she would have to run, but it would be too late, she wouldn't be able to escape.

As Mr Mendez moves raggedly up the street Hannah cranes her neck to peek around the corner. At first, she can see nothing beyond Mr Mendez. Then suddenly, she sees the man again, coming down the other side of the street. She retreats and presses herself against the building, her body shuddering, thankful for the solid wall. She snatches another quick look and sees that he is continuing on down the street, past his car, as if he has another errand. His hair is flattened down by the rain and his face is impossible to see. If he continues on his path he will reach the corner, look to the right and see Hannah.

She sprints down the road, away from the corner, the umbrella twisting and waving in front of her. She runs to an old brown pick-up truck, parked in such a way that she can hide behind it and still see out. She sees the man reach the corner and glance from side to side before crossing over. No matter how hard she stares she cannot make out his features. But Rob would dress like that. He would duck his head into his coat like that. He would come looking for her, like that . . . .

As he disappears from view, Hannah turns. She runs slowly down the street, cursing the cumbersome umbrella, but not willing to relinquish the protection it offers. She runs until the ache in her side becomes an insistent stabbing, then she slows her pace, trying to catch her breath. From time to time, she looks behind her, but no one is following. Her sobs come in strangled clusters that she stops by pressing a hand to her mouth. There are no cars and no people on the road when she crosses over to Jack's house. For a moment she fights with the garden gate, pushing and shaking until it opens. Then she runs up the front stairs, throws herself through the door, slams it shut and bolts it. Outside, the umbrella lies where it has fallen, on its side. Beyond the porch the rain makes a dull screen of water, pouring patiently out of the sky.

HARRY

San's arrival in the downpour doesn't surprise Harry. He likes to be considered reliable. It is a point of pride for him. Still, she shakes her head as she sees the little boat materialize out of the greyness. The day is so monotonous and dark that she welcomes the flash of faded red cutting through the water, trailed by the crisp white wake.

Big Mack is already down at the boatshed fiddling with one of the logs. He got it partway into the shed the night before, but he wants to have it completely in place by the time San arrives. It's been a long time since the island has seen so much human activity. Perhaps it's been waiting for that. Perhaps Harry has guarded it too jealously all her life, blanketing a seed of community that could have been growing.

She puts the last of the breakfast dishes into the drying rack and pulls the plug in the sink. She turns and wipes the counters and the table, then notices a stain on the wood from Mack's coffee cup. She frowns and rubs at the mark, trying to eradicate it. It resists and she gives up, rinsing the rag and drying her hands on a towel.

She wants to go and see what San and Mack are doing. Her curiosity niggles at her, but she decides to wait. A friendship will flourish more easily if they are left alone. At lunchtime she will go down and offer them soup and see what they have done. For now, on this grey day, while no one is about, she is going to have a bath. She wanted to have one last night, but she offered it to Mack instead. It was a good idea. He was in much better spirits after that. He might want one again tonight, so Harry will take hers now.

She turns on the kitchen tap and lets it run for a few seconds. The water is scalding and she is careful not to burn her fingers as she fills her hotwater bottle. This is part of the bathing ritual. She places the hotwater bottle in the folds of her towel. The air in the bath house is cool, but a warm towel can make up for that. There is little point in having a woodstove there, when it's used for such short periods of time. It's only in the middle of winter that she misses it anyway. The hot towel is the next best thing.

She exchanges her clothes for her robe and her shoes for her slippers, but as she heads for the door, she grabs her woollen toque from the hook and tucks it under her arm, just in case. The covered way protects her from the rain and she is still dry when she pushes open the heavy cedar door, with its smooth driftwood handle. It surprises her to find that the bath is clean. She doesn't expect men to think of that. But then, her experience of men is limited and out of date; due for revision.

She turns on the taps and watches the steam billow out into the room like a sudden summer fog. The windows quickly become opaque and the rain vanishes, replaced by whiteness. She leans across the bath and opens the round window that she calls her breathing hole. Then she plumps up the cushion that rests on a section of tree trunk and sits down to wait.

This bath house is her luxury. It is the first thing she has done for herself that has gone beyond mere survival. Everything else on the island has a purpose related to necessity, but the bath is for pleasure. She used to bathe in a tin washtub in front of the fireplace. In summer she would shower under the garden hose after it had been warmed by the sun. That kind of bathing may have got her clean, but it was never enjoyable. Not like this!

Harry reaches in and swirls the water with her hand. It's almost right, just a little hotter. She turns off the cold tap and stands up to undress. Then she puts one foot into the bath and feels the familiar rush of pleasure. She puts the other foot in and sits on the side of the bath, waiting for the last dose of hot water to render the temperature almost scalding. Moments later, she sinks into the tub, sighing out loud as her shoulders go under and the water rushes around her neck and the base of her skull. This is the pinnacle of her day—this sudden immersion in water, when heat probes its glowing fingers into the marrow of her bones and whisks away the pain and stiffness of age. She stretches out and relaxes, breathing in the cool fresh air from the window, which flows down onto her face and stirs the steam into swirls and eddies.

Even Hannah approved of this bath house when she first arrived at Christmas. Harry massages her swollen knuckles in the hot water. She has been trying to imagine Hannah's face, her reaction on reading the letter. Did she shout for joy? Scream in anger? Laugh? Cry? As with most matters relating to her daughter, Harry has no idea. On one level she feels as if she knows Hannah so well, but on another she feels lost, completely at sea and unable to read the signs. She is also uncertain of her own motives. In a way, she wanted to show Hannah that her prejudices are unfounded; that she shares in Big Mack's heritage, whatever that means.

But there was more to it than that. In her old age, Harry's longing for Alain has not diminished. She wonders about him constantly, dreams about him, pictures him coming to her, full of love, saying that he should never have left, that his life was never the same again. Sometimes she feels his embrace in her sleep and the depth of the feeling shocks her. She has never told anyone about this. Who is there to tell? At the time of writing the letter, it seemed good that Hannah should be the one to know. It is a fragile thread of truth, one of many that could be spun into a cord, something more substantial.

So now she is waiting. She is used to waiting. She bides her time, leaving her deepest thoughts closeted. She busies herself around the house, stacking firewood, sweeping, dusting, gardening. She listens to the radio and reads books. And all that time, her questions sit on the shelf until she deems it safe to consider them. Only in the last few years have her thoughts of Alain taken on this life of their own. It annoys Harry. She is losing control. But it is a bittersweet annoyance. The memory of love is so palpable. From time to time she finds herself longing to be held—just held—by someone who loves her. Whom she loves in return. It would be such a relief! She can feel her body longing to relax and receive this embrace. She wonders how long she can continue to dream this way, without any hope of her dreams being realised.

For a moment, when Hannah returned to Fortune Island, Harry thought she had found the embrace she was looking for. Aside from a couple of dim old photos, Hannah is the only proof that Alain ever existed. Perhaps there is enough of Alain in Hannah that the magic still works. She can feel him in her love for their daughter. It frustrates Harry that Hannah is so close, yet so unreachable. The recent disagreement between the two of them rises up, black and crooked, like the blasted fir tree on the far side of the bay. Harry cannot ignore it. It sways into her thoughts constantly, especially when she is talking to Big Mack. Resolving it is critical, especially now that Harry has learned about the New Year's Eve cargo van. The thought of this new injustice drives her wild. She finds it amazing that Big Mack has not been stomping around the house, thumping his fist and demanding the driver be caught. His outlook is fatalistic, a strange mixture of hope and resignation.

Harry turns her face to the breathing hole, inhaling welcome cool air. The question is: how much should one trust in fate? Mack is so disillusioned about life that he seems to feel any action he takes will make things worse; that improvement will only happen if events are left to take their course. He has come here, to Fortune Island, because it was the only place he could go that wasn't jail. Despite herself, Harry is enjoying sharing her home, but she can't shake the feeling that this is just an interlude for him. Whatever he does while he is here will have little bearing on his life after he leaves.

It is impossible to predict the events in life that will have the greatest, most lasting effects. Harry's father's death had been terrible—a young girl's first experience of grief. But it did not affect the pattern of her life, the way her mother's remarriage did. Mack is full of grief at his mother's disappearance, but his life has been more affected by his family's silence. His mother vanished for him because he could not mention her name—because none of them mentioned her name, remembered her ways, searched for her. In protecting themselves, the members of his family have done the greatest damage. This irony makes Harry consider her own choices. Would Hannah have been shaped differently if Harry had persisted in remembering Alain out loud? In choosing independence, did Harry miss something? Did she shut out potential love? She watches the steam curl in the draught, then leans forwards and reaches for the wash cloth. Some things she will never know.

BIG MACK

The saw is loud in the woodshed, despite the wide-open hangar doors. San and Mack wear ear muffs as they wield the heavy saw with the milling bar attached. The milling has been going smoothly and they have made several beams in a variety of dimensions. San brought with him the plans for his boat shed, which he showed Mack right away, explaining the requirements. The shed will be large, with skylights and room for a loft. The design is neatly drawn in pencil, with straight, sharp lines and legible notes. Every piece of wood is listed on the back and San has been ticking them off whenever a new beam is made.

Mack can't imagine San doing all this by himself. Some of the beams are hard for *him* to lift and he is twice San's size. It is definitely easier with two people. Right now, though, San is working and Mack is standing by the open doors watching the rain. He bailed San's little boat once this morning and it already looks low in the water again. He's thankful that he left his canoe upside down on the dock at home. It wouldn't sink to the bottom, just fill to the gunwales and wallow at the dock, awash, but it's a nuisance when boats get like that.

There is no wind in the harbour, yet the water moves in a quick grey dance as the raindrops pelt down, then bounce back up. In fact, it's impossible to make out individual raindrops, just lines of rain, like the tassles on a dancer's shawl. Despite the noise, it is good to be in the shelter of the shed. There are a few drips here and there, the kind that you only find when it rains like this. Other than that, there's a welcome through-breeze and there's plenty of room to move around. It's not as though they're bumping into each other all the time.

"This shed is the basis for my design," San had said that morning. "I need something bigger, but I like the proportions of this."

Mack had nodded, looking around at the neat rows of wood,

remembering the time he spent here over Christmas. It reminded him of Hannah, an instant of closeness that almost immediately floated away, out of reach. He wishes again that he could remember what happened on the night Boy died. He wishes they could find the asshole that framed him. Was it really Kevin McKay? Another memory of that night drifts back to him. He can't quite place it but he knows that Kevin was there.

"You look far away," comes San's voice.

Mack turns around in surprise. The saw has stopped, but he didn't notice, he was so busy thinking. "Yeah," he says, taking another look at the rain.

"Why are you staying here?" San asks.

Mack knew the question would come eventually. So far he has given no reasons for his visit. He'd like to tell San, but the more he talks about it, the more upset he gets.

"It's a long story," he sighs.

San nods and follows Mack's gaze back out to the bay. "Harry said you were here on a conditional release from jail."

"So she told you," Mack says.

"Some. And now I'm asking you."

"Why?"

"Well, we're going to be working together for a while," San shrugs. "Before I moved out here, I lived in the city. I lived an okay life, but I saw things that I didn't like. Injustice. I tried to help. I spent a lot of my time on the streets, but I couldn't stop what was happening. In the end I gave up. That's why I moved out here. I was sick of people."

"Well, I'm sick of people, alright. You know what it's like at home. Everyone looking at me, ready to believe the worst. Then there's the fuckin' racists in town, coasting along with their easy lives, thinking they can get away with murder at someone else's expense. But it's not that, either. What gets me is what this is doing to my family. My sister's in the city, sitting by a hospital bed. She could be there for months. She's probably frightened that they're going to ask her to pull the plug on her son, Boy, the most defenseless kid for miles around. I would never hurt him. How could I hurt somebody whose face splits in half with happiness every time he looks at you?"

San nods and says nothing.

"Then there's my dad and my own boys. I've let them down. I didn't mean to, but I can't change a thing. They still love me, but they trusted me to be there for them. And now I'm not. I could see the difference right away when I got home from the jail. It's all falling apart and I'm standing here, looking at the rain, helping you mill lumber as if none of that exists. I feel like I'm in another world. It's unreal. I go along fine for hours at a time, then all of a sudden it hits me and I wonder what the hell I'm doing."

San listens and nods. There's a look in his eyes that says he understands. After a while he speaks. "You can't torment yourself about the people who need you. Acknowledge your mistakes, fix them if you can, but keep them in one part of your mind. Don't let them take over. Keep the rest of your mind clear. If you can't think straight, you're no use to anyone, least of all yourself."

San's quiet voice blends with the rain. Mack is still standing in the doorway, staring out. It's funny how he's spent his life fixing things for other people, but not for himself. San's words float around in his head, resonating. In between the words he sees the beginning of a way. A way to make it through life, even if he ends up in jail. Possibilities spill into his mind, crowding his thoughts. He turns to San, smiles and thanks him. Then he walks over to one end of the newly-cut beam and moves it out of the way.

LONNY

When the rain stops, it's as if someone has flipped a switch. It goes from being a downpour to nothing, in seconds flat. The sky clears and the wind starts to pick up from the west. Lonny pulls on his shoes and coat and goes outside. There's only a couple of daylight hours left and he wants to find Uncle Silas. Grandpa has said that he won't take the boat up to Fortune Island because Boy is not completely well yet. Lonny doesn't think that's fair. Uncle is worried about Boy. And Grandpa isn't being nice enough to go and tell him that Boy's awake. "It costs money to go up there, you know," Grandpa said. "Do I look like I have lots of money? We'll go there when it's time to bring him back."

But Lonny wants to go there now and maybe Uncle Silas will take him. He saw Silas down at the other end of the village today and a while ago he thought he saw him going over to Sara's. That's a good place to start looking. He might find Sam there, too. As he nears Sara's house he wonders what he's going to say. He needs to make Uncle Silas see how important it is to tell Uncle Mack about Boy. He walks slowly up the stairs and knocks on the door. There's no answer, but he's sure Sara's home. The lights are on and he can hear music. He opens the door and pokes his head inside.

"Auntie?" he calls.

There are footsteps in the corridor and he hears some mumbled noises from the back bedroom.

"It's me, Lonny," he says, a little louder this time.

"Just a minute," Sara's voice floats down the hall.

"I'm sorry," says Lonny when he sees her. "I didn't know you were sick." She's standing there with her arms folded, wearing her bathrobe, and her hair is all messy. Sara usually dresses up real smart, so he can tell she's not feeling well.

"I'm sorry," he says again. "I was looking for Uncle Silas. Have you seen him?"

"Uh-uh."

"Oh, I thought I saw him coming over here."

"He left."

"Oh. You don't know. . . ." Lonny's voice trails off as he sees Sara look at her watch.

"I'll be going now," he says. "I hope you get better soon."

Sara raises her eyebrows and lifts one hand off her other arm. Then she turns and heads back down the corridor. As he shuts the door, Lonny's sure he hears her giggling. He hears another voice, too. A deeper one. He shrugs to himself and walks towards the dock. Maybe he'll find Silas down here.

It's funny that Saturday's gone so fast because it felt like it was going so slowly at first. The rain made him stay inside and he watched TV all morning. Grandpa let him watch cartoons, which he doesn't always let Lonny do. Even so, the morning seemed to drag on forever. Maybe because he was wishing he was with Uncle, not here.

Lonny climbs up onto the *North Wind* and tries to open the door to the cabin. It's locked with a padlock on the outside. For a moment he fiddles with the padlock, but he can see that it's firmly closed. He sidles along the edge of the boat to the front window. Bending down, he looks inside, but he can't see Uncle Silas. He puts his palms against the glass and pushes, but the window must be locked, too. He gives one last push and suddenly it slides.

Holy! He can get into the boat this way! Lonny looks over his shoulder to make sure nobody's looking. Then he squeezes through the window and into the cabin. Inside, everything is tidy as usual. He climbs up onto the captain's chair and rests his hands on the steering wheel. He gives it a little wiggle, then moves his right hand over to the throttle lever. It's so much fun to drive a boat! Lonny knows where the key goes and how to make it start up. Uncle leaves it running for a long time before he goes anywhere in the boat. He says it has to warm up. Grandpa keeps the key tied to an old fishing lure in his coat pocket. If Lonny had the key right now, he could just drive right out of here. Leave Grandpa and

Uncle Silas behind. He knows where Fortune Island is. He could go there himself! The thought is exciting, but it's almost dark now and it would be scary to go by himself in the dark.

Lonny drops down off the captain's chair and noses around the boat. In the front berth he finds a sleeping bag. Not one he recognizes. It's put away all neat and tidy, but it makes him wonder if someone has been sleeping on the boat. Grandpa would be so mad if he found out! Come to think of it, Grandpa would be pretty mad if Lonny took the boat somewhere. He might not speak to Lonny for a whole year. Lonny might not be allowed to live in Grandpa's house. Then what would happen?

Lonny climbs back out the window and slides it shut again. He doesn't push it too hard, in case he wants to come back again sometime. He jumps down onto the dock and walks back up the ramp. Lights are starting to come on in people's houses. There are still a few Christmas lights up, too. Lights make the houses seem warm and friendly, but Lonny knows that that's not always the way they are. Some houses frighten him because of the parties that go on in them. He tries to avoid those houses. As he walks up the path he sees Sam, going home.

"Hey Sam!" he calls.

Sam turns and stares at him. He doesn't smile.

"What's the matter?" asks Lonny.

"Nothing. Why?"

"You look sad. Or mad."

"It's nothing."

"You going home?"

"I guess. I don't really feel like it though."

"How come?"

"It's private."

"Is it because Auntie's sick?"

"What do you mean she's sick?"

"Well, she is isn't she? She got out of bed when I went to your house to look for Uncle Silas."

"Did you find him?"

"Nope."

"Then you didn't look hard enough."

"What do you mean?"

"It doesn't matter. It's none of your business."

Lonny can tell that Sam is upset. He's fiddling with the tape on his hockey stick, not looking up.

"D'you want to come to Grandpa's with me?" Lonny asks. "You can phone your mom from there."

"Okay."

As they walk silently up the path together, Lonny sees a star beginning to whiten in the fading blue sky. That first star always makes Lonny feel sad. Seems like it makes Sam sad, too.

HANNAH

"What did the car look like?"

"It was black."

"What else did you notice about it?"

"It wasn't rented. It was newish. BC plates."

"Do you remember the plate number?"

"No, Jack. I don't. I panicked, okay? I couldn't think about anything."

"And anyone else would of done the same. I'm just asking so's I know."

"I'm sorry. I'm over-reacting."

"Are you? I've never seen you frightened like this before."

"I just . . . I just don't know . . . . Maybe it's not him. I can't say that for sure. But maybe it is."

"And if it is him? Do you figure he'd be violent?"

"I . . . ."

Hannah leans over the kitchen table and drops her head on her arms, unable to say more. Her shoulders shake but there is little sound. Jack does not move from his place across the table. He watches and says nothing. Finally she lifts her head again, blows her nose and wipes her eyes.

"I don't know," she says in a small voice. "It all depends."

"On what?"

"On how his life is going; on whether he's with someone new; on if he suspects I'm pregnant; on his drug situation."

"And if it is him and he don't find you this time, you think he'll try again?"

Hannah rubs her temples and stares into space.

"I can't answer that. I don't even know if this is him. I was too chicken to find out. I could just be basing everything on a stupid over-reaction."

"Well, why don't we go look for him? This isn't a big town, eh.

There's only a handful of streets and one hotel. We'll dress up and drive."

"Except I don't want you involved in this. It's my problem. I'll go by myself."

"Well, you could if I'd lend you the truck. But—fact is—I have to come, too. You can hide and spy and give me directions. I'll drive. Four eyes will be better than two. Besides, I'll know if I see a stranger, or if that car belongs to a local. You need to know who you saw and you need me to help you."

"Jack, this whole thing is stupid and sordid. I didn't mean to bring it to your doorstep. I don't know what I thought I was doing by coming here."

"You were coming home, girl! To your family. To a safe place. That's what home is for. And that's what family's for. You came all this way to survive and I won't be doing my job if I don't help you. So you can think what you like, but we'll go out together."

Hannah moves her fingers to her scalp. She hangs her head again.

"I'm supposed to start work tomorrow, but I can't. I'll have to cancel. I'm going to go to Fortune Island. I'll take the water taxi as soon as I can. I'm going for sanity's sake, even if we don't find him tonight. And if we do find him, then you're coming to Fortune Island with me."

"Ach, I wouldn't do that."

"Well, you have to, if you're going to drive me around town tonight. That's the deal."

Jack sighs and leans back in his chair.

"Okay," he says. "I get to drive you around. Then, when we find something, or nothing, I'll do as I'm told."

Hannah pushes her chair back from the table and gets up. In places, her hair has stuck to her face.

"I'm going to wash my face," she says. "Then we'll go."

In the truck, she crouches down, a baseball cap pulled over her forehead. They drive the streets in a pattern, checking every driveway, every alley. Twice they see a car that looks familiar to Hannah, but each time Jack identifies it. "Oh, that's Larry's new car;" or, "Young Gilbert fancies himself in that thing." Hanson Bay used to have a pretty ragtag collection of old cars and pick-ups, but people have become wealthier. There are the usual old beaters, crumbling with rust, but there's a lot of shiny paint around, too.

"Those crab fishermen are doing pretty good, these days," says Jack. "They're trying to outcompete each other for the biggest, toughest truck."

Hannah doesn't answer. She knows these roads, these houses, these people. She's forgotten a lot of names and there are a lot of new people, too, but she's not looking for trucks. She curses herself again for not remembering the plate number.

"Let's do the hotel now," says Jack as they near the main part of town.

"Okay. Let's go behind it first. Down the alley."

They drive slowly down the narrow, rutted lane and Jack pulls into the parking lot. A handful of cars are parked there: two station wagons, an old Camaro and a sedan, up on blocks. Jack looks at Hannah and she shrugs. He backs out into the lane again and continues down the road, turns left and left again to cruise by the front of the hotel. Hannah checks both sides of the road, but there is nothing. The rectangular walls of the hotel loom up from the street. In daylight, Hannah knows, the once-white paint is grey and peeling. Rob would never sleep in a place like this. She starts to feel helpless. He could be anywhere: sleeping in his car down a logging road, or in his bed at home. This search is starting to seem silly. She's still nervous though. Even if they don't find anything, she'll be glad to get away for a night or two. At least she'll be able to sleep at Harry's.

When they have exhausted every street and driveway they turn for home. Hannah stares out of her window, dragging her finger slowly back and forth along the dash. Suddenly, she sits up.

"Hey, who's that?"

A black car is on their right, waiting to turn. Hannah can't make out the driver's face, but the shape is familiar. The car seems right. Jack pushes his nose towards the glass and indicates a right turn. Hannah scrunches down in the seat, pulling down her hat, but staring with one eye.

"That's Liam Sanford," says Jack. "He's one of the new teachers at the school. He's only been here since the start of the school year."

Hannah sits up, staring openly now. The man sees them and raises his hand in greeting. Hannah catches a glimpse of dark hair, a dark coat with a collar. The car disappears into the darkness and she dissolves into tears.

"I'm sorry."

"Sorry for what?"

"For over-reacting. For making all this fuss. I should have been brave enough. I should have walked right up to him in the street. Followed him into the post office. My reactions are all wrong. They're always wrong."

"So you thought that was him?"

"Uh-huh."

"Reactions aren't wrong, eh, Hannah. People should follow their instincts more than they do. Sometimes, it's thinking that makes things go awry. This evening's been good. A bit of excitement, but helpful. If this hadn't happened, I'd never of known how scared you were. You told me about Rob in such a regular way."

"It's easy to forget things when they're not right in your face."

They are quiet for a while, just the engine puttering. Jack turns into his own parking spot and shuts off the truck.

"Still planning a trip to Harry's?" he asks.

"Yes."

"I'm glad."

Hannah takes a deep breath. "I think I am, too."

Jack opens his door and steps out into the night. "Come on," he says. "Let's go and book you a boat ride."

HARRY

Mack is quiet after his day of work. He sits across from Harry, saying little, not inviting conversation. Harry takes out her glasses and places them on her nose. Then she picks up her pen and pulls the kerosene lamp closer.

Harry has decided to lay down parts of her life in writing. She has kept journals before, but journals are personal, not for public scrutiny. She's not sure who her audience will be. Possibly Hannah. Or no one at all. It doesn't matter. The important thing is that she will have done it, if only for herself. Order is the problem. Harry has never liked chronologies and she doesn't think of her life in that way. Instead she sees the shapes of things, hanging together, like Earth when seen from space: continents, ocean, islands—they don't line up in order of appearance. They're just there. Like the events in Harry's life. So for now, Harry is going to write a page a night, maybe more if things go smoothly. She doesn't want to rush it, though. She wants to be precise, even if it means making several attempts.

For some reason, tonight she has decided to set the record straight about Cutter. The other day, in the Seagull, he treated her with such disgust—a tramp, a witch; the woman who didn't sleep with him. She thinks back to Lionel Nieder telling her about Cutter's lies. Lionel was an unexpected friend for Harry around that time. He stuck up for her, made a point of talking to her on the street, disputed inaccuracies when she wasn't there to defend herself. Harry wonders where he is now. He left Hanson Bay about ten years ago, without telling anyone he was going.

When she met Alain, Lionel became friends with him, too, and the three of them would go fishing together after work. Harry smiles, remembering those trips. Alain was the worst fisherman! He had no instinct for it whatsoever. Whenever he hooked the bottom, which he did often, she would joke that the farmer in him was trying to plant the lures. "We're not ploughing!" Lionel would add.

"Pfft!" Harry laughs out loud. Her hand rests on the blank sheet of paper and her eyes look through the darkness at her past.

"Huh?" says Big Mack.

Harry gazes across the room at Mack. She smiles. "Memories. Sometimes it's hard to believe the things that have happened."

Mack nods, his eyebrows raised, his fingers tapping the ends of the arm rests. He still seems faraway.

"The past is like a story," Harry continues, "that I've been told, over and over. I get to know some of it so well. Then I stumble over something that isn't part of the main plot. Something small, that I've forgotten. And suddenly I'm in that other part of my life, the unofficial version, the part that is the most real. It makes me wonder about my brain—where I keep all this stuff, you know? It's incredible, really."

A small rush of wind pushes at the window, making Harry glance over her shoulder. Mack looks over, too.

"Another one," he says, meaning a storm.

"I think so," she replies. "They seem to come in threes. One down, two to go. Probably be howling by morning. I wonder if San will make it?"

"Even if he doesn't, I can get some stuff done. He's left the list and the gear." Mack rubs his fingers, one by one. "So what were you thinking about?" he asks.

"Oh, nothing," Harry answers, pauses, then adds, "well, something, I guess."

"Huh."

"I just . . . I was remembering . . . . Have you ever met a person who really didn't know how to fish?"

"Not really."

"This guy I knew—there was no point even giving him a lure. Except that he wanted to catch something so badly. He'd get so excited, pulling and pulling. Never any sign of a fight on the line. Then he'd bring up a rock, or a starfish—some piece of the bottom. The rest of us would be having a fine old time, hauling in ling cod. Then he'd *really* catch the bottom. Bust the line. And he'd always try to persuade us that he'd just caught the biggest fish—so big that it got away. He'd ask us for a new lure, so that he could have a second chance to catch it. If we laughed at him, he'd be so disappointed, so we always had to give him another lure. Tie it on for him, even."

Mack smiles. "I've always had good luck with fish."

"Is that what it is? Luck?"

"Well, my dad taught me lots, but there's still a little bit of luck in there."

Harry looks back at the blank page under her hands. Was it just bad luck that she fell for Alain? Or did she not know enough? She picks the pen up and looks at it, then puts it down and pushes her chair away from the table.

"I want to write some of my memories down," she say, standing up, "but they sweep me away. I can't write and think at the same time."

"I don't believe in writing things down," Mack says.

"I have to. I forget what happened yesterday if I don't write it down."

"Writing makes you forget. If it's important, you should memorize it."

"But I can't memorize everything."

"That's because you should tell people. Pass it on. My kids are always asking me to tell them about the time that such-and-such a thing happened. They know the stories better than me, by now."

Harry looks around her at the walls of the cabin. Do the walls know her stories? Have the words seeped out from the pages of her journals, along the cracks of wood, into the structure of her cabin? Her eyes come to rest on Mack, squeezed into an armchair, looking at her with one eye, assessing her like a crow. She wonders if he is offering himself as a listener, volunteering. She wonders if, after all these years, she can tell someone the real stories. And if she can, will it be him?

BIG MACK

Mack listens carefully to Harry's words. He hasn't smoked pot for a long time now, and he finds himself more able to concentrate. For a while after work he was stuck with a foot in each of his worlds, confused. San's words kept coming back to him: how, if he can't think straight, then he's no help to anyone. Now he's trying to think straight—maybe even help Harry. It's funny to think that she might need help, as tough as she is. But her stories make her real. She's been through stuff, too. She tells him what it was like to grow up on a farm with a mother and father who loved her. He's never been away from the coast, but he could picture her there. When he asks her if she has any photos, she digs for a while in a box, and comes up with a brownish-looking snapshot of a cabin, three people in front of it, her mother, her father and Harry.

"You look so serious!" he tells her, squinting to make out the people. The young Harry is wearing a dress. Her hair is pulled back into a braid and her bangs are cut straight across. "Haven't changed your hair much," he can't resist adding.

Harry's fingers go to her forehead and she touches her hair. "Let me see that again," she says, reaching with the other hand.

Mack passes over the photograph and she holds it away from her eyes, examining it as if she has never seen it before. "I've always looked serious," she says. "People are constantly telling me to smile, it's not the end of the world—when I'm not sad or angry or anything. It's just what my face does."

"Like your father," Mack says.

"Do you think so? People always told me I looked like Mother."

"They just saw the hair. Your face is like your dad's."

Harry rubs her fingers around the white border of the photograph, touching it like it's the most precious thing she owns. "He died five weeks later."

When she says that, about her father dying, Harry's face goes blank. Mack is watching carefully, trying to figure out how much it means to her. He is expecting to see sadness; tears, even. Instead he sees nothing, the way his own father looks sometimes. But with the old man, the muscles tighten in his face, guarding the skin, forbidding it to change. With Harry, there is only emptiness as if the emotions have been poured away.

"How did he die?" he asks.

She continues staring, rubbing the edge of the photo. "They thought it was a heart attack. We don't really know. We didn't see it happen. I found him in the barn, next to a bale of hay. He looked peaceful, as if he was tired and had sat down for a rest. He was leaning into the bale of hay, his arm resting along the top of it. His head was resting on his arm. At first I didn't want to wake him, so I snuck up closer. I was going to find a piece of straw and tickle his nose, but something stopped me. I don't know how I knew. I may have seen a dead animal before, but I certainly didn't understand death. I think it was his face. There was saliva on one side. I ran to get Mother. I said: 'Papa's in the barn! He's in the barn!' She didn't understand. 'Of course he's in the barn,' she said. I remember shouting, 'No! No! He's in the barn!' I didn't know what else to say. I was too young and too confused. I pulled her by the arm and then she knew something was wrong. When I look back at it, I was like a dog, whining and barking and finally latching on and tugging."

Mack doesn't interrupt. The greatest respect he can show her is to listen without saying a word. Harry's a good listener herself, but she still interrupts sometimes, trying to fix things before she's heard the whole story. That's kind-of a white person thing, though. Having to respond.

"The worst thing about Papa dying," Harry continues, "was putting him in the earth. It haunted me. I couldn't shake the idea that he was asleep. I panicked about what would happen when he woke up. Mother told me that dead people don't wake up, but that didn't help. I would hear him calling me, several times a night. 'We have to go!' I'd tell Mother. 'He needs us!' Finally she slapped me. Hard. I was so shocked, because she'd never done that before. But we were both exhausted from grief and overwork and lack of sleep. She screamed at me to shut up. 'How many times do I have to tell you he's dead?' she yelled. 'Dead! Now get back to bed. Dead people don't need our help. And that body in that coffin is not your father any more. Get that straight.' I still had the dreams after that, but I didn't tell her. I barely slept, in case I dreamed. Sometimes I wonder how I survived."

Harry's face is still blank, but now Mack can see the look for what it is, a kind of expression. Her face is empty because her father's death exhausted her—emptied her out. He remembers his own dreams when he was six years old. He dreamed about finding his mother, the way Harry had found her father. The universal nightmare of loss. He's glad he doesn't have those nightmares anymore. He wonders if Harry still has them, but he has a feeling that she's done with talking for the evening. One more question might put her over the edge. He decides to go for a bath and leave her alone. He won't go just yet, though. He watches her face until it relaxes.

LONNY

Lonny has taken the clock into his room, so he knows that it's only three in the morning. The night is taking forever and his legs quiver with pent-up energy. He wants to go! His plan is all arranged. Tomorrow—well, today!—when Grandpa goes to church, Lonny is going down to the dock. He'll take the key for the *North Wind* and start the motor. It's the weekend and no one will hear him. Grandpa will be walking to town in the dark, not hitch-hiking. He never hitch-hikes. He walks pretty slowly, but he refuses to get a ride to church. It's part of his whole Sunday that he has to walk. Once in a while, he gets a ride back. Someone from the church insists and he can't turn them down.

Grandpa won't take Lonny to Fortune Island, even though Lonny knows something new and important that just can't wait. So, if nobody will help him, Lonny will go on his own. He doesn't want to go at night because he might get lost. He needs to wait for the morning, when it's almost light. But if someone sees him leaving, they might stop him. Most mornings he'd be worried about Grandpa watching the water from his chair by the window, but Sunday is perfect because Grandpa won't be there.

Lonny hugs himself in the dark, imagining the trip tomorrow, how happy Uncle will be. Harry will be happy with him, too. Maybe she'll even make him some cookies. He feels under the mattress for the keys to the boat. It was exciting taking them out of Grandpa's coat pocket. He feels a little bad about it, but he had to do it. It's not like he's hurting anyone.

Every so often there's a gust of wind that flings rain at Lonny's window. Then he doesn't hear anything else for a while. He hopes it won't be stormy, because that will make things harder. As he lies there, he realises that he should probably be on the boat right now. What if Raylene is around when he tries to sneak away? He sits up. Too bad he doesn't have a flashlight. He needs to see where all his stuff is, but he doesn't want to turn on the light. He feels around the room for his clothes, touching them to figure out what they are. In the end he gives up; there're too many dirty clothes scattered around with the clean ones. He feels his way over to the light switch and turns it on. He looks around him at the mess, then crawls over his mattress picking out sweat pants, a hooded sweatshirt, dry socks and a clean t-shirt. His coat and shoes and hat are by the front door. If he leaves his bedroom door open a crack, he might have enough light to see his shoes without waking anyone up.

The door seems to make so much noise as he opens it! Closing it is worse. He stands still for a long time waiting for the noise to be forgotten. Then he tiptoes over to the front door and sees his runners where he'd hoped they would be. He grabs them with one hand and his coat with the other. Then he tiptoes back to his room and switches off the light. More creaking. Again, he waits for silence. Then he pushes his feet into the shoes and heads for the front door.

It's locked. Of course it's locked! And he won't be able to lock it behind him, so Grandpa will know that somebody went out. Lonny's heart beats hard and he stares at the door handle. The kitchen door is probably locked, too. His bedroom window is too high off the ground and too close to Raylene's room. He wouldn't want to wake her up. He goes to the front window. The sliding part opens far enough for him to get through it. He can drop his feet onto the railing for the stairs. It'll be slippery, but he can hold onto the window sill. He lifts the catch and slides the window open. The noise seems loud, but he doesn't wait around this time. He breathes in as he slips through the window and turns around. He holds on tight as his feet reach the railing and slip, just as he thought they would. But he's prepared and he works at it until he gets a good grip, then carefully slides the window shut behind him. After that it's a cinch to drop down to the stairs and walk out into the night. It's dark, all right. Lonny stumbles in the ruts and falls into some blackberry bushes. The noise wakes a dog: "Rrrrrrrr-uff," it snaps out a warning bark.

The dogs! Oh no! What is Lonny going to do about all the dogs? They'll be outside for the night, protecting the houses that feed them. What if they pile on him? He stays where he is, very still. He'll have to go slow. Real slow. After all, it doesn't matter if it takes him all night to reach the boat. He takes a deep breath and closes his eyes. He's patient. He can wait a long time. He makes a list in his head of all the places that dogs hang out, whose houses they sleep under. Then he moves, ever so slightly, out of the berry bush, hearing the rip of his jacket. On hands and knees he starts his journey to the boat, while the rest of the village sleeps.

HANNAH

The cabin of the water taxi smells of salt, fuel and dampness. The VHF radio is blaring out the weather forecast: gale force south-to-southeasterlies, building to storm force this evening. The north is expecting hurricane force—normal for that tip of the island. Hannah wonders why anyone would want to live up there. It's such an inhospitable area.

Right now the wind is blowing, but the sky is patchy. The morning is dark and the last quarter moon gleams through the clouds in the south, beside a bright star. Even though it is beautiful, there is something sad about seeing the moon in the morning. As if the planet is never going to tilt back towards the sun. As a little girl, Hannah didn't mind the long winter nights. She began to dislike them when she started school in Hanson Bay and had to walk through the morning gloom to get to class. In Whitehorse, there was even less daylight in the winter, but the snow made things brighter—sparkled with hope. Fools' gold.

The boat sputters, then roars as the driver, Wayne, plays with the throttle. Then he strides out of the cabin and casts off. They idle away from the dock, into the greyness. The chop is steep, broadside to them. Wayne takes a slurp of his coffee and Hannah sees some of it lingering on his moustache. He puts the mug in a holder and pushes the throttle as far as it can go. The boat rears up, like the stallion it's named for, and takes off, galloping through the water and bumping over the waves. This boat is so fast they'll be at Fortune Island in about twenty-five minutes. By then, Hannah will be sore from all the banging. She shifts her position and looks out of the window. As they near Bailey's Rock, she sees a big red seiner on her left. It looks like the one she had travelled on before, the *North Wind*. She wonders where it's going, but not for long. The water taxi cuts as close as it can to the rock, then turns and speeds onwards. Arcs of spray obscure the already-dim view, leaving Hannah with quick glimpses, now and then.

She braces herself and thinks about her visit. She will be polite to Mack, but distant. She hopes things will not be too strained.

"I just look out the window when people annoy me," Louise said, when she was talking about the clinic. "It's so easy to tune them out. Then you smile and ask some silly question and they forget what they were saying. Works like a charm."

Hannah is going to try this technique whenever she feels herself rising to Harry's bait. She'll look out the window, then change the subject. In her imagination, the barrier between herself and her mother lies at the entrance to their mutual world. It became a barrier when Hannah tried to leave that world. If they can get past it, she can try to come back. She and her mother could forge an entirely new relationship, one that she is now sure that she wants. In her pocket is her letter. She plans to hand deliver it to show that she's keeping with Harry's theme. It signifies reciprocation, the starting point in a chaos of dead ends.

At Kingfisher Rock the swell freights in from the open ocean, tossing the tough aluminum boat and burying it in green water. Hannah leaves her seat and stands in the aisle, one hand on either side, holding on. When the boat slams down off a wave, she lets her knees buckle and absorb the force. The conditions aren't too bad, but Wayne is an impatient driver. She considers asking him to slow down, but he probably has to get back for another run. Her presence in the aisle seems to send its own message, though. Wayne glances over his shoulder and sees her, then puts his hand to the throttle. The boat slows, but only slightly.

By the time they near Fortune Island, Hannah has a cramp in her thumb from holding on. Wayne has finished his coffee and is fiddling in his chest pocket for a pack of smokes. He takes them out and lays them on the dash. If he lights one up, Hannah will have to go out onto the back deck. She's barely hanging on to her breakfast as it is. The ride is smoother now, though. The inlet is free of swell, only whitecaps to contend with. Wayne speeds around the point, into Deep Bay, not slowing the boat until they are nearly at the dock. The sudden stop creates a steep wash that slams into the dock and sets it rocking. The wash almost swamps a little red boat that Hannah doesn't recognize. Wayne lights his cigarette and goes out, then grabs the tie-up line and pulls the boat in. Hannah decides to wait until the bouncing has lessened before she leaves the cabin.

As she steps out, she sees that Wayne is looking over towards the boatshed. Two figures are visible in the doorway, one large and one small. She hears the tail end of a comment, shouted across the water . . . almost sunk my boat . . . learn some manners! Wayne shrugs at Hannah and pushes off again. He doesn't wave, or say goodbye, but he drives slowly until he reaches the entrance to the bay. Then she hears the roar of the engine as it screams up to maximum speed. She turns towards the boatshed again, but this time there is only one person there. She's not sure who it is, but he waves and she waves back. Just then Rustum comes barking and whining down to the dock, his tail thumping against the ramp railings. Hannah holds out her hand to stop him from jumping on her. Then she strokes his ears briefly and picks up her bag.

"Go!" she tells him, pointing towards the cabin. As she looks up the ramp she sees Harry standing at the top. Hannah takes a deep breath and smiles, then walks slowly upwards. At the top, she stops, wondering if she should hug Harry, whose arms are by her sides.

"I've come to stay for a few days," Hannah says. "I hope that's okay." Then she reaches in her pocket and pulls out her letter in its envelope. As she hands it over, she sees a tremor in her mother's hands.

"It's hard to have a postal relationship with you," she says lightly, "when no boats come out here."

Harry's hand is in her pocket, holding the letter. The brief smile she gives Hannah does not erase the anxious set of her forehead. Together, they walk towards the cabin.

"I'll sleep on the floor," Hannah says. "Hey, who's the other person here?"

"You didn't recognize San?"

"Oh, of course! I'll go down and say Hi to him."

"Maybe you should wait."

"Why? What do you mean?"

"Well, they're busy milling. You'd be interrupting."

"You think I'm going to go and get in an argument with Mack."

"I don't think it will be comfortable for him that you're here."

Hannah remembers Louise's advice, so she looks around at the trees and tries to tune Mother out.

"You can't write a letter like that and not expect me to have questions," she says.

Harry pauses on the path.

"You're right. I didn't think that through."

"You didn't expect me to react?"

"Not so quickly," Harry admits. "You've never shown any interest in your father before."

Hannah opens the cabin door for her mother, then follows her into the mudroom. As she unties her shoes she wonders why this visit isn't going the way she had imagined. She had known it would be awkward, but she'd thought she'd at least feel welcome.

"Mother," she says, coming into the warmth of the cabin. "We need to start off on the right foot, otherwise things will only get worse."

Harry fills the kettle and lights the burner. The tremor is still there, in her fingers, Hannah can see it from across the room.

Harry doesn't look at Hannah for a while. Then she says, "If it wasn't for Mack, I'd be weeping with joy to have you here. But the way things stand, this will be an uneasy visit for all of us. You and Mack distrust one another. It doesn't make sense to me. I don't believe it's built on anything solid, but I know that it isn't going to go away overnight. Mack's been let down by everyone in his life, with a few exceptions. I don't want to add to that list. Your presence here is a slap in his face."

Hannah opens her mouth, but no words come out. She hasn't thought of it like this. Sure, she thought things would be uncomfortable between her and Mack, but she didn't mean to be lording it over him. She was so busy thinking about herself and her father and Harry and Rob, she hadn't really considered Mack. She drops onto a chair and runs her fingers over the worn cloth. Harry is pulling out cups, spoons, the teapot. Wayne's water taxi is probably back in Hanson Bay by now. The whole thing is a mess.

While she is thinking, Hannah's hand trails over her abdomen. Suddenly she remembers the other reason she has come here, the one truth that can patch this up. She looks over at Harry and tries to make eye contact.

HARRY

When Harry first sees the *Silver Stallion* barrelling towards Fortune Island, her heart shrivels. It's like an unexpected courier coming to the door. Water taxis bring news, not always good.

Her first thought, of course, is Boy. Has he died? If so, what happens next? Hannah says Mack confessed to a crime; Mack says he was framed. Neither of these options seem credible to Harry, even though they're both possible. Unfortunately, the most likely scenario is that Mack will go to jail, despite any case built in his defense.

Harry taps the counter with her index finger and watches the boat zoom by. Rustum is barking in the mudroom, trying to get out, but she decides to keep him in for a while longer. She looks at the yeast foaming in the little jug of water. It has to be used this minute. She pours it down the drain and rinses out the cup. She'll try again when she has time. Meanwhile she should go down to the dock. She pulls on her boots and coat. Rustum is pushing at the door and dancing around. She lets him go and follows him down the path.

When she sees Hannah, her heart shrivels a little more. She glances over at the *Polynesia* and decides that Hannah will have to sleep there. Even though Mack is sleeping in Hannah's room, it is his home for a month, maybe more, maybe less. It would be wrong to ask him to move. No, if Hannah comes on a trip like this, she will have to take her lumps.

Harry tries to put aside her fears and feel happy about her daughter's visit. After all, doesn't she want resolution between them? When Hannah gives her a small envelope, she almost tears it open on the spot, wondering what the letter inside it says. She stares at her daughter's face and lets herself remember Alain: the prominent cheekbones, his height and colouring. For the first time since Hannah was a baby, she finds herself marvelling at the wonder of creation: two bodies passing into one.

415

As they walk up the path, Harry tries to regain composure, but her breath still comes unevenly and her chest feels tight. She chastises herself for not being more welcoming. Her own child should always be welcome! But the stubborn side of her resists. This is not a happy situation. She tells Hannah this, bluntly, anticipating the shouting that will arise between them. When it does not come, she is surprised, but relieved. Still, she carries on, preparing tea and drumming home the fact that Hannah's timing is poorly thought-out.

When Hannah doesn't respond, she dares to look at her, expecting the worst—anger, hysteria, tears; instead, she sees a relaxed-looking woman, gazing back, softly. She is so surprised that she stares, looking at Hannah as if she has never seen her before.

And she hasn't. Not this Hannah, the one who says: "I'm carrying a baby. I'm going to be a mother."

Harry freezes, unsure if she has heard correctly. Hannah continues to smile, as her hand touches her abdomen, where new life lies concealed. Suddenly, the air seems to leave Harry's chest all at once, in a big whoosh. She clutches herself and bends over, trying to breathe it back in. Winded, she gasps and wheezes. She feels Hannah's arms gripping her, walking her to a chair. She feels Hannah's hand at her temple, sliding down to her shoulder. She feels the sweat prickle her neck. She can't speak, but she wants to say she's sorry, that she understands why Hannah has come, that she loves her. Hannah crouches beside Harry, cradling her shoulders in a way that seems to tell of love. Slowly Harry's breath comes back, the pounding in her chest begins to taper off. She hears the scream of the kettle in the background. She tries to get up, to turn it off, but her knees don't seem to be working.

"Turn it off," she gasps and Hannah smiles and squeezes her shoulders, then straightens up and turns away. From the corner of her eye, Harry sees Hannah pouring the water into the teapot. Harry tries to calm down. It's only a baby after all! No reason to react like this. She counts in her head, four seconds to inhale, four seconds pause, four seconds to exhale, four seconds pause. It seems to work. She inhales and pauses.

"Tell me," she says. Then exhales.

Hannah laughs. "That's what I came here for! I want *you* to tell *me*. Everything. Your life, my life, Alain Savard."

Harry gasps—a little *huh!*—and moves her head so that she can see Hannah. Life is so unpredictable. You have to be careful what you wish for. She counts in fours and considers. She decides that she has the right to ask some questions of her own.

"Whose is it?" she asks.

"It doesn't matter. I'm going to be a single mother. I'm not going to tell him."

"But who?" Harry persists.

"Him," Hannah says in a small voice. "Rob. The guy I ran away from."

Harry nods, wonders if Hannah has run far enough away. Then she wonders how Hannah will manage the baby.

"You can come here," she says. "I'll help you."

"I don't know how I'm going to do things, yet. I'm still trying to get used to the idea. I'm hoping I can work enough hours to get maternity leave."

Harry giggles, thinking how wrong she's been. Hannah has not done everything the prescribed way.

"What?" asks Hannah.

Harry waves her hand, shooing Hannah's question away.

"No," says Hannah. "What's so funny? This is serious."

"Oh, it's very serious," Harry agrees, her mouth in a straight line.

"You think it's funny that I'm in this situation?"

"Not funny, no. Ironic."

"Oh, wonderful. Why?"

"Well, I was always sure that I didn't have grandchildren because I hadn't received a wedding invitation, one of those ones on a white card with swirly letters. Mothers think they know their children so well and we don't. We don't know anything."

"That's not true. You know too much. That's why we argue. The other day, when I was talking to Jack about Ada's death, and your love for my father, I felt as if someone had pulled a blindfold off me. I realised how wrapped up in myself I've been. My problems are so . . . so small. My world has been so small."

Harry feels herself sagging at Hannah's words—a feeling of intense relief.

"Your world *was* small," she says. "Because of me. I wanted to protect you, so I kept you here on the island when you should have been out there, fending for yourself. Because of that, you had to learn your lessons ten years later than everyone else." Harry is sitting up straight, now. She pushes herself out of the chair and stands, legs steady. She moves into the kitchen and lifts the teapot. "I cursed you with my blindness," she says, hoarsely, as she pours. "I knew that I was escaping from the world, but I thought I was being brave and resourceful. I never saw that I was hiding, that I would hide here forever. I didn't see that I was hiding you, too. I didn't want history to repeat itself. But it has."

Hannah is quiet, holding the cup she has been given. "Do you think," she says, brushing her fingers down to her belly, "she'll be a struggler, too?"

Harry takes her cup back over to her chair and sits down. "Well," she muses. "There's you and me and Jack. That's three different people trying to influence her. Maybe she stands a chance. But, maybe she'll be a boy and we won't have a clue what to do with him."

"Oh God!" Hannah laughs. "Not a boy! Please, not a boy!"

"Why? You think girls are easier? Let me tell you . . . ."

They sit and talk—mother and daughter, eyes wide with hindsight. Harry imagines looking down at the cosy living room, seeing two women, each surrounded by rainbow light, the colours

418

matching in some places, clashing in others. And a third light glowing in the middle, making the colours blend.

MACK

"What the hell is she doing here?" Mack growls, throwing down the file that he was using to sharpen the saw. He slips back into the shadows of the shed, anger pounding in his arms. Behind him, San waves across the water, to the dock.

"It's Hannah," San says. "She's come to see her mother. I haven't seen her since she was a teenager."

"She's a bitch, that's what she is," bites Mack.

"Whoa!" San's eyes open wide and he stares at Mack.

"It's not enough that she's accused me of beating Boy. Now she's followed me here, to rub it in. The water taxi's left. That means she's staying over."

San picks up the file that Mack threw on the floor. He leans over the saw and begins to file the chain. Over his shoulder he says: "She saved Boy's life. That's a good thing, isn't it?"

Mack paces the floor, kicking at sawdust.

"She said I admitted it; that I said it was all my fault. What does she know? I'm being framed, Goddammit! Some asshole out there is laughing his face off because he's just got off scot-free. Pin it on a Native. That's all you have to do."

"Have you talked to Hannah?"

"No."

"Then you don't know her side of the story?"

"I don't give a damn about her side of the story."

"Well, maybe you should. Maybe this is your chance to find out. Maybe it's her chance to hear your side of the story, too."

"So now you're on her side?" Mack explodes. "Well, you can do your own damn milling!" He strides towards the door.

"Listen to me." San's voice is soft and calm. "I grew up the same way you did. I've seen what you're up against. My heart is with you. But I've known Hannah since she was a little girl. She has her own struggles, but she tries to do what's right. You need to show her what is right. She can't learn that from any other person."

420

Mack pauses in the doorway, feeling the wind on his face and a sprinkling of rain. His shoulders slump and he fiddles with his fingers.

"You owe it to your family."

At the mention of his family, Mack sees his boys, their bright faces full of life. He remembers Sam's fib about the firewood; he see Lonny's angry looks. His boys need him to be there. He stands in the doorway, listening to the wind. Words fall away, out of his mind. He sees San's family, laughing on the beach. Then he sees his own family laughing on a beach, too. He wonders if he can make it happen. Not if he goes to jail.

He thinks about Hannah and tries to see the whole thing as a misunderstanding. He can't quite believe it, but he decides he'll speak to her, if only because it's a small island.

He pulls back from the doorway and turns to face San, who is still staring at him, a warm light in his eyes. Mack doesn't say anything. Words seem too bothersome.

LONNY

Steering the *North Wind* is a lot different than Lonny remembered. At first, when he left the dock, he bumped into two other boats, because the tide moved him around so much. He couldn't tell if he'd done any damage, but he was going pretty slow. He's amazed how long it seems to take for the boat to turn. At one point, he had run outside and pushed off a second time, but the boat was going forward and he almost fell in. That made his heart race and his hands shake. What if the boat left without him? How would he explain that to Grandpa?

Lonny is standing on a crate in front of the wheel. He can't see the water right in front of the boat, but he can see the rocks and beaches. There's a chance that he's going the wrong way, because steering is much harder than it looks. The water seems to go on and on forever and there aren't any signs that say Turn Here.

Now he's crossing a channel and the waves are different. There're the waves from the wind and the waves from the sea. The sea waves roll under the boat, so he has to hold the wheel tight. The rocking has never bothered him before, but now that he's by himself—driving!—it makes him feel nervous. The boat tilts way over, then rolls back again. Lonny can only tell how far he's come when he looks behind him. He can barely see Hanson Bay now. His fingers are cold and sweaty where he's holding on to the throttle. Sometimes he experiments and makes the boat go faster, but he prefers to go slow because he's not sure of the way.

How come he was so sure he could do this? It's hard! He's concentrating as much as he can, but there's so much water. The reefs could be anywhere. He could be driving over a reef right now and the boat would sink underneath him. He would get too cold and then he would drown. He looks around the cabin for a life jacket. Does Grandpa even have lifejackets? he wonders. When he looks back out the window he sees a piece of wood floating in front of the boat, hidden in the waves. He pulls the steering wheel to the right, but not fast enough. The log hits the boat with a thud, making Lonny jump. He breathes quickly and wipes his hands on his pants because they're getting so slippery. The log could make a hole in the boat. The boat might start to leak. What would he do if that happened?

Ahead of him Lonny sees the waves, looking like lines of soldiers. The white spray is the smoke from the guns going off. The army is attacking the beach on the other side of the channel, endless troops all going the same way. Lonny hopes the waves aren't going to get bigger. He still has to go past that rock where they caught the *tush-co*. It's always rough there.

Suddenly, he sees a boat in the distance. It's a water taxi. He's so happy to see it! It's coming straight towards him and he watches it grow bigger, charging through the water, throwing up spray. He tries to imagine himself driving such a fast boat. That would be so cool! Sam would be impressed. It doesn't matter that Lonny's a little frightened of going fast. He'll get braver when he gets used driving and when he knows his way. The water taxi zooms past him and he waves at the driver, who doesn't wave back. He's happy, though, because there's a wake for him to follow. He squints into the distance and tries to remember the way the water taxi came. It curved around from the point. He follows the white line and hums a little tune.

Hm hm hm, hm hm hm, life goes on—Hah!
Hm hm hm hm life goes on

It's the same tune that Old Leo was singing when he was splitting firewood. It's the kind of tune you hum when there's a job to be done.

Lonny thinks about Uncle. He hopes that Uncle is not too homesick. Apart from staying at Harry's, Lonny has only been away from home once. He stayed with Auntie Lila in the city. It was fun for the first day, but by the second day he didn't like it so much any more. Auntie went shopping all the time and it got boring. They trailed around from one place to the next. He was with Boy that time and it was his job to keep Boy from getting lost. It was hard work; Lonny almost got lost himself.

By the time the white trail disappears, Lonny can see the fishing rock poking up out of the sea. From time to time it is covered by waves and vanishes like a magic trick. The waves must be big, because Lonny has never seen that rock disappear before. Even though it frightens him, he's glad to see the rock. It gives him something to aim for. He knows that once he gets past it, he can turn and head for Fortune Island. The water's deep around there and he won't have to worry about hitting reefs.

The *North Wind* heads out into open water with Lonny concentrating hard at the wheel. It must be because of the waves that the boat is going slower. Lonny tightens his grip on the throttle and pushes it forward a tiny bit. The boat doesn't go faster; in fact, it slows down more. Lonny stares at the sea—at the wind and waves that are pushing him towards Kingfisher Rock. Bit by bit, the *North Wind's* engine gets quieter and the boat goes slower. Suddenly the engine gives a little cough. Then it dies. The boat is completely quiet, except for the sound of the water washing up onto its stern. Lonny stands on his box, gripping the wheel, wondering what to do.

HANNAH

Hannah stands by her mother, watching her make bread. Harry's knuckles look like wooden burls as her fingers relentlessly poke into the dough, pressing and turning, pressing and turning.

"Here," says Harry. "You do it."

"It's okay. I like watching."

"You just don't want to get your fingers dirty," Harry grumbles.

"Hey! I just . . . I just don't know how."

Harry pulls her fingers out of the dough and goes towards the sink. She nudges the tap on with her wrist and rubs her hands under the stream of water. Hannah sees a dark, ropey vein, knotting its way down her mother's arm, over her wrist, onto her hand. Is that what my hands will look like when I'm old?

"Wash your hands under warm water first. Never knead bread with cold hands."

Harry fiddles with the taps, feeling the water with one hand. Then she nods at Hannah. Hannah stares back, then moves slowly to the taps. She can't believe she's doing this. She's never been interested in making bread before. Harry was right when she made that quip about Hannah getting her fingers dirty. The thought of all that gunk under her nails is gruesome. Still, she warms her hands and dries them, then moves tentatively over to the bowl. The dough is warm and soft, elastic but not gooey. Hannah squeezes it between her fingers and presses her palms together, suddenly enjoying the feel of it.

"Now punch it," Harry says, over her shoulder. "Give it everything you've got."

Hannah pushes her fist into the dough.

"Harder. Much harder."

She slams her fist into it.

"That's more like it. But never knead in anger. It would upset your grandmother."

Hannah glances over her shoulder at her mother. "You're putting me off."

Harry takes a step back. "I'll leave you to it, then."

By the time Harry comes back, the dough is even more pliable than before. Hannah has been enjoying herself. Kneading bread is quite different from what she'd imagined. She likes the idea of her grandmother giving advice. Does Harry use the same words?

They place the bowl of dough in its rising place by the stove and cover it with a cloth. The rain has set in now, Hannah can hear it dancing on the chimney cap.

"I thought you should sleep in the boat," Harry says.

Hannah frowns, thinking of the wind and the rain. She won't be able to sleep if it's stormy. The boat will pull on the lines and tilt with the gusts. The gear will rattle and scream. No, she won't be able to sleep. She almost argues, but she remembers what Harry said about Mack. She remembers that Mack and his boys stayed on their boat in the Christmas storm. They didn't complain.

"Can I start warming it up, then?" she asks.

"It shouldn't be too damp. We used it the day before yesterday. But go ahead, light the stove if you want. There's plenty of diesel."

Hannah gets up and goes to the door. "Can I borrow your boots?"

"Do they fit you?"

She slips her feet into them. A little tight in the toe, but wearable.

"I thought you had bigger feet than mine?" Harry asks.

"I guess not. Can I borrow your raincoat, too?"

"Good grief! Anyone would think you were a tourist."

"I am. Are there any matches on the boat?"

"You don't need them. The stove's got a pilot light, remember? Take Rustum," she adds. "He needs some fresh air."

Hannah pulls the hood of the raincoat over her head and opens the door.

When she gets to the boat, she finds that the conditions are not as bad as she had feared. The dock is much more protected than the house, except at high tide. She lights the stove and opens a window on the lee side. Then she pulls the little mattress out of the front berth and leaves it out to dry. No matter how often a boat is used there is always dampness. She closes the door and steps back onto the dock, looking over at the woodshed. A chainsaw is going. She wonders what they're doing.

Despite Harry's warning, Hannah decides to go over to the shed. She hasn't seen San for years, and as for Mack, well, she needs to acknowledge him. She climbs the ramp and turns left, away from the house. Her feet tread down the path and the noise of the saw gets louder.

She stands in the doorway and sees that Mack and San are milling a log into beams. Mack is pulling the blade through the wood with steady arms. His eyes are focused on the job at hand, occasionally darting forwards or backwards to assess how he's doing. He looks the same as he did at Christmas—strong, intense, glowing with health. She thinks back to the face she saw in the police car. That was not the same man. That's the problem with this situation. The Mack she saw then was not the Mack she knows. She stays by the door and doesn't move. She remembers talking to *this* Mack in *this* shed, holding out her hands, wondering if he would take them. Instead, a hum of energy pulsed between them and died away. Seeing him again, she remembers that feeling. All trace of it had evaporated when she left Fortune Island. Afterwards, she couldn't remember why she had felt so drawn to him.

San looks up and sees her. He smiles, but he doesn't wave. He doesn't want to disturb Big Mack. Hannah understands. She stays where she is and smiles back. Rain dribbles off the roof, onto her raincoat and down the backs of her boots. She takes a step forwards and continues to wait.

Finally, the beam is cut and there is sudden silence. Big Mack puts down the saw and gestures to San. Together, they move the beam. As they put it down, San says something that Hannah can't hear. Mack glances over at her. His eyes flash, black and angry. He looks away again.

That look makes Hannah feel cold to her bones. She wonders if she should go back to the cabin.

"Hannah!" says San, coming over, making her feel better. He gives her a quick hug and looks her up and down. "I always knew you were going to be taller than me, but not this much. You're making me feel short!"

Hannah smiles and asks about his family. He gives her the details. There is a new child, one she hasn't met yet. "We call him Bear," San tells her. "He's pretty cute. He adores Big Mack." Here, San beckons Mack over with his whole arm. "You guys need to meet," he says, looking from Hannah to Mack.

"We've already met," says Mack, under his breath from across the floor.

Hannah looks down, wishing she had gone back to the cabin.

"No," says San. "You guys need to meet again."

Hannah is startled. She wasn't expecting this. How much does San know? And who told him? She feels as if she's about to go on trial, be questioned about her decisions.

"It's okay," he says. "I don't want you hash it out. You need to start from the beginning. Leave your stories behind."

"My story is why I'm here," says Mack, shifting his weight, his great arms locked across his chest.

"We're all here because of our stories. Hannah probably has a few of her own."

"I wouldn't have come here," Hannah interrupts, trying to explain. "But I had to. I didn't come to make trouble. I wasn't thinking straight. I'm sorry. I've got the stove going in the boat. I'm going to stay there. I won't get in your way."

When she says this, Mack looks at her without the venom she

saw before. She looks back at him for as long as she can. There's a lift to his eyebrows that shows some curiosity. He shrugs. "It's your home. You can do what you like."

"It used to be my home," Hannah corrects him. "I ran away from here. I can't call it home any more." She swallows, wondering why she said that.

San's eyes fly between the two of them, reminding Hannah of his presence. For a moment, she had almost forgotten he was there.

Mack's hair flops down to his eyebrows, hiding the scar on his forehead. Hannah stares at the raven blackness of it and thinks of Alain Savard. She takes in the cedar-coloured skin and white teeth. She wants to say "my father is Métis," but she can't. It would be stupid, irrelevant. She closes her mouth and drops her eyes to the floor.

"Maybe this evening you can ask Mack about his life?" San suggests. "Get to know him a little. He can ask you some questions, too."

Hannah shrinks at the idea of such a stilted, constructed evening, but San looks stern, as if he won't give up. Mack is looking past Hannah's right ear, staring at the rain. She catches his eye and nods a slight yes. He does the same, then turns back into the shed.

"Don't let me interrupt you any more," Hannah tells San. "It was good to see you. Say hello to Clarissa for me. And the kids." Before he has a chance to reply, she turns away from him, into the rain and the wind. Rustum leads the way home, through the clamshells.

Home?

HARRY

When Hannah says that she's been down to the shed, Harry turns on her heel, furious.

"Why?" she demands.

Hannah steps away from her, wide-eyed. She doesn't answer, just stares at Harry.

"I'm sorry." Harry softens her tone.

"Don't you see? I had to."

"Had to what?"

"Break the ice. Get it over with."

"And how did you do that?" Harry's tone is sour.

"You really don't trust me, do you?"

"Around Mack, you're a mystery. You insist he's guilty. You say I'm not safe here, alone with him."

"That was a mistake. He obviously thinks a lot of you. I can see he wouldn't hurt you in these circumstances. I . . . I shouldn't have said that."

"Darn right." Harry wonders if she should have made this last comment, but it's too late. The words are out. The peaceful flow of mother-daughter unity has hit a rough patch already. "He thinks a lot of Boy, too," she continues, anyway. "So why do you think he would hurt him?"

"Mother!" Hannah explodes. "As long as I'm here, there will be peace between Mack and me. So, drop it!"

Harry drops it. She takes her glasses off and leans back in her chair, rubbing the bridge of her nose. The recipe book she was looking at lies open on the page for date squares. Rain splatters on the window behind her and she wonders how strong the storm will be this time.

Across the room, Hannah curls into an armchair and pulls a blanket over her knees. In her hands, she has a tattered paperback copy of *The Once And Future King*.

"You loved that book when you were little," Harry says.

"I probably still do."

"You especially loved it when the Wart became a fish and swam in the moat."

"I was jealous of him for having Merlin. I wanted a Merlin."

"I think we all do."

Harry gazes over at her bookshelf and sees a library book that she still hasn't read. The librarian is forgiving when Harry's books come back late, but she really should return this book on the next trip to town. The stormy afternoon stretches out in front of them, confining them to the cabin. She decides to go for a smoke, then read. She hasn't smoked much today, she's been too busy with Hannah. Her fingers shake slightly as she holds the paper out to receive the tobacco. Hannah doesn't look up at her as she goes to mudroom, pulling out her yellow plastic lighter. She closes the door behind her and opens the outer door, watching the afternoon draw in and the branches dance their erratic, wind-blown ballet.

When the men come up from the shed, the smell of fresh-hewn cedar fills the house.

"Are you going to be safe going home?" Harry asks San.

"I'll be fine," he says. "That's why I'm leaving early. I've got the bigger boat today and the wind will be behind me. It's not as if I'm going out there," he gestures to the south. "As soon as I'm around the point I'll be flying."

"Do you have a radio?"

"A little handheld one."

"I'll switch mine on. If you run into any difficulties, you can try calling. Call me when you get home, too. Then I'll know you're safe."

San smiles at her. A little grin that says he will appease an old lady. She doesn't care. His safety is her responsibility.

"You better go now," she says. "But take these for the kids." She hands him a lumpy paper bag.

"You don't have to do this," he tells her.

431

"Don't try and stop me!" she cautions. "I like doing it. Now, scat! Go home before it gets dark."

She makes a joke out of shooing him towards the door and he goes, looking over his shoulder, ducking his head in mock terror.

"And don't come back until the storm's over!" she yells out the door at him.

His answer is just a sound, battered by a rising wind.

Harry switches on the VHF radio and stands by the kitchen window, watching San's boat disappear into the greyness.

"How long do you think it will take him to get there?" she asks Mack.

"Oh, twenty minutes. Something like that."

"Shall we lay bets on it?"

"I don't have anything to bet."

"We could do forfeits."

"What's that?"

"The person who wins can dare the other people to do something silly. It's a good game."

"Oh."

Mack sits at the kitchen table, staring out of the window. Hannah is still in an armchair by the stove. She stood up when Mack and San came in, but now she has retreated to the world of King Arthur.

When the VHF crackles to life, Harry rushes for it, her fingers trembling. It's too soon for San to have reached Swan Bay. He must be in trouble.

Mack jumps up from his chair and comes towards Harry. "That's my dad!" he says. Harry pauses for a moment, fumbling with the handpiece.

"Fortune Island. Go ahead."

"You're finally there. This is Mack Stanley. I've been calling and calling. Have you seen my boat up your way?"

"The *North Wind*? No. Why?"

There's a pause on the radio. "Jesus!" Mack says, grabbing the handset away from Harry. "Somebody stole the boat?"

"It might have been Lonny, coming to see you." Old Mack's voice goes fuzzy, then fades out.

"What? Lonny?"

Hannah looks up from her book. "That big red boat?" she asks. "I saw it this morning, heading this way."

"Hang on a minute, Dad," Mack says loudly. "Someone saw it this morning."

"Just when it was getting light," Hannah adds.

"Just when it was getting light."

A big sigh comes over the airwaves. "I only noticed the boat was gone a little while ago. He must of taken it when I was at church."

"There's no sign of it here."

"It hardly had any fuel. I was going to fuel it up on Monday, before I came to get you."

"You were coming to get me?"

"Lonny was too impatient. He was trying to beat me to it."

"I don't understand."

"Lila phoned. Boy woke up. He says you never hurt him. They dropped the charges. I tried to get you on the radio all day yesterday. You must of had it shut off."

Mack doesn't say anything. He drops the handset and Harry grabs it as it swings on its wire. Mack touches his fingers to his cheeks; his eyes are glazed and he stares straight ahead.

Hannah stares at him from across the room.

Harry takes over, turning up the volume and fiddling with the buttons, trying to make a clear connection. "So what did happen?" she asks.

"Boy was following my son. The fireworks went off. He thought they were explosions, or someone was shooting at him. He got real scared." Old Mack pauses and Harry imagines him taking a drag of a cigarette. "I guess he tried to run away. He slipped on some ice

433

and hit his face on a rock wall. He was able to get up and run a bit further. Then he collapsed. He doesn't remember anything after that." Pause. "The RCMP asked the questions. They're satisfied it was an accident. Lonny heard about it. He kept bugging me to come and get Mack, but I was waiting for my cheque."

Harry looks intently at the radio. She tries to focus on the crisis. "How far do you think Lonny could have got with the fuel you had?"

"Hmmm." Pause. "Maybe halfway."

"We'll go out right now," Harry tells him.

"It's all my fault," says Big Mack.

"I'm gonna come on the water taxi," Old Mack tells them. "A few other boats from here are coming, too."

"We'll go out to Kingfisher, then follow the wind. Maybe we'll see you out there. We'll stay on this channel."

"*Choo.*"

"*Choo.*"

Harry puts the handset back on its hook and starts planning the trip in her head. When she turns around she sees that Hannah and Mack are staring at one another, expressionless.

"What are you waiting for?" she yells at them. "Lonny's out there somewhere! Let's go!"

Hannah stands up; her book falls to the floor. Her eyes are still locked on Mack's. "Wait!" she says to Harry, then looks back to Mack. "You said it was all your fault. Those are the same words you used that night. Don't use them any more. It's like you *want* to get into trouble for things that aren't your fault."

"Enough!" says Harry. "Both of you. Out! Mack, you start the boat, please. I'll catch up in a moment."

Harry watches them scramble into warm clothes. She opens a chest and takes out a wool sweater, wool long johns and several blankets. She packs them into a canvas bag. In the mudroom she searches for her long-range spotlight and two other, smaller flashlights. Then she bends down and picks up her first aid kit.

She has one on the boat, but this one is better equipped. Who knows what they're getting into?

Lastly, after pulling on her own boots and coat, she leans out of the door and delivers a piercing wolf whistle. In moments, Rustum comes barrelling up the path. She pulls him inside. "You have to stay," she tells him. "It's a bad night and there won't be room for you. Rescuing one person will be quite enough." She strokes his ears briefly, then squeezes backwards out of the door, pushing it firmly shut, despite Rustum's whines of protest. She hefts the canvas bag and heads off down the path to the waiting boat.

BIG MACK

When Mack hears the news, a big hand seems to grab his throat and pin him to the wall. Although he always knew he wasn't guilty, some doubts had still been plaguing him. How can you prove that you're innocent when you don't remember a thing? What surprises him, though, is that nobody's guilty. It was an accident, pure and simple. How come he never thought of that? In a weird way he *wanted* someone to be guilty. He'd felt so much better ever since he thought that Kevin McKay might have done it.

They dropped the charges. Those words are such a relief. Mack pictures his little family back together, all his new resolutions working out, nothing going wrong, ever again. For a moment he even forgets that Lonny is drifting around out there, alone in the storm. When he remembers, it is like a shot of adrenaline. His mind races ahead, wondering where the boat could be. He tries not to picture Kingfisher Rock.

While Mack's mind swirls with these thoughts, Hannah apologizes. She's sincere, but Mack barely hears her. Lonny needs him.

He turns the key and the boat starts. It's warm in the cabin because the stove's been going for a while. Hannah is outside, fiddling with the lines. Harry is still up at the house. Mack shifts his weight from foot to foot—Hurry up! Let's go!—then lets the throttle ease, until the boat idles quietly. He jumps onto the back deck and looks around for a tow rope. There isn't one. There are lots of ropes on the *North Wind*, but Mack might not be able to board the boat. He'll need to throw Lonny a line and have him cleat it off at the bow.

"We need rope," he says to Hannah.

She points at the little shed on the dock and he moves there, fast. When he gets back he has a large coil of rope over his shoulder. Harry is taking things out of a bag and putting them away: clothes, blankets, safety stuff. She's obviously been thinking ahead.

"You drive," Mack says to her. "I'm going to fix this rope." He leans out of the door and motions to Hannah to let them go. She pushes off, then hops on board.

"What about binoculars?" she asks.

Mack hasn't thought about them, but they could be useful. Only for another hour or so. Harry pulls out a battered pair, the centre strut broken, and hands them to Hannah.

"They don't work so well," she says.

"It's okay," Hannah answers. "It's just to catch sight of that red colour."

Harry drives the *Polynesia* out of Deep Bay, turning south towards Kingfisher Rock. Mack thinks how the three of them must look. One old white lady, one big Native guy and a young white woman. Not your average rescuers. Mack doesn't care. They're going to look for Lonny. That's all that matters.

LONNY

The boat turns sideways to the waves as soon as the engine dies. Lonny keeps trying to steer, but it's no use. The wind is too strong. Kingfisher Rock gets closer and closer, like a spider pulling him into the watery centre of its crashing white web. Sometimes Lonny closes his eyes because he doesn't want to look. Often, he can't see, anyway. The windows are all fogged up and the waves are so big! Some of them splash right over the boat. The thought of banging into Kingfisher Rock makes Lonny pee without wanting to. He can smell it now, as he goes to the back of the boat and peeks through the little window in the door. The water is still washing over the back, surging forward, then retreating. When he looks back at the front windows he sees a dark shadow on the right. He knows it's the rock. He clings to the back door knob and closes his eyes. His fingers are so cold and rigid, he wonders if he'll be able to pry them off the door knob when the boat hits the rock and he has to get out.

Behind his closed eyes, the world gets darker and darker. He stops breathing, waiting for the crash to come.

It takes him a while to realise that he isn't going to hit the rock. When nothing happens, he opens one eye and peeks out of the back door, amazed to see the rock behind him. He got close, but not close enough. Lonny starts shaking and can't stop. He runs back to his box at the front and his fingers jump up and down on the steering wheel. His teeth chatter. He knows he was lucky, but he just feels cold and scared.

Eventually, Lonny remembers the anchor. Of course, the anchor! He lets go of the steering wheel and gets down from the crate again. Now, he wonders how he can get to the bow of the boat without getting washed overboard. Maybe he can tie himself to a rope and tie the rope to the boat. He knows good knots. He opens a closet, looking for a lifejacket. He doesn't see one. Then he pulls on his coat and goes to the drawer, looking for a knife. There's a small one that looks sharp and he puts it in his coat pocket. He takes a deep breath and opens the door. Instantly the handle is pulled out of his fingers and the door flies open. Wind and rain roar in his ears and blow him backwards. The wind screams in the rigging—a high pitched noise, like angry ghosts. A wave washes over the deck and he imagines himself being thrown overboard. He knows for a fact that he won't be able to swim very long in this water.

He looks at the mast, which is close to the door. Some pieces of rope are looped around it. He could tie himself onto them and then climb onto the roof. The waves won't get him up there. Just the wind. He reaches out and untangles a piece of rope. Then he ties it around his waist, remembering the bowline that he practised on Grandpa's neck tie. He loops the other end of the rope back around the mast and climbs up, holding on tight. The rigging flaps and shrieks. The cabin roof is scary because there's nothing to hold onto. Lonny watches a gust of wind come over the water, black and feathery, coming to get him. The gust hits hard and the boat tilts over. Lonny lies flat on the roof, praying he'll be okay. As soon as the gust passes, he scrambles to the front and drops down. He grabs onto a large cleat and holds tight as another gust hits. Then he looks around for the anchor. It's confusing; there's a big roll of chain and the end of it goes into a groove at the front of the boat. He can't see the anchor. Then he remembers that the anchor pokes out the front of the boat. It's not a little anchor that he can chuck overboard. It's a great big thing that needs a winch.

He ties his safety line to the cleat and leans right over the bow of the boat. Below him, the water rises and plunges away. He stares at it for a long time. The blades of the anchor stick out of the bow and he reaches for them. He holds on and tugs, but nothing happens. The anchor doesn't budge. He tugs again, straining as hard as he can without falling in. It isn't going to work. He comes back to the roll of chain and stares at it. Uncle made it work when they anchored out in Silent Inlet, but that was so long ago. Lonny wishes he could remember what happened. There's no lever to make it turn. He tugs on the end of the chain, but it doesn't unravel. It makes him want to cry, but he can't. When he looks around him he can see the mouth of the big inlet he went up with Grandpa. He's drifting towards it. The inlet has rocky sides. The boat could bash against the rocks and break. If he can't use this anchor, maybe he can find something else to throw overboard—anything to slow him down.

He decides to go back inside, but this time he goes the easy way, inching along the lee side of the cabin, closing his eyes when the gusts hit and holding on tight. When he reaches the cabin door he opens it and steps inside. Then he unties the rope from his waist, bracing himself in the doorway as a wave hits.

The feel of the rope in his hand suddenly clears his mind of fright. He holds the free end and stares at it, thinking hard.

BIG MACK

Mack looks back down to the rope on his lap, which he is splicing into a heavy loop. Hannah takes the binoculars and goes outside, squelching past him in runners that are already soaked. When the boat turns broadside to the waves, spray washes over it and Hannah comes dashing back in again, soaked.

"How are we going to see anything?" she wails, pulling her wet jeans away from her thighs and standing braced by the stove.

"We'll get upwind," Harry says over her shoulder. "Then we'll turn our back to the storm. We should be able to see something then."

Mack finishes off the splice and puts the rope down, under the table. He squeezes up to the front and peers out. There is only grey water and white spray. The windshield wipers flip back and forth, allowing brief moments of clarity. He wonders how the *Polynesia* will do in a storm. She seems seaworthy, but you never know.

"Do you have a pump hooked up?" he asks Harry.

"There's one in the engine room."

"Do you ever use it?"

"Not much."

"Does it still work?"

"I think so."

Mack considers going to get it, but that means shutting off the engine. He should have thought of it before he left. Bilge pumps are notorious for quitting when you need them.

He keeps his eyes on the water, searching from left to right in a steady pattern. He wonders how far Lonny got before running out of gas. If he got as far as Kingfisher, they'll need to search further north. If he didn't make it that far, he might have washed up on the rock itself. Mack's heart thumps—two big beats—right up into his throat. Harry is driving towards the rock. The water is more exposed now, the swell heaving under the whitecaps. He cups his hand and leans as close to the glass as he can. The boat's cabin is so small that he has to crane his neck to keep his head away from the ceiling.

Hannah moves away from the stove and comes to stand between Mack and Harry. She stares ahead, holding onto the dash, small muscles puckering around her eyes. She doesn't turn to look at Mack and he resumes his search pattern, trying not to see her as he does so. He can feel her presence, though. Twice, he misses a section of water and has to start again.

Harry slows the boat as the waves increase and they near Kingfisher Rock. Mack wonders if they would really be able to tow the *North Wind*, in these conditions, with this boat. Waves slap over the back deck and occasionally bury the bow. Harry steers well, looking for patches of calm, accelerating into the waves when they come. She turns upwind of the rock and Mack wipes the windshield with his sleeve trying to see better. There's no trace of red anywhere near the rock.

"Can you see anything with the binoculars?" he asks Hannah.

She lifts them to her eyes, lurching as a wave hits. "There's too much movement," she says, dropping them again and looking at Mack. "They're no use."

Mack thinks of Lonny all alone in the boat. If only he would use the radio! But Mack seldom bothers with the radio, himself, and it's placed up high, above Lonny's line of vision. He may not see it, let alone know how to use it. If the boat's still afloat, then Lonny's probably sitting in the cabin, holding tight with skinny arms, his eyes full of fear, wondering what to do.

Use the radio! Mack thinks, trying to transmit his thoughts the way a whale sends noises from its forehead. Perhaps if Mack thinks of Lonny hard enough, he'll get the message and send Mack something in return. Mack stares at the water and concentrates on his thoughts. It's going to be okay, Lonny. I'm free. I love you. I'm coming to find you.

"Hold on tight, I'm going to turn!" yells Harry. And for one crazy moment the boat heels over, as a wave takes them broadside.

Hannah tumbles into Mack, who is pressed against the window. Harry's feet slide out from under her, but she keeps a grip of the wheel and suddenly, the worst is past, they are heading downwind. The rock shows clearly between waves and there are no signs of wooden debris. The sick feeling in Mack's stomach lessens for an instant. Then it builds again.

"He must be up the inlet somewhere!" Harry yells again, gesturing north with her forehead.

"Let's go!" Mack shouts. Then he clears the glass with his sleeve again and looks at Hannah. "I'll concentrate on this side. You look straight ahead."

Hannah looks back at him, grey eyes rising towards the crease in her forehead. "We'll find him," she says, although he barely hears the words. She turns and resumes searching.

"Lonny!" bellows Harry. "Hang in there! We're coming to get you!" Mack looks at his co-searchers, these people who are on his side. The warmth of them soothes his fear. He feels as though he's in a dream, with no idea how he got here, no idea where he's going, no sense. He's going to find Lonny, though. Suddenly, he's sure of that.

LONNY

Lonny can't count the hours he's been here, standing in the cabin doorway, staring at the waves. He can't feel his feet anymore. His right hand is numb, too, where it's holding the end of the rope. He's soaked from head to foot. In a way, he's paralysed. His thoughts have pinned him here and now he can't move.

The wind is worse, now, but the waves are smaller. As soon as he got into the inlet, the sea waves died off, but the chop still sprays past him in a steady rhythm.

Shh. Shh. Shh.

That noise makes him think of being a baby again. He doesn't remember much about being a baby, but there's a feeling of being held—rocked, maybe—and the thought of it makes him sad. Suddenly, he's so sad for his mother and his father. He wishes he could remember what it was like to have them. Maybe, if he'd known he was going to lose them, he would have tried harder to memorize the way they were. As it is, there's not much he can think of, except the fighting. And he doesn't want to think about that.

Lonny's stuck with the thought that even if he doesn't get killed by the storm, Grandpa's boat will be wrecked and it will be his fault. Grandpa will never be able to buy another boat, so he won't have a job any more. Grandpa would never forgive him for wrecking the boat. It's his most precious thing.

Lonny thinks of his grandpa's skinny face and staring eyes, the way he shakes when he's angry. It would be so terrible to make him angry. Lonny feels like a failure. It doesn't seem to matter that Uncle's free. He'll be mad at Lonny, too. What Lonny's done is so dumb! No one will ever forgive him.

He stares at the end of the rope, watching it flip around in the wind. For some reason, when he first saw that piece of rope, it made him think of the time when some of the older boys hung a dog from a tree behind the village. When Sam told Lonny about

444

it, they went to see. It was gross. The dog's mouth was open and its tongue was hanging out. It's body was limp and dangling. Lonny thinks about it whenever there's a suicide at home. Last year it was his cousin, who was only seventeen. He heard that Fergus hung himself in a closet. Lonny could never understand why he had done it. He was good looking and popular. He was a great basketball player. Someone said he was sorry about some money he stole. Someone else said he just thought nobody cared.

Shh. Shh. Shh.

The piece of rope twitches in Lonny's fingers. It seems to call him, inviting him to escape from everything. Nobody could be mad at him if he were dead. They would get to the boat and find him and then they would be sorry for wanting to be mad. It would be his way of saying he's sorry for taking the boat, for being an extra person in everybody else's family.

Lonny looks up at the boom, hanging out over the back deck. He could make a loop, then throw the rope over the boom and cleat it off. He would have to get up high, though, so that he could fall down. Maybe he could stand on the crate, then push it away. Maybe the waves would push it away and Lonny would fall and it would be like sleeping.

Shh. Shh. Shh.

Nobody at home has talked to Lonny about the kids who have killed themselves. Uncle said something like, "Don't you ever do that." But he didn't explain what it meant, or why they did it. He knows it really bothers Uncle, because of how he gets when it happens—all silent and dark—so that Lonny and Sam don't go near him for a while. But there must be a reason why people do it. Maybe they just feel like no one loves them. Or maybe they've made mistakes they can't fix. Like Lonny's dad. Lonny overheard his auntie talking about his dad one time. She was saying that at least he would be safe in jail. Safe from himself, "Him and his death wish." Lonny's not sure what she meant, but he knows that his father might have tried to kill himself. Uncle has said that

445

Lonny shouldn't blame his dad for his mother's death. He said that one day he would explain what happened, but not yet. Lonny wonders if his dad ever tried to hang himself.

He pulls his hand inside and rubs it with his other hand until the fingers can move. Then he fiddles with the rope, trying to make a loop, like the one on the dog's neck. His fingers are stiff and jumpy. They don't do as they're told. Lonny looks out and sees that the boat is moving towards the silent grey cliffs at the end of the inlet. As he fiddles with the rope, he wonders if there are any swans there. If he hangs himself maybe he can become a swan.

Shh. Shh. Shh.

He makes a loop. Then he rests it on the door knob. The water catches his eye and he sees a big gust pushing a little black tornado of spray in the fading light. The little tornado spins towards the boat, hitting it and pushing Lonny backwards. He grabs the mast and holds on, salt spray filling his eyes. His heart pounds and he wonders why he wanted to hold on, why he didn't just let go and fall into the water. Wouldn't that be easier? No planning, just a little slip, then he'd be flying like a swan.

If he fell in, though, it would just look like an accident. Lonny wants to let everyone know that he's sorry. He tries to control his legs and arms as they jump around with cold. The gust sets his teeth chattering, completely out of his control.

He goes back into the boat and jumps up and down for a while, flapping his arms until they relax a little. Then he goes over to the steering wheel and picks up the milk crate he had been standing on. A cold feeling stabs into him, colder than the rain and the wind. Colder than his chattering teeth and shivering limbs. Lonny tries to breathe slowly, but he can't. He holds the crate in his arms and tears fill his eyes. He imagines his mother, holding him when he was a baby, making sweet noises, stroking his hair.

Shh. Shh. Shh.

He can hear her outside, shushing him, soothing him. He can hear her calling him. He can find her under the boom, but he

446

needs the crate. He walks towards the cabin door and up the steps. He holds the crate tenderly. He loves cradling it, pouring his heart into it, feeling the pressure of it against his chest. A gust pushes the boat and he falls against the side of the door. He stays there a moment, staring out at the rain and wind, staring at his mother, flying towards him, a beautiful swan, with bright eyes that look right at him. He cries as he sees her, and reaches for her with one arm. Then he steps out onto the deck, grabs the loop of rope and tucks it into the crate. He finds a good spot, under the boom and puts the crate down, sitting on it and holding the rope in both hands. The spray wets his eyes, but he can see his mother through it. Her feathers are so white. She is so beautiful.

Through his tears he realises that he has seen her more than once. She is not always the same. The shape of her shifts and changes. She is still white, but now she's no longer a swan. She's a boat, a sweet white boat. The spray rises up around her. Bright lights gleam out towards him, green and red. He sits on the crate, watching her cut through the water towards him. She's calling him. He can hear her, but her voice has changed, too. It's deeper now. She sounds like Uncle.

Lonnnnnyyyyyy! she calls, her voice filling him with joy. Lonnnnnyyyyyy!

Salt water fills his eyes, from tears and waves. It's hard to see anything, but this white shape, bearing down on him, calling his name through the rushing wind, calling as if he's loved and wanted. Calling him home.

He puts down the rope and opens his mouth to the storm.

"I'm heeeerrre!" he yells as loud as he can. "I'm heeeerrre!"

Joanna Streetly was born in Trinidad and educated in England. She has spent the last sixteen years afloat among the communities of Clayoquot Sound, where she works as a freelance writer, illustrator, editor and kayak guide. She is the author of *Paddling Through Time* and the editor of *Salt In Our Blood*. *Silent Inlet* is her first novel.